I0579154

This is a work of fiction. All characters and events are either a product of the author's imagination or used fictitiously, and any resemblance to real people or events is entirely coincidental.

TO STEAL THE WORLD

Copyright © 2020 by Beth Alvarez

First Edition: January 2020

NEVER LOST

Copyright © 2020 by Beth Alvarez

First Edition: December 2020

TO STEAL THE CROWN

Copyright © 2020 by Beth Alvarez

First Edition: February 2020

DON'T STEAL FROM DEMONS

Copyright © 2020 by Beth Alvarez

First Edition: December 2020

TO STEAL THE QUEEN

Copyright © 2020 by Beth Alvarez

First Edition: June 2020

All rights reserved.

No part of this book may be reproduced in any form or by any electronic or mechanical means, including information storage and retrieval systems, without written permission from the author, except for the use of brief quotations in a book review.

Omnibus First Edition: December 2020

Cover art by Jose Alvarez

ISBN: 978-1-952145-11-7

WESTKINGS HEIST

THE COMPLETE SERIES

BETH ALVAREZ

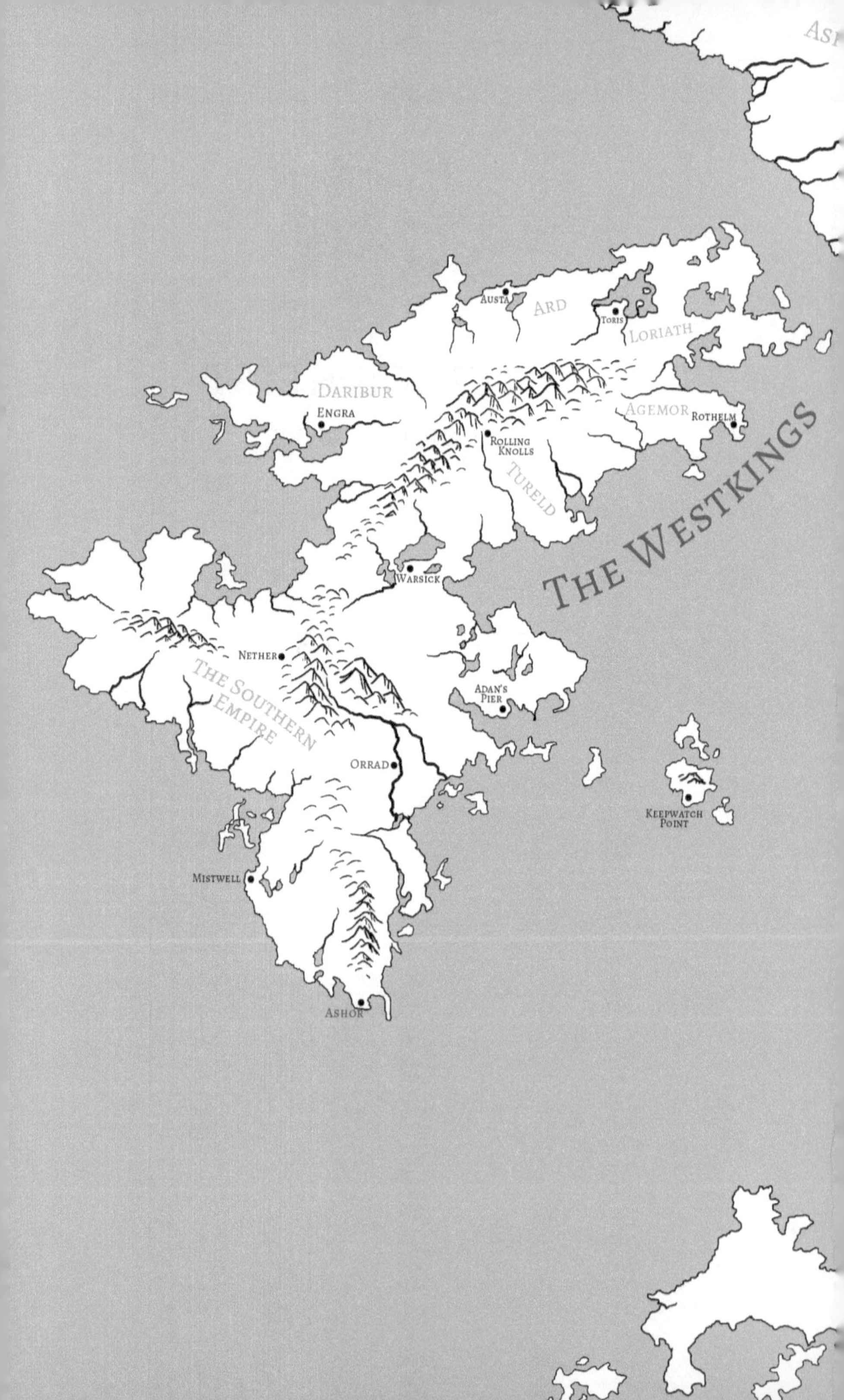

ASH
ARD
AUSTA
TORIS
LORIATH
DARIBUR
ENGRA
AGEMOR
ROTHELM
ROLLING KNOLLS
TURELD
THE WESTKINGS
WARSICK
THE SOUTHERN EMPIRE
NETHER
ADAN'S PIER
ORRAD
KEEPWATCH POINT
MISTWELL
ASHOR

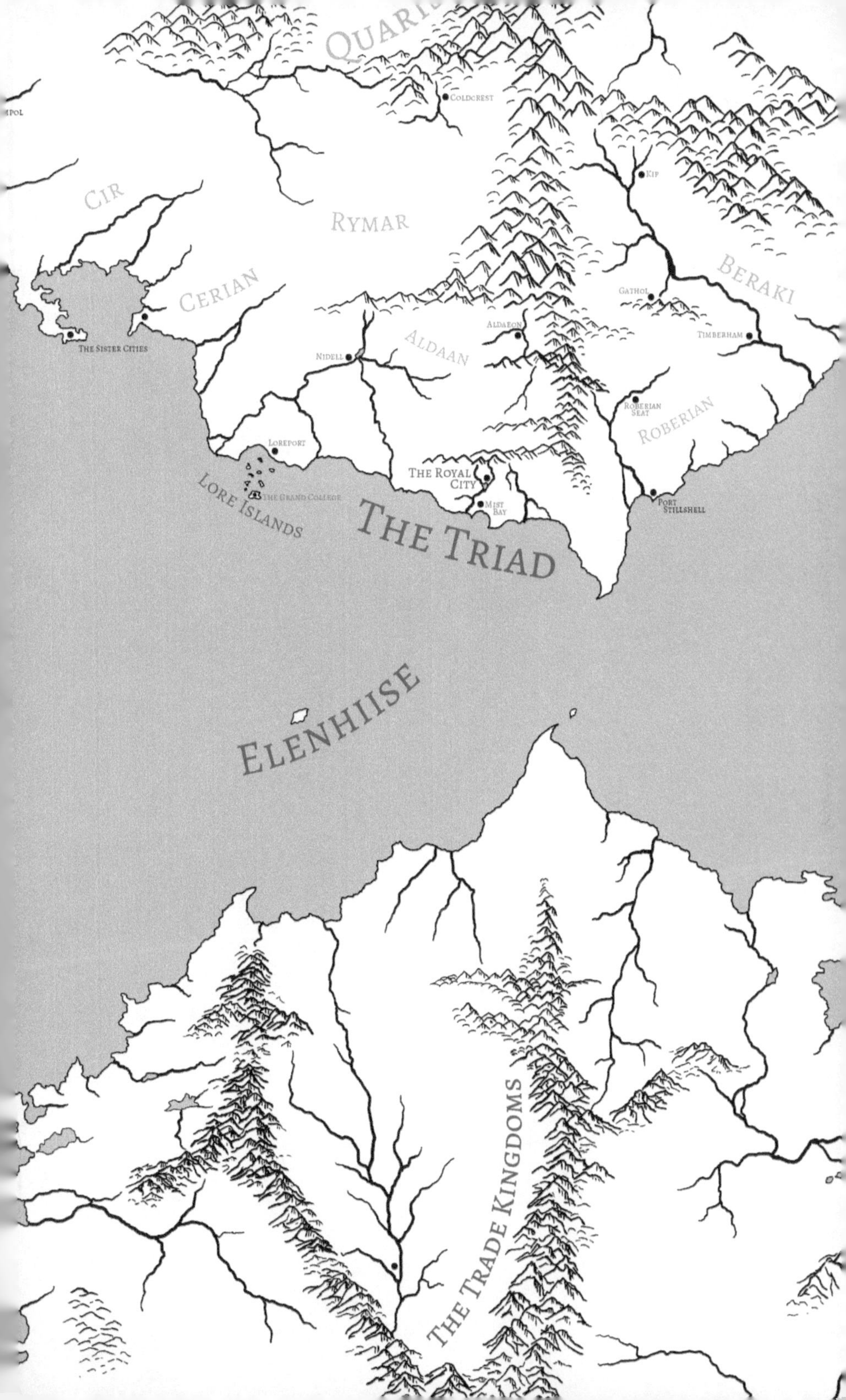
QUARI
COLDCREST
KIP
CIR
RYMAR
GATHOL
BERAKI
CERIAN
ALDAEON
TIMBERHAM
THE SISTER CITIES
NIDELL
ALDAAN
ROBERIAN SEAT
ROBERIAN
LOREPORT
THE ROYAL CITY
PORT STILLSHELL
LORE ISLANDS
THE GRAND COLLEGE
MIST BAY
THE TRIAD
ELÉNHIISE
THE TRADE KINGDOMS

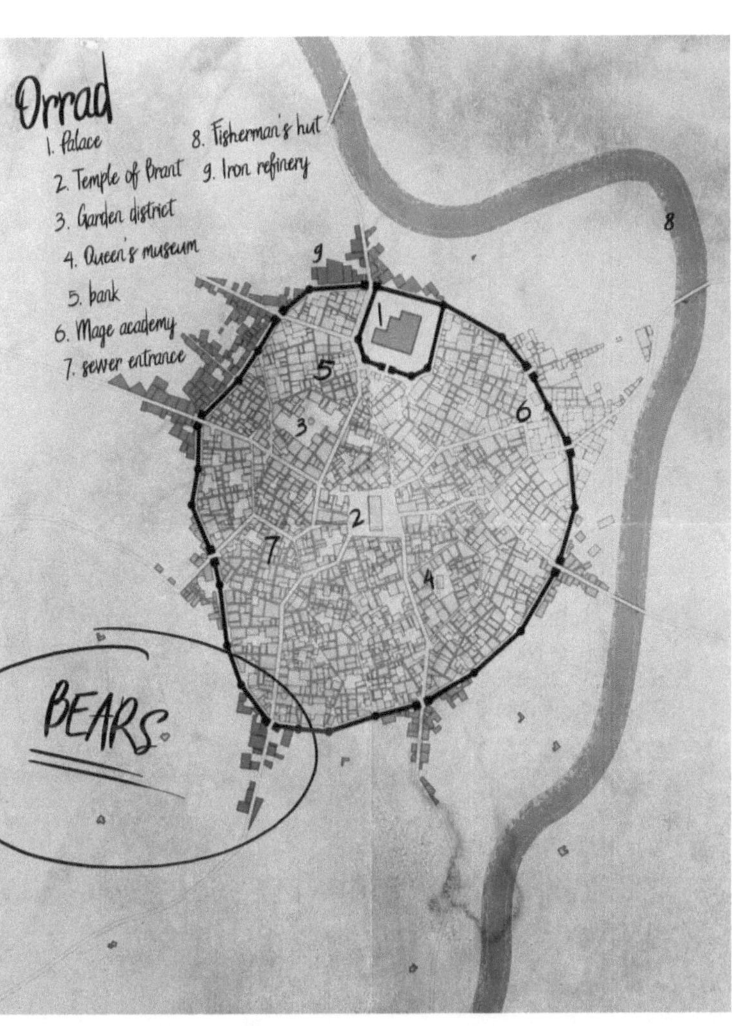

Orrad
1. Palace
2. Temple of Brant
3. Garden district
4. Queen's museum
5. bank
6. Mage academy
7. sewer entrance
8. Fisherman's hut
9. Iron refinery
BEARS

CONTENTS

TO STEAL THE WORLD

THE FIRST HEIST

CHAPTER 1

A THIN PLUME OF GRAY-BLUE SMOKE COILED ABOVE TAHL'S upturned palm. No matter how many times he tried to summon fire, he never got farther than smoke. The rest of his power—his Gift, everyone called it—hovered just beyond his reach. It didn't stop him from trying, but he wondered sometimes whether the mages called such feeble magic a Gift as mockery instead of compliment.

He blew the wisps of smoke into the morning air and curled his slim fingers into the palm of his hand. It didn't matter; he'd given up on magecraft the first month after he'd been admitted to the academy. Or rather, they'd given up on him. Still, the ability to conjure fire struck him as useful, especially in his profession. Now and then, everyone needed a distraction to save their hide.

The smoke he'd managed disappeared overhead, swallowed by the thick plumes that billowed from the bakery's chimney. The cool, shadowy sides of chimneys were Tahl's favorite places to practice. Not only did they disguise his pathetic power, but they provided a comfortable shelter and an interesting view. The city below hummed with life, but it wasn't the city that interested him.

A man paused at the mouth of a narrow alley some distance away. To everyone else, he was all but invisible, his furtive glances into the wider streets easy to mistake for mindfulness. He stepped back into the alley as a cart rumbled past. Then he slid across the cobblestones, as casually as every other pedestrian, and vanished around the corner.

Tahl slid to the far side of the chimney and waited for the man to emerge on the other side. He had watched the man for days. His target walked with a comfortable confidence among the crowds. If he'd known Tahl had figured him out, perhaps he would have run.

The bakery's aged wooden shakes creaked as Tahl slipped to the roof's edge—not the edge that hung over the capital's main street, but the back edge, where firewood sat stacked to the eaves. One of the baker's apprentices crossed the yard with a sack of flour on his shoulder to accompany the white powder that frosted his dark clothes. Most of the capital's wealthy wore bright, garish colors. The working class appeared drab by comparison. Tahl's own wardrobe varied, depending on who he needed to be. Today, he could have been a baker's apprentice, dressed in dark browns that let him blend in with the city's roofs. Some of the roofs, that was; the garden district, where the wealthiest lived, favored clay tiles in a deep red-gold. To the north, those tiles glowed in the morning light, a beacon to guide him to his planned rendezvous.

The apprentice disappeared into the bakery and Tahl thrust himself from the edge of the roof. His toes hit the bare earth and he sprang forward into a roll to defer the impact. He popped to his feet and dusted his clothes as he darted out the back gate. The first roll of the day was always the most pleasant, but the acrobatics were best saved for later. If things went sour, he'd need them.

Orrad, the capital city, had been his home for a handful of years, but the streets sometimes still felt like a maze. Tahl was more comfortable on the rooftops, but he avoided them during the day. He was no one, unnoticed, unthreatening, and he intended to keep it that way. Aside from taking a morning perch to practice his smoke and get a view of the city, he kept his feet on the ground, which was far more likely to keep his head attached to his shoulders. Atoras, the ruler of the southernmost Westkings Empire, was known for his ruthlessness and ill temper. The practice of docking a caught thief's fingers that was utilized in the east was gracious and merciful in comparison to the penalties Tahl had seen enacted on his fellows here.

Soft chimes rose above the noise of the crowds and Tahl lingered at the edge of the street. His mark was somewhere farther ahead, but the people parted for an entourage of priestesses and crowded the sides of the wide avenue.

The quintet of women walked single file. Their bare feet made no sound on the cobblestones, but the soft, melodious sound of the wooden chimes that hung from their wrists announced their presence to anyone who could hear. Tahl turned his head to watch; he still found the priestesses a curious sight. On the southern coast, where he'd grown up, the Children of Brant were all but unknown. But Orrad was home to the largest temple in the Westkings, and their influence over the city was undeniable. Some thieves—namely those pushed into the profession by necessity—took issue with the Creator, but Tahl had never devoted much thought toward Brant or his disciples. He was curious, more than anything. No matter how many times he saw the priestesses in the city, he never could figure out how they knew where they were going with those translucent, pale green silk scarves over their heads.

Then the priestesses passed, and the crowds closed behind them. Tahl joined them, pushing through the bustle like everyone else. The procession had stalled him, but he knew his mark's route by heart.

Most marks weren't worth following for weeks on end, but this one was different. Special. And if Tahl was right, this one was the first key to changing his fortune.

Not far up the main road, Tahl darted into a gap between buildings. The winding trail was meant for rainwater drainage, rather than people, but he was slim enough to fit without trouble. His shoulders brushed the rough stone walls and he shifted to angle his right shoulder forward, so his dominant hand would lead. He'd never encountered trouble in the streets; it wasn't uncommon for the working class to take whatever shortcuts through the city they could find, and there was no reason for anyone to believe him anything else. Still, he wasn't foolish enough to put himself at a disadvantage, should he encounter one of the city's less amicable inhabitants in the alleys.

Tahl emerged not far from the garden district, its walls a stark white above the gray stone homes of the lower class. Though inhabited by the city's elite and walled off to protect it, the garden district was open to the public. Tall bronze gates stood open at the cardinal points to allow access to the district, and while the north and south gates hosted guardhouses, there were not always sentries at the gates. Tahl had memorized the guard rotations—as had his mark, he was sure. When Tahl crossed into the garden district, the south gate was empty.

The cloying scent of morning flowers greeted him the moment the gardens themselves came into view. Trees dressed in white and pink blossoms clustered around the central fountain. Their petals coated the water and clogged the thing until nothing more than a trickle spilled from the basins in the tree-shaped statue's branches. Spring pollen coated everything and made it hard to cover one's tracks, but it had rained the night before, and most of the road was clear. The rain was why Tahl had chosen today to move.

It was Somnday; the end of the week and the day of rest for those who could afford time off. The one day of the week Tahl was certain there would be no one at work in the gardens that sprawled around the tall, white stone houses. He ducked behind the thirteenth house from the south gate, where the gardens were shady and thorny flowering vines crept up the stone toward the third floor of the house. He'd studied those vines elsewhere in the city, memorized how far apart the thorns were spaced.

Tahl drew a breath and climbed.

The railing on the balcony above was clean, washed by the rain the night before. He left no handprints. Across the balcony, doors with fine glass panes waited. Inside, the curtains over the doors were drawn, a unique challenge to overcome. Tahl slipped his thinnest knife from his left sleeve and crouched beside the doors to listen. He couldn't risk standing; Somnday or not, the garden district would have traffic, and he couldn't let himself be spotted by neighbors.

Thin as it was, his knife almost didn't fit in the crack beside the door. His mark was no fool; the doors were barred, instead of latched. Not a hindrance to anyone who wished to enter by force, as Tahl could have wrapped his fist and smashed one of the thin panes of glass to grant all the access he needed. Petty burglars might have taken the easy route, regardless of whether or not the noise would alert the house's occupants to the crime. Most nobles were weak and fearful and wouldn't confront a burglar on their own. With this mark, the barred door meant caution, not fear.

The knife caught the end of the wooden bar and Tahl wiggled it upward. It was hard, heavy work and several times, the tip of the knife threatened to slip from its place, wedged in the grain of the wood. Persistent, he slid the end of the bar upward. The glass was a boon; it let him see exactly where his knife was. The bar lifted over the edge of its bracket and he eased the knife forward. The bar shifted and teetered, then balanced atop its iron bracket.

Tahl held his breath. He thrust open the other door and caught the bar before it fell. The curtains rippled and he froze until they stilled. Beyond, the room was quiet.

Somewhere below, on the second floor, was where he needed to be. Despite that certainty, he did not know where he was going. He closed the door and eased the bar back into place before he dared to peer out from behind the curtain. A fine bedroom lay on the other side. Foolish, he thought; the least defensible place in the house. But it was empty, and Tahl crossed to the door with haste. Not long, now. His mark would be crossing the garden, reaching the front door.

He put a hand to his pocket and waited until he was sure the hall beyond was empty to remove and uncork the tiny glass vial. The oil inside was sweet-scented, but thin; it penetrated hinges faster than anything else he'd tried. When he drew the door open a moment later, it was silent.

The hall beyond the bedroom ran north and south with tall windows at either end. He cut south without hesitation. He didn't have time to think, only to act. A flight of stairs waited around the corner. He stepped out and recoiled. A maid balanced linens in one arm, watching her skirts as she scaled the stairs. Tahl sprinted north instead, the soft toes of his doeskin boots silent on the thick carpet. Another stairway, this one empty. He ducked around the corner and tip-toed down the steps.

The office waited on the other side of the house. Tahl slipped through the parlor in the corner and into the wide office, a shadow in the morning light. Loud footsteps on the stairs below announced his mark's arrival, and when the office door swung open, Tahl stood before the tall eastern windows, gazing at the garden fountain beyond.

The nobleman froze. "Who are you? How did you get in here?" he demanded. "Nella! Nella, what is this?"

"Bahar Eseri," Tahl said as he turned from the garden. "Chief of the southern empire's thieves guild."

The man's eyes widened and he closed the door before his maid could respond. "What do you want?"

Tahl's eyes narrowed. "I want in."

CHAPTER 2

"In?" Bahar stared as if he hadn't heard. Then, suddenly, he burst into laughter. "I haven't a clue what you're talking about, boy. Now, you've got one chance to tell me the truth about what you're after and how you got into my house. Did Nella let you in? I told her I wouldn't see guests."

"Your maid doesn't know I'm here." Tahl paced away from the windows. "I thought you'd prefer to keep it that way, since you keep all your business secret."

The nobleman scoffed. "Whatever you think you know about my business, you're wrong." He stalked to his desk and unstoppered a cut glass decanter.

"What you do during the day, perhaps." Tahl shrugged. "You manage an import company focused on goods brought in from the northern empires. A substantial portion of your business is legitimate, which provides a comfortable front and convenient cover for the portions that are not, as the stolen goods that move through your distribution facilities can be classified as bookkeeping errors."

The corners of Bahar's mouth twitched downward.

"You inherited the company from your father at a young age," Tahl continued, "after he was killed in an accident in a warehouse. A considerable amount of your family fortune went to the families of the others killed in the incident, after Emperor Atoras found working conditions unsafe and ordered you pay reparations. Given how comfortable you were in a lavish lifestyle, you sought alternative means to bolster your income. You began to falsify numbers when you were sixteen, and began to operate as a fence when you were seventeen."

"Ridiculous." Bahar filled his snifter halfway. "Such accusations could get a man killed."

"Yet you haven't stopped me."

The nobleman sipped his dark red liquor.

Tahl inched closer. "Founding the guild was your idea. With your trade connections, a network of informants was easy to establish. You organized your clients and contacts over the course of several years. By the time you were twenty-five, you'd become the leader of a group no one could pin down. A ghost who couldn't be found guilty, because your trade company helped evidence disappear, and no one in their right mind would blame one of Orrad's social elite for the aggressive theft that plagues the city."

Swallow by swallow, Bahar drained his glass. He slammed it back onto his desk. "You're creative, I'll give you that. I enjoyed your story. I'm sure the guards will enjoy it just as much."

He lunged over the desk and caught Tahl by the shirt. His hands were like vicegrips, his curled fingers strong as steel. Tahl ducked under his arm and swiped an elbow down onto Bahar's back. The nobleman crashed to the floor and Tahl danced backwards.

"You need me," Tahl said over the man's angry roar.

"Need you?" Bahar bellowed. "Why would I need you?"

Tahl raised a hand and rolled a gold signet ring between his fingers. "Because you don't have anyone like me."

Bahar's chest heaved as he stared at the ring. He resisted, unwilling to remove his eyes from Tahl, but the need for certainty won. His gaze fell to his hand and the pale indentation on his finger where the ring had been.

"Like I said." Tahl flicked the ring toward him with a shrug. "You need me."

The signet ring bounced off Bahar's fingers and pinged against the desk. His eyes followed it as it rolled across the floor. "I could have your head, boy."

"You could," Tahl agreed. "But you won't. Because no one's ever been able to find you before, and you know how valuable that makes me."

The nobleman's eyes narrowed. He rested a hand against the edge of his desk and bent to pick up his ring. "You have a strange method of convincing people to cooperate."

Tahl smirked. "And you haven't called the guards yet, so I'd say it works."

Grunting, Bahar straightened and twisted the ring back onto his finger. "I've grown curious. You're looking for a guild. Why bother? If you're as skilled as you think you are, why not work alone?"

"Do you work alone, Lord Eseri?" Tahl raised a brow. "You could, perhaps, manage all your imports by yourself. But that wouldn't be effective, would it? You want to scale. You want to build efficiency. You want someone else to do the work that's beneath your skill level and keep the best fruits of your labor for yourself. Do you think my business is any different?"

"No," the noble said, easing himself into his chair and letting a thoughtful eye linger on the thief. "I suppose not."

Tahl spread his hands. "There you go."

For a time, neither spoke. Then Bahar leaned back in his chair, tapping a finger against the edge of his desk. "There's one thing you failed to consider, though."

Progress. Tahl hid his satisfaction and opted to raise a brow instead.

"The guild doesn't accept outsiders." A shadow of weariness crossed Bahar's face and for a moment, he looked older than his silver-flecked hair suggested. "Imagine, letting a stranger into a group so carefully cultivated over a span of decades. Their safety depends on secrecy. A thief doesn't seek them to be admitted to their ranks. They wait for the guild to approach them."

"So you admit you've been discovered?" Tahl asked.

A harsh grin split the older man's features. "I admit I know of the guild. Every businessman in Orrad does, but to speak of them is to risk bringing the wrath of Atoras down on your head. But, no. You have the wrong man."

A single, fleeting moment of panic clawed at Tahl's heart. He caught it and wrestled it into submission. No matter how skilled he was, the instinct of fight or flight was hard to defeat. "Impossible."

"I applaud your confidence," Bahar said, "but there's nothing I can do for you. If you're as skilled as you claim, hit the streets again. Make your work noticed. The guild will find you when they believe you'll be an asset."

Tahl lifted his chin. "A thief who makes himself easy to find is a thief who doesn't live long."

A dark chuckle escaped the nobleman. "Indeed."

"Name your mark," Tahl said. "Everything has a price."

"*My* mark?" Bahar pressed his fingers to his chest, wrinkling the vermilion silk of his vest. Funny; Tahl could have sworn there had been an ink stain on the side of the man's hand when he swiped the ring. "I told you, I'm not involved."

"Then why haven't you thrown me out or alerted the guards outside?"

"Because I know better than to cross the guild." The older man shook his head, a shadow in his dark eyes. "They could ruin a man like me with a thought. As for throwing you out..." He leaned back in his chair and frowned. "I've told you what I know, and if I am to be honest, you're young and I am not. I doubt I could lay hands on you. But you will leave of your own accord."

Tahl half-listened, his thoughts still on the ink. Lord Eseri hadn't had ink on his hands when he walked through the city; he must have paused to write something before he reached his office. A message to a courier at the door, perhaps. Tahl tucked away a mental note to exit through the front door—after he inspected the inkwells along the way.

"You're right," he agreed after a moment. "You've been helpful, even if you haven't given me the answers I hoped for." He couldn't fault the noble for standing his ground and pushing to hide his identity. He'd just said it himself—a thief who was easy to find didn't live long. Any number of people were after Bahar's head. Until now, no one had found him. Tahl strode toward the door. "Of course... If you *were* part of the thieves guild, what would it take to impress you?"

Bahar sneered. "The world."

Tahl gave a single nod. "Noted." He slipped out of the office and stalked past the maid, whose mouth dropped open when she saw him. Her eyes followed him to the stairs and he stifled his amusement. Not a mark had been left behind to show how he got inside, but he didn't doubt Bahar would force the woman to scour the place in search of some clue. He bounded down the stairs to the first floor and paused at a small secretary desk near the entryway. It was tidy, but clearly received use, its surface stained with old ink.

One by one, he unstoppered the three ink bottles that sat on the secretary and ran his fingers around their rims. One red, two black. Satisfied, he exited and turned south. By the time he passed the district gate, the smudge on his second finger was gone.

Tahl smirked.

Disappearing ink.

———

ORRAD WAS NOT as comfortable as his home city of Ashor on the southern coast, but Tahl had grown used to it. He still preferred the salt air and sea winds, but the capital had its own charm. The air was ever cool and scented with pine, and the wide, cold river that flowed from the gray mountains reminded him of home.

Unsurprisingly, the bridge across the Ranton river was his favored refuge. He leaned his elbows against the stone balustrade and laced his fingers together. He'd washed his hands, but hints of red and black ink still stained his first and third fingers. He rubbed the pad of his clean middle finger against his knuckle.

Despite that single twinge of uncertainty in Lord Eseri's office, Tahl's confidence he was on the right track never wavered. Discovery of the disappearing ink had been an added frustration instead of a confidence boost. Bahar Eseri was the leader of the guild; there was no doubt about that. Tahl had spoken to any number of thieves in the city. By all accounts, the nobleman held the power to admit anyone he pleased. He should have been impressed instead of angry or dismissive. He hadn't even offered a real answer for Tahl's question of what it would take.

No matter. If he wished to give dismissive answers, he'd receive dismissive results. *After all*, Tahl mused as he pushed himself from the balustrade and made his way home, *the world is easier to take from someone than they think.*

To call his room modest was generous, but Tahl preferred his drafty attic space over the dank stone room he'd had at the academy. Orrad's mages were supposed to be the most powerful in the Westkings, yet they couldn't keep mildew from the corners of their stronghold. At least the attic was dry.

He unrolled a map across the rough table and drummed his fingers against its edges. Finding Bahar had been the hard part; he'd located the guild headquarters the first day he'd decided to look. Nestled comfortably within a high-traffic area on the fringes of the mercantile district, it had been circled in blue on his map for a month. Bahar's home was a contrasting red. Tahl hadn't liked the color; he found it too often associated with challenge. But he had only so many colors in the little box of mostly-used wax crayons he'd gotten from an artist who often set up on the south side of the bridge, where an outcropping of stone gave a good view of the docks. Yellow was too pale to show up on the dark paper. Tahl rubbed his fingertips together as he surveyed his box. Eventually, he took a nub of deep ochre wax. When he had the resources, he'd ask the artist for more colors.

In spite of his wealth—or perhaps because of it—Lord Eseri had never married. He had no children that anyone knew of, no lovers, and no immediate family alive. His life revolved around his business, both above and under the table.

"Going after his assets is too predictable," Tahl muttered to himself as he searched the map and scoured his own thoughts for ideas. "Money is his world, but anyone can steal money." His fingers rapped against the edge of the map and he worried his lower lip between his teeth.

One after another, he marked places of interest in ochre. Whatever the mark, it had to be someplace with high security, or his skill wouldn't be noticed. There were museums, armories, auction houses. All of them likely to be involved in Bahar's business. Enough to draw notice, sure, but enough to shake the man's foundations? Tahl scrubbed a hand through his hair and then rubbed his eyes. All too obvious, none too damaging.

Maybe he was looking at this the wrong way. Maybe his focus was too immediate to the noble. Tahl's fingertips dragged his lower eyelids down and he stared at a point near the center of the map, one he'd chosen not to mark.

That's it. He dragged his ochre wax around the place. Threatening a man like Bahar did no good. Threatening the establishment he obeyed without realizing—now *there* was a solution.

SOMETIMES THE SMOKE TINGLED. IT WAS THE CLOSEST TAHL EVER got to the sensation he imagined came with fire. He wiggled his fingers, twisting the plumes into spirals. The smoke did not have to form in the palms of his hands, but he'd grown adept at making shapes that way. He could weave anything; the shape of a bird, the outline of a man. The mages at the academy considered it a parlor trick, instead of real magecraft. He shaped a bat and cast it into the sky. Its wings beat as if it lived, until it dissipated into the clean night air. Whether or not they believed it was useful, he knew it was. For a thief, nothing helped more than a distraction.

One of many reasons thievery flourished in the academy, Tahl supposed. They were secretive, but they relied on their magic too much, using it to break locks or carve holes in glass. It worked well enough within the academy, but outside, their magic was what gave them away. Every mage could sense their power; when they worked their magic to break and enter, they exposed themselves to every other mage in the vicinity.

Tahl, on the other hand, held power so feeble that his presence—and even his most complicated, dense smokeworks—bore no more essence of fire than a lit candle or burning tobacco pipe. The academy mages had claimed he was too weak to train, unable to learn, and cast him out. But not, he thought with a smirk, before he found his new trade.

Under the cover of darkness, the rooftops made a better home than the streets. Thieves like him weren't the only ones who prowled Orrad after dark. He'd watched a pair of roughs for the better part of an hour as they stalked around corners and between buildings. Anywhere they served alcohol, there were easy targets, and the pair had circled the inn Tahl perched on for a good amount of time.

There was a certain amount of predictability in the way those sort of muggers worked. They disguised themselves with a comrade and made conversation as they walked, moving in patterns that suggested they roamed between the taverns and inns in search of more drink. They rarely took a drop themselves, instead focused on tracking when patrons entered and predicting when they would leave.

The people they targeted bore patterns, too. They favored the working class over nobles; a less wealthy quarry, but less dangerous, too. Few who challenged nobles escaped the guard, which made Tahl's interaction with Lord Eseri all the more interesting. The brutes also preyed on people of smaller stature, which worked endlessly in Tahl's favor.

His marks rounded the corner and disappeared on the last round of their patrol, and Tahl slid from the inn's roof to its yard. He always landed in the back; it was softer there, dirt instead of cobbles, and it gave him time to rehearse. A trough stood out back for horses and burden beasts, the water ice-cold. Scrubbing his face with it always added just the right amount of red to his complexion to make him look soused, and the wet dribbles down the front of his shirt from where the water ran off his chin never hurt. He untucked his shirt just so and unfastened a button on his trousers, then staggered toward the front of the inn with a hand on his belt.

Just as his feet reached the street, his marks rounded the

corner on their return. Tahl pretended he didn't see them, pausing at the corner to hitch his belt tighter.

"Oi," one of the brutes called, his voice thick with feigned intoxication. "Necessary out back?"

Tahl sniffed loudly. "There's a stable," he slurred, "and that's good enough."

The man slapped his comrade's chest and motioned toward the back as if to suggest they go.

"Just watch the mule," Tahl said as they approached. "He's not so mindful of his feet."

They spun and surged toward him.

Predictable.

Tahl dropped to the ground and swept their feet out from under them with one leg. A flick of his hands slid his knives out from the sheaths strapped to his forearms and into his hands.

Groaning, one of the men rolled onto his stomach and pushed himself to his hands and knees. Tahl darted forward and caught him with a kick to the stomach, and he sprawled again.

Behind him, the other man clambered to his feet and roared in anger. But anger dulled his judgment and when Tahl spun on him, he lunged forward. Tahl's arm shot forth, driving the heel of his palm into the brute's nose. The man howled and staggered backwards and Tahl darted again, his knives ready. Instead of the man, he targeted the purse at his belt. Coins spilled to the ground with a bright jingle and bounced in every direction.

"Go!" the other thug choked as he struggled to his feet. He tried to run, but couldn't do more than stagger. His partner stumbled after him, clutching his crushed nose and groaning in pain.

Tahl flicked a salute toward their backs and gathered their lost coins. It was a good haul; a month's wages for most workers. Two copper pennies glinted in the light that spilled from the inn at his back. He considered them for a moment, then turned toward the inn's door. As many bullies and robbers that lurked in the night, there were others, too—less fortunate and less skilled than him—who deserved a lucky break. He wiped his palm against his trousers and slipped inside.

The would-be muggers were right in their assessment of the inn's inhabitants. Nearly two dozen men bowed over their drink, some so unsteady on their chairs that Tahl didn't know how they'd survive getting to their feet. But, as with most places that served alcohol this near to the river gate, the room held only working class people. Putting his head down, Tahl let himself blend in as he crept to an empty space at the end of one table. He sat and pressed a silver coin to the tabletop with his thumb.

"Again?" a small, unimpressed voice asked beside him.

Tahl smirked at the girl as she thunked a wooden mug down in front of him. "A man's gotta eat. Besides, they make it easy."

"You're barely a man," the girl retorted.

"And you're barely old enough to be serving tables, but here you are." He spread his hands placatingly. "Food, Nia. Please. I'm hungry."

She rolled her eyes, but pushed her way back to the kitchen.

Despite the enjoyment she derived from picking at him, Niada was one of few people in Orrad Tahl genuinely liked. Their shared profession was one reason for it, though the rest of their bond had come from her role as an informant. The girl worked as a barmaid in any and every establishment that would take her, though they were few and far between. With rowdy drunks abound, the role of barmaid wasn't always the safest, and Niada was young—a handful of years younger than Tahl. Between her age and her small stature for her twelve years, few barkeeps were willing to take her on. Still, she managed to find work, and in some ways, her age worked to her benefit. Lips were loose after a few pints of ale, and no one paid mind to a little girl carrying tankards between tables.

"Here." A wooden plate clattered to the table in front of him, spilling gravy. Niada looked down her nose at him and held out her hand.

Tahl pushed the silver coin across the table and left it. "There's more for you, if you want to work for it."

"Of the two of us, who works more?" She sat down at the other side of the table.

"Why work more when you can work smart? I'm the one with the full purse." The riverside inns didn't serve as good of food as those near the garden district, but Tahl was too hungry to care. He speared a half-dozen slices of spiced carrot with his fork and jammed them into his mouth.

Niada sniffed. "At least I have food whenever I want it."

"Fair," he muttered between bites. "I need information."

"Which is why you gave me a whole pim today, and not two half-mites for your meal." She rolled the coin between her fingers.

"And if you want the two half-mites, you'll help me out." The carrots were overcooked. Tahl moved on to the fish and its oily gravy.

The girl motioned for him to continue.

He gulped down the near-flavorless food with a grimace. "I found him."

Her dark brows climbed. "Today?"

Tahl nodded. "On my own, thank you very much."

"You can't get mad at me for that. It was a dumb idea to begin with."

"Well, dumb or not, it happened. But he won't let me in." Deciding the carrots were preferable to the fish, he turned his plate.

She smirked. "Called it. You owe me another pim."

"I never actually took that bet." He paused to chew. Niada leaned forward over the table. That eager to hear the rest of the story, was she? He slowed down, forcing her to wait. The anticipation on her face morphed into frustration.

At last, he swallowed. "The gravy's not saving that fish, by the way."

"You don't even like fish!"

"All the more reason for it to need saving." Tahl wiped his mouth with the back of his hand. "He didn't turn me in, which is how I know I scared him. Not enough to get him to let me in, but enough that he was worried what would happen if I spoke to the guards. But since he didn't want to cooperate, I think it's time to do more than scare him."

Niada's green eyes shone with delight. Her eyes were another kinship between them. With both of them dark-haired and green-eyed, Niada could have passed for his sister. Of course, as a northerner, her complexion was too pale. "What's the plan?"

"Barmaid! Drink!" came a raucous voice from across the room.

The girl grimaced and thrust herself from her seat, but she held up a finger to ask Tahl to wait. He craned his neck to watch her work while he finished his meal, whether or not he liked it.

He really didn't like fish—at least, not in Orrad. The whiskered bottom-feeders they dragged out of the river tasted like mud.

Eventually, Niada returned. "Talk fast," she whispered. "I'm still working."

"I'll have you get me a drink in a moment. I need ideas. Something big, something most people would think impossible." The coins in his pocket clinked when he shifted to remove one.

"Liar," she said. "You've already got a plan. I know you."

He shrugged. "I have half a plan. I need a suggestion for the other half. Something that would cause a stir."

"The opal in the queen's crown."

Tahl rolled his eyes. "I'm serious."

"Then you'll like the information I just got this morning." Her eyes twinkled.

"Which is?"

"Ah-ah." The girl held out a hand. "Mites first."

Scowling, he pushed a single copper half-mite into her palm.

Niada's brow furrowed, but he pointed at the bar. "Drink," he ordered.

When she returned with a mug of water, he smirked. A good thief never drank—at least, not outside the comfort of their own home. She sat and leaned close. "The Temple of Brant brought a collection of artifacts from the north. They're to be used for something during the equinox service, I think, but until the equinox, they'll be on display in the Queen's Museum."

"I like where this is going," Tahl murmured over the rim of his cup.

She nodded. "They brought an artifact they're calling the Seed of Brant."

He slapped the table. "Done. That's all I needed."

"What's my part?" she asked, eager.

"That was your part." He passed her a second coin. "Now you just listen."

"That's not fair!" Niada protested. "You never let me help with anything!"

Tahl ticked a finger at her. "You are helping. You just helped. I can't have you on this, this is mine. If I don't do this one alone, it won't mean anything, it won't make any difference. Understand?"

The girl crossed her arms and slouched, pouting.

His shoulders slumped in defeat. "I'll take you next time."

A tiny spark of hope lit in her eyes. "Promise?"

With a little more flourish than necessary, he pressed a spread hand to his chest in a gesture of honesty. "Promise."

"Okay." She rose and collected his empty dishes. "But I'm going to hold you to that."

Tahl stood and tucked his hands into his pockets to silence his stolen coins. He strolled outside and sucked in a deep lungful of night air.

"Seed of the Lifetree, huh," he murmured to himself, gazing at the stars. He couldn't have timed things better if he'd tried.

CHAPTER 4

THE ARTIST LICKED HIS LIPS AND EYED THE COINS IN TAHL'S PALM. Sweat broke on the man's brow. "The whole set?"

"That would make it easier to learn, wouldn't it? Having all the colors handy?" The two pims in his hand glinted in the light when Tahl flexed his hand. Truthfully, the bright chalk pastels in the box between them weren't worth half what he offered, given their apparent quality, but they would be more useful than wax. Chalk could be erased, which would spare his maps. It also wouldn't melt when his rented room over the stable got hot, come summertime. He could have stolen the chalk ten times over while the man worked at his drawing, but the fellow was a skilled artist. Though no one yet recognized the artist when he worked near the river, Tahl doubted that would be the case forever. Building a rapport was wiser. Eventually, skilled artists moved within noble circles, and that made them useful friends.

"I—I suppose," the artist said.

Tahl lowered his hand. "Is something wrong?" The pair of silver coins were probably close to what the man made in a week. His hesitation made no sense.

The man flashed him a nervous smile. "No. I mean, not exactly. I mean, just... just sentimentality. As an artist, your tools become an extension of yourself. You'll understand once you gain experience."

"Ah." Tahl already understood. He felt the same way about his two favorite knives. "Could you tell me where you bought them, then? I can get some of my own."

Relief washed over the artist's face. "That, I can do."

The directions he gave were clear and simple—another reason to befriend the man, Tahl decided as he walked. Connections were useful, but connections who could navigate within the maze-like museums and manors in the wealthiest parts of the city were priceless.

Near the boundary between the mercantile district and the gardens, Tahl found the little market stall with its stock of paints, chalks, and other artistic supplies. He intended to pay; Tahl had a soft spot for the arts, one he'd always attributed to his mother's passion for painting. It was the merchant himself that changed his mind. The man wore silks finer than those Lord Eseri sported, and the prices on his materials were easily three times what they should have been. Business was business, but to flaunt such excess when most students of the arts struggled to feed themselves was tasteless.

Tahl lingered beside a pastry cart nearby until a larger group of pedestrians came into view. Timing was everything. He moved as they approached, allowed their passage to push him to the edge of the street. As they passed, he turned his head as if to watch them in curiosity. The merchant followed suit. A flick of Tahl's fingers slid a small box of colored chalks off its stack and into his pocket. The merchant looked back as if to question what Tahl had seen, but Tahl never took his eyes off the group. Instead, he hurried after them, as if to join someone he'd recognized. The pedestrians never noticed him at their heels. They rounded a corner, Tahl with them, and then he broke away.

Boring. Uneventful. All in all, every time he stole something, Tahl was reminded of why he sought the guild.

Most thievery was beneath him. The brawls were interesting;

they restored challenge. But pickpocketing and petty thievery had lost their risk and danger long ago. The big heists—now those were fun. He liked the jobs that kept him on his toes, that put beads of sweat on his brow and down his spine. The jobs that made his heart race and let fear grip his belly.

Those jobs, unfortunately, didn't come often, and scarcity didn't pay the bills. His attic room above the horse stalls wasn't luxurious, but it certainly wasn't free. The guild had resources. Lodgings. And tools much better than low-quality colored chalks, he was sure. The guild offered security—and less time spent to ensure subsistence meant more time he could spend on real jobs.

When Tahl reached home, he stopped at the foot of the ladder to his room. The hatch at the top of the ladder was open. A short cycle of possibilities ran through his head. With as good as he was at covering his tracks, there was no chance Bahar Eseri or any of his lackeys had stopped by. The noblewoman who let him rent the room sent her servants up now and then to ensure the space was clean; no concern, as he wasn't foolish enough to leave anything incriminating where it could be found. Which meant the last possibility... well, it was the most likely. Tahl resigned himself to it on the way up.

A blade flashed toward the back of his head and his wrist snapped up with a knife of his own to deflect it. "Sloppy," he said, deadpan.

Niada huffed. "I want to know your plan."

He crawled up and shut the hatch. "You'll hear about it in the morning. It's happening tonight."

"Tell me!" she insisted.

"So you can piggyback off my success and keep me from getting in?" Tahl shook his head.

Her face twisted into a pout. "I can help. I have information."

The chalks rattled in their box as he pulled it from his pocket. Tahl turned it over, investigating, before he pushed the end of the box with both thumbs to slide it from its cover. The box itself was thin wood, but the cover was some sort of thick paper. He hadn't seen its like before and he studied its texture with his fingertips. Imported, it seemed; the fibers were like nothing he'd observed in the Westkings. International trade connections were an aspect of befriending an artist he hadn't yet considered.

"I want in, too," Niada said in a small voice.

"I'll be sure to put in a good word for you." Tahl took a piece of blue chalk and closed the box. "Is that the only reason you're here?"

The girl shook her head. "There's a rumor going around. I thought you ought to know. They say there's something big coming, and it might draw unwanted attention to the guild. All guild members are to watch and interfere if they see anything going on outside of guild business."

"Is that so?" He couldn't help a wry smile. "Sounds like I've spooked the guildmaster."

Niada rubbed her arms. "Promise you won't do anything stupid, okay? I know you want this, but... Tahl, you're the only one who takes me seriously. I don't want anything to happen."

"Thanks for the confidence." Most of the attic was unfinished, but the corner that hosted his rough bed was insulated with blocks of straw. He shifted the straw aside to remove a long wooden box from behind it. It would have been easy to keep more behind the straw, but it would have been easy to find. All he kept there was the long, shallow box that held his maps.

"Promise," she insisted. "I'm serious."

"I promise," he said as he unfurled the map onto his table. He circled the Queen's Museum with chalk and scattered lines and symbols in the streets around it. Niada watched, anxious, but the notes would tell her nothing. Like most thieves, Tahl kept his own code. He'd never recorded a cipher for it. The translation existed only in his mind.

"So you're really going after the Seed, huh?" She kept her

voice low. Though the hatch was closed, their voices carried into the stable below.

His chalk stopped mid-stroke. "I think it's time for you to go."

Shrugging, she turned toward the hatch. "I didn't think you'd go for it, since it was my suggestion."

When she didn't leave, he put his things aside and opened the hatch for her. "Nothing's set in stone yet. Go."

"Tahl—" she started.

"I'm changing clothes now," he warned, sliding a hand underneath his shirt.

Alarmed and disgusted, Niada scurried down the ladder and slammed the hatch behind her.

That trick wouldn't work forever. Someday, probably soon, she wouldn't find boys disgusting. He dreaded what he'd have to do to protect her then. Tahl bolted the hatch and pulled his box of gear out from under the bed.

The first thing that went on was his small collection of knives. One on either arm and one on each leg. Though he had lightweight leather armor, he left it in the wide, shallow box and opted for his best gear instead. Leather was good for mobility, but it was noisy. He pulled his heist shirt on over his head.

That he had a dedicated *heist shirt* was amusing, to say the least, but it was the best piece of gear he could have asked for. Inky blue and lightweight, it was knitted from the finest wool. Its thousands of tiny stitches stretched and flexed to hold the fabric close against his skin without restricting movement. He slid a finger into the high-necked collar and ran it back and forth to help the cloth lay smooth up to his chin. It insulated, but breathed, which made it suitable for any weather. It had also cost him a small fortune and earned a number of suspicious looks from the woman he'd hired to make it. But no matter. It was worth every pim.

The matching pants sported pockets inside and out. He checked each pocket with care to ensure they were empty. Then he retrieved a box from under a loose floorboard and began to fill his pockets with tools.

Wire. String. Darts with wrapped tips. Lock picks and wrench. Vials of oil. A little box of fire inch-sticks imported from the Chain Islands of Raeldan. They were cheating, soaked in sulfur so they lit easy, but they were a useful crutch with his limited magic. Item after item vanished into his pockets and Tahl finished by strapping a dagger to each of his thighs. When he finished, he stretched and twisted to ensure nothing rattled or jingled. Then he pulled on his shoes.

Like his clothing, the shoes had been custom made. Dyed to match the rest of his outfit, they were the softest doeskin, both comfortable and stealthy. He wiggled his toes into place—the shoe's big toe was split from the rest to grant more dexterity in climbing—and tugged the back up around his ankle and over the cuff of his pant leg. It fastened in the back with hidden metal hooks.

To his grief, his bag was dark brown instead of blue, but it would suffice. The last of his gear went into the bag and he slung it over his shoulder. Only then, after he was ready, did he notice the little basket of tavern food Niada had left by the back leg of the table.

Tahl lowered his bag back to the floor. All that preparation, and he'd forgotten the most important thing: making sure he had the strength for everything he had to do.

"I'll definitely put in a good word for you," he muttered as he pushed the map from the table and sat down to eat.

The sunset glowed red on the horizon when he licked his fingers clean and took his bag once more.

By daybreak, one way or another, his deeds would be on the lips of everyone in Orrad.

CHAPTER 5

SLOW, DEEP BREATH FILLED TAHL'S LUNGS. HIS ARMS STRETCHED overhead, fingertips toward the ceiling. Then he bent at the waist, back and arms straight as he sank down, down, until his hands splayed flat against the floor. He exhaled. Every stretch was necessary. He longed to be on the roofs, but the more time he spent on preparation, the less likely he was to get hurt.

Most of his body sported bruises, and he had his share of scars. The acrobatics were what injured him, more often than not. The city wasn't made for vaulting rooftops, and when he misjudged, the landings were never kind. He couldn't afford any missteps tonight.

Between stretches, he committed his maps to memory. He tried not to write things down, if he could help it; the few notes he kept in his room were kept scattered. Nothing made sense without the other pieces. It was the easiest way to ensure secrecy.

He laced his fingers together behind his back and extended his arms behind him. Pleasant warmth spread in his chest and back when the muscles pulled. When he touched the floor again, he felt no strain in his back or the backs of his knees.

It was time.

The horses in the stable below his room barely noticed his presence. They'd grown used to his coming and going, and with familiarity came disinterest. Tahl slipped out the stable door and scaled the stately house beside it.

The first time he set foot in Orrad, he'd noticed the city was built in a way that proclaimed they did not care about thieves. Affluent as his parents were, they would have been horrified to know he'd always been fascinated by the stalking shadows that ruled the night. He'd taken to practicing acrobatics long before he'd known the academy would reject him, forcing him to employ the skills he'd learned between the classes he'd failed.

He'd expected his parents to show pity. Instead, they'd scorned him for his failures. They'd both been successful mages. How could their only son lack any power at all?

The first few weeks had been hard, but Tahl was a fast learner, and he adapted. The roofs had felt foreign under his feet then. Now, he swore they were his true home. He sucked in a breath and, with a running start, vaulted from one roof to the next.

He knew how to land, how to slide, how to push his momentum into the next leap. He'd pushed too far, learned his limits, learned to prepare. Tonight, all his practice would come to fruition. The worst part was, everyone who saw him would think he'd failed.

Some distance from his home, he stopped and crouched on the darker side of a roof. He crept to its edge and peered into the streets below. Getting down was always harder than getting up, and the chances of being seen were greater. The moon was fuller than he liked, which meant the night was brighter, but he supposed it could be worse. Orrad was on the east side of the Westkings, which meant the city never saw the sliver of the second moon that sat perpetually on the horizon in the far west. He'd never been there and probably never would, but he'd heard in Raeldan, the moon hung in the sky both night and day.

Surviving the light of two moons—now that would be a challenge.

He probed each handhold before he took it. Though scaling down the wall was harder than climbing, he reached the ground fast and sprinted the short distance to his next climb. There were only a few wide breaks where it was impossible to cross the rooftops to continue through the city. When he dismounted again, it was just outside the garden district.

Not all the city's nobles could afford to live within the garden walls. Others chose to live just outside as a matter of frugality. Tahl's first mark of the night was beside the gate. He lingered in the shadows between houses and watched the guard station for a time. The location gave rise to interesting difficulties. Torchlight flickered outside the guard station, casting a warm glow across the front and north side of the house. The back of the building was visible from the walkway along the top of the garden wall. The only part of the place bathed in shadow was a narrow alley directly across from where Tahl stood. Naturally, with the tiny gap between the tall houses, that was the one part of the building that bore no windows. The back would have to be good enough.

Tahl lingered, stretching and bouncing soundlessly on his toes. He'd given himself as big a window of time as he could for each step of his plan, but that meant finding ways to stay warmed up. Eventually, the guard at the gate disappeared into the guard house for a change of shift, and Tahl darted across the street.

The moment he reached the narrow alley between houses, he climbed.

The varied stones at the corners of the walls were interesting, pleasing to the eye, and made his job easier—as did the next house over being only an arm's reach away. He wedged his toes between the stones on the back corner of either house and propelled himself upward until he was halfway up the third floor. From his perch, he could lean his head back and see where windows dotted the back wall. Shutters guarded most, but two windows in the center of the third floor were left unshuttered. An oversight? Or a sign of occupancy?

Something moved behind the building and Tahl shifted to free his foot from the second house. He pressed close to the wall and focused on his breath. Slow, steady, even. The slower his breath, the less he trembled with effort.

A shadow stirred on the ground below, intent on the back of the house. Tahl eased his foot back to brace himself between houses again. He leaned out, just enough to get a better look.

You've got to be kidding. He fought back a groan. Of all the nights to encounter another thief, why now? Why *here?*

The thief vanished into the house on ground level and Tahl swung around the corner. No matter how sure of hand and foot he was, he could only move across the side of the stone building so fast. He ducked under one of the shuttered windows and aimed for the nearer of those left open. He needed speed now. Balanced on the edge of the window sill, he searched the edges of the frame until he found the latch. It was a single pane, hinged on one side instead of split down the middle, and every second he spent fuddling with opening the blasted thing was too much. The time he'd allowed himself for this leg of his mission no longer mattered.

Tahl hit the floor harder than he intended, wincing at the thud. Voices echoed elsewhere in the house, their conversation and laughter enough to mask the sounds of his movement. He allowed himself to breathe and left the window open as he darted into the hall.

He hadn't had time to case the house; he could only pray what he needed wasn't on the main floor. There had to be an office, a parlor, a workspace somewhere. Yet door after door opened to reveal sleeping quarters. Tahl bit back an oath.

Brant forbid something work out easy, tonight of all nights. He descended to the second floor with his teeth clenched and froze when he hit the hall.

At the far end of the hallway, his new rival stared with wide eyes for all of a heartbeat before he dodged into a room. Instinct gnawed at him and Tahl darted after the other thief. His tip-toed dash was soundless and when he appeared in the doorway, the other thief yelped.

A stroke of luck. The room was a library, with a desk at the far end of the room—exactly what Tahl hoped to find.

"The key is mine!" the other thief snarled in a whisper, brandishing a dagger in challenge.

Tahl's brow furrowed and he pulled the door closed behind him, leaving only the thinnest sliver of light to pour in from the hall. "Key?" he whispered back.

The man's face slackened in confusion. *Man* might have been a generous term, Tahl decided after his eyes had a moment to adjust. The other thief was perhaps a year or two older than he was—and at seventeen, Tahl was barely considered an adult.

"The guild's challenge," the young man replied. "You aren't part of it?"

Tahl shook his head and relaxed his stance. The other thief copied him unconsciously, lowering his dagger.

"I don't even know what you're talking about," Tahl said.

The thief raised a brow. "Then why are you here?"

"This man's part of an imports company. I'm after his logbooks." Tahl pointed toward the desk and the man relaxed further. "You're with the guild?"

"It's part of the admittance challenge every thief goes through. If you don't even know about the hunt for the key, you're nowhere near ready. It'd rust to nothing before you found the first clues."

A small, unpleasant sense of irritation pricked at Tahl's spine. He stood straighter. "That's all potential recruits are required to do? Complete a treasure hunt they learned about through word of mouth?"

The thief shrugged. "If you've not got that far, I can't help you, mate. Good luck with your logbooks."

"Good luck with your key," Tahl replied dryly as he circled the stranger and opened the drawers on the desk. "When you find it, tell Guildmaster Eseri I send my regards."

The young man spun toward him with his mouth agape. Before he could protest, Tahl pressed a finger to his lips and hugged the book he was after to his chest. He backed to the windows behind the library desk, then twirled to fling them open.

"Hey!" the thief called before he caught himself. His hand clapped over his mouth and he wheeled toward the door.

Tahl caught the window sill in his free hand and swung outside. He hung on just long enough to slide the log book under his skintight shirt. Then his toes dug into the wall and he kicked off hard, twisting in midair to land in a roll. He tumbled across the narrow garden and stumbled when he rolled onto his feet.

Sloppy, he mentally hissed. The book slipped and he pulled it from his shirt as he dashed back the way he'd come.

Behind him, a guard dog bayed and angry voices rose in the night.

CHAPTER 6

THE FIRST THING TAHL WAS GOING TO INVEST IN AFTER THIS venture was a better bag.

As soon as he'd made it back onto the roofs, he'd tucked the log book in with his gear and slung the straps over his shoulders again. But the straps were too narrow and stiff to be truly comfortable, and with every running leap he took, it chafed a little more through the thin knit of his shirt. There had been the part where he'd rolled over it, too—normally not a problem, but he'd landed just the right way for something to turn sideways and dig into his back when he'd tumbled. Now every step jolted the bag and its contents against the rising bruise.

He got what he deserved. If he was honest, he deserved worse. A skilled thief knew when to show off, and that hadn't been the time. It had, however, been a wise time to run. What allotted time was left in the first leg of his mission had been spent hiding on the far side of a roof until the guards were suitably distracted. They hadn't removed anyone from the house, which meant—Tahl assumed—the other thief had escaped. Good; he didn't know what sort of clues the man hoped to find, but he hadn't wanted the fellow to be caught.

Tahl trotted along the peak of a roof and paused at the end.

The building below sported a flat terrace instead of tiles or shakes. He considered jumping, then thought better of it and climbed down, instead. In warmer weather, the terrace might have been a welcome nighttime retreat, but the spring air still held a bit of a bite. All the better, he figured; the fewer people who were out, the better. He stalked across the terrace to crouch at the corner and slide his bag from his shoulder. The waterskin inside was small, but it was better than nothing. He allowed himself a single swig, held it in his mouth and let it trickle down his throat as his eyes drifted across the city.

Orrad hosted a number of impressive buildings, but with the arrival of the temple's artifacts, the Queen's Museum had become magnificent. Beacons of mage-light lit the tall building's exterior in shades of gold, dulling the light of the stars overhead. Tahl couldn't see them from the terrace where he took a second sip of water, but he could imagine the pine boughs and bright berries woven into garlands and draped around the museum's entrance. Symbols of the Lifetree. He'd seen them but hadn't wondered why they were there instead of the temple. Foolish. He'd let his goal of finding the guildmaster and joining the guild distract him from what was happening in the city. He wouldn't make that mistake again.

As he capped his waterskin and returned it to his bag, Tahl traced the rooftops with his eyes. The museum couldn't be approached directly, not with those mage-lights on it. Safer to sweep northeast first, approach from the back. Like the temple and the palace, the museum faced south to welcome the most light in its doors. There were messages within the city's layout, whether intentional or not. Everything considered good, just, sat in north-south alignment. The academy, which considered itself respectable but hid dealings that spoke otherwise, faced west and sat sideways. Comical, Tahl thought, that both the thieves' guild headquarters and Lord Eseri's mansion sat crooked, off-kilter from the grid.

The building immediately ahead sported a roof with a

reasonable slope. Tahl started there, bounding from the terrace to that rooftop, and the next, and the next. The more momentum he retained, the better. The cold night air made his chest burn, the humidity heavy in his lungs. The rest of him felt light, the soft patter of his steps all but lost in his senses. With every jump, his heart soared. With every landing, he felt a surge of victory.

Guards circled wide streets below. Tahl altered his path, cut farther north. The muscles in his legs burned, but he was close. Getting there was the easy part. He veered east to compensate for his detour. It worked better this way; he had to dismount from the roofs one way or another, and the neighborhoods that surrounded the north side of the museum took him closer to the building than his original approach.

He didn't want to slow, but the alternative was plunging into the cobblestone street that was too wide to vault. Reluctant, he stalled, halting only when his toes reached the edge of the last roof. There he crouched, forcing his breath to remain slow and even. Gasps for air were noisy and useless.

The Queen's Museum loomed ahead, taller than the three-story buildings that comprised most of the rest of the city, yet not as tall as the palace or Brant's temple. It was hard to say where the artifacts would be inside, but he had no reason to worry just yet. Museums tended to be prideful of their displays. With something as rare and valuable as temple artifacts, they'd likely set up an exhibit and point signs straight toward it.

Tahl had seen exhibits once or twice and held a rough idea of where they might be, but his knowledge of the museum still lacked. Admission was expensive, which kept most of the working class at bay. Atoras was like most emperors in that respect—he withheld knowledge from the peasantry, fearing the advantage it may give them. As a mage, pitiful as his ability was, Tahl's education was on par with that of most nobles. That the size of his purse was all that restrained him from enjoying the social luxuries of his peers sometimes rankled.

But not for long, he reassured himself as he retreated to the lee of the roof. The shadows were a luxury, themselves. Tahl adjusted his hold on the edge of the roof several times before he swung a leg down to scout for toe holds. *By tomorrow morning, everything will change.*

If he survived.

His feet reached the ground and he crouched beside the wall. An aching heat had started in his shoulders and thighs. *And we're not even to the hard part yet,* he mused. A few seconds for stretches were all he could spare. Then he slipped around the corner of the building and tucked his hands into his pockets as he strolled into the wide avenue illuminated by the looming museum's glow.

He wanted to run. A lesser thief might have. But even dressed as oddly as he was, he drew less attention if he walked. The guards roamed farther down, too far to see him clearly. From a distance, no one would notice the cut of his clothes. He could have been anyone, walking home from an evening's work, walking home from a courtship dinner. Still, his pulse accelerated as he crossed the road. Only when he ducked into the shadows on the other side did he again feel safe.

What would it be like, to spend every night gripped by that kind of fear? To sink into danger—the real danger that came with a heist, instead of the uninspiring risk of injury that came with petty theft?

For a single, fleeting instant, the consuming heat of anger swelled in Tahl's heart. Bahar Eseri had weaseled his way into leadership of the guild through politics and business, not skill. Then he admitted members through simple tests instead of true challenges, building his own empire of petty thieves who could never hope to taste the bitter fear of what Tahl was about to do.

To steal from the temple was to blight one's soul, planting a festering rot that would eventually consume them. It was a fool's errand, a descent into depravity that could shock a man even so arrogant as Lord Eseri.

He's blighted, himself, no doubt, Tahl muttered silently to himself. *I could ask for better company.* He slid into a final alleyway and emerged at the edge of the museum's broad plaza.

The Queen's Museum grazed the sky, its mage-lights blotting the heavens above to empty blackness. Ironic, given the treasures the place held. If the Lifetree's branches were the gate to Heaven, then to block out its stars in honor of Brant's artifacts was an act of blasphemy.

All around the building, armored guards marched in rows of three. Tahl sank back into the shadows as they approached. When he put his head down to hide his face, he all but disappeared. But he watched.

They moved in steady rhythm, perfectly spaced so that no one could slip by. At every corner of the building, more guards stood ready, spears resting against the cobbles. Tahl had planned to climb the north facing wall and gain entry through the roof, but he'd forgotten the museum bore two entrances, both north and south. Acting casual helped him cross streets, but it would do nothing to help him get inside. A side approach was his only option.

He watched the guards cycle past, his toe tapping a steady, soundless rhythm against the ground. They all marched the same direction, northward up the west side, where Tahl would have to climb. He'd have to move southward, toward the main entrance, and catch the gap where the party marched on and left the south corner exposed.

Exposed save the guards posted at the corner, that was. He'd need something to distract them, pull their attention toward the entrance. That would provide an opening of almost a minute before the next team of guards would round the corner. One minute to climb high enough that he wouldn't be seen.

I've worked on tighter schedules, he reassured himself as he backtracked into the alley and moved farther south. It would have been easier to judge how far he needed to go if he'd been on the roofs, but he wasn't about to risk being seen before he even made it to the museum. When the illuminated building's corner soared over the top of the building beside him, he squeezed into the gap between two houses and padded closer.

The distraction would be the easy part. *As if any of this is going to be easy from now forward.* Tahl let a group of guards pass the corner and braced himself to act after the next one. His heart thumped against his ribcage, tried to urge his breath to race along with it. He struggled to maintain control of his breathing as he summoned what little magic he had.

The guards passed.

Tahl forced his magic to manifest. A teeming swarm of smoke bats formed over one of the massive mage-lights, darting and weaving so it was impossible to tell where they'd come from. Their hazy wings threw writhing shadows against the front of the museum, obscuring the windows. An ill omen.

At the south corner, one of the guards nudged his partner and pointed with his spear. They raised their voices to scold the creatures and, when the swarm didn't dissipate, raised their spears to bang on the bottom of the massive brass sconce that held the mage-light against the wall.

Tahl bolted for the building. His magic wouldn't last long, and his opening would evaporate with it. His fingers dug into the tiny gaps between the stone blocks and he leveraged himself up fast. Only a few handholds in, he jabbed his fingers into a gap and winced when a fingernail cracked. *Climbing claws,* he added to his mental list. *Before the next job, I'm getting climbing claws.*

Not that he needed them. He was used to the cuts and scrapes and chips in his nails, all of them hard-earned. His toes were protected, though, and the soft, pliable doeskin gripped the wall just as well as his own skin might. He pushed himself left, the countdown ticking loudly in his head. Voices neared the corner, signaling the guards' return. Grimacing, Tahl hauled himself up beside one of the solid brass sconces just as the guards rounded the corner. Elsewhere, on the edge of his senses, he felt his smoke unravel.

Below, footsteps clacked against the stone and a trio of guards strolled past.

Tahl pressed himself closer to the corner where the mage-light's sconce met the wall. The sconce had looked smaller from the ground. When he was right beside it, the thing was taller than him. Its left side made a perfect hiding spot, out of sight when the guards rounded the corner, and he doubted any of them would look directly at a mage-light of that strength, anyway.

Except now I have to figure out how to go unnoticed with the light shining directly on me. Maybe he hadn't thought that all the way through. Straight up was the best option, but would leave him most visible, casting a massive shadow up the wall for all of Orrad to see. He shifted farther left instead. There was no escaping the lights, but there was a narrow cone of shadow that crept up between the two nearest lights. Their meeting point was weakest. If he was fast and cautious, perhaps he could make it through. Beyond that point, the roof was only a few feet away.

The next team of guards passed underneath him and Tahl waited until they reached the next mage-light before he started upward at an angle. His movement wasn't noisy, but movement drew the eye. With all the odd, arching shapes and different colors of stone that made up the museum's exterior wall, a still shadow was more likely to go unnoticed. He froze when the next trio passed.

His shoulders already screamed, his upper arms burned. His legs fared better—difficult as the climb was, his nightly rooftop running had conditioned his legs well. Worst was the bruise in his lower back where he'd landed on his bag. Those muscles groaned; their straining protest was enough to put a fleeting regret in the forefront of his mind. He couldn't afford to pay it any mind. He'd have time to hurt tomorrow. The next handhold put him at the meeting of the two mage-lights' beams.

Here goes.

He swung into the light. His toes wedged between two

particularly uneven stones and he thrust himself upward, stretching beyond what he thought he could reach.

A shrill whistle burst from the guards on the ground, now far below.

That didn't take long. Tahl's amused smile morphed into a grimace. The top was no more than four feet off.

A stone cracked against the wall, narrowly missing his leg.

Slings! He overextended his reach, his arms too exerted to pull him that far. He pulled back and found a closer handhold. *At least they're not arrows.*

More stones whistled through the air. Tahl reached for a crevice and jerked back his hand. A fist-sized rock smashed into the stone where his fingers would have been. Maybe aiming for the shadows had been a bad idea. If he'd been right in the light, the guards wouldn't have been able to aim while staring past the blinding mage-light.

Something popped against his side. Heat and pain radiated outward a split second later, driving the air from Tahl's lungs. *Blight it all!* He gasped, lunging upward and seizing the edge of the roof. With the last of the strength in his arms, he dragged himself up and over the small guard wall and wheezed when he crashed onto the flat stone on the other side. Exhaustion hit him like a lead weight. He couldn't afford to rest. Grunting, he rolled over and pushed himself up. The far south end of the roof hosted a service door. Cupping a hand over the welt on his side where the stone hit, he ran.

Locked. Of course it was.

He dropped to his knees and shrugged his bag forward, ignoring the burn in his shoulders. The guards would be up the same stairs and after him in a moment; he couldn't spare the precious minutes needed to pick the lock. Instead, he wrapped his fingers around a crude metal shiv and slammed it into the keyhole. One hard wrench and the metal gave an unpleasant crack as the mechanism broke. The lock and handle both fell and

Tahl stuck his hand in through the hole to check for a bar on the other side. Nothing.

At least that much went right. The door creaked open and he darted inside. Pain pulsed in the soft tissue of his side. He hated to think what that bruise would look like in the morning, but he wasn't bleeding, and the pain wasn't so unbearable that he couldn't keep moving. No internal damage, then. At least he hoped.

The squared spiral staircase inside led to a narrow maintenance hall, exactly the sort of place Tahl didn't want to be. Shouted orders and thundering footsteps already echoed inside the museum. He ran until light flickered at the end of the dark passage and sprawling shadows of armored men reached his eyes. He stretched out his arms to plant his palms flat against the walls. His feet followed, one after the other, and he shimmied upward until his back touched the ceiling. When he turned his head to hide his face, he became invisible.

A mask, too, he added to his list. *At least for my lower face.* His job was getting expensive.

A pair of guards in red livery marched up the hall and his stomach sank. Those weren't normal guards—those were members of Emperor Atoras's Elite. *Here to placate the temple, no doubt.* Tahl's envisioned plan ticked up a few notches in difficulty. He was sure it could be worse, but at the moment, he wasn't certain how.

Neither of the men who passed beneath him carried a light. *So who has the light, I wonder?* Tahl waited for them to turn the first corner on the stairs before he dropped and sprinted to the end of the hall. With the luck he'd had tonight, it didn't seem likely the lightbearer was just a member of the museum staff. The Elite always worked in pairs; it was safe to assume there were at least two more somewhere in the museum. Looking for him.

Running hurt his side. He stopped at the doorway and braced himself against it as he caught his breath. Scaling the wall in the shadows instead of direct light had definitely been a mistake. Now he had to complete the job with a handicap, and he'd brought it upon his own stupid self. Maybe Lord Eseri had been right to scorn him.

He shook his head hard, dislodging that idea before it could settle. No; he'd outpaced all the other thieves in the academy's basement ages ago, and more than one of them had already been members of the guild. He was more than skilled enough. And Lord Eseri—he'd never pulled a heist in his life.

Tahl swiped the back of his hand over his sweating brow and delved into the museum. He'd never seen a maze quite like the odd rooms and twisted halls that created the exhibits. During his time in the academy, he'd read about a labyrinth the mages said existed on a remote trade island in the center of the Lantaaran ocean. He doubted it existed, but if it did, it couldn't be worse than this.

After hours as it was, most of the rooms were dark. He couldn't have asked for a greater blessing. Light through a doorway ahead warned him of a guard's approach and he ducked behind a sculpture to avoid notice. The man hurried past without a glance, clearly on his way to join the Emperor's Elite Tahl had just evaded. The moment the mage-light vanished into the next room, Tahl sprinted on.

More sculptures rose as twisted shadows in the dark, monsters that seemed to chase him from room to room. Portraits by master painters lined narrow halls, their accusatory eyes enough to make his skin crawl. Museums were fine by daylight, he decided, but he wouldn't be eager to return.

Beside the doorway to another room, a small placard on a stand pointed the way to the temple artifacts, and green banners emblazoned with symbols of Brant beckoned him forth. Tahl followed, his heart thumping in his throat.

Voices echoed in the museum's halls, announcing the arrival of reinforcements. Tahl couldn't go any faster, his breath ragged and his side aching so it was all he could do to stay on his feet.

Then the temple's exhibit spread before him, its priceless artifacts sheltered under the finest mage-made glass.

Relief washed over him. *Almost done.* All that remained was to locate his chosen artifact among the displays.

Tahl wove between sculptures of trees to reach the glass cases, scanning their contents as he walked. Most contained things he thought worthless—bits of stone and what looked like useless branches. Books lay scattered between them, open to carefully chosen pages. Pieces of textiles hung on delicate racks, pitiful compared to the grand tapestries on the walls. Right in the middle of it all, he saw the Seed.

For a moment, he thought it a rock. It looked like one, shaped like the polished gemstone eggs that were utterly useless and decorated the mantels of far too many nobles. Yet it was different. Its gleaming surface shone, iridescent like a tiger's eye stone, but undoubtedly wood. A slight ridge ran down the center of its edge—it wasn't quite ovoid, but a bit wider than it was deep—and its tip bore a point with a distinctive split where the shell came together.

"Brant's shaking branches," Tahl whispered to himself. "It really is a seed." He swung his bag off his shoulder to dig inside. The case was sealed; he slit the rubbery material at its corners with a razor-thin knife. The substance hummed under his fingers, seething with magic he was only just able to detect. Life energy; protective wards meant to preserve whatever was sheltered inside. Ignoring it, he retrieved his lock picks from his bag. The latch on the case was small and simple, easy to undo. The threat of soul-blight was enough to keep most people away.

A long shadow sprawled over him the moment the case came open. "Here! To me!" the guard roared as he tore his sword from its sheath.

Tahl bit back a curse and jammed his picks back into his bag hard enough to tear one strap from his fingertips. Items spilled across the floor when the bag tipped and this time, he didn't restrain his profanity. He spun and snatched the Seed from its cradle. "Catch!"

The guard's sword fell from his hand, his face stricken with fear as the Seed arced through the air.

Tahl hiked his bag over his shoulder and bolted.

A second guard stepped into the doorway. Tahl skidded to a stop and pirouetted back the other direction. He bounded over his lost belongings on his way to the other exit and stifled a shout when one of the Emperor's Elite blocked his way.

The Elite drew his sword so fast, Tahl almost didn't have a chance to free his dagger. He almost crumpled under the weight of the blow, the forceful peal of metal against metal echoing through the whole museum. Tahl could fight, but not an Elite— not with a dagger. But the exit was on the other side, and he didn't have a choice.

He feinted forward and ducked the Elite's arm. He had no chance of landing any blows, and any he might would do nothing to the mage-enhanced armor underneath the red livery.

The Elite twisted after him and swept the ground with a leg. Tahl leaped a second too late. His toes caught the Elite's greaves and he stumbled before casting himself into a clumsy roll. He sprawled sideways, one leg hitting a tree statue hard enough to make him howl. Pain shot up his leg and into his hip when he found his feet. Then the Elite was on him again, his sword flashing overhead in a downward arc.

Tahl reeled backwards, but not far enough. The sword caught his face, dragged across his cheek under his eye.

Smoke exploded all around him, flooding the room, blotting out every trace of light. The Elite and the other two guards hacked and coughed, clutching their chests. They fell to the floor to gasp for breath as the smoke wafted upward.

Second by long, precious second, the blue-gray smoke faded.

The Elite lifted his head, but it was already too late.

Tahl was gone.

CHAPTER 7

Tahl limped and gripped his side, but he couldn't help grinning as he dragged himself over a roof's peak and sat to regain his breath. He couldn't rest long, but he was also sure he deserved it.

The guards would congratulate themselves on deterring the thief. The Elite would receive a dressing-down when his superiors learned said thief had escaped. The Seed would be nestled back into its cradle, the preservation wards restored, and the Museum would crow over their right to display something so precious that someone dared break into the legendary Queen's Museum to steal it.

And the logbook—documenting a great number of Lord Eseri's dirty deals—still lay on the museum floor.

Tahl swiped a hand over his right cheek and grimaced. Blood coated his hand, cold and sticky. The cut burned something fierce, and his face and neck itched where the blood ran and crusted over. He'd planned to be caught, but not by the Elite. Escaping with just a slice across his face was extreme fortune, though it created new problems. He didn't have to see it to know it would scar, and unusual scars were the mortal enemy of a thief who wanted to remain unnoticed. Brushing his sticky hand against his pants, he stood. Niada would know what to do. Disguises were one of her specialties.

But that was a problem for later. He spared a few moments to stretch and prepare his muscles for another round of abuse. His body ached, but the night wasn't over yet.

He started a sprint—more subdued than before, less energetic, less graceful when he bounded from roof to roof. Every landing felt heavy, like the weight of his own weariness tried to pull him to the ground. He couldn't let it. He couldn't break. The hardest vault was still ahead.

The rooftops carried him northwest, far from the museum and the search hounds that howled in the night. They wouldn't find him; he didn't fear their calls. The hounds the guard employed were half the reason he utilized the rooftops the way he did. The beasts couldn't follow up the three-story buildings to pursue his scent and Orrad was too vast a city for them to pick it up once it was lost.

Ahead, the garden district loomed, a broad and open circle of green in the midst of dreary roofs.

One more, he told himself, his mental voice as taxed as the rest of him. *One more mark, and then it's done.*

With every ounce of strength left in him, he sped across the last roof overlooking the garden district's walls and launched himself from the tiled edge. The moment his feet left the roof, he regretted the decision to jump. He sailed over the wall and landed hard in a thick patch of monkey grass, rolling twice before he came to a stop, flat on his back.

A long, slow groan of pain escaped his throat. The gash in his face throbbed, as did the bruises in his back and side. He still hadn't dared look at his side, but he didn't have to see it to know it would hurt for weeks. The strength ebbed out of his limbs and for a long moment, he rested.

If only he could linger. The garden district was only a safe place to catch his breath because they believed no one could enter without notice. With the guardhouses at the gates and the patrols that walked the walls at regular intervals, it was almost true. In the shadows, he blended into the grasses and regained his breath, but the rest of his mission still called.

Aside from the patrols along the tops of the walls, guards rarely walked the rest of the district. Tahl staggered out from behind a house and limped his way across the plaza to the fountain in the center. He sat on the edge of its basin and dipped his hands in the water. It was ice cold, clean and refreshing. Exactly what he needed.

He cupped water in both hands and scrubbed the blood from his face and neck. Pale petals clung to his skin, softly fragrant and oddly soothing. He washed his hands and wiped his face again before he allowed himself to look at the fountain.

Water hardly trickled from the upper tiers. The anchored magic that sustained the water flow was frivolous, but still present, drawing upward despite the clog of petals that kept the water from moving through the fountain's inner workings. Its power hummed at the edge of his senses. As did a hint of interference. Something out of place, something that didn't belong. Something that kept the cycling magic from working the way it ought.

Curious, Tahl pulled up his sleeve and leaned forward. He plunged his arm into the cold water, into the narrow mouth that led to the column where the water was meant to flow. The channel was clogged with twigs and petals, things far too small to stop the fountain on their own. Then his fingers met something else; something rough, cold, and hard. He searched out its shape, his brow furrowed. It stuck tight and he worked to wiggle it free. The second the obstruction came loose, petals and twigs sucked into the fountain and water spewed from its top. Tahl leaned back and opened his hand.

Flat across his palm lay a large, rusted key.

For a moment, all he did was stare. A key, jammed inside a

fountain directly in front of the guildmaster's house. It was so obvious it hurt.

A laugh escaped him before Tahl could catch it, and his eyes swept up to the thirteenth house on the west side. Did Lord Eseri keep watch? Hover over his desk and stare out the windows, hoping to see whoever puzzled things out? He almost hoped so. The mental image of Lord Eseri's face twisted with anger as it pressed against the glass was reward enough. Tahl slid the key into his pocket, instead of his bag, and turned north.

All things considered, moving into the final leg of his mission from the garden district made things more difficult. Guards waited at the north gate. Undoubtedly, they patrolled where he was headed, too. But the lack of a guard presence actually *inside* the district made it a necessary respite. Tahl walked instead of running, drank the last of his water, and—most importantly— finally caught his breath. When the north gate came into view, he wasn't rejuvenated, but he'd gained his second wind.

Just beyond the district's gate, a stately building just tall enough to tower over the nearby houses and businesses stood against the sky. Its white stone facade was impressive in the daytime, but menacing at night. It was no surprise Orrad's most prestigious bank would be placed just outside the homes of its clientele. No surprise that the street beyond the gate teemed with guards, either. The whole city was guaranteed to be on high alert after his disappearance from the museum. Which meant that this, finally, would be a job worth calling a challenge.

One last time, Tahl delved into the shadows. When the sun rose, they'd be a part of him forever. A legend, a legacy he could leave behind.

He slipped behind the row of houses. One of the last houses bore a larger private garden with flowering bushes near the wall. He ducked into a cluster of bushes and tried to ignore the sickly sweet fragrance of its blooms. He knew the patrol patterns by heart. They were constant, dependable, and regular. It didn't matter that he didn't know the time—soon enough, a guard strode by. Tahl couldn't see him from the foliage, but the cadence of his booted footsteps and the creak of his lightweight armor gave him away. The sound drifted west and then south, around the curve of the garden wall. Satisfied, Tahl emerged.

The wall was not impressive—at least, not compared to the museum's walls or the towering white building he pressed toward now. It still rose nearly twenty feet from the ground. The stones were smooth and tightly mortared, but there were still dips between them, and what little purchase they granted his fingertips was enough. He scrambled up the wall and over the low stone guardrail.

Instead of vaulting over the side, he trekked south, leaving ample distance between himself and the guard ahead. Some short distance from the point where he'd mounted the wall, he stopped and pulled a rope from his bag. He'd seen another thief use a hook, once; some three-pronged, clawed monstrosity that created an anchor for a rope anywhere it caught. Someday, he'd have to get one of those. For now, he set his sights on a raised stone finial on the end of a balcony's rail. It was a perfect crossing point, so long as the anchor on this side held.

Without a claw to rely on, he twisted the rope into a loop and checked to ensure it would pull tight. He gave it a twirl, testing to make sure it didn't slip tight too soon. Then he spun the rope overhead and tossed the looped end across the gap.

Too low. It hit the balcony's rail and fell. Undeterred, he adjusted the rope and tried again. This time, it snagged the finial and pulled taut.

No time left. The next patrol would be by soon. He tugged the rope a little tighter and tied it to the wall's rail in the most secure place he could find. *Don't break,* he silently ordered as he slid over the rail and wrapped his limbs around the rope. It strained beneath his weight, but held.

Hand over hand, he inched along the rope like a dark caterpillar, hanging precariously over the street below. Against the dark sky, he was all but invisible, and people moved beneath him without notice. He crawled onto the balcony and allowed himself a breath of relief. The knot on the rope was too tight to undo. He sawed through it with his favorite knife instead and the loose end fell to the street below. Not that he feared anyone would follow. Orrad's roofs were his.

Tahl scaled the remainder of the building with ease, not as fast as before, but with renewed strength and certainty. *But don't get too confident,* he reminded himself. *This isn't over yet.*

The key in his pocket thumped against his leg as he sprinted across the roof and leaped to the next. Each touch of the iron stirred his ire anew. Such a simple task, it was almost insulting. No wonder he'd missed it. He'd been so focused on impressing the guildmaster that he'd overlooked the menial effort they expected thieves to put forth in order to join.

But if that was all they expected, Lord Eseri *should* have been impressed. He should have quaked in his boots. Tahl couldn't help the small, angry voice that lodged itself in his head. *Do you regret it yet, Bahar? Do you see what I'm doing? After tonight, you won't have any boots left.*

Few places bore security like Orrad's bank. For any other reason, Tahl would have balked at the idea of infiltrating the place. It was a challenge, no doubt, but hardly worth the payoff. Until now.

Any job can be worth the effort when the stakes are personal. A new flood of strength poured through him and he took the last leap, from the last residential rooftop to the bank's peaked portico. He landed with a crack. His feet slid and he dropped to his knees to dig his fingers into the roof tiles.

For an instant, everything was still. Then the soft melody of wooden chimes rose into the night air. Tahl turned his head.

A long line of green-robed priestesses, at least fifty strong, snaked down the wide avenue that led past the bank and northward, toward the palace. He couldn't help but stare. He'd never seen priestesses out at night, and never so many at once. Below, the guards who had filled the plaza now flanked the street to watch the priestesses pass. Even those at the bank's door turned away from their post to watch the procession. Their chimes wafted, sweet and haunting, and curiosity clawed at Tahl's heart like a starving beast. But he couldn't indulge it. Instead, he gave a silent prayer of thanks for the distraction and fought his way to the rooftop.

Unlike the museum, the bank bore no rooftop access doors. Tahl didn't need one. He climbed just until the peak sheltered him from view of the priestesses and guards, then slid his worst dagger from its sheath on his leg. The blade was mostly dull and already chipped; it earned another gouge in its edge when he drove it under a roof tile and wrenched it upward. The tile cracked and fell to pieces, exposing the vulnerability beneath.

Wood. If only he'd been capable of starting a fire.

Tahl bit back that frustration and forced himself to focus. There was a weak place in the roof; he'd seen it when it had been patched following a storm, late last summer. He fractured several more tiles and put the pieces aside, wedging them in other tiles so they wouldn't fall. After three more, the seam in the wood repair came into view.

His dagger just fit between the boards. Tahl wiggled it under and heaved against it, prying the board up a bit at a time. Eventually, it popped free, its squawk of protest lost beneath the priestesses' chimes. The second board came free easier. He dislodged a third and dropped into the attic feet first.

Dust swarmed the air around him and the need to cough tightened his throat. He fought it back, tears welling in his eyes. A few hard swallows helped the feeling subside, but the tears left tracks down his face that caught the dust and stained his skin.

Faint moonlight streamed in through the hole in the roof. Weak as it was, it was enough to illuminate the access hatch some short distance away. He stalked across the joists to open it. Below, a ladder descended into a tiny, lightless room he could only assume was a closet.

Tahl tiptoed down the rungs and let his hands explore the walls. A ridge and crack beneath his fingertips revealed the shape of a door. No hinges on this side; the closet was too small for the door to open inward. His palm flattened against the surface and he searched a moment before his thumb bumped against the handle. Locked. No surprise.

This time, he had no need for haste. He leaned close to the door, listened as his picks ticked against the pins inside the lock. Unlike those he'd dealt with at the museum, this was sophisticated. Only the best for Orrad's wealthiest.

The lock came open when he twisted and the door swung outward in perfect silence. He'd expected to emerge in a hall somewhere, but instead, he stood in a darkened office. The space was meticulously organized, cold and pristine. Orrad's bankers saved the lavish trappings for their homes, it seemed—and for the first floor, where they needed to impress their clients. Tahl had only seen the interior of the bank once, when he'd still been part of the academy. The exhibition of wealth hadn't bothered him then. But then, he'd also thought he would remain part of that world.

He was ready to return. To the prestige, the dignity, the comfort. No one wanted to subsist, but aside from literacy and his feeble magic, he had no socially acceptable skills.

But that didn't stop Bahar Eseri from being successful, did it? he mused.

The office door, too, was locked. Tahl tempered his impatience. He couldn't just barrel out into the hallway and hope for the best. The upper floors had windows; it stood to reason they would have night guards on patrol. When the lock clicked, he eased the door open, grateful for the superior maintenance that kept the doors moving on soundless hinges. His oils were still in his pocket, but they were useless if all the doors opened outward.

Tahl peered into the hall from a sliver of an opening. As he'd expected, a guard stood at the far end of the hall, at the top of the stairs that led to the floors below. Right where he needed to be. He stepped back to peer through the crack beside the hinges. Little was visible, but it was enough. He sank backwards and drew the door with him. *Easy enough.*

Farther down the hall, more offices waited in tidy rows. He focused on the one he'd seen and closed his eyes. Fire magic seemed harder at night. According to the mages at the academy, it was because the element grew weaker without a source of heat close at hand. Tahl had always thought that foolish. The traces of energy he needed were fewer in the environment, true, but *he* was a source of heat, and carried everything he needed with him.

Coils of smoke wound themselves outward from his point of focus. He felt them as they spread and thickened, a low cover that cloaked the floor. He built it upward. Thick, billowing clouds flooded the room down the hall. Fine beads of sweat broke on his brow as Tahl reached the edge of his strength and released the smoke. It spilled outward, flowed under the door and scented the air. His smoke always bore a faint hint of sulphur, acrid and hard to miss.

The guard sniffed, soft at first, then long and hard. His head swiveled and he jumped from his post to race up the hallway. He fumbled with the lock and thrust the door open. The smoke poured free.

Tahl held his breath and darted out of the office. Halfway down the stairs, where the air was clear, he allowed himself to suck in a breath. He would let the smoke linger, let the guard search for its source. He wasn't foolish enough to assume the guard would return to his post when the air cleared.

More offices and sitting rooms waited on the second floor, but here, expensive vases, tapestries, and potted exotic plants lined the walls. He ducked into the shadow of a plant with broad fronds. Another guard waited at the stairs that led to his destination. Tahl braced himself and searched for strength. Weak as his power was, magic was draining, and he'd already relied on it a great deal. Instead of the offices, he focused on the stairway behind him, churning up clouds of smoke that spilled downward and trailed along the ceiling of the second floor hall.

It took longer for the second guard to notice, but when he did, he hurried past the plant—and Tahl. "Edren?" the man called, voice thick with concern. Upstairs, a series of coughs answered. The guard swore and took the stairs by twos.

The plush carpet silenced the soft pad of Tahl's feet. He bolted down the hall and stalked down the steps to linger at the bottom, just beside the wall. If he remembered right, the guard station was just around the corner. Smoke wouldn't work this time. He had nowhere else to hide. He caught his lower lip with his teeth and worried it, the way he did when he needed ideas.

A quiet snort and grumble gave his answer.

The guard was *sleeping*? Tahl caught his breath and bit his tongue to bridle a laugh. *And they say Brant doesn't favor thieves.*

He swung around the corner and ran for the iron grid that barred the way to the vaults. Power hummed here, vibrant even in his dull magic senses. A ward to prevent tampering. *New meaning to warded lock, there.* He let his hands hover before the bars, let the magic permeate his form. In most civilized countries, mages were bound by law to serve the ruler whose country they inhabited. At worst, they were neutral parties, held by honor to protect society. The northern mages were neutral, but Atoras was a ruthless leader who bound the empire's mages to his service. Tahl would have been one of them, had he been stronger—any mage of recognizable strength was, and any mage at his level... Well, as far as Tahl knew, there weren't any. Magic was dangerous, but the academy trained and retained anyone with a teachable Gift.

Which means there have to be more unteachable mages out there. Mages like me. Mages who bore just enough skill to be dangerous. Tahl's eyes narrowed as he singled out the edge of the ward. Some of them felt like bubbles. With the right kind of prick, they would burst.

Imagine, he thought as he focused his power into a single, sharp point. *Enough mages like me, and we could undermine the entire empire.*

He pushed.

The ward warped and flexed under the needle of his magic. He didn't know if it would alert the mage who created the ward in the first place, but it didn't matter. The mages lived outside the academy, and the academy was too far away for them to change anything. His power pressed further and the ward burst. Magic fizzed in the air, like the tingle of bubbles popping against his skin. It dissipated as he slid his favorite pick into the grid's lock.

Without the magic to protect it, a lock was all it was. Like any other. The real difficulty lay beyond, in the individual vaults the bank so proudly displayed.

The grid door popped open and Tahl slid inside. Beside the door, a book of names hung on a peg in the wall. He lifted the cover and spared a glance for its pages. The bankers wouldn't have been foolish enough to mark which vault belonged to which patron, but a symbol followed each surname. Lord Eseri's name sported a simple circumflex.

Tahl tilted his head. The others were a little clearer; crude depictions of animals, a wagon's wheel, a crown. *A crown would be too easy. Everyone knows Atoras is the fourth emperor.* He glanced at the fourth vault, then back to the book. The tiny chevron mark seemed obvious, yet he drew a blank. Was it supposed to be an arrow? He tilted his head back to look at the ceiling. Nothing. Just a plain plastered ceiling. *Unless it means farther up. The offices? The roof?*

The roof.

He spun and ran for the numbered vaults. A roof. A house. *Number thirteen.* He skidded to a stop in front of it and pressed his chest and cheek against the vault door. No wards. More tentatively, his fingertips went to the strange, rounded lock in the center. He'd never seen anything like it, but with how the bank bragged about their security, he wasn't surprised. But a lock was a lock. It wouldn't keep him out.

No wards protected the lock, either. The mechanism moved. A slim silver ring pushed forward and back on a wide knob, spun freely from side to side, but didn't come off the front. There were no keyholes to be seen. Tahl closed his eyes and listened as he moved the pieces.

Something inside rattled. That was different. He flattened his free hand against the vault door and explored with more than just his hearing. Calling his magic forth again pushed him to the brink of exhaustion, but he needed it. Maybe he didn't have strength or power, but he had ideas, and those were worth something more. When he turned the dial, the metal creaked.

Friction.

Heat.

For an instant, the lock's inner workings illuminated in the extra senses that came with his Gift.

The knob under his hand was composed of more rings, stacked atop one another. Each of the five rings turned individually, moved some part of the lock. He pushed and twisted, manipulated one ring at a time until the last one dropped into place. Abruptly, the knob came loose and pushed inward until it was flush with the vault's door. The door clanked, groaned, and finally slid open.

Beyond, it was too dark to see. Tahl padded inside, his footsteps muted by something soft on the floor. *Leave it to nobles to put fine rugs inside strongrooms.* He retrieved a handful of inch-sticks from his pocket. To anyone else, they were useless without flint, but Tahl's smoke—and feeble heat—were enough to make them ignite. It sparked and hissed and he winced against the flare of light. The tiny flame didn't travel far, but it was enough. The little light glinted off the treasures organized inside. Gem-studded weapons and gilded armor decorated racks in the corners. Pieces of artwork sat propped against the walls. On the far end of the vault, barrels—entire barrels—of coins from numerous countries sat, waiting for a man who would never spend them.

Tahl shook his head. The inch-stick singed his fingers and he shook it out before he lit another. In the center of the vault, he knelt and drew a small, folded piece of paper from his pocket.

"Bardan! Everything all right?" The words echoed through the empty bank. Outside the vaults, the sleeping guard snorted and choked as he jerked awake.

Time's up. Tahl left the paper on the floor and lay the iron key from the fountain atop it. He stood and his eyes caught on a set of scales beside the barrels of coin. They were garish beyond belief, cast in gold with silver inlays and gems at the peak of the fulcrum. A grin twisted his mouth. He shook out the second flame and snatched the scale from its shelf.

"The gate!" a guard roared beyond the open grid door.

Tahl jumped out of the thirteenth vault and slammed its door closed as he reached for his magic. The floor seemed to rock beneath his feet.

One last time, come on. Just once more.

He seized the threads of energy within himself. Everything in his head spun, upsetting his balance. He staggered against the row of gleaming metal doors.

Come on...!

The faint glimmer of power he retained grew brighter with his determination. It flickered, flared, and finally answered his call. Triumph poured through him as smoke spilled from his hands to fill the bank's first floor with curling clouds of gray-blue.

CHAPTER 8

THOUGH HE WAS NOT NORMALLY A PESSIMIST, BAHAR ESERI DID NOT think it unreasonable to label last night a disaster. The city had been teeming with guards ever since, and he still hadn't gotten an answer as to when they would disappear. It had brought his business to a screeching halt. The delays would cost him thousands of pims—more than most men earned in a lifetime.

He clenched his fists at his sides as he stalked down the corridor to his underground office. The cheerful warmth of the springtime air hadn't touched his headquarters, the stone tunnels as cold and dank as ever. He supposed it didn't matter. What did matter was pulling the shattered pieces of his schedule back together.

Thieves would always exist outside the guild. They always had. But Orrad was his domain, and to say he was displeased did not quite capture Bahar's feelings. He wasn't angry, but annoyance prickled down his spine like the crawling feet of the camel crickets that infested the back halls of the guild headquarters.

He knew who it was. He'd known the moment one of his guild's officers sent a page to alert him to the attempted thievery in the museum. It took a fool to go after the temple. That the artifacts had been the target told him everything he needed to know. Bahar had long ago ordered that the temples be avoided. He did not fear curses, but Brant's disciples were numerous, and together they had enough power to crush the guild with a thought.

Still, it wasn't the target that bothered him. It was that the attempt had been bungled. The thief had escaped, but he'd cast undue attention on the guild. Within the span of an hour, everything ground to a halt, his best thieves abandoning their assignments for fear of the increased guard presence across the city. Bahar shouldered open the door to his office and grunted at the darkness. Everyone knew he expected the lamps in his office to be lit.

"Light," he barked over his shoulder.

Someone scrambled from a hall nearby with a lantern in hand. His steward. Good. The small man ducked ahead and moved from lantern to lantern to light the wicks. The warm, golden light did nothing to chase away the chill.

Bahar turned his head away until his eyes adjusted. The mask that hid his face from the guild rubbed uncomfortably when he twisted, but he ignored it. "Has he been apprehended?"

"No, Guildmaster, I don't believe so."

Another displeased grunt. Until someone caught the boy, the guild's people would be reluctant to work. Bahar rounded his desk and paused. A striking gold-and-silver set of scales like that he used in his personal strongroom sat beside his logbooks. He fingered the brightly colored gems at its top. "What is this?"

The steward licked his lips. "I'm not certain, sir. A gift from one of the initiates, perhaps?"

Bahar frowned.

"Excuse me, Guildmaster?" a journeyman asked from the door.

"Never a moment's peace," Bahar muttered. "What?"

The journeyman thief straightened. "A messenger was sent to

your home, sir, bearing a message from the bank. They say it is urgent and you must come immediately."

A chill ran through him and Bahar glanced back toward the scales. No; he shook the idea from his head. It was coincidence.

"Very well," he said as he abandoned his desk. "Continue collecting information on the status of our members. I want everyone working within Orrad accounted for by nightfall."

"Yes, sir." The journeyman bobbed his head and disappeared around the corner.

The steward adjusted his spectacles and peered at the scales. "What do you wish me to do in your absence, sir?"

Bahar paused in the doorway. "Remain informed. And put that in the guild's strongroom. Remind the novices I won't be won over so easily."

"Yes, Guildmaster." The small man bowed in acknowledgement, then bowed again when Bahar dismissed him with a flick of his fingers.

Perhaps the worst part of this, Bahar decided, would be the number of novice thieves who would take a wrong notion from the night's events. Some would want to complete the job, prove their superiority to the whelp who tried and failed to gain the guildmaster's respect. He'd have to issue a reminder that the temple was to be left alone.

Then there would be the newcomers who would surface and claim they had been the ones to attempt the remarkable feat—which had gained the attention of the entire city. Useless and misguided, but something he'd have to deal with, nonetheless. He took his favored exit from the guild headquarters, through a hidden passage in the back of a warehouse through which he conducted legitimate business. His peers applauded his devotion to ensuring his warehouses ran smoothly; he made a point of visiting all of them regularly, so those that contained illicit activity never attracted suspicion. That was the way he liked things: unnoticed.

When he walked the city, Bahar walked it as a noble, nothing more. The nods and greetings he received were filled with the respect he deserved. Members of the guild—the few who knew his identity—never acknowledged him when he was without his mask and cowl. Truthfully, he resented any acknowledgement of his life outside the guild when he wore his disguise, but he was willing to let his journeyman's blunder slide. There were few places where life and business overlapped. The bank was one of them. Better not to take chances.

A clerk waited at the foot of the bank's front steps, surrounded by guards. Too many guards.

Bahar forced a smile. "Gentlemen. Is all well?"

The clerk worried his hands. "Good morning, Lord Eseri. Please, come inside." He nodded toward the main room of the bank, which was, Bahar noticed belatedly, filled only with clerks and guards, including a handful of Elite. A sense of uneasiness welled in his stomach.

Once inside, the clerk lowered his voice. "I don't know how to say this, my lord, but there has been a... how should I say it... breach."

"A breach?" A new sensation crept down Bahar's spine— cold claws of dread.

"Yes. We don't know how or why." The clerk led the way past the showy grid door and into the hall of vaults. "The door was closed when I arrived, but the guards heard it slam. We investigated the contents of each vault, we've been working at it since the middle of the night. But only one vault was targeted."

They stopped outside the vault Bahar had held since he'd claimed his family's business. It stood open by scant inches.

Bahar gritted his teeth and stepped inside.

The clerk followed, his head down in what Bahar hoped was shame. They should be ashamed; the bank was supposed to have guards. Wards. How could anyone get past the wards without the bank's employed mage present?

"The most curious thing is," the clerk continued, "all the artifacts, art, and weapons are accounted for, and whoever it was, he or she left... that." His hand lifted, one stubby finger directed at something on the floor.

A small, folded note with a rusted key atop it.

Bahar crouched beside it. He'd seen that key before. He'd jammed it into the garden district's fountain himself. With effort, he made himself pick it up. "Where were the guards?"

"Present," the clerk said. "The building filled with smoke that had no apparent source, but they saw and heard nothing else. Not even footsteps. It was as if it were a... well, a ghost."

Slowly, Bahar stood and unfolded the paper. It was coarse, cheap, offensive to his fingers, but the simple note inside made his blood run cold.

You had your chance.

Long moments snaked past in silence. He lifted his head and his eyes fell on an empty space beside his barrels of loose coin.

His gold-and-silver scale was gone.

"Lord Eseri?" someone asked.

Bahar turned to face the red-cloaked Elite. Three more appeared at his flank, their spears ready.

The leader motioned for him to follow. "If you'll come with me?"

Flush with anger, Bahar jammed the key into his pocket and squared his shoulders. "What is the meaning of this?"

"That was not a suggestion, Lord Eseri," the Elite said. "Or, should I say Guildmaster?"

Full panic gripped him and squeezed the air from his lungs. Bahar struggled to find words.

The Elite didn't give him a chance to speak. "For crimes against the crown of Emperor Atoras, Bahar Eseri, leader of the thieves' guild, you are under arrest."

CHAPTER 9

THE HATCH INTO TAHL'S ROOM CLUNKED OPEN WITH NO PREAMBLE. He jolted awake, his favorite knife in hand before he saw Niada's head pop through the hole. Groaning, he jammed the knife back under his pillow and collapsed back into bed.

"You're still sleeping?" Niada clicked her tongue in disapproval. "It's practically noon."

"I don't care what time it is," Tahl groaned into his pillow. "I'm exhausted."

She closed the hatch and padded over to his bedside. "I would imagine you are. You know you have to tell me about it now, though." As a peace offering, she extended a small packet made of grease-stained paper.

Tahl eyed it for only a moment before he turned back over and accepted.

"Oof." She cringed at sight of the dark-scabbed gash across his face. "That should have been seen right away."

"It should have, but I shouldn't. Not with the city on high alert." The academy and temple both had healers, but he couldn't risk being caught on the streets after everything was over. Even if it meant a scar was guaranteed.

Niada made a small, sad sound in her throat. "How did it happen?"

"One of the emperor's Elite," he replied as he pulled his treat from its paper wrapping. A thin slice of sweet pastry, slathered in whipped butter and sprinkled with coarse sugar. Nothing had ever looked so good.

"In that case, you're lucky you're alive at all." She sat on the edge of the bed, regarding him with curiosity. "So how does it feel to be the Ghost of Orrad?"

He raised a brow. "Is that what they're calling me?"

"It caught on pretty quickly. Started before the sun came up, I think."

"How do you know it was me?" The butter melted against his warm fingers. He cupped a hand under the treat to catch crumbs as he took a bite.

She shrugged. "You're the only person I know of who does those kind of smoke tricks. I guess you were smart to keep that a secret from most people. Every guard in the city is after your head."

No surprise there. "Which is why I'll need your help figuring out how to deal with this." He gestured to the wound on his face with his little finger. "I was fast with the smokescreen, I don't think he saw where he got me, but I know he knows he did."

"There's a kind of soft wax that can be used to cover scars. Once it's healed, I'll teach you how." She watched him eat with a neutral expression, but sadness dulled her eyes. Despite how good she was at playing roles, she never could hide her feelings. Perhaps she'd grow better at it with age.

"What?" Tahl asked.

"Everyone in the city is talking about what you've done. I think every single crime in the city last night has been attributed to you. But I don't think it's going to help you get into the guild. I'm not sure there's even going to be a guild, after today."

"What makes you say that?"

She hesitated, rubbing her fingers as if to coax warmth into them. "Lord Bahar Eseri was arrested this morning. They say he's the guildmaster. The moment word got out, the thieves' network started to fall apart."

"Oh." Tahl stuffed the last of his pastry into his mouth.

Her hesitance grew. "You don't seem surprised."

"I already knew." He licked his fingers clean. "At least, I knew it was coming."

Niada cocked her head. "How could you know?"

"Because," he shrugged, "that was the heist."

Her eyes searched his face for answers she couldn't piece together.

"I told you I found him," Tahl said. "I visited him in his home office, told him I wanted in the guild. He pretended he didn't know what I was talking about. I don't fault him for playing dumb, but considering no one had ever discovered his identity, he shouldn't have been so dismissive."

The color left her face. "You didn't."

"I asked him for a challenge. What I'd have to steal to be let in. He said I'd have to steal the world." His eyes darkened. "So I stole his."

"I don't understand," Niada almost whined. "If you just meant to have him arrested, why the heists? Why the bank? The museum?"

"Because no one in Orrad would respect a thief who just walked up to the Elite and told them the guildmaster's identity. The Elite probably wouldn't even believe them. I'd come across the identities of some of Eseri's partners while looking for him. One was old, getting feeble-minded. He kept records in his house to aid his memory. I took one. Planted it in the museum, made it look like a mistake. It pointed fingers at Eseri without my involvement. The bank was to ensure the Elite would be able to find him. Where better than a vault full of stolen wealth?"

She frowned. "If that's the case, why not the guild headquarters?"

"My fight was with Lord Eseri," he said. "Not the guild."

"Why the museum? Stealing those artifacts—"

"—Could curse me, I know." He flashed her a grin. "But with the temple angry and everything pointing back to Eseri, no amount of government corruption could keep him safe."

Niada's shoulders slumped and she shook her head. "Out of everything you've ever done, Tahl, this is unbelievable."

"But I did it." He grinned, then winced when the expression pulled at his injured face.

"For all the good it did you," she harrumphed. "The guild won't have you now. If a thief steals from a thief, what does that make him?"

"Untrustworthy," Tahl said. "Or, a force to be reckoned with, depending on how you see it."

Her eyes narrowed.

"Orrad's afraid of the Ghost now." He pushed himself from his bed and trudged to the table, where a plain stoneware pitcher of water waited beside a cracked cup. For a fleeting moment, he envisioned them as silver instead. *Soon.* "The guild will probably crumble. There will be infighting, disagreements over who should lead. It'll splinter into smaller groups. They'll struggle. And then they'll have their chance to unite."

She leaned back. "Under the Ghost?"

"Under the Ghost." He poured himself a drink. The water was warm and stale, but in the wake of his victory, it was as satisfying as wine.

Once again, she shook her head. "Unbelievable."

"I'm sure that's what the fragments of the guild will think when they see us." He paused, just long enough for her to lift her head with a question in her eyes. "You know. The Ghost of Orrad and his second-in-command."

Niada's face lit with delight and she leaped from the bed. "Really?"

He touched his fingers to his chest in a display of honesty. "I wouldn't want anyone else."

She squealed with delight and spun to pull the wooden box

from underneath the bed. "Come on, then. We'd better get started."

Tahl blinked. "What are you doing?"

"Getting you a quick disguise so we can get that cut on your face healed. The sooner you're back at full strength, the sooner we can do this." She pulled a small bundle of bandages from the back of the box and dashed over to join him at the table. "Sit down, let me wrap your face."

He did as he was told. "Don't you think this'll look a bit conspicuous?"

"No. We'll tell anyone who stops us that you've got fly larvae in your eye and need to see a healer at the temple immediately. They'll be too disgusted to ask any more questions."

Tahl grunted in disgust, himself.

"Exactly." She laughed, winding the bandage around his head, covering both his eye and injury. Her little fingers were nimble and it wasn't long before she tucked in the ends of the bandage and pulled him to his feet. "Come on."

He didn't want to; he wanted to sleep. There was no staving off Niada after she set her mind on something, though, and he reluctantly let her pull him along.

Beyond his quiet stable-loft room, the city looked no different than ever—save that he looked at it with only one eye—but the guard presence was undeniable. It would linger for some time, he expected, then fade away with the memory of everything that had happened. The Ghost of Orrad would vanish for a time. When he resurfaced, perhaps a few months down the road, it would be to reunify in the shadows that would consume the rest of his life.

Already, he felt out of place in the daylight. Orrad's rooftops were his home. Night was where he belonged.

"You're making that face," Niada said.

Tahl blinked his uncovered eye. "What face?"

"The one you had in the inn the other night. The one you get when your plans get bigger than you are."

He hadn't realized that expression existed. "I'll try to keep my delusions of grandeur less visible from now on."

Near the temple, he was no longer the only one sporting bandages. Not every malady could be healed, but everyone trekked to the temple for care at some point in their lives. Until now, Tahl had never needed their services. He tried not to sulk over it being something so minor. If not for his newfound need to hide, he wouldn't have sought healing at all.

Guards stood outside the temple for the first time he could recall. A station spurred by his actions the night before, he was sure. If the temple's artifacts weren't safe, nothing was. Niada dragged him up the stairs and latched onto the robes of the first cleric she saw. "Please, you have to help my brother! He's been injured, it'll scar so badly he'll never find a wife."

Tahl struggled not to snort.

"Patience, child," the cleric replied with a series of soothing hand gestures. "Sit at the foot of the altar. You shall be seen."

The faintest hint of mischief flitted over Niada's face as she turned to escort Tahl to the far end of the temple. A handful of injured and ill people already waited on the stairs below the altar. She sat among them. Tahl remained on his feet.

"You should sit." She patted the empty space on the stone stair beside her.

He crossed his arms. "If I sit, I'll fall asleep. Don't forget I was awake all night."

"Suit yourself." She flicked a hand in dismissal.

Even standing, Tahl felt his head dip as the quiet peace of the temple washed over him. He braced himself where he stood and let his eyes slide closed for a moment of rest. It wasn't long before the soft clink of wooden chimes chased away his drowsiness.

"You've come for aid?" a soft, feminine voice asked.

Niada scrambled to her feet and bowed to the veiled priestess. "He needs healing, my lady, and confession."

Tahl shot her a one-eyed glare at the same time the priestess turned toward him. Though her face was hidden by the green fabric draped over her head and held by a crown of fresh flowers, he had the distinct impression she saw him. Perhaps through him. The idea gave him a chill.

"What have you done?" the priestess intoned, her voice as musical as the chimes that hung from her wrists.

Perhaps inviting Niada to be his second-in-command had been a mistake. He could only imagine the trouble she'd get him in, thinking she spoke for them both. "I cannot make myself voice it here, as confession ought to be between me and Brant," he said, "but the Lifetree knows my sins. Forgive me, Priestess. Um, that is, may Brant forgive me."

The priestess lifted her chin, the rest of her so still she might have been a statue, if not for the way her veil shifted with every current of air. Finally, she raised a hand and laid it on his face.

He sensed her power as it poured through him like the shock of cold water poured over his head. He shuddered and gasped and she drew her hand back.

"There is a spark in you," she murmured. "Small, but there."

The pain in his face had already subsided. Tahl fingered the bandages in wonder. "I was put out of the academy. They said I didn't have what it took to become a mage."

The priestess shook her head and hooked her fingers in the shape of the two crescent moons—a symbol to represent their creator. "The academy does not know everything. Mind your spark. Watch it closely. For a spark may easily turn to flames and consume that which it should have illuminated."

Another chill took him, spawned by something in her words. Superstition claimed the priestesses bore foresight. He didn't believe it, but the statement was so eerily predictive that he understood how the rumors began.

"Go, now," the priestess said, as placidly as if the warning had never passed her lips. "You are whole, by the blessing of Brant."

"What about his sins?" Niada protested.

"He bears nothing that is not already forgiven. Peace be with you."

"And with you," Tahl replied as the priestess turned away. After she moved on, he spun to glower at his companion.

She shrank back. "What?"

"Are you trying to get me killed?" he whispered as he reached for the bandages on his face.

Niada hopped forward to stop him. "I'm trying to help you!" She caught his arm and steered him back toward the entrance. "If you'd been cursed—"

"I didn't do anything to *be* cursed, Nia."

"But you stole—"

He pressed a finger to his lips and she hushed, though her face was sullen. She really was like a little sister. "I didn't take anything. I never intended to, either. All I needed was a high-profile distraction, and nothing could have worked better than that."

"So after all that, you didn't even steal anything?" she asked in a whisper as they slipped back into the city's crowds.

"I didn't say that," Tahl replied, somewhat defensively. "I just didn't steal what you think I stole."

Niada pursed her lips, but said nothing more.

As they walked, he couldn't help letting his fingers snake up underneath the bandages on his face. Despite the healing, traces of scarring remained. His own fault, since magic only mended wounds seamlessly when they received immediate attention. The mark ran across the bridge of his nose and down his right cheek at an angle, curving up again toward the corner of his eye. Something of a checkmark, he supposed, and entirely too recognizable. That wax Niada mentioned would be invaluable.

"It's funny," he said as he concluded his inspection and withdrew his fingers. "The guildmaster arrested, the guild collapsing, and all I stole was a book."

NEVER LOST

A WESTKINGS HEIST SHORT STORY

CHAPTER 1

"YOU COME HERE OFTEN." THE SOUND OF THE PRIESTESS'S VOICE was no surprise after the soft melody of wooden chimes had announced her presence, yet somehow, Tahl hadn't expected her to speak. He glanced up, regarding her translucent head covering with a pensive frown. He never would understand how the priestesses walked with such confidence. Even with his reflexes and skills, he wouldn't be so confident walking blindfolded.

"It's a nice place to be," he said after a time, making no effort to rise from the cool floor. He'd been rolling a pim between his fingers when she'd decided to creep up on him, and he returned to flipping the silver coin across his knuckles after he'd concluded his cursory pondering over whatever sixth sense the priestesses had. After all the months he'd spent sitting in the same place, he'd still never seen a priestess without a pale green silk sheet over her head. For that matter, the flowers in the woven crowns they wore atop the veils never seemed to wilt, either.

A soft giggle escaped her throat. "It is." She crouched beside him, resting her elbows on her knees as her skirts pooled around her bare feet.

Tahl's eyes drifted to the wooden chimes that hung from her wrists. The weights that dangled from the clappers touched the floor, the soothing clink of the wooden tubes muted. "You're here every night."

"And you are not, so how would you know?" Her tone was playful, teasing, and he tried to picture the smile that might go with it. She straightened her chimes. "But you are here a lot. Always at the same time, always before sunrise, when the rest of the world sleeps. Yet you do not seek the clergy, nor do you offer prayers."

"I don't speak with the priestesses tending the temple, either," Tahl said. "This is a first."

This time, the sound the priestess made was thoughtful. "A failing on my part. I have never thought to speak to you before."

His coin grew still between his fingers once more. "I don't really want the attention."

"Yet you come," she said. "Many, many nights."

Tahl rubbed the edge of the coin with his thumb. He could just feel it between the fleshy pads of his fingers, warm and smooth, save for a single nick in the edge that had grown familiar. There was no reason to tell the priestess anything, yet he couldn't help feeling he owed her some sort of explanation. "It's quiet here. I like to sit here and think, while all the rest of Orrad dreams."

"And when do you dream?"

His lips twitched with a hint of a smile. "All the time."

A quiet moment passed. "What do you dream in these waking moments?"

That little smile evaporated.

"Forgive me," the priestess said hastily, rising to her feet. "It is not my place to ask. I shall leave you in peace."

She'd gone no more than a handful of steps before a clawing sense of guilt churned Tahl's words loose.

"Being… appreciated," he said. "Being someone who deserves to sit here."

The priestess paused. Her head swiveled back toward him, though her face remained hidden. The movement made the chimes at her wrists sway. Tahl could have sworn the sounds they made seemed curious.

Sheepish, he looked away.

Slowly, the priestess turned to face him fully. "Everyone deserves to sit here. Brant's temple is welcoming to all."

"Is it?" He couldn't help the doubtful, sarcastic twist to his voice. "I doubt the Lifetree would want me here if he knew where I spent the rest of the night."

The tilt of the priestess's head told him that had been intriguing, not frightening. But she did not question him, and for a long time, she did not speak. Even the wooden chimes that hung from her wrists grew silent.

Belatedly, Tahl realized her stillness had made him hold his breath. He filled his lungs and released the air as a sigh. This wasn't like him. He wasn't sulky, and he didn't care what the priestesses–or Brant–thought of his profession. He liked what he did. He liked the challenge, liked the thrill, liked the occasional luxuries his thievery brought. The silver pim tumbled between his fingers at an agitated pace.

At last, the priestess spoke. "The temple is not a refuge solely for the holy, but for those who hurt, as well. We are never so lost as we think."

He did not reply. Instead, he tucked in his chin, his eyes trained on the altar before him. He always sat at the foot of the steps, gazing up at the altar on the dais, where candles flickered through the still of night.

"The sun is rising." Her tone was gentle, soothing, free of accusation. "May it rise on your soul as well." The priestess bowed her head and hooked two fingers in the double crescent that represented Brant's canopy. Then she turned, her skirts and veil rippling like waves on the Ranton river as she disappeared between the pews.

Tahl stared after her for a long time. But he couldn't linger, and eventually, he rose from his cross-legged position on the floor and stretched his legs. If the sun was rising, it meant he was out of time to sit and dream. Kind as her words had been, the priestess's words meant little. His soul was swathed in the night.

He stepped onto the dais and left his last pim in the poor box.

TO STEAL THE CROWN

THE SECOND HEIST

CHAPTER 1

THE CITY HAD CHANGED, AND NOT FOR THE BETTER. TAHL LOUNGED against the rail of a balcony and watched the people below.

On the surface, to the unsuspecting eye, all was well and the city thrived. Business went on as usual. New imports companies had sprung up to fill the void left by Bahar Eseri's arrest and the crumbling of his business empire, and more businesses meant more commerce, more ships that came and went from the river harbor, more people who ventured in from the countryside to find work as dockhands.

Tahl had never cared about the surface. He thrived on what happened in the city's underbelly, where truth between the dishonest shared a fuller picture.

Orrad was afraid.

He heard it in the whispers between thieves, saw it in the anxious glances citizens cast toward others in the street. The city's markets were full to bursting during the day, but there had once been a thriving community of people who ventured out after dark. Taverns had hummed with life after the day's work. Nobles held parties that continued into the small hours of the morning. Now, even the guards walked with uncertainty.

The worst of it was that no one knew he was to blame.

Tahl pushed himself back from the railing and retreated from the balcony's edge.

In the past three days, he'd seen a half-dozen muggings from a single vantage point. Crime surged, thieves more brazen than ever. It was a symptom of a problem the city officials didn't understand. With Bahar Eseri's arrest, Orrad's thieves guild had fallen apart. Without the organization and protection the guild offered, each and every thief in the southernmost Westkings Empire was left to fend for themselves. No pooling of resources. No structured assignments. Desperation among the thieves made the city unsafe for both thieves and average citizens.

And I did it, Tahl thought with a grim smile.

One more stage of his plan, he reminded himself. Destabilizing the city had been deliberate, but he admitted it was hard to watch, and the price had been higher than he expected.

Anyone could have expected the number of thieves who tried to claim the name he'd made for himself, but he never would have imagined so many false Ghosts would be captured. Even today, people flocked to the palace to see the sentencing of another pretender.

Tahl warred with the sense of responsibility that reared its head each time he heard about another arrest. Part of him knew it wasn't his fault if others tried to steal his title and ended up imprisoned beneath the palace—or worse. Yet if he hadn't spent the past several months in hiding, no one would have had to suffer.

Still, it had not been the right time. The city needed to struggle. The thieves needed to know desperation. Only then could he unite them under his banner.

Metaphorical banner, he mused as he pushed open the door and stalked into the house. The worst thing he could do was make himself noticeable. Near as he could figure, the emperor's judges had identified all the thieves they'd arrested as fakes. They lined the cells of Orrad's prison, scheduled for execution, as was the customary punishment for thieves. Had they found the true Ghost, Tahl had no doubt his gallows would be mounted in the plaza outside the Queen's Museum the same day.

He no more than stepped into the hallway than he came face to face with his employer.

"Oh," the old woman squeaked. Her eyes flicked to the room he'd just emerged from. "Were you out on the balcony again?"

Tahl stuffed his hands into his pockets. "Yes, ma'am. I had a minute after I finished. You know I can't help it."

She chuckled and reached to pat his cheek. To his relief, she went for the left. "I know, I know. The city is beautiful, even from a balcony as small as mine. Are you off for the day, then?"

"As long as you don't need anything else, ma'am." He mustered a smile. Ebitha was a pleasant woman, grandmotherly, but formal. She didn't appreciate it when he dallied after work was finished, but she was too polite to begrudge him his city-gazing.

"No, it's quite all right. Just see to the horses tonight before you're off to bed. Best of luck today." The corners of her eyes crinkled with her smile.

"Of course, ma'am. Thank you, ma'am." Tahl ducked his head in respect and trotted down the stairs before she found more work for him to do.

He was grateful for Ebitha's accommodating spirit. He'd rented the room above her stable for ages, but she'd become his employer after the heist that put the Ghost on the map. Though he still practiced his acrobatics and sneaking and stayed abreast of the news, the time he spent thieving had been slim while he tried to avoid notice. As a result, it had grown harder and harder to pay his rent. Fortunately—or unfortunately, depending on the task she found—there was no shortage of odd jobs around a wealthy widow's home for a strapping young stable boy to handle.

Tahl was disinclined to complain. The work kept his rent paid and the old widow let him eat scraps from the kitchen. It was worse than the subsistence he'd suffered through before the guild he'd desperately wanted to join collapsed, but it kept him alive. That was reason enough to be grateful. He pushed out the front door and breathed deep.

Summer's kiss had left Orrad hot, but it paled in comparison to the heat Tahl had grown up in along the southern coast. He rolled up his sleeves and walked comfortably in the sun.

Even near Ebitha's estate, the streets were crowded. Heavy carts laden with crates of imports rumbled up and down every road and forced pedestrians to the sides of the streets. Tahl picked a cart to follow at random. It was best to keep up appearances, and eventually, each load of cargo ended up at a dock, a shop, or a warehouse of some sort.

Immediately following his heist, Tahl had told Ebitha he'd worked for Lord Eseri and found himself jobless in the wake of the man's arrest. She had pitied him, and he had promised he would continue to look for proper employment while he saw to her house and her precious horses.

It was half truth, too. He had looked. Not for the warehouse or shipping jobs he'd insinuated, but for exceptionally easy pickpocketing jobs—and for the opportunity he needed to build a new thieves guild. He hadn't known what that opportunity would be, and the longer he waited, the more restless he became. Finally, he was left to wonder if the opportunity would arrive at all, or if he was meant to forge it on his own. The more time that crept by, the more he suspected it was the latter.

The cart he'd chosen to follow bumped its way down a narrow avenue, toward one of the smaller docks on the Ranton river. Disinterested, Tahl peeled away to cut through an alley instead. Just north, alongside the eastern gate, waited an inn he frequented. He doubted he would be fortunate enough to find his informant there, but it was always worth a look.

By some unfathomable stroke of luck, he spotted her between the tables.

Tahl kept his head down and his hands in his pockets as he

trudged over to take a seat. He used to sit in the middle of the room, eager to hear everything that was going on. Now he positioned himself well away from the noise. He slipped a copper half-mite from his pocket as he sat and pressed the coin to the tabletop with his thumb.

A moment later, the barmaid's shadow passed over him.

"You're getting stingy," Niada muttered as she took the coin and stuffed it into her apron. "What'll it be?"

"Water," Tahl said. "Come on, Nia. You know that."

She shrugged. "You're the one who sets the appearances, I'm just trying to help you keep them." Her eyes narrowed. "You're getting better with the wax."

He winced at the mention of his scar. Despite daily practice, he still had difficulty covering the checkmark-shaped gash that traveled over the bridge of his nose and across his right cheek. "The color match is better, too," he said with a hint of pride. He'd used most of his chalks to make it happen, but he couldn't trust anyone to help him. Aside from Niada, that was. He still didn't know where she got the wax, but he was grateful to have it, even if he hoped he someday wouldn't need it.

"I think you need a bit more powder, though. The shine is a little strong. You may want a box of powder like the noble ladies use." Niada tipped her head in the direction of the kitchen. "Food today?"

"No fish," he replied.

"No promises." Her fingers fluttered in dismissal and she trudged off to fetch his food and drink.

It wasn't hard to tell she was mad at him.

Tahl rested his elbows on the table and fought back a sigh. The last thing he wanted to do was upset Nia. She was the closest thing to family he had in Orrad, even if she did grate on his nerves worse than his blood sisters did. Had, he corrected himself silently; he hadn't seen his family in years.

Regardless of what he wanted, he assumed it was too late. She was already mad. Niada had been short with him for weeks, and not only because he'd grown tight-fisted with his coins. That, he refused to feel guilt over. Food was at the top of his list of necessities and it was hard enough to keep food on his table, even with the scraps he picked from Ebitha's kitchen.

When Niada returned, she thumped a plate down in front of him.

Fish. Again.

Tahl groaned and slouched in his seat.

She shrugged as if helpless. "You pay with a half-mite, you get a half-mite worth of food. You know what they say about beggars."

"But we aren't beggars, are we?" He stared her in the eye as he jabbed his fork into the greasy meat and twisted a chunk free.

Niada crossed her arms. "I'm not. I'm not really sure what you are, anymore."

"Well, that's potentially the most dramatic thing you've ever said." Tahl shoved his fork into his mouth and fought back a shudder. The fish was worse every time he ate it.

"You know what I mean," she said, exasperated. Her voice crept up in volume and he raised his brows at her until she tightened her arms across her thin torso and scowled. "When are you going to do something?"

He swallowed hard and scraped his tongue against his teeth as another shudder coursed through him. "Tomorrow. Today, if I feel like it."

"Don't make fun of me, Tahl."

"I mean it," he said. "And I'm still waiting on my water, so maybe if you get me that, I'll tell you what I'm thinking."

Niada's eyes narrowed, but she turned to retrieve his drink. He watched after her with a frown. She was a little taller, he thought; still bony, still a child, but that wouldn't be the case forever. As she developed her thieving skills, she'd be a useful accomplice while working, but he'd miss the way information fell easily on her young ears.

She scuffed her feet against the floor on her way back.

"Here." She shoved the rough wooden mug into his hands. "Water."

"Thank you," Tahl said, more politely than he felt she deserved. "Do you have a minute?"

Her fingers flicked toward the room. It was relatively empty, this early in the day.

He took several gulps to wash the taste of the fish from his mouth. "Do you remember when I was getting ready for work before? You gave me a suggestion. The opal—"

"—In the queen's crown. I remember." Her toes tapped softly against the floor, more a sign of irritation than impatience.

"Right." Tahl ticked a finger at her. "I was thinking about that. About how long it's been. And I don't know about you, but I'm sick of fish."

Niada shifted. He'd piqued her interest, it seemed. "So you're looking for ideas?"

"You already gave me one. I just said."

"The opal? I wasn't serious, Tahl. What you did was dangerous enough."

They quieted as a patron rose and moved past them.

"I didn't say the opal," he whispered when they were isolated again.

Her shoulders hitched up toward her ears in an exaggerated shrug. "So?"

"I'm going to steal the crown."

CHAPTER 2

Out of the entirety of Orrad, the rooftops were where he felt most at home. They had been his refuge, his domain, the one place he felt wholly free.

Yet he'd only just begun to venture back to them. The weeks immediately after the Ghost's first strike, even the rooftops had been swarmed by guards. He supposed he only had himself to blame. The roof was how he'd gotten into not just the Queen's Museum, but the bank, too. The bank's broken roof tiles and dislodged planks had been unavoidable. He simply hadn't had time to put them back. Even if he had, the tiles were still broken, and that would have given away his point of entry eventually.

The thatching underneath him was more prickly than he'd expected. Tahl shifted to ease his discomfort, but it just resulted in him being poked somewhere else. His return to the rooftops should have been triumphant, a part of the Ghost's grand return.

Instead, he lounged against the crude cobblestone chimney of a farmer's cottage, half a mile from Orrad's walls.

"Aye, I think that did it," the farmer called from the ground below. "I don't see anything, anymore."

Tahl nodded and inched his way toward the edge. "If it starts leaking again, I'll take another look." He fought the urge to bound off the eaves and tumble in the thick grasses below. He swung down instead, relatively sedate, to drop to the ground with a quiet thump.

"Much appreciated, lad." The farmer grinned as he scratched his beard. "Where'd you learn to climb like that, anyway? Might mistake you for a squirrel with all that scurrying."

"My parents took me to see a circus when I was young. I wanted to be one of the acrobats." Tahl spread his arms and pretended to walk a tightrope. His feet followed the furrow in the ground where the rain fell off the roof.

The farmer laughed. "I've no doubt you could, lad. No circuses anymore, though. Not since..." He trailed off and shut his mouth, as if he'd said something he shouldn't.

Tahl cocked his head. "Since what?"

"Ah, a lot's changed in these past few months. I'm sure you've noticed, lad. The emperor, Brant bless him, is just taking all sorts of precautions. Tighter checks at the guard gates. More restrictions on traveling caravans and peddlers. Not just in Orrad, mind. Being outside the city like I am, I've seen more than my share of folk turned away at the gates."

That, Tahl hadn't heard. "He doesn't think... you know... is in the city anymore?"

"I don't think he knows. I don't think anyone knows, and that's the problem." The farmer shook his head sadly. "Aye, trade's better than ever, but who does that really help, lad? Never thought one man could scare an emperor so bad, but I suppose I never thought one man would have the temple out for his head."

A small twinge of guilt plucked at Tahl's heart.

"Ah, but it's no matter I suppose," the farmer said as he straightened and adjusted his broad-brimmed hat. "Things will settle. They always do."

"Yeah," Tahl agreed in a murmur. He accepted his sack of

vegetables and bade the farmer goodbye before he cut a path toward the forest through the grass.

Actions were like ripples, someone once told him. He wanted to attribute the words to his mother, but he wasn't certain. It didn't matter—the phrase was relevant no matter who'd said it. The effects of actions tended to spread, and sometimes it took no more than a pebble to start them.

His aim had been small: dethrone Bahar Eseri as guildmaster, destabilize the thieves guild, dismantle everything Lord Eseri had built. It was a petty, personal vendetta, a response to the guildmaster's snub. Tahl never considered it might spread beyond that. He meant to rebuild the guild, of course; that had been part of his initial goal. But the idea that he—*he*, a teenager cast out from the mage academy—could frighten Emperor Atoras himself? He'd never fathomed the ripples could reach so far.

All the more reason his new plan was ambitious. Tahl allowed himself the smallest of smirks as he trekked into the trees.

There were a number of small game trails that wound their way through the woods, and he had grown familiar with quite a few since he'd taken to using forest clearings as a new place to practice his magic. It was a better place to do it than on the roofs in Orrad, he admitted. There were fewer eyes and ears in the woods, and on the occasion he did cross paths with other people, it was easy to explain his presence. He always had a bag with him. Today, it was the farmer's burlap sack with a few vegetables inside. Other times, he used a satchel. But every day he ventured into the woods to practice, he spent enough time foraging for wild fruits and nuts that he had a reasonable explanation for being out there on his own.

Today, he stuck closer to the wider trade road that meandered between the trees. The clearing he sought was far enough back in the underbrush that he didn't imagine he'd have any visitors, but he didn't want to be so far off the path that the one visitor he expected couldn't find him.

Not long after Tahl settled at the foot of a tree to practice spinning smoke shapes from his fingertips, Niada emerged from the brambles at the clearing's edge.

He twisted a plume of smoke into the shape of a butterfly and sent it to bat its wings around her head.

Flustered, she slapped it away. A moment later, she slapped a mosquito, too. It left a crimson smear across her arm. "There you are."

"Exactly where I said I'd be," Tahl replied. Normally, he practiced alone. Having spectators rarely worked well. Magic took a great deal of concentration, and his Gift was weak enough without distraction robbing him of his focus.

Sniffing, she rubbed her arm and trudged across the clearing. Both her arms were covered in scratches from thorns and welts from insect bites. "How can you stand coming out here?"

"Long sleeves help." He paused to unroll his. "Of course, then you bear the risk of overheating."

"I think I'd rather stay in the city."

"I would, too, but until things settle down, this is best." He flicked another smoke shape at her. This time, it resembled a sparrow.

The smoke hit her shoulder and dissipated. She brushed at her shirt as if she'd felt it. "I think you're getting better at that."

"Doesn't feel like it," Tahl muttered. "I feel like I've gotten worse. All these weeks of doing nothing, no chances to really push my limits or train like I want to?" He shook his head. "It feels like I'm wasting away."

"Maybe you are," she goaded as she inched closer and pinched his arm. "I don't think you're as strong as you were."

He grunted and pulled away. "That just means I have to start now. Get out here every day and practice, while I get the information I need for this heist."

Niada's eyes glittered. "That's what I'm here for, right?" She dropped to the ground in front of him and swung a small satchel around from her back so she could dig through its contents. He really was rusty. He hadn't noticed the strap of her bag at all.

She produced a small notebook. "I got some information from a palace guard. Not a lot, but I wrote it down. Or I tried, anyway." A hint of color rose in her cheeks. Like most commoners, she wasn't exactly literate. Tahl had taught her as much as he could, but certain things—such as spelling and grammar—were difficult to improve without access to books. Even had he stolen a few from some haughty noble's library, it would have been too conspicuous for a young girl working as a barmaid to carry books around.

"I'm sure it's fine," Tahl lied. Half the time, he couldn't decipher what she'd tried to write. The trick was getting her to read her notes back to him, instead.

Niada paged through the ratty notebook until she found what she wanted. "Here. I got a little bit about schedules, and which parts of the palace are open when. I thought maybe we could use that and go investigate the castle on our own."

"That's better than I expected, honestly." He cocked his head to look at the page. The scrawled letters had improved in form since he'd seen her handwriting last. A set of numbers in the corner caught his eye and he leaned down to tap the edge of the page. "What's that?"

"The number of guards on duty during each shift."

Tahl released a low whistle.

"I know," Niada murmured.

"Well, I can't say getting past them will be the easiest thing I've ever done, but it's not impossible. I don't think anything is." He committed the numbers to memory. Once he had a chance to see the castle's grounds for himself, he'd be able to evaluate what they actually meant. A large number of guards could be little threat at all if there were gaps in their patrols and posts.

She studied his face for a time while he tried to decipher her notes. "I've wanted to ask since yesterday, but I didn't want to make you mad."

"You are good at doing that," Tahl mused.

Her nose crinkled. "I'm being serious. I just wondered... I mean, I know you were somebody, back before the academy. You never said much, but you can read. Did... were you raised for something like this? Becoming a king?"

Startled, he stared at her a moment before he let out a laugh. "What? I'm not stealing the empire, Nia! I'm stealing the crown. The literal crown, the thing on Atoras's head?"

Her cheeks brightened. "How was I supposed to know?"

"Because I told you? I specifically said I was going to steal the crown."

"And Lord Eseri wanted you to steal the world, and you ended up pulling a heist based entirely on some weird metaphor." She raised her hands in a sign of defeat.

"Fair," Tahl laughed. "All right, I'll give you that one. But no. I don't want the Westkings Empire. Just the guild."

"Which you're going to have to rebuild from nothing," Niada reminded him. She paged through her notebook. "I was thinking about that, too. About uniting all the thieves under your leadership. I came up with some designs."

His brow furrowed. "Designs?"

"For your emblem." She turned the notebook so she could see. A handful of simple symbols filled the page, the charcoal smudged until some were unrecognizable.

"Lord Eseri didn't have an emblem."

"Lord Eseri didn't have a name," she retorted. "You're the Ghost, Tahl. You're something special."

"Not yet," he said.

Niada frowned. "Don't you want to look at them?"

"Not really, no." He stepped back to give himself more space. They couldn't sit in the forest forever, and he needed to practice. "I'd rather talk about how we're going to get into the palace."

Her face fell. "All right."

Magic tingled at the tips of his fingers as he spun a handful of shapes. Wisps of smoke resembling mice scattered across the grass, darting and weaving beneath twigs and fallen leaves. "Just entering should be easy. Castles are busy places, they won't notice a few extra faces. The trick is figuring out where those faces are least likely to draw attention."

One of his shadow mice crawled over the top of Niada's shoe. She ignored it, staring at the notebook in her hands.

Tahl stopped. He'd used that to pester her before; she hated the mice more than anything. "Nia?"

"I'm listening," she murmured.

"Are you?"

She nodded.

"I'm going to need you for this one, Nia. I'm counting on you to help me work my way through the castle so I can make this happen. And I'll need you to keep gathering information, too. That could be the most important thing I need you to help me with."

Niada nodded again.

His brows drew together. "You still want to be the guild's second-in-command, don't you?"

"I do," she said softly. She tucked a loose strand of dark hair behind her ear. "I'll keep listening. I'll see if I can get work at some of the places the guards drink. That should help. Just..." Her fingers plucked at the edges of her notebook's open pages.

"Just what?"

With the greatest care, she tore the page of drawings from her notebook and folded it in half. "Just consider it, okay?" She pushed the paper into his hand and turned away. "You don't have to like it, but people need something to look up to. It gives them hope, you know?"

Tahl blinked at her back as she retreated between the trees. Her feelings were hurt. She always sulked when that happened. A twinge of guilt tickled in his chest. He hadn't meant anything by it. They were just drawings, silly symbols that would draw too much attention.

"Hope," he murmured thoughtfully as he curled his fingers around the crumpled paper. Thieves were the villains. How could they give anyone hope?

CHAPTER 3

Orrad's palace was the seat of power in the Westkings. Not only the southern empire, but the entirety of the region. The two segments of land that formed the Westkings were hardly connected and easy to divide into north and south. The bridge between them was so narrow, Tahl had often wondered why they were considered the same continent. But while the northern region was ruled by a dozen or so monarchies, the south was dominated by a single ruler—Emperor Atoras.

The southern half of the Westkings was, as far as Tahl knew, the largest empire in the known world. Judging by the palace that loomed ahead of him, Atoras knew exactly what sort of power he held. It rose from the earth with sheer, blocky walls, its windows few and far off the ground. There were no true balconies, and only a single terrace jutted out toward the courtyard. Tahl studied the building with a careful eye as he approached. He couldn't stay in one place long enough to have the view he really wanted, and only so much was visible beyond the high curtain walls that separated the fortress from the rest of the city.

That was what it was, Tahl concluded. A fortress, rather than a palace. A monstrous thing of sharp lines and high stone that sheltered a ruthless emperor who had more to fear than anyone else in the world. It was easy to assume kings and emperors had enough power to claim safety. Few things were farther from the truth.

The sun shifted until it became too blinding to look toward the palace. Tahl lowered his eyes to take in the guards along the curtain wall instead. The gate ahead stood wide to welcome business. Guards flanked the entrance to the tunnel that led beneath the wall to the courtyard where all manner of people scuttled about. A farrier inspected a horse's hooves beside a wagon where children helped unload baskets of summer fruit. Beyond, a man gathered broken pottery into a handcart. It was something like a second market, and Tahl had never seen a need to investigate it before. His work was done elsewhere in the city, where he rubbed elbows with commoners and occasionally robbed the rich.

Satisfied by his first look, he continued past the gate, though he let his eyes linger like a curious stable boy might. For most, entry to the palace was something they could only dream of. For him, it was a challenge, and he'd need time to determine the best point of entry. Then he passed beyond the point where he could see inside, and the cool shadow of the curtain wall enveloped him.

Something brushed his arm and he spun toward it, one hand over his hip, where a dagger's hilt jabbed his side beneath his shirt.

A man in a hat tried to dart away, cementing his guilt in Tahl's mind. He all but disappeared into the crowded streets.

Tahl's eyes narrowed. He watched that hat until it vanished and, uneasy, turned to lose himself in the crowd as well.

Fewer people walked near the castle walls. In addition to the guards that patrolled the wall's top, a handful of men in armor walked the cobblestone roads that flanked the fortress. Climbing wouldn't be an option, but options were, for the moment, the least of Tahl's concerns. He slipped into an empty alleyway to check his pockets, silently cursing how distracted he'd let himself become. He was supposed to be the Ghost, the most fearsome thief in Orrad, if not the whole of the Westkings. He knew better than to gawk and lose track of his surroundings. Yet he had, and someone had gotten close—too close.

What few coins he had remained in his pockets. Nothing had been taken. Just a brush against a pedestrian, nothing more. Now that Tahl thought of it, perhaps he'd been the one to brush up against the man in the hat, instead of it being the other way around. He'd been moving without watching where he was going. It was plausible. Yet so was the idea of the other man being a thief.

All the more reason to bring the city under control. Tahl smiled grimly to himself as he checked his knives. They, too, were secure.

And what if they hadn't been? He cursed himself for the uncertainty. Niada had often accused him of going soft in the past few weeks. He hated to admit she might be right. Nothing kept him on his toes quite like knowing the city's guards could take him at any second. If he wasn't thieving, there was no reason for them to give him a second glance.

The wax that hid his scar gave him a sense of security. By now, the scar was so well healed and the fight in the Queen's Museum so far behind him that there was little chance the Emperor's Elite would remember they'd marked his face. His desire to take up the mantle of the Ghost in an official capacity was the only reason he continued to hide it. The Ghost would bear the scar; Tahl would not. His fingers drifted to the soft wax without thought and he puzzled over the texture. He'd noticed the shine, but hadn't known what to do about it. Perhaps Nia was right about the powder, too.

A shadow moved over the mouth of the alley. Tahl straightened and when his eyes fell on the man who blocked the entrance, his jaw almost dropped open. The man in the hat stood before him, brandishing a dagger.

"Your coin," the man said, his voice deep and hoarse. "Now."

Tahl moved back a half step. "You really think you're going to get anything from robbing peasants?"

"I said, your coin," the stranger growled.

With a flick of his hand, Tahl freed his knife from his belt. "Come and get it."

A wicked sneer twisted the man's upper lip. "Who do you think you are, boy? Don't you know who I am?"

"Thugs are a half-dozen for a half-mite in Orrad," Tahl replied, unamused.

Sharp, rasping laughter welled up in the mugger's throat. "I'm no mere thug, boy. Last chance. Hand over your coin, and you can tell everyone you saw the Ghost of Orrad and lived."

Tahl's eyebrows shot up. "You've got to be kidding." His eyes searched the brute's face. The man was serious, his stern, angry face made all the more serious by the jagged, ugly scar that marred his right cheek. The fellow jabbed his dagger forward in threat.

"Well," Tahl mused, "you've got the scar, I'll give you that much."

The stranger's facade faltered. "What?"

"Didn't you know?" Tahl quirked a brow. "The Ghost has a scar on his face, given to him by the Emperor's Elite. I thought everybody would know that."

The false Ghost gaped.

With the speed of a viper, Tahl lashed out with his free hand to snare his opponent's wrist. He twisted hard and a howl of pain tore free of the man's throat as his dagger clattered to the ground. Tahl spun, wrenching the man's arm behind his back. His foot landed on the false Ghost's knife and he kicked it backwards into the alley behind him.

"Now," Tahl whispered as he brought his dagger's point to the corner of his attacker's jaw, "you've got two options. One, you tuck tail and run, leave the common folk alone, and give up this ridiculous charade of being the Ghost. Or two, you try to fight me, and I sink this dagger into the artery below your ear. Which sounds better?" His blade rasped against the man's skin, eliciting a soft yelp of fear.

"One of Eseri's men, were you?" the false Ghost whispered.

A muscle in Tahl's jaw twitched. "Eseri missed his chance to recruit me. Or maybe I missed my chance to join his guild. I guess it doesn't matter now, does it?"

"N-no," the man stammered. "I suppose it don't." He raised his free hand, trembling, in a signal of defeat.

Tahl shoved hard and let go, propelling the stranger out of the alley. In two heartbeats, Tahl stowed his dagger and scaled the wall beside him to hide in a recess behind a chimney. When the false Ghost turned, the alley was empty, and the man's mouth fell open.

Amateur. Tahl sighed at the thought. He clung to the wall until the man retreated into the crowds. Then, slowly, he eased his way back to the ground.

His inaction had become a greater problem than he realized. Tahl's lips puckered with his sour frown as he retrieved the man's dagger from the alleyway and turned it over in hand. It was poor quality iron, not even steel, and the blade was so notched and dull it couldn't have cut fruit.

"And this is what Orrad is afraid of now," Tahl muttered to himself. He tucked the ugly knife into his belt beside his own blade. It wasn't very good, but Niada always knew someone willing to buy a blade, regardless of the condition it was in. *Maybe she'd be a good fence.* He hadn't taken much time to consider what sort of duties he'd assign to go with her position as second-in-command. Perhaps it was time he did.

Time I did more than that, he admitted to himself. To see the city full of false Ghosts was one thing. Being accosted by one himself had never crossed his mind as a possibility. *And if I weren't going slack in my skills, it wouldn't have happened.* He was still fast enough, when he needed to be. Nimble on roofs and walls, though he dared not climb to the rooftops within the city limits. But he'd grown nervous in his time hiding and that, he decided, was the problem. Nervousness led to distraction, and distraction led to mistakes.

And really, what do I have to be nervous about? Everything has worked according to plan so far. The guards hadn't found him. He'd gained proficiency in disguising his scar, even if he would have to prowl the market later for that powder. The city had destabilized and become desperate, and all the false Ghosts only emphasized the existence of a real one. *Who has done nothing for months,* Tahl thought with a hint of disappointment.

He worked his way through the city streets, more attentive than ever after his moments-long scuffle with the man in the hat. Tahl frowned to himself. He'd only just thought up his plan. Now he had to revise it in the same day. The heist was supposed to be his grand return to the public eye. Something shocking, sudden, to shake Orrad to its core. Yet being shaken was the last thing his city needed. Orrad craved strength, unity. It craved the gentle, guiding hand of a steady guild that could simultaneously rule its underbelly with an iron fist.

And so the beginnings of a new guild comes first, he silently concluded.

When Tahl reached Ebitha's modest stable, the evening sun warmed the city in shades of gold. He cleaned the stalls and tended the horses, his mind elsewhere. By the time he climbed to his modest room above the stable to wash and eat his evening meal, he'd made up his mind.

His heist clothing lay neatly folded in the box he pulled from under his bed. Tahl removed the deep blue shirt first. A small block of fragrant, reddish wood clattered to the floor when he unfolded it, and he scooped it back into the box with his belongings. Keeping the wood nestled in the folds of his clothes was a trick he'd learned from the locals, useful for deterring moths and tiny carpet beetles from the precious, finely-knit fabric. He'd grown fond of the smell, though it came with the disadvantage of the faint scent of cedar clinging to him like a second skin. A good thief shouldn't smell like anything, though he supposed if he had to choose, cedar was an acceptable option. Better than smelling like the horses, at least.

Tahl stripped out of his normal clothes and slipped into the soft comfort of his close-fitting thief's garb. He stretched his arms overhead and savored the pull of the muscles in his sides and back before he sank forward, folded in half at the waist, to press his palms flat to the floor. The backs of his knees ached. Slow breath filled his lungs until his ribs creaked and strained to contain it all. A long breath out eased the strain in his back and knees. Longer stretches brought warmth and mobility into his limbs. Finally, he sank to the floor beside his box of meager belongings and sat cross-legged as he drew a small object wrapped in cloth from the corner of the box.

His fingers traced the edges of the mirror shard as he folded back the cloth. He'd found it in an alleyway and kept it to make shaving easier. It had proven useful for when he smoothed wax over his scar, too. Now, he used it to peel the wax from his cheek and the bridge of his nose.

Once he'd had healing and the color diminished, it wasn't as bad as he'd thought it would be. The edges had buckled inward instead of jutting out, and the depression in his skin was silvery-pink and easy to fill. Tahl couldn't help but wonder if it would have been more imposing if it protruded, but he didn't devote it much thought. Instead, he wiped his face clean and put his things away.

As he pushed the box back under his bed, something pale protruding from the pocket of his everyday trousers caught his eye. He caught it with two fingers, and the paper rasped as he pulled it free. Niada's sketches. Simple but striking, now that he looked at them in the weak lamplight of his home.

He folded the paper and tucked it into his bag of supplies.

The horses hardly whickered as Tahl slipped out through the stables. His footsteps across the yard were soft, almost soundless, and his pulse accelerated in anticipation of the first move.

Silent, he sprang from the ground and caught a familiar handhold in the side of Ebitha's tall house. The split toe of his soft deerskin shoes made it easy to find purchase with his feet and he scaled the wall in seconds. Atop the roof, the deep ridges between the tiles made perfect handholds for him to leverage himself up past the overhang.

The moon hung low in the sky as he crept to the ridge of the roof and stood tall, looking over the sprawling city below.

All right, he thought as he drew a deep breath and prepared for the rooftop voyage. *Let's give them something to be afraid of.*

The Ghost turned east.

CHAPTER 4

Dawn's first muddy light brought the city to life. Tahl was up with the sun despite his late night. Ebitha met him at the back door, where he stood with a bucket of fresh-drawn well water in hand.

"You're in good spirits this morning," the old woman remarked as she accepted the wooden pail and squinted up at his face.

Tahl grinned back at her. "Good things sprang from yesterday."

Her eyes brightened. "Found work, have you?"

"Yes, ma'am." He stepped back and hooked his thumbs in his pockets. "I'm to start right away."

"About time! They say all the trade growth is good for the city, but I don't know what good it does when every manner of ruffian is in from the country. I'm sure there are some good ones among them, but it's hard for the young ones when there's so much more competition for work." She extended an arm to pat his cheek and he tilted his head to land her touch closer to his jaw, lest she leave marks in the wax over his scar. He disguised the movement with a smile.

"I appreciate everything you've done for me, Ebitha. I couldn't have made ends meet without your help. I'm happy to look after the horses until you can sort out finding a new stableboy."

The old woman's cheer faltered. "Ah, perhaps. I've been thinking about the horses, these past few days. It's been years since I could ride, and they're so expensive to maintain. I've started to wonder if I'd be better off letting them go."

Tahl blinked. Few things meant as much to the woman as her horses. She had purchased them as yearlings and they'd been with her a good decade. As well cared-for as they were, he expected all three had at least another fifteen years left in them. "They still make you happy, don't they?"

"They do," Ebitha replied haltingly. She drew breath as if to say more, then the sparkle in her eyes faded and she sighed instead. "Well, no matter. I'll think on that a minute yet. Best wishes for your first day of work, lad. I'm sure your manager will be impressed."

"Thank you, ma'am. I'm not sure when I'll be in tonight, but I'll see the horses are cared for before I sleep." He retreated a step before he flicked his fingers in a quick goodbye.

People filtered into the streets from the buildings around him and Tahl slipped into the growing throng with a practiced ease. In his brown trousers and unbleached cotton shirt, he looked like every other warehouse hand or porter on the street as they trudged off to start the day's work. Unlike them, he walked with a cheery bounce in his step.

Part of him felt bad for misleading Ebitha. He'd never been out of work, save the restrictions he'd put on his own activity. But he'd needed a reason to justify the tightening of his purse strings and the extra hours he spent in his room above the stable. Likewise, he felt a need to explain the sudden lack of his presence in the coming days. Especially when it meant someone else would need to tend the horses. He liked the animals, even if they were both impractical and unnecessary within the city limits. Everyone was given to their follies.

Tahl wondered at why she might consider selling the horses—he assumed that was what she meant, rather than turning them loose outside the city—after so many years together, but he could puzzle over that when he ran out of things to do.

The streets that ran eastward cut a jagged path, zigzagging across the city. He stuck to the widest avenue and cocked an ear toward the people clustered at the street's edge, where vendors hawked wares and citizens shared news in conspiratorial tones. Several whispers caught his attention and Tahl suppressed the urge to smirk. He'd wondered what the response would be, but a part of him already knew.

On the eastern side of the city, crowds gathered to gawk at the tall stone face of the mage academy, where a half dozen novice mages with scrub brushes worked to eliminate the black mark emblazoned across the building.

The crest was tall, a sweeping hook that resembled a cowl. A lone mark representing an eye glowered out from the shelter of its curve.

Armored guards stood in a loose half ring around the front of the mage academy, preventing anyone from coming near. Behind them, a senior mage—a Master, he thought—barked orders to the students who scrubbed.

Again, Tahl resisted the overwhelming desire to smirk. Under normal circumstances, he suspected the mages would have used their power to blast the emblem off the front of the academy. But he'd used his own magic to create it, etching soot into the stone. Residual magic couldn't be unwound, the flows of power already long since gone. And there was the etching, besides. Even after the novices finished scrubbing, a shadow of the mark—his mark—would remain on the academy's face.

"You used it," a small voice said beside him, full of wonder and a hint of admiration. He'd been glad to spot Niada among the crowd and had positioned himself where she'd easily catch sight of him.

"Well," Tahl said, almost dismissively, "people need something to look up to."

"What changed your mind?"

He shrugged. "The Ghost."

Nia's brows drew together in confusion.

"I'll explain later," he murmured. "Are you free today?"

"I have a morning shift at The Last Drop." Her hand fluttered in the air overhead and she produced her apron as if from thin air. "But I'm free after that."

Tahl chuckled. "I saw the bulge in your sleeve."

"You did not, you liar. I wound it around my arm this time. It was perfectly flat."

"Not at your elbow." He tweaked her arm between his forefinger and thumb. "We need a new headquarters. Meet me at the west gate when you're finished. We're going exploring."

A sparkle lit Niada's green eyes. "Deal."

With a wink, he retreated through the crowd.

"A MORNING SHIFT implies you'll be done before afternoon," Tahl complained as Niada approached the gate. He'd lingered long enough that the guards had come to heckle him more than once. The last thing he wanted was their attention.

"It normally does," Nia called back, but a mischievous smirk twisted her mouth. "I don't think you'll be disappointed once we've had a chance to talk."

Tahl's eyes flicked toward the guards beside the gate. She rolled her eyes in complaint at the reminder.

"Where are we going today?" she asked, smoothly abandoning the subject.

"Back into the city." He caught her arm and turned her toward the south.

Her jaw took a stubborn set and she pulled back. "Why'd you make me come all the way over here, then?"

"Because I was working outside the west gate today." Tahl pulled her arm again and gave her a coaxing look. "I still have to eat, you know."

Sullen, she gave up and followed him. "You're the one making things difficult for yourself, you know."

"I know, I know. I'm working on it, okay?" He stuck out his tongue in the ultimate of juvenile responses, but it had its desired effect. Nia giggled and trotted up alongside him.

He led her through a handful of twisting, turning alleyways and did not speak again until he deemed them safely outside where they could be heard.

"Eseri's guild met in one of his warehouses," Tahl said, mindful to keep his voice low even though he saw no signs of anyone in the alley ahead or behind. "I don't have a warehouse, so we need another option. There's a place I thought we should investigate. It might work. There are entrances all over the city. It would be hard to defend, but defense isn't the point. It would be easy to escape if it were raided."

Nia's nose crinkled. "Where is it? I've never heard of anywhere like that."

Tahl came to a stop above a ring of stone topped with a wooden cover. He gestured grandly with both hands.

She stared. "What is it?"

"A sewer." He pushed the cover with his foot and it slid a few inches, providing enough space to get his fingers under it and move it aside.

Her mouth twisted with uncertainty. "A what?"

"An underground channel that was supposed to keep the city cleaner. Extra water was supposed to go down drains in the streets to reduce flooding. People were supposed to connect latrines to it. I guess it works in other places, but the water table in Orrad is too high because of how close we are to the Ranton." Tahl dropped to his knees and turned to scout for the rough ladder he knew was there. His toe caught on it and he worked his way down. "The Ranton ended up being the biggest problem. Some of the channels they dug ended up flooding because the river makes the ground water too high. You hit water six feet down, and this is ten."

Nia leaned forward, silhouetted against the sky as she watched him descend. "So they abandoned it?"

"Yep." His boots hit the ground and Tahl stepped back to make room for Nia to join him. "Some of the tunnels collapsed and they filled them in from above. And some got hooked to latrines, but since the sewers connect to the river, the water ended up being contaminated and folk got sick. The mages insisted it was because of the waste being flushed into the river water, so Atoras called off the whole project."

"Seems like a waste." Short as her legs were, she struggled down the wide-spaced rungs of the ladder, but she breathed in relief and accomplishment when she reached the ground. Despite the high water table, the bottom of the tunnel was dry, if dirty and cluttered with leaves. "Are there any water drains in the streets? I don't think I've seen them."

Tahl nudged her aside and took a few steps up the ladder to replace the lid. "Nope. But you can see where they were. They were afraid the tunnels would collapse if they kept getting water into them, or that people would dump things they shouldn't into the sewer. There are big stone blocks where they pulled the grates back out."

"So there's just tunnels down here with no purpose." She paused as the lid scraped halfway over the entrance. "What are you doing?"

"Closing it so no one knows we're down here." He grunted as he heaved the heavy lid back into place and sealed them in darkness. "I think there are some beggars who come down here for shelter, but they'll all be out on the streets looking for money, this time of day. Most of the entrances are sealed off right now, so we shouldn't run into anyone else."

Nia scoffed. "Like we'd be able to see them. Neither one of us brought a lantern."

"We don't need it." Tahl fished a coin from his pocket. "But you can't tell anyone you saw me do this, understand?"

"Saw you do what? I can't see anything, Tahl!"

He ignored her protest and trained his thoughts on the small coin in his hand. This was one of the only tricks he practiced in his loft above the stables, one that wouldn't show and wasn't impressive enough that anyone would notice the magic at work. Weak as his power was, there were still a few practical things he could make it do.

The coin in his palm grew warm as he shifted power into it. A sense of cold ran down his arm as he transferred his own strength into the threads of magic that trickled into the coin. Ever so slowly, it began to glow. A hint of red light outlined his fingers. The light swelled, and he let his grip ease, his fingers separating to let narrow beams shine through.

Niada gasped. "What *is* that?"

"A coin," he replied with a grin as he rolled it between his fingers. It was incandescent, too bright to look at directly, but cast more than enough light by which to see. "It's a mage-light."

A hint of wonder colored her expression. "You've never done that before."

"Well, thieves and shadow go together better than thieves and light. I haven't had many reasons to use it." Tahl bounced the light in his palm and then pointed it toward the path ahead, using his hand to shield them from the direct light. "This way."

They padded down the shadowy tunnel together, Nia close at his heels. All the while, her eyes were fixed on his hand and the light that issued from the coin.

"How many new things have you learned to do?" she asked in a whisper.

He raised a brow. "What makes you think this is new? I can do lots of things. Most mages can do lots of things. I just couldn't do anything at a high enough level to be useful." The last word escaped with a hint of venom. He couldn't help it; those had been their words. Too low a level, they said. Too weak to ever be useful. It still raised his hackles every time he remembered. One hand drifted to the back of his neck, unconsciously smoothing the prickle of irritation that bunched in his shoulders and crawled up his scalp.

"You never showed me, that's all," Nia murmured.

"That's because it's called a secret." He flicked his hand sideways to flash her eyes with the light. With a startled yelp, she fell back, hands to her face.

"What was that for?" she cried.

Tahl closed his hand a little more, blocking off extra light when he aimed it back toward the ground. "If you're going to look into someone else's business, you'd better be ready for things you don't want to see."

A sullen silence grew in the wake of his words. Content to let her brood, Tahl turned into an adjacent tunnel.

He hadn't visited the sewers more than twice, and while he'd drawn a few crude maps of the tunnels and entrances he'd found, he didn't have any real idea how big the sewer system was. Most of the entrances were sealed, but he suspected it wouldn't be hard to chisel the mortar out from around the stones and work out some sort of trick to open and close them without needing a great deal of strength. Though Tahl figured himself clever enough, he didn't have as strong an education regarding complex mechanics as he would have liked. He didn't doubt he'd puzzle out something eventually, but with fortune, there would be others he could delegate such jobs to once the guild was reestablished.

"What's that?" Nia asked, interrupting his thoughts.

Tahl paused to inspect what she pointed at. A tall iron grate sat in an alcove in the wall. At first glance, he thought it merely for ventilation, but then the slender hinges along one bar caught his attention. He made a small sound in his throat as he turned the light toward it. "A gate. Wonder where that goes. Should we look?"

She cocked her slim hips to one side and crossed her arms. "I thought exploring was the point."

"Yeah, but if you want to chicken out, now's the time." He ran the fingers of his free hand over the hinges. They weren't as rusted as he would have expected, but a touch revealed the presence of grease. He wiped his fingertips on the coarse stone of the wall. "It's pretty old. The lubricant feels tarry. But it should open." Assuming he could find the latch, that was. The other side of the grate bore no obvious lock.

"Down here." Nia crouched beside him and dug a tangle of half-decayed leaves from the bottom bar, where a pin driven into the stone lay half hidden. She dusted her hands against her skirt and grasped the pin. "Won't budge."

Tahl nudged her aside with his leg and bent to wrap his empty hand around the angled top. The pin was stuck fast in the stone. "Step back."

She scuttled backwards until her back touched the wall.

Tahl, too, stepped back. He gripped the top of the gate for support and then launched his heel full force at the pin.

The gate clanked and shuddered. He kicked it again and the pin shifted beneath the heel of his boot.

"Got it." He leaned over to jerk the pin free. Rust and mud caked the bottom half and fell away in large chunks when he touched it.

"Looks like it's been there for ages." Nia took the pin from his hand as he jerked the gate. The hinges moaned a long protest as the gate's bottom scraped through dirt and rotten leaves.

"Well, not ages. Just as long as the sewer's been here. It's younger than us, anyway." Tahl held the mage-light out ahead of him and motioned for her to go first.

She shook her head vigorously and stepped back. "You've got the light. You go."

"Sure?" He offered the glowing coin on his palm.

Nia winced and turned away from the brilliant light. She considered it for a moment, then tossed the gate pin to the tunnel floor and gave her head a shake. "Thanks, but I'll leave the magic to the mage."

Shrugging, he ducked under the top edge of the gate's frame and strode onward.

The tunnel beyond the gate was unremarkable. Dark lines on the stone along the bottom of the walls marked where water had run for however many years the sewers had been there. The water line was lower than he'd expected, but then again, most of the drains were blocked off. The ground underfoot was damp, if not muddy, which meant there had to be access to the city somewhere down the passage.

"Are you sure this is connected to Orrad?" Nia asked, as if to question his thoughts.

Tahl paused to trace the turns they'd taken in his mind. "We're headed... south? No, back west. We just turned again." Unlike the rest of the sewer, this tunnel lacked the twists and turns he'd expected. It ran straight for as far as he could see— which was farther than he'd expected. The stone walls were light, save the darkened stains along the bottom, and the light cast from his coin bounced well ahead down the passage.

Nia squinted at the shadows beyond where the mage-light reached. "Why run the sewers that far? There's nothing out there but farms and forest."

"Maybe it doesn't run the way I thought," Tahl mused. "I thought it fed into the tunnel we were in, because the dirt that was all ridged up at the bottom of the grate seemed like it was collected on the back side. Like it was catching on the grate as water poured in. But maybe that's not it."

"It could go the other way." Nia nodded as if it had been her idea. "Maybe the water pours from the other tunnels into this one. Like a drain out... somewhere. I thought you said it went to the Ranton, though?"

He'd thought it did. "Maybe only part. Maybe the rest pours

out here. There are creeks that run through the forest, little tributaries that feed into the river. Maybe this is supposed to catch the overflow, when there's too much water for the sewer system to feed everything into the Ranton."

With a snort, she kicked a clump of dirt toward the stains on the walls. "Doesn't look like that's a problem."

"Well it wouldn't be, not with the drains all plugged. It—" Tahl stopped short and his feet stilled. She walked straight into his back and squeaked in alarm.

"What?"

He inched aside and pointed ahead.

The bright cut stone of the walls ended abruptly, replaced by deep, muddy brown rock and a yawning hole that swallowed all light.

Tahl expected her to be dismayed. Instead, Nia scuttled to the edge of the tunnel and leered out into the shadow with a gasp of delight.

"I can't believe it!" she cried.

Hesitant but curious, Tahl crept after her.

Before them, the tunnel fell away in chiseled terraces, rather than a sheer drop. Beyond the last terrace—a shade too tall to be comfortably called steps—the light glinted off the damp stone floor of a cave. Something dripped occasionally, a soft and steady *plink* in the silence.

"Wow," Tahl said. The single word echoed back, more skeptical than he thought he'd sounded.

"I didn't know there were caves outside Orrad," Nia said in a rush. She hopped down onto the first terrace and almost lost her footing. Her arms shot out to the sides to restore her balance.

More cautious, Tahl stepped down behind her. The stone was slick and the dank must of mildew rose to meet his nostrils. He held the coin at arm's length, letting the mage-light reveal more of the cavern ahead. It was generously sized, perhaps half the length of the sanctuary inside the Temple of Brant.

Nia spun to face him. "We could set up here. Put a lock on

that gate so that only initiates with a copy of the key could get in. No one would think to come this far."

"We'd have to scrape every bit of mud out of the bottom of the tunnel, or the footprints would be a dead giveaway," Tahl replied, tone flat. "But maybe. I think we need to see more." He pushed past her to take the next step down. Descending the terraces was difficult, each level knee-high. It was a long, uncomfortable descent, not enough to warrant crouching to slide down, but enough to put unpleasant amounts of pressure on his knees. Mindful of the risk for injury, he opted to slide down the next level as a precaution.

Nia followed his lead. "We'd have to put some blocks here to make it easier to get up and down."

"Do you hear that?" He cocked his head as she grew still beside him. A soft whoosh carried through the cave from somewhere to the left. Wind or water, he wasn't sure, but it could be another opening. "This way."

She trotted close at his heels as he led the way. "We would have room for beds down here. Maybe we could wall off some sections of the cavern and have real sleeping quarters."

"And a treasury," Tahl said. "The last thing we want is any thieves in the guild having free access to everything we scrape together."

Nia sniffed as if she didn't appreciate the addition. "How is that supposed to work, anyway? People in the guild have expenses too. You can't just take all their money."

"Nobody takes all their money." Tahl fought the urge to roll his eyes. "They bring in their goods and gold, the treasurer takes it and weighs it, and they get their fair share of coin back."

"What's stopping them from keeping their gold for themselves?"

"It's dirty, usually. The goods always are. They need the protection of a fence and few thieves in the city have that right now. The guild won't be too concerned about pocket change. If they scrape together a few pims on their own, they're welcome to keep it, but anything big? That goes through the guild."

She considered that with a thoughtful tilt of her head. "Almost everyone who visits in the taverns I work at pays with pims."

"That's because Orrad's official currency is silver." He gave her shoulder a playful nudge. "If anyone's paying with actual gold, that's always a problem. There's gold currency floating around, sure, but almost all of it is from the northern kingdoms. Atoras has done his best to suck up as much gold as he can."

"What do you suppose he wants to use it for?" Nia's eyes took a distant look and he could almost picture the thoughts that had to be running through her head. Piles of gold and gold-plated treasures heaped around inside the castle, the very place they planned to infiltrate.

"I have some theories, but it's too soon to speculate. Over here." The mage-light in his hand revealed an opening into a sloped tunnel. It ran uphill and while a pool of water sat at its mouth, the tunnel itself appeared dry. "The sound's coming from here. I'm pretty sure it's wind."

If the tunnel opened into the fields west of the city, it would be the luckiest find Tahl could imagine. An easy avenue for escape from the city opened countless new opportunities. Smuggling, for one. It wasn't his specialty, but it had lined Bahar Eseri's pockets well, and Tahl was sure he could find someone to manage an operation within the new guild. New passages and recesses opened up along the way, promising countless hiding places for his thieves.

"I couldn't imagine anything more perfect," he murmured to himself as they walked.

Nia frowned. "What was that?"

"I was just saying—"

"No," she interrupted, her eyes skimming past him to search the nooks and crannies behind them. "I thought I heard..." She trailed off, uncertain.

Tahl turned and the light that radiated from his coin glinted off something in the dark. His stomach dropped to his boots. "Run."

"What—" Nia started, but he clamped a hand on her shoulder and spun her toward the darkness.

"Run!"

CHAPTER 5

"Go!" Tahl shoved Nia ahead as the beast's furious snarl reverberated in the tunnels. The path ahead was dark, save the fifteen feet or so illuminated by his mage-light. Or was it ten feet? He skidded hard in the gravelly dirt and altered his course to follow Nia down a new passage. His mage-light was fading and he didn't dare stop to recharge it.

Behind them, heavy breath and heavier footfalls signaled the beast's location.

Tahl wasn't sure what it was. Big, furry, and angry, no doubt. Too large to be a wolf, but he wasn't as familiar with the empire's wildlife as he supposed he ought to be. Whatever was chasing them, from the sound of its footfalls, they couldn't outrun it for long.

Its den had been in the worst possible position. Angled so it could rocket out after them, and their only choice was to flee farther down an unknown passage. Even had they managed to get past it to retrace their steps, there were the long tunnels of the sewer to contend with.

"It can't be that far," he said between breaths, though he didn't know if he meant to reassure Niada or himself.

Nia did not reply. The patter of her feet against the packed tunnel path came twice as fast as his. Her steps covered half as much ground. Tahl could have outpaced her easily. To do so would have sentenced her to death. Instead, he put a hand to her back when she faltered and pushed her onward.

The mage-light in his hand guttered. That was unusual. When magic gave out, it typically faded slowly, it didn't flicker like a dying flame.

And there are much more convenient times to think about that, he chastised himself. Ahead, the path split. Above the heavy thudding of the monster at their heels, the whisper of grasses and leaves in the wind caught his ear. They had to be close to the surface. How else would the beast have made the cave its home?

A soft stirring of air brushed his cheek. "Left!" he barked as they hit the split. Inexplicably, Nia veered right.

Cursing, Tahl skidded to a stop and threw a look over his shoulder. Down the passage, glinting eyes reflected the dying light cast from his coin. The monster thundered forward and Tahl lingered as long as he dared. The beast's shadowed maw opened, revealing glistening teeth.

"Bear," Tahl spat. "Bear!" He didn't know if Nia could hear him. Part of him hoped not—if she'd gotten far enough, the rock would absorb any sound he made.

Undisturbed by its identification, the bear barreled toward him. Tahl did the only thing that crossed his mind.

With all his might, he flung his mage-light at the bear.

The brilliant coin struck the beast square in the eye. The bear faltered a step and bellowed, more in anger than distress.

Tahl grimaced and spun away. *Smart.* His only source of light now lay behind him, on the other side of an angry bear who stalled for only a moment before it resumed its chase. A few more steps plowed Tahl into a stone wall. He skirted to its edge and charged forward again, an ache of mingled breathlessness and panic gripping his chest.

The bear's sight was no better than his and as Tahl scrambled farther up the passage, the ground underfoot shuddered with the impact of the beast striking the wall.

Great. I'll just crash it to death. He fought back a grimace and let his fingers rake the damp walls. It offered little assistance in finding his way forward. If he thought he had a moment, he would have made another light. The loping footfalls behind him reminded him he didn't even have a second.

Another twist. He followed the wall around the curve and his shoulder slammed into stone. His teeth clacked together to hold more curses at bay. Somewhere ahead, the darkness began to look more gray. Whatever lay ahead had to be better than the bear at his back.

Tahl willed his footing to be sure, even as he felt the weight of the bear's gait hit the ground behind him. An oak leaf skittered across the floor, carried by the wind, and he granted himself a fleeting moment to be aware he'd seen it.

Another twist. Daylight poured into the tunnel ahead. With renewed vigor, Tahl pumped his burning legs and prayed it would be enough.

He burst from the cave's entrance and stumbled two steps before he fell to the rocky hillside. Seconds too late, he shifted into a roll and tumbled through the scree. Jagged edges of broken stone gouged the exposed flesh of his arms and scraped or bruised everything else. One more somersault and, by some miracle, he landed on his feet.

Maybe the Lifetree did favor thieves.

Too breathless to offer prayers of thanks, he staggered forward and regained his stride. His left leg protested but he refused to break his stride. A tree waited ahead and Tahl vaulted to catch the lowest branch. With a grace that hid his injuries, he sprang from limb to limb until he was certain he perched too high for the bear to follow, the branches hardly able to support his weight.

The fall had given him some headway. The bear trundled down the slope, snarling and snuffling as it followed his scent through the rock. With the blood that trickled from Tahl's skinned knuckles and the cuts on his arms, he expected it was an easy track to follow.

The bear stopped at the bottom of the tree and bawled. Its agitation had lessened, but it gazed up at him as it reared onto its hind legs and placed a paw against the trunk, seemingly considering whether it was worth pursuing him up a tree.

Tahl wiped blood from his hand and drew slow, deep breaths. Gradually, the discomfort in his chest eased.

At least the bear had followed him and not Nia. As much as he wanted to will the creature away, he didn't want it to return to its den just yet. A few more minutes would give her enough of a head start that she could find her way back out of the cave.

And if she doesn't? He grimaced as the thought sprang into his mind unbidden. He had no intention of leaving Nia to fend for herself, but he wasn't equipped to deal with a bear.

As if on cue, the bear released a low, frustrated moan. Deciding Tahl wasn't worth pursuing, it dropped to all fours and turned away. Bored, it lumbered farther down the slope.

Tahl let his head drop back against the trunk of the tree as a deep sigh of relief escaped his lips.

"What were you saying about perfect?" a small voice called from a short distance away.

Startled, Tahl straightened and scanned the ground.

"Over here."

His eyes snapped up to a tree some twenty feet away, where Nia clung to the top branches, her skirts bunched around her knees.

Tahl's brow furrowed. "How did you—"

"Turns out mine was the shortcut. I got here first." A smug smirk twisted the corners of her mouth.

He returned it with a grin. "I don't know about you, but I still think it's perfect. I can't imagine anything better for keeping guards off our trail."

Nia rolled her eyes and sagged against her tree. "You're the worst, Tahl."

"You love me anyway," he retorted.

"Yeah, right."

———

THEY LIMPED BACK to the city walls together as the sun sank behind their backs. Or rather, Tahl limped; Nia trudged, unharmed but weary after their escape. She eyed the guards at the western gate with some trepidation, but they weren't interested in her. Tahl grimaced when one of the guards waved for him to stop.

"Trouble on the road?" the guard asked, his voice gruff.

"We got chased by a bear," Nia provided helpfully. "He fell."

The guard's brows rose.

"It didn't get me," Tahl grumbled and glowered her direction.

"It almost did." She returned his glare with a neutral look.

He cleared his throat. "Just a warning, the bears don't want to share their early season berries. There's a big one in a den down that slope, a little ways to the south. It's not too close to the road, but you might want to let travelers know, just so the berry brambles don't tempt them off the path."

The guard grunted and turned his head when Tahl pointed the right direction. "I see."

Tahl gave a stiff nod and jammed his hands into his pockets as he slinked past.

Once they'd turned the first corner inside Orrad's walls, Nia nudged his arm. "Why'd you tell them where the cave is? We won't be able to use it now."

"Were you really thinking we'd use it?" He held up his hands to display his bloodied knuckles. "There is a bear inside."

She tucked in her chin and looked sullen.

"I know what I'm doing, okay?" Tahl lowered his voice. "We can still use the tunnel for emergencies, if we need to escape or slip in and out of the city, but it's definitely not getting used for anything else. A bear might be worth the risk if it slows down someone who's chasing me, but that's it."

Nia huffed. "But you told—"

"I know," he replied before she could finish. "Because the more people who know there's a bear that lives over there, the fewer people will be nosing around. It works out better for us. Nobody's going exploring a cave if they know there's a bear inside, and nobody's got the means to hunt a bear except the guards. They're not going to bother."

A doubtful twist took the corners of Nia's mouth, but she said nothing else about it. Instead, her eyes settled on his scraped and bloodied arms. "Maybe we should go to the temple and get you healed."

"I've had worse."

"Yeah, but you need to be at the top of your game for what we're doing next." She put a little too much emphasis on the last word. A few passersby cast her curious looks.

Tahl snorted. "As long as I don't slip down any more rocky hills, I'll be fine."

"It's not like you to slip."

"It's also not like me to get chased by bears, but that happened, didn't it?" He turned her down a wider road than he'd planned on taking. It was a more innocuous path than the winding alleys he preferred, and the people whose heads had turned when they overheard Niada lost interest. "We still need to decide on a place to go, though. I've got an idea for that."

She perked up. "You do? What is it?"

He led her back to the sewer grate they'd entered through and she stared at it, confused.

The cover had settled back as if nothing ever dislodged it. Tahl shifted it aside again and started down the ladder. Before his head disappeared into the hole, he paused to reach across the dusty ground and pluck a pebble from the earth. "Coming?"

Nia picked at the front of her skirt. "What about the bear?"

"We're not going back that direction. I know the way to a particular place in the city from here. That's our destination." He let go of the ladder and dropped to the sewer tunnel's floor without making a sound. "Coming?"

Uncertain as she looked, she still followed.

Tahl closed the entrance behind her and poured his focus into the pebble in his hand. He regretted losing the copper coin he'd flung at the bear's face, even if it had bought him a few seconds. That half-mite was supposed to provide his supper. Without it, he'd need to rely on Nia's charity, and he doubted she felt particularly charitable after he'd led the two of them off to be chased.

"This way," he murmured as the pebble flared with light. It wasn't as brilliant as the coin had been; the pebble was smaller and he was tired. His magic always suffered first when his energy began to drop.

Niada trailed close behind him, though she was understandably less enthusiastic about their second trip underground.

He led her a different way this time, winding toward the east instead of the west. The underground tunnels were more direct than the roadways above, and he counted the branching passages they strode past in order to keep his bearings.

"Where are we going?" Nia asked, voice quiet.

"The Queen's Museum." There was little point in keeping it secret. "There's an outlet to the sewer within the building. I think they meant to build some sort of fancy lavatory and connect that part of the museum to the sewer. They tiled over it, but I'm pretty sure we can open it up again."

She squinted distrustfully at his back. He didn't have to look to see it. There was a familiar heat and weight to her gaze when she looked at him that way.

"How do you know?" she asked.

"It was one of the entry routes I considered when I broke in to distract the guard with the Seed." Tahl flashed a grin over his shoulder. She rolled her eyes in response. Fine. She didn't need to revel in his successes like he did. Of course, it hadn't gone perfectly. That venture was what had earned him his scar.

The rest of the walk was quiet. Eventually, he led her down a dead end and pointed at a large, square block of stone in the ceiling. "That's it. We just need to pry that out." He motioned for Nia's hand. When she extended it, he pushed the mage-light into her palm. "Hold that."

"Not giving me much choice," she muttered.

Ignoring the complaint, Tahl pulled a knife from his belt. He'd figured the low-quality blade the false Ghost had threatened him with would be useful, but he'd thought its use would come from putting a few mites in his pocket. Instead, he jammed the blade between the large stone and the rest of the ceiling to chip away the mortar.

It was slow, frustrating work, and long minutes dragged by before the stone had any give when he pushed on it.

"Lucky the ceiling is so low," he mumbled to himself as he worked the blade deeper. "If I were as short as you, I couldn't reach it."

Nia's cheeks puffed with indignation. "I'm still growing."

Tahl shrugged and pushed the stone upward. It shifted. Chunks of broken mortar rained down on his head and he turned his face toward the earth to keep it out of his eyes. Again, he pushed, and the stone slid up and to the side. "There we go."

Curious, Nia crept forward. The space above the new hole was dark. "I thought the museum was open."

"It should be." That was part of his plan for exploration, at least. If the museum was filled with visitors, a few more voices wouldn't be noticed. He laced his fingers together and braced his hands against his thigh to make a foothold. "Come on. Climb up."

She eyed him, wary.

"It's easier for both of us if you go first. You can't get up there on your own and it's easier for me to lift you than to pull you up." He tapped his thigh and laced his fingers again. "Come on. Take the light up."

"If I get caught—"

"You won't get caught. At least, not if you're half as good a thief as you think you are."

Her nose crinkled with offense, but it spurred her into motion. She nestled her toes into his hold and pushed herself up.

Tahl kept his head down as her skirts went over the top of him. She usually wore leggings under her skirts, just in case she needed to make a quick escape, but there were few ideas less pleasant than getting a glimpse up his honorary sister's legs.

Nia disappeared into the space above. The shadows around the mage-light took a bluish tint.

With the sewer's ceiling as low as it was, it wasn't difficult for Tahl to catch the edge of the hole and drag himself up into the museum. The space was tight, and he realized with a start that his shoulders were a shade wider than they used to be. Maybe he was still growing, too. That put all sorts of unpleasant thoughts in his head. If he outgrew his heist outfit, could the old woman who knitted the thing adjust it? A full new outfit was out of the question. It had cost more than an average man earned in a year.

The room he emerged into was as dark as he'd expected. When the addition of lavatories failed, the space had been converted to storage. Wooden frames of unfinished walls cast skeletal shadows across the crates and sheet-covered sculptures stowed in the large, incomplete space.

"Big area to leave empty," Nia murmured. Low as her voice was, it carried in the quiet emptiness.

Tahl shrugged. "Museums can never have too much storage. They can't have everything on display all the time, you know."

"Why not?"

"There's too much stuff. Things that have to be cleaned and restored, too, and things they remove from display because of the times. Depending on the state of things in the empire, some artifacts and pieces of artwork are considered too sensitive to share." He crept to a crate and pried at the lid, curious to see what was inside. It was nailed down fast. A thick coat of dust on its surface indicated it had been stored for some time. He brushed his hand against his trousers and his dusty fingers left streaks of gray. "Besides, sometimes they get things on loan, like the artifacts they had from the temple. They had to take stuff down to make room for that exhibit."

"Looks like some of it's never going back up." Nia frowned at the massive stacks of crates.

Tahl paced toward the door. "I'm not surprised. We're not near the exhibits."

She followed with the light. It glowed steady, a surprise of its own, given how tired he'd grown before he made it. "Where are we?"

"The basement. Or, sort of. This level is halfway underground, according to the diagram I found in the hall of records." The door was locked when he tested the knob. Perfect.

Nia blinked. "We have a hall of records?"

"We have a lot of things," Tahl replied mildly. "This room was supposed to be where the plumbing went. Pipes fashioned to connect to all the lavatories, which were going to be just above us. I think they planned to have water cisterns in here too, if I remember right, but I'm not sure how they thought they were going to get that water up to the lavatories to use it."

"And we're going to just crawl through a hole in the floor every day?" Skepticism oozed from her tone and for a moment, Tahl reconsidered the wisdom of working with an adolescent. He wasn't much older, but he'd left the attitude behind when he'd been ejected from the mage academy.

"Yes." He shoved a box aside. "If we get creative in rearranging, nobody will know we're here. Judging by the dust on the floor, no one's been in here for years."

She crossed her arms. Her fingers shielded most of the light from the pebble in her hand. "And when they do decide to come calling?"

"Then we'll hopefully be built up big enough that we'll have allies on the inside." Tahl flashed her a grin and stepped back, his arms spread wide. "So I think this is it. Our new headquarters. The new guild, led by the Ghost of Orrad. What do you think?"

"I think," Nia said, "we need to talk about how this guild is supposed to get together."

"They'll come to us."

"How do you figure?"

He shrugged, surveying the room like a man appreciating his holdings. "Because two days from now, the Ghost will be wearing the crown."

The words carried a certain weight, and he paused to appreciate them after they left his mouth. One day to heal. A day and a half to plan. A hint of a smile worked its way onto his lips.

A FULL DAY OF PLANNING WAS SIMULTANEOUSLY NOT ENOUGH AND more time than Tahl needed. His research efforts proved fruitless within the first few hours. If there were diagrams of the palace, they weren't anywhere he would find them. The hall of records showed nothing of value. The museum's library showed nothing at all. It wasn't the first time he'd winged something, but winging the theft of the emperor's crown was madness.

At least no one had to *know* that he had no clue what he was doing. Niada didn't need to know there was a complete lack of strategy beyond what got them in the door. They'd split up not long after that. Nia would face little risk. The worst that could befall her was a scolding and being physically removed from the palace grounds. But him... Tahl shook his head. There was no room for failure.

He checked his daggers for the dozenth time, a quick tap to each hilt to make sure they were still in place. Without his heist outfit, he felt strangely naked, but the dark, inky blue fabric would have been so wildly out of place that he'd never make it through the door. Instead, he wore average street clothes, the simple brown trousers and unbleached cotton shirt he wore for most day-to-day business. The heist clothes were more comfortable, but the worn outfit he sported was broken in and didn't hinder his movement much. It was the best he could manage.

"Ready?" Nia's small voice piped from the alley behind him. She'd probably meant to startle him, creeping up from behind like she did. Too bad Tahl had heard her coming. He didn't reward her with so much as a twitch.

"I've been ready." He spared her a glance. Instead of the skirt she'd sported the day before, she wore comfortable riding breeches and knee-high doeskin boots, suitable for a young girl working menial stable jobs. Though it was sensible for what they intended to do, he fought an inward cringe. Orrad sported its own fashion sense and while close-fitting breeches weren't unusual attire for women in the capital city, they always struck him as strange compared to what women on the coast wore—the loose, billowing trousers that tied around the waist. "Don't those chafe?" he asked without thinking.

Niada raised a brow. "They're more practical than what you're wearing. They won't get caught on anything."

Fair as the assessment was, Tahl bit his tongue to hold back a retort. He was an expert thief. He didn't get *caught* on things. "Fine. Let's go." He allowed himself one more tap to each dagger hidden on his person, then turned toward the palace looming against the northern sky.

A steady stream of business flowed through the front gate, though it had dwindled as the day went on. There were fewer deliveries to be made in the late afternoon, which was both convenient and problematic. Deliverymen would be tired this late in the day, eager to recruit help and conclude their day's work early. The lack of bustle inside would make it harder to move around unnoticed, but Tahl clung to the idea of using nightfall to hide his escape. The later they got started, the better.

"There's one," Nia whispered. She glanced up, seeking his approval. When he nodded, she darted forward to put herself in the way of a small wagon. The driver reined his mule back with an irritable protest.

"Unload your goods for a half-mite," Niada offered in her most cheerful voice.

The driver sneered. "You couldn't lift a single sack of flour with those arms."

She shook her head. "Not just me. My brother, too." Her thumb jerked toward Tahl and he presented himself appropriately. Their coincidental shared dark hair and green eyes had often come in handy for schemes like this. His darker complexion was easily explained away with the claim he worked the farms outside the city.

The driver gave Tahl a quick look up-and-down and sneered. "Feh. Arms that size aren't worth a half-mite."

Nia cringed, but Tahl only raised a brow at the derision. The wagon lumbered past to disappear through the palace gates.

"Sorry," Niada murmured, presumably for the driver's insult.

Unbothered, Tahl shrugged. "He didn't have the money."

"What makes you think that?"

"He didn't even have a purse on him, for one thing." He flashed her a grin. "If you've got to pull a man's fortune from his pockets, he doesn't have enough to be worth robbing."

She didn't appear convinced, but she didn't argue.

Several more deliveries passed before an old farmer paused to consider their offer. His lone ox as worn as he was, and he rubbed the beast's shoulder as if to apologize for the weight of its burden. Even the tongue of his wagon was heaped with bags of grain, forcing the farmer to walk on foot.

"Well," the old man sighed at last, "I'd be grateful for the hand, full honest, but I haven't got a mite to spare."

"We'll work for food, too," Tahl put in before Nia could protest. "Has all your grain been paid for, or could we get a measure?"

The farmer trudged back to his wagon and slapped a sack. "Barley for the emperor's stables. I brought an extra, always do, in case one gets torn. Help me get all of it stored in the royal stables and I'll give you a half peck from what's left over."

Unlike Tahl, Niada had no shortage of food, but her eyes lit up. She could be a convincing actor at times. "Really?"

The old man nodded and twitched the reins against his ox's back. "Long as we're done by sundown, I'd say it's fair."

"No problems there, sir." Tahl nudged Nia's arm and they fell in step alongside the lurching wagon. "We're stronger than we look."

They paused at the gate for the guards to inspect the load. The armored men poked and prodded at the supplies while questioning the farmer. They gave Tahl and Niada a cursory glance, but didn't find them threatening. Good.

"Look close when we get inside," Tahl murmured. "We may never have a chance to make a delivery to the palace again." The hint of awe he injected into his voice earned a small chuckle from the guard who stood nearby. Nia nodded once, her eyes round. She got his meaning. Watch for vulnerabilities. Watch for information.

"All clear," one of the guards announced with a wave of his hand. The gate behind him was open, and armed men moved aside to clear the path. The guard offered Tahl a wry smile as he returned to his post. "Enjoy your peek, farm boy. If you're lucky, you might get to see the horses."

Tahl flashed him a grin as the farmer clucked to his ox. The wagon groaned as it set into motion again.

The shadow of the gate was cool enough that a shiver slid down Tahl's spine as they passed through. The walls were deeper than he'd thought. Not relevant, given he planned to escape over the top of them when all was said and done. Taking the gate out would have been idiotic. His gaze drifted to the top of the arched tunnel, where narrow slits stared back like accusing eyes.

They passed the second portcullis and the castle yard opened in front of them. The farmer turned his ox to the left. Smooth stone tiled the ground before the keep and to the far right, where men sparred and practiced archery outside what Tahl could only assume was the barracks. He took it all in with a carefully staged look of wonder on his face. Beside him, Nia's eyes were so big that he wasn't sure she was pretending.

"You get used to it after a while," the farmer said with a pleasant chuckle. "I've delivered grain for the emperor's horses for close on thirty years now."

"That's a long time. Atoras hasn't even been on the throne that long, has he?" Tahl ran a quick tally of guards in his head. The number was every bit as ugly as Nia had written down.

"Aye. It's been an honor to serve Emperor Atoras and his father both." The farmer grinned at him. "Fine horses, too. Always a pleasure to see. Sometimes they have them out in the yard. Those are the best days."

Tahl's thoughts were already elsewhere when he nodded. "I hope I get to see them." The layout of the yard was different than what he'd expected from the outside. The northwestern corner hosted what had to be the stables. The ornate stone structure was surrounded by a green paddock half the size of Orrad's garden district. White horses grazed behind the fence, but it was an opening in the curtain wall behind the grass that caught Tahl's eye. "The horses have their own gate?"

"Emperor Atoras has three dozen horses, lad. Where did you think they go to graze?" The farmer stifled a laugh. "They've a large, private pasture on the promontory just outside the city. The emperor's farriers and smiths sit alongside it. Safest place for the finest horses in the Westkings. Easy to defend, impossible to get them out without passing the guard towers on the west side."

"I never knew," Tahl said, thoughtful. "Do you think the farriers would take an apprentice?"

"He's good with horses," Nia added from behind him, reminding him of her presence at his back.

The farmer shrugged. "Couldn't say. Might be worth asking while you're here, though. Never a better chance."

Tahl flashed him a grin and nodded his agreement. "What about you?" he asked, turning his attention to Niada. "See anything interesting?"

She hesitated and Tahl raised a brow. Was it that she hadn't seen anything, or was she trying to think of an inconspicuous way to frame it? "Laundry maids," she said after a time.

Both Tahl's brows crept upward. Nia blushed so furiously, he thought for a moment the expression might be genuine.

"Well, it's something I can do," she blurted. "Work's easier to find for strapping boys."

The farmer listened to their exchange with a curious glint in his eye. "A bit young to be looking for work, aren't you, miss? You should still be on your mama's apron strings."

Niada's face fell and this time, Tahl knew the expression was real. "Blackhead plague," she murmured. "Four years ago, now. We were on Papa's farmstead then. I wasn't as sick as the rest. They sent me to the temple. The priestesses saw to me, but by the time I was well enough to take them back..." She trailed off, her head bowed.

Tahl reached back to grip her shoulder in a quiet show of solidarity. The truth was always easier to maintain than a fabricated story, but sharing the truth wasn't always easy. "I was in the academy then," he added for the farmer's benefit. All of Nia's family had perished. He hadn't so much as gotten sick.

The farmer didn't hide his surprise. "The academy? What are you doing looking for work with horses, then?"

Now it was Tahl's turn to sober. Before he could say anything, the farmer raised a hand.

"Those soul-blighted rich mages," the man grumbled as the wagon creaked to a stop outside the paddock gates. A man in stable livery came to let them in. "All that matters to them is wealth and class. I'm sorry, lad. I'm sure you saw the academy as your way forward."

"My family made a lot of sacrifices to get me there," Tahl said, a tinge of remorse in his voice. That was the hardest part of the truth to face. They'd pushed to send him, pushed to get him into the capital, then turned their backs the moment he'd failed. All he had ever been was another badge of honor, a bargaining chip in the political games noble houses played. The moment he'd been cast out of the academy, he'd become useless.

He changed the subject as the gate squeaked open and they rumbled toward the feed room at the end of the stables. "If you don't mind, I think I'll slip back and talk to the farriers when I'm done."

"And I could talk to the maids," Nia chimed in.

The farmer shrugged. "No business of mine what you do, so long as you do good work for me beforehand."

"Thank you, sir." Tahl's eyes flicked to Nia. She grinned back and nodded.

For the next fifteen minutes, Tahl pretended to be enamored with the horses and doing his best not to let them be a distraction. Niada climbed onto the wagon and pushed the sacks around for the men to take, and Tahl hefted two sacks at a time, earning a few appreciative remarks on his wiry strength. He resisted the urge to say he'd been stronger. Within a few weeks, he expected he'd be back to full strength again. Training in the woods had nothing on actually running the city's rooftops. Hauling himself up walls and over balconies for hours on end seemed like a tantalizing reward ahead of him.

As he had so often in recent days, Tahl had to stop the small inner voice that said his lack of training had been self-inflicted. Not ideal, he reminded himself, but part of the plan. Now he was inside the palace walls. The first hurdle had already been crossed.

While they hauled sacks of grain out of the wagon and into the stable, Tahl let his eyes roam. He'd thought the walls challenging from the outside. Now he saw they were challenging on the inside, too. The ugly things were mortared smooth and meticulously maintained, not a ledge or handhold in sight. The only buildings that sat close enough to the walls to reach them were low, like the stable, and a leap from the roof's edge still would have fallen short of the walkway.

No wonder Orrad never fell in the Claiming Wars, Tahl mused. Every institute had weaknesses, but from where he stood, he couldn't see any. But most fortifications were designed to keep people out, not in. Right now, figuring out how to overcome the problem of getting into the castle was more important than figuring out how to scale the walls.

Visiting the farrier gave him an excuse to part ways with the farmer, and a believable one for the man to give the guards when he left without his assistants. Though Tahl was loath to let Nia involve herself too deeply in the trouble yet to come, he was willing to entertain her participation for now. Anything that helped his chances of getting inside was a boon.

Niada wrestled one of the few remaining sacks off the wagon by herself, hoisted it onto her shoulders and trotted it to the stables.

"Tough little thing," the farmer remarked.

Tahl nodded. "She's had to be." He dragged the last pair of sacks to the feed room by himself. They'd collect their payment first, he decided, then they'd split up and he would pray the rear of the palace offered some easy way in.

When he returned to the wagon, the farmer was already halfway through filling a small sack with their grain. Tahl waited patiently, thanked the man for his generosity, and allowed himself a fleeting moment to regret he'd had to expend any energy in something so menial as moving horse feed.

"Best of luck landing an apprenticeship." The farmer clapped a hand to Tahl's shoulder. The corners of his eyes crinkled with kindness.

Someday, Tahl promised himself, *I'll find a way to repay people like this.* The people who had offered him kindness after he'd been expelled from the academy were few, but they were precious in his eyes. They'd helped change his fortunes, and with luck, someday he'd be able to aid theirs.

"Fair travels," Tahl replied as he passed the sack of barley to Nia. She started to wrinkle her nose, but caught herself and her expression morphed into the grimace of someone unprepared for the weight thrust into their arms.

The farmer clucked at his ox, and the beast lumbered toward the front gate.

"Let's split now," Tahl murmured. "I'll go around the back. You go back up front and see if you can find those laundry maids."

She hefted the barley in her arms. "What do I do with this?"

"Hang on to it for now. If nothing else, it'll make a good breakfast when all this is over." He waved her off and tucked his hands into his pockets as he turned toward the rear gate. "Stay safe."

"You, too," Nia said.

The back of the palace was no less defensible than the front, Tahl noted with a grim smile. The windows were few. There were none at ground level, and those in the middle were scarcely a hand wide. More like arrow loops than windows. The upper floors of the palace bore true windows, wide things with glass panes and curtains, and he suspected those were the suites where the nobles spent their time. But the walls were chiseled smooth, just like everything else. The joints between the large stones were so precisely mortared that he didn't think he could catch a ridge with so much as a fingernail.

A hook and rope could get me up to an arrow slit, perhaps, he mused, *but I didn't bring those, did I?*

Above him, the fortress glowed gold as the sun dipped into the late afternoon sky. The curtain wall cast long, cold shadows across the yard. More than once, his eyes darted to the gate that led to the promontory where the emperor's horses would be grazing. Instinct told him the horses were important to his mission, though he couldn't fathom how. The emperor's white horses were dangerously recognizable. Even if he managed to steal one for his escape, he wouldn't be able to evade attention with it.

There were still other peasants within the walls, so the guards ignored him as he explored. With a fixed look of purpose on his face, he was unlikely to be disturbed, but once the sun set and the gates closed to business, he'd no longer have any reason to be wandering about.

A door along the back wall opened and the noisy clatter of pans spilled out into the golden evening. A young man trudged out with a bucket, rubbing the back of his head. The sullen frown he wore and the way his feet dragged across the stone made it clear he'd rather be elsewhere. The bucket swung from his fingertips.

Tahl had noted the low, square stone wall that rimmed a well, but hadn't paid it much mind. He quickened his pace and swooped the bucket out of the youth's hand. "I'll get it."

The boy—not much younger than Tahl himself—gave him a startled glance. A lack of recognition shone in his guarded eyes, but a moment later, he apparently decided it didn't matter. "Thanks," he grumbled, still rubbing the back of his head as he slipped off to sulk.

Tahl leaned over the wall to scoop a bucket of water from the well. It was no more than an arm's length down, which surprised him, given the castle's altitude over the river. If the well was spring-fed, perhaps there were passages to explore under the castle proper. That thought lingered no more than an instant. If there were caverns under the palace, it was nowhere he wanted to be after the scrape with the bear. He ducked in the back door with a silent note of how the wood was girded with iron. Even the kitchens could be defensible.

Inside, the kitchens were crammed with people and Tahl had to lift the bucket overhead to keep it from sloshing over someone. Scullery maids scrubbed dishes buried under mountains of suds, a luxury he'd never seen elsewhere in the city. More sat near the hearth, scouring cast iron with handfuls of salt. Appealing fragrances graced his nose from every direction. A man worked dough with his fists while a woman beside him braided more into loaves. A half-dozen people manned spits and kettles above roaring fires, and in the middle of it all, a boy worked with a mop.

"Here," Tahl said as he deposited the pail of water on a wooden counter beside a particularly surly woman and darted past before she had time to reply. He ducked under a tray and twirled behind a maid on his way to the door. The corridor beyond sported heavy traffic, but they were all serving staff, strangers in clothing similar to his. He thought it a blessing until a man stepped into his path and seized him by the collar, his face red with fury.

"What are you doing out of uniform?" the man bellowed, giving him a shake.

Tahl stumbled a step and gaped. "I was just—I spilled something, the laundry—"

"Get back into it!" The man shoved him into a passing page, who yelped and skittered away.

Fighting the urge to defend himself, Tahl put his head down and hurried onward. Laundry was a good excuse, and would get him back with Nia, assuming she'd found her way inside too. He didn't know who the man had mistaken him for, but a uniform seemed like a sound idea. More than one young man scuttled past him in some sort of livery. Blending in could only make things easier.

A few hallways away, Tahl paused and caught a boy by the arm. "Brant's branches, it's a maze in here! Where's the laundry, again? It's only my third day and if I'm late again, the stablemaster will have my head."

The boy paled. "You're just getting into uniform *now?* Stablemaster Hammon will gut you like a fish, is what he'll do."

"I know," Tahl groaned. "The girl who took it, she gave me directions, but—"

Before he could finish, the boy caught his arm and turned him the appropriate direction. "Second hall, turn left. When you get to a staircase, take it down. The laundry pools are there. You'll hear the girls."

"Thank you." Tahl slapped the boy's shoulder in appreciation and lit off in a sprint befitting his supposed situation.

There were fewer people in the second hall and after Tahl had gone a short way, he noted his assessment of the palace's interior had been wrong. The boy seemed to agree with him, but the palace was built with corridors in utilitarian lines, a network of passages interconnected and arranged for efficiency. Despite the design's obvious intention to reduce foot traffic down certain paths, the workers had clearly developed preferences that kept them crowded. A desire for human contact, perhaps, or a need to be seen and acknowledged as they carried out their work. Tahl's lips twitched with amusement. He'd rather be invisible, even when he wasn't doing anything suspicious. Fewer eyes meant more freedom. He liked to feel his notoriety in other ways.

A staircase opened to one side. Tahl took the steps by twos. True to what the boy had said, the sound of laundry maids giggling reached his ears by the time he hit the hallway.

Before he could round the corner into the room from where the voices came, Niada emerged with a bundle of gray cloth in her arms. She froze when she saw him.

"What are you doing here?" she whispered.

"Looking for you. I wanted to make sure you got back out of the palace before I go any farther."

A wrinkle of worry formed between her brows. "Do you know what you're doing yet?"

"Sort of. I need a uniform if I'm going to keep sneaking around." He brushed a hand down the front of his shirt as if self-conscious.

Nia lifted the garments she held. "I just got you one. I was coming to find you."

"I like that we both went straight to the uniform idea," Tahl murmured as he took the clothing from her arms. His fingers rasped against the smooth material. Weeks of manual labor had given him new calluses and for the first time, he was made aware of their presence.

"This way." She jerked her head to the side and led the way farther down the hall. A short distance from the laundry pools, she opened the door to a storage closet and ushered him inside. "You can change in here."

He ducked in after her and reached for the buttons on his shirt. "Don't look."

"That's disgusting. Nobody wants to see you, anyway." The door clicked shut and Nia lingered beside it, staring at the crack where the wood met the stone doorframe.

Tahl stripped out of his everyday clothes as fast as he could. The uniform she'd brought him belonged to a guard. He didn't know whether that was brilliant or foolhardy. Either way, the outfit was a good fit, a testament to Niada's attention to detail. He adjusted his knives on his person before he put his boots back on. To him, they stood out like a red flag, dark brown instead of the black the guards wore in uniform. "Is there some boot black down here? I need it."

She cast a hesitant glance over her shoulder, as if checking to make sure he was decent before she turned to face him. "Boot black?"

He pointed at his toes.

"I haven't seen any." A note of apology colored her voice. "I think you're just going to have to wing it this time, Tahl."

Which he could do, and did often, though he preferred a solid plan. He scooped his discarded clothing from the floor and folded it. Something crinkled in his pocket and he paused. In the midst of everything else, he'd forgotten. A small envelope rested in the pocket of his trousers. He drew it free and clasped it tight.

Nia cocked her head. "What's that?"

"For you." He extended the envelope to her. The wrinkled

paper under his fingers almost didn't feel real. "Instructions for what comes next. But don't read it until the heist is over."

Her face fell. "I don't read that well, Tahl. You know I don't."

"You do well enough. I used small words. You'll be fine." He pushed the note into her hand. "Just take it. It's part of the plan and you'll need it."

"Okay." She sounded uncertain, but she took it anyway. Her fingertips traced the edge of the envelope's wax-sealed flap before she tucked it into her pocket and reached to take his clothes.

"You still have the barley?" he asked.

She nodded.

Tahl held on to the edge of his folded shirt. "Do what you need to here to get out without being noticed, then take this and the grain to my room at Ebitha's estate. Read the note tomorrow at noon to finish the plan. Understand?"

"I got it." Her eyes flicked over him before they settled on his face with a hint of sadness in their green depths.

The way she looked at him made him uneasy. "What?" Was his uniform that incorrect?

"It's just weird," she said, "seeing you look like the world you were born into. This could have been you, you know? Maybe this, instead of the mage academy. Your parents might have sent you to be a cadet."

It might have been a better choice. Tahl was better suited to scouting than magecraft, though he struggled to make his magic useful anyway. "The world I was born into doesn't matter, Nia," he said. "What matters is the world I'm in now. Are we good?"

"Almost." She held up a finger and inched close enough to reach for his face. He started to pull back, but she was insistent, her eyes trained on his cheek. Her fingernails found the edge of the wax that filled his scar and bit by bit, she peeled it off.

He blinked at her, confused.

"There." She balled the used wax in her hand and offered him a smile. "Now you're ready."

"Why'd you do that?" His hand went to his face, traced the groove that dipped under his right eye and skimmed the bridge of his nose.

Nia padded back to the door and shot him a grin. "Because when you get out of here, the face they see is what's going to be on all your wanted posters. Don't forget, Tahl. From now on, you're the Ghost."

CHAPTER 7

In another life, perhaps Tahl *would* have been a guard. He preferred the idea of an adventurous outpost on the untamed western coast, but he was comfortable enough in the crisp gray of a palace guard. He anticipated problems, but most of the palace staff put their heads down when he strode past, as if they expected abuse. Perhaps it wasn't far-fetched. Orrad's guard was as cruel as rumors held Atoras himself to be. Tahl was inclined to believe it. A hard man would want to work with hard men, to have them represent his power over the empire.

Somehow, the disposition of a leader had never crossed Tahl's mind. Bahar Eseri had been a cold and formal businessman. As result, his guild had been tightly structured and functioned like a business, itself. But what would the Ghost's guild be like? What was *he* like?

Maybe that's a question for Nia. In his head, he'd already taken to letting her handle the organization end of the guild. It seemed like the best solution, given her natural inclination to want involvement. Being the one who organized everything would let her have a finger in every pie.

But that was a worry for later. Right now, he had to find the emperor's quarters. His chances of swiping the crown directly from the emperor's head were nonexistent. His best hope was to pilfer it from wherever Atoras left it at night. Proud as the emperor must be, he couldn't hate himself enough to try to sleep with the crown on.

The windows were upstairs, so Tahl worked his way through the halls in search of a way up. A guard crossed an intersection in front of him and Tahl paused to study his appearance. Aside from the black boots, the only real difference was the weapon at the man's waist. Though the city guards carried short swords, this man in the palace had a long knife instead. Tahl considered that as he transferred his longest dagger to his belt and carried on.

A wide stairway cut upward to the next floor. Maintaining a sense of purpose was hard when he didn't know where he was going, but Tahl kept his chin up and his stride long. He'd almost reached the top of the staircase when a man in gray with an officer's stripes on his shoulders appeared in front of him.

The officer put out a hand. "Where are you going?"

Tahl stopped, but caught himself before his expression faltered. "I was told to report upstairs, sir."

"Upstairs? To who?"

"Just upstairs, sir. They didn't say."

The officer's eyes narrowed. "Who sent you?"

Tahl straightened a shade and brought his heels closer together. "I was at the stable gate, sir."

A low groan escaped the officer's throat. "Not the stablemaster again. Nobody cares about his bloody fences."

"I was just told to report, sir."

"Fine." The man rolled his eyes. "Go up."

Tahl shifted on the stairs, uncertain.

The officer's lip peeled back in a snarl. "What?"

"They didn't tell me who to report to, sir. I assumed you would know where I'm expected."

Though Tahl expected the officer to yell at him, the man

instead drew a breath as if to shout, then paused. His eyes narrowed. "Who are you?"

The question set Tahl's heart to racing. He straightened a little more and racked his memory for a believable story. His uniform bore no insignia. He decided not to push his luck. "Private Chal, sir." The name was the first that sprang to mind. Somehow, he doubted his childhood friend from the southern coast would mind.

"Private?" the officer asked. One of his brows lifted a hair.

Tahl wished he could remember what the different insignia meant. The stripes on the man's shoulders meant nothing to him. "Just recently graduated, sir." He allowed himself a nervous lick of his lips. It wasn't unrealistic for a newcomer to be intimidated. "This is my first post, sir."

"I don't remember a Chal on the list of new guards."

Tahl didn't dare smile. "I'll do my best to be more memorable in the future, sir."

The man's gaze fixed on Tahl's scar, as if he committed it to memory. Let him, Tahl thought. By the time they realized who he was, he'd be long gone. Nia had been smart to remove the wax. By morning, the Ghost's face would be on countless flyers. Assuming he made it out alive, that was.

"Upstairs," the officer said finally, easing back on his heels. "Third floor. Corporal Denen should be going over records in the library."

Tahl bowed his head in appreciative respect. "Thank you, sir." He stepped aside to let the man pass. Once the officer was halfway down the stairs, Tahl turned to sprint onward. He had no intention of seeing Corporal Denen, much less reporting to the man, but the existence of a library that far into the palace was interesting. Depending on how labyrinthine the shelves were, it might make a good place to hide—and an easy excuse, should he be caught. It seemed plausible that a mere private might be assigned to research that could go on well into the night.

He expected resistance as he progressed through the palace,

but found none, which was fortunate. He didn't know where the library was and cracked numerous doors in his search. The serving staff paid him little mind; one benefit of his stolen uniform.

Tahl considered trying to push farther into the palace and find the emperor's rooms. The library was a good fallback if he couldn't find them. It seemed like a reasonable plan, anyway. Satisfied with his decision, he trekked up the last flight of stairs.

By now, he had a reasonable map of the palace in his head. He'd avoided areas like the throne room or formal dining halls, but those were large spaces that were impossible to miss. A good portion of the middle floors were devoted to business and functionality, while most of what he'd seen in the recesses of the first floor—and the basement—were devoted to supply storage and simple rooms for the serving staff. As he moved through the third floor, the offices were replaced with fine lodgings, likely meant for nobles, officers, or visiting dignitaries. That left the top floor of the castle for the royal family.

At the top of the stairs, the fine furnishings began. The vivid red Emperor Atoras favored colored everything in sight—the plush rugs underfoot, tall tapestries on the walls, even a vase of fresh flowers set against a wall. Hallways split from the top of the stairs and Tahl considered his options. Judging by what he knew of the structure, he was farther to the west side. To his right had to be the castle's only balcony, and its entrance was likely somewhere near the emperor's quarters.

Tahl turned right and kept his pace quick and confident. He hadn't gone far before he reached the balcony's doors, and they were so unlike anything he'd ever seen that he stopped to stare.

The tall pair of doors were made of etched glass, so clear it had to have been crafted by mages. The images that frosted its surface were detailed beyond belief, portrayals of flowers and vines so delicate they seemed at war with the stern palace that surrounded them. Beyond the glass, a garden sprawled across the balcony.

The exotic flowers and shrubs called out to be inspected and Tahl's natural curiosity tingled. But he wasn't there to see gardens. He forced himself to move on.

Farther down the hall, a single guard stood beside a broad, ornately carved wooden door. The only door worth a guard, he noted. No mystery who that belonged to. At least they'd made the finding part easy.

Now to get past that guard, Tahl mused. He'd anticipated that difficulty from the beginning, yet now that it faced him, part of him balked. Worst was knowing that even if getting into the emperor's quarters was a challenge, the real challenge began when he tried to *leave.* He was no fool and didn't believe he'd be able to grab the crown and vanish without being noticed. Getting his hands on his mark was always the easiest part of the job. Getting away with it was different.

You're not a thief until you have it in hand. He slid back a step and retreated to the garden doors to gaze outside. A moment to plan how he would proceed couldn't hurt. He clasped his hands behind his back and studied the shape of the balcony and the garden he'd never known was there.

"What are you doing?" called the guard by the door.

So much for a moment to think. Tahl leaned back to look the guard's way. "Just looking," he called back. "I'm on break."

"You're on break and you wanted to look at flowers?" The man sounded skeptical.

Tahl shrugged and reached for the door. Even the handles were glass, beautiful twisted things that resembled leaves. He pulled, and the doors rattled. Locked. He didn't know how and couldn't see a mechanism, but it clanked again when he gave it another tug. "Don't you ever get curious? I've never been out there. The view of the city must be amazing."

The guard considered that, his head tilted to one side.

"Imagine being wealthy enough to have a garden like that to begin with." Tahl let his hand drop. He crept up the hall to join the man. "But I guess you're used to seeing it. It probably loses its wonder after a while. This is my first station, so everything is..."

"Overwhelming," the guard supplied, a knowing look in his eyes.

"Exactly." Tahl's thumbs itched to hook in his pockets, but that seemed too casual for a guard in a crisp uniform, so he kept his hands relaxed by his sides. "So I've been using my breaks to explore a bit. I feel like they don't mind as much if I'm in uniform. Someone might object to me poking around the castle when I'm off duty."

The guard grunted. "Probably so."

Tahl rocked on his heels and let his gaze wander. The guard didn't seem to mind his innocent chatter. In fact, he seemed grateful. How long had he been on duty, watching an empty room? The hallway was dead silent, and had been since Tahl arrived.

"So these are the royal quarters, right? Have you seen inside? Are they big?" The inanity of the question was so rich that even Tahl almost winced.

The corner of the guard's eye tightened a shade, but he sighed and shrugged. "Like you'd expect. Man rules the whole southern portion of the Westkings, practically a continent on its own. His quarters reflect it."

Tahl nodded along, as if his suspicions were being confirmed. "My family's estate was by no means small, but I bet the whole house could fit in the top floor of Orrad's castle, if you could slice it up like that. I don't know... seems like it would get lonely."

"Lonely?" the guard repeated.

"Well, it's just his, right? The rest of the royal family has their own space?" Tahl waved a hand toward the other doors—conspicuously unguarded doors—that lined the hall. "I can't imagine having that much space and no one to share it with."

"I suppose that's true," the guard agreed in a slow drawl. "They don't pay us well enough for a space much bigger than the emperor's private water closet, but even my little space would be lonesome without my wife." A hint of a smile cracked through his bored expression.

Tahl grinned, less at the expression and more at the piece of valuable information wiggled free. Atoras was alone in his quarters at night. No one else to look out for. "You smirk like a newlywed."

"Six months." The man's smile turned sheepish. "Hoping for a little one soon. Ah, but you're too young to care about that yet."

"Too early for me to settle down," Tahl agreed, "but I'm happy for you. Congratulations." He paused to glance toward the glass doors, to see the way the light had shifted on the floor. "I think my break's up. Nice talking."

"Yeah," the guard agreed with another sigh. "Nice change of pace. It's a long shift up here, quiet as it is."

"Is it? I'll swing back some time. Maybe you can give me some recommendations for parts of the castle I should explore." Tahl took several steps backwards before he turned back the way he'd come. "Enjoy your evening."

The guard didn't reply, but Tahl had meant it sincerely. The man had seemed amicable enough. With fortune, perhaps he wouldn't be the guard on duty when night fell.

CHAPTER 8

upper floor of the palace were unguarded. Tahl dipped back to
the staircase to wait for a moment. It wouldn't take long for his
new friend to turn his attention elsewhere. After sufficient time
had passed, Tahl slipped back into the hallway and crept to a
nearby door. It wasn't locked, and he crept inside without notice.

The room beyond appeared to be guest quarters, clean but
bland in decorating. Judging by where he stood, he suspected he
was two suites down from the emperor's rooms. It was a good
hiding place, assuming Atoras had no visitors today, and Tahl
stalked to the window to get his bearings. The horse gate in the
north wall was visible from where he stood. It might have been
promising for an escape if he hadn't been on the fourth floor.
And still not in the emperor's quarters.

His fingers explored the window frame while a frown tugged
at his face. If the windows didn't open, any hope of using them
was pointless. At the side, he found an odd protrusion. When he
flicked it, a soft click sounded and the window parted down the
center to swing open. He'd seen the seam between the two panes
of mage-made glass, but had assumed it was simply a design

choice instead of a parting line. Perhaps the balcony doors opened the same way.

"Useful," he muttered to himself as he leaned forward. He didn't dare let himself be seen hanging out the window, but he pressed his shoulder to the wall beside it and waited until the yard below was clear. Then he allowed himself a moment to check the wall on the other side.

The windows to the emperor's quarters would be to the right. He saw a window perhaps ten feet away, but the wall surrounding it was perfectly smooth. No way to reach it and no way to make handholds. Even if he'd had a pick of some sort—a tool he'd used to scale difficult buildings in the past—he wouldn't have been able to find mortared seams wide enough to jab the thing into.

"In and out the front door it is, then." Tahl closed the window and marveled at the way the latch snapped shut on its own. If he weren't there to rob the place, he'd be tempted to stay and study it. With a new guild headquarters to outfit, it seemed wise to keep an eye open for unique additions.

Tahl crept back to the door and leaned close to listen. Unsurprisingly, the hall beyond was silent. No footfalls. No conversation. Now and then, he caught the soft scuff of boots against the carpet as the lone guard shifted.

A distraction would be enough. Tahl wasn't averse to fighting, but this wasn't like slipping past the city guard. Getting caught entering the emperor's chambers would mean certain death. Another execution, no different from any number of false Ghosts who had already hung.

He ran through his memory of the hall. There was another door not far beyond the emperor's, one he could picture clearly. A door was a better distraction than the hall itself.

Tahl closed his eyes and gathered his energy. He hadn't yet relied on his magic. He'd hoped he wouldn't need to. It had saved his hide a dozen times during his last heist, but that had been out in the city. Atoras had his own personal court mages and although Tahl's power was weak enough that most mages paid him no mind, the last thing he wanted to do was draw the attention of a mage who might sense his presence.

The thoughts made his concentration falter. He brushed them away, cleared his mind, and tried again. For anyone else, this would have been so simple. All he had to do was picture the door, an anchor for the magic he wanted to work. Tahl pushed his toes against the door he hid behind, imagining the crack at the bottom. He focused there, pooling his power.

Though he couldn't see it, he felt the magic take shape. Smoke grew from nothing. Small wisps at first, nothing noticeable. Then the plumes thickened into dense, billowing clouds and poured from under the door.

Down the hall, the guard let out a sound—or maybe a word —of surprise.

Tahl fed the magic as much strength as he could manage in a moment's time, then tied off the flow of energy. He only had a few seconds. His boots touched the carpet in the hall just as the guard disappeared into the thick, enveloping smoke.

Even in boots, he could be silent. Tahl darted up the hall, mindful of each step. Three seconds. Four. He reached the door and prayed it would open.

It was unlocked. Tahl held his breath as he ducked inside and closed himself in. His first glance into the emperor's rooms made him pause for a half beat. Even for an emperor, the opulence was enough to be shocking. Fighting his urge to gape, Tahl darted across the suite. There was no time to spare, and he had to make a decision.

The suite only offered a handful of places to hide. A tall wardrobe stood against the near wall. A number of chests sat near the windows, and the bed did not sit up off the ground. All of them were too obvious of choices.

His eyes darted to the corner, where a massive brown bear reared on its hind legs and stood angled toward the door, as if to challenge any intruders.

Challenge accepted. Tahl jerked his dagger from his belt and bolted across the room to slide behind it. The blade sank deep into the back of the taxidermy beast. He hoped his instinct was right. It was too big to fill with sawdust alone; the weight would have made it impossible to move. His dagger resisted, the fur and hide thicker than he'd expected. A moment later, the blade thunked against a beam of wood and Tahl grinned. He pulled the dagger back until it cut just along the surface, then plunged deeper.

Outside, more voices clamored in the hall. Booted footsteps passed the door on their way to investigate the smoke, which had already begun to dissipate. The cut in the bear's back was no more than two feet, but it had to be enough. Tahl jammed his dagger back into its sheath and wiggled through the gap.

Large as the bear was on the outside, the inside was cramped. A wooden frame held the bear in position and sawdust stuffed its limbs, leaving only a small hollow cavity for him to curl inside. Tahl squeezed in and tried to make himself comfortable, then adjusted the hole in the bear skin to hide his entry.

The voices returned to the emperor's door. The rattle of armor filled the room as guards strode inside to investigate.

"Check the closet," someone ordered. Booted feet moved everywhere and Tahl closed his eyes. With the sound of their feet filling the room, he couldn't help but envision a half-dozen scurrying lizards creeping across the floor and up the walls.

Dust tickled his nose and he rubbed it firmly to discourage a sneeze.

Outside his bear, furniture creaked and chest lids clacked, reaffirming his choice to hide elsewhere. Still as he sat, the bear did not so much as shift.

"Nothing," another guard said. A window rattled, and sounds of consternation came from more than one throat.

"No evidence of a smoke bomb, either. What else could it be?"

"Don't know." Four different voices so far.

"Check the other room for a magnifier." Five voices.

"What?"

"If the sun hits it just right, the light can burn things."

"That's a myth."

"It's not, either. My cousin and I used to steal my father's loupe from his workshop and use it to burn ants."

"You always were a beast, weren't you?"

A few friendly laughs answered, and the footsteps that moved back toward the door sounded more relaxed. By now, the whole upper floor had been scoured.

The door clacked shut and Tahl buried his face in the sleeve of his stolen uniform, willing himself not to sneeze.

The sun had only just begun to set.

He was in for a long wait.

THE CREAK of the door startled Tahl awake. He didn't know how long he'd been asleep—he hadn't intended to fall asleep to begin with.

Voices trailed into the emperor's quarters, carrying a dull conversation about political matters that were so trivial, Tahl didn't know why they had the emperor's attention to begin with. Atoras was a hard man, the fourth in a line of warrior rulers who had subdued the Westkings under their thumbs. A dispute over fishing ships—from what Tahl could make out—seemed far beneath his notice.

Tahl moved ever so slightly. His whole body ached in protest, cramped inside the upright bear for a number of hours. Stiff, sore muscles could only hinder him. He had little room to stretch, but he tried anyway, shifting from one side to another, twisting in slow motion, careful not to rock or rattle his hiding place.

The conversation concluded but people remained. The rustle of fabric and patter of slippered feet filled the air. Maids, perhaps, turning down the blankets and helping Atoras prepare for bed. A soft giggle confirmed the suspicion.

Stabbing pain shot through Tahl's calf when he tried to flex his ankle. He bit his tongue hard and fought to remain silent as he pointed his heel and pulled his toes toward his shin, forcing the charley horse in his leg to release. Had he been caught skulking around the palace in a stolen uniform earlier, he might have escaped with a mere reprimand. Were he caught now, he had no doubt it would end with his death.

The cramp subsided and he let out a long, slow breath through his nose.

The room grew quiet. A faint light glowed beyond the slice in the bear hide, but after a time, that too faded. Judging by the dark that fell, it was safe to slide out, but Tahl waited anyway. Each moment brought more discomfort, more suffering, but he remained still. Eventually, a soft snore radiated from the space behind Tahl's back.

At last, he allowed himself to emerge. One foot after the other slid out through the slit in the bear's back. His booted toes found the wooden base beneath the beast and he twisted to slide out backwards. Dust stirred in his wake, clogging his throat and tickling his nose. He held his breath and waited for the sensations to pass, though fighting the urge to cough put tears in his eyes.

With the curtains drawn, Tahl could barely see, but a shadow lay in the canopied bed. The crown had to be nearby. He searched the room in the dark. Atoras's crown was a gaudy thing; he'd seen it in paintings. Crusted with jewels as it was, it shouldn't be hard to find it. Yet nothing glinted in the dark.

Tahl kept his breath steady as he stepped out from behind the bear, his boots muted by the plush carpet underfoot. He stalked closer to the bed, loomed over the end of it like a shadow. Like a ghost, he thought with a small hint of amusement.

Before him, Emperor Atoras slept.

The man's face was stony, even in sleep. Anger creased his

brow and bitterness twisted his mouth. The emperor ruled with a cold heart and an iron fist. Yet he lay helpless, prone, and Tahl couldn't help but marvel.

Getting to the emperor had been easy. Easier than anything Tahl could recall doing during a theft. Were he an assassin and not a thief, he could draw his dagger, slit the man's throat or plunge the blade into his heart before he had a chance to wake. Tahl could seize the kingdom, the crown, just as Niada thought he intended.

Beside the emperor's head, a gleam stole Tahl's attention.

The crown, cradled on the second pillow.

Lucky for you, I'm just a thief.

Silent as snowfall, Tahl leaned across the bed and wrapped his fingers around the crown. A tingle of something brushed his senses. Magic, he thought, though subtle, and he couldn't tell what it was supposed to do. Curious, considering he felt nothing from the emperor himself. The crown's enchantment would have to be unraveled another day.

Tahl sank back and gave the emperor one last long look. The man did not stir, though the craggy anger in his face had grown a little more defined. Tahl couldn't help but imagine the pure rage that would twist Atoras's features when he woke.

With luck, I won't be here. Tahl turned toward the door and considered it briefly. Outside, shadows of boots stirred, blocking part of the sliver of light that seeped in under the door's edge. In and out had seemed easier when the way was unguarded. He could summon more smoke in the hall, but the guards would be more likely to rush in to aid Atoras than to go investigate. That left one other avenue for escape.

The curtains whispered against his uniform as Tahl ducked behind them to unlock the window beside the stuffed bear. His fingers found the latch at the edge of the window, the same as the one in the guest room, and he winced as it snapped open.

Behind him, the emperor still snored.

The latch was all that made noise. The panes of glass parted and glided open, as soundless as an owl's wings. Tahl hitched up one leg and rested a boot on the window sill as he leaned forward and looked to the left. The guest room window was too far away, and there were no windows on that side of the emperor's suite. He craned his neck to look right instead. Closer by, another window ledge waited. Below, the courtyard seemed farther away than ever. He doubted he'd survive the fall. *Just means I gotta get this right.*

He slid the crown up his arm to secure it and keep it out of the way.

It had been a while, but he'd made harder jumps. Farther, higher, but perhaps not to such a small ledge.

Doesn't matter, he reassured himself. *You've got this.*

His other foot lifted to the sill and he shifted to press the sole of his boot against the window jamb. His heartbeat accelerated and he fought to keep his breath even. The muscles in his legs and shoulders tensed like the coils of a compressed spring. A strange tightness took his throat, and Tahl closed his eyes for an instant. *Brant have mercy on me if I fail.*

He jumped.

His shoulder skirted the wall and his boot clipped the ledge. Panic surged in his chest as he slipped off. His fingers caught the ledge and his body slammed against the wall. Breath escaped for a single stunned, painful moment. Then Tahl wheezed and willed his fingertips to dig into the stone. Slowly, he dragged himself upward. There was nothing to hold on to but the ledge. His boots scraped against the smooth stone. The worn soles stabilized him, but did little to help him climb.

Tahl's shoulders passed the ledge and he slammed an arm onto the window's outer sill. Already, a fine sheen of sweat broke out on his brow. A shimmy of his other arm put a knife in his hand. He jammed it between the window and the wall, scraping up and down in search of the latch he knew was there. His arm trembled beneath his weight.

The latch popped and the window swung outward against his arm.

A soft gasp was all that escaped as the window shoved him free.

Tahl swung hard to the left and cracked against the wall again, his knife wedged in the window frame all that kept him from plunging to his death. The crown clattered against the stone, the glinting jewels beside his head mocking him.

He braced his boots against the wall and thrust upward hard, swinging his other arm over the ledge. His fingers found a lip on the other side, beneath the window, and he clung to it with all his might. The knife remained stuck and Tahl silently blessed the master smith who must have forged it.

Releasing the knife, he snapped his other arm in through the window and scrambled upward. His boots squeaked against the stone of the palace's outer wall. One more kick sent him up and over and he tumbled into the room in a graceful somersault, bursting beyond the curtains to land in a crouch with his head tucked and one hand pressed to the floor.

His pulse roared in his ears and his heart tried to beat a hole in his chest. Tahl allowed himself a triumphant grin.

He lifted his head and he swore his heart skipped a beat.

A woman in white nightclothes stood between him and the door.

Tahl froze.

Her gaze darted from his face to the crown he still carried on his arm and her dark eyes widened more than he thought possible.

Panic returned and his stomach lurched. Tahl had seen her face a thousand times. It adorned every poster in the lobby of the museum and decorated the surface of every copper mite he'd ever earned—or stolen. She was strikingly beautiful, but he hadn't expected her to be young.

He rose to his feet.

The queen's expression grew steely. She lifted her chin and

stared him straight in the eye as a cold defiance spread over her face.

Before he could speak or even draw breath, she stepped aside.

Tahl's eyes darted between her and the door and his brows drew together in confusion.

Her head tilted as if to question what he was waiting for. Her attention lingered on the crown, but she said nothing.

In silence, he stalked forward to open the door. With his hand against the latch, Tahl drew a breath, looked at the crown on his arm, and realized he'd set himself up for failure.

Niada should have left the barley. He could have used the bag.

"Time to be famous," Tahl muttered. He shoved out into the hallway and veered left.

He didn't know what waited that direction, but the emperor's quarters were to the right. The rough floor plan of the castle he'd assembled in his head told him nothing, but he didn't dare try to shoulder his way past the guards with the crown around his arm.

The crown shifted as he thought of it and he crooked his elbow to keep it in place.

"Hey," a voice barked behind him.

Tahl tucked his chin and kept walking. Belatedly, he considered that emerging from the queen's quarters in the dead of night was quite possibly worse than bursting out of the emperor's quarters and catching the men in the hall off guard.

"Hey!" the man repeated, louder. Booted steps hurried after him and Tahl picked up his pace.

Behind him, the guard broke into a run, and Tahl stifled a curse.

There had to be another way down, if only a narrow servant's stairway. The hall stretched on for what seemed forever before it took an abrupt turn. He darted around the corner and froze.

Instead of another wide hallway, he found a small alcove with a narrow door.

Armor rattled in the hallway, betraying the guard's position. Tahl jerked the door open, praying for an escape route.

It was a latrine.

"Lifetree's mercy!" he spat. So much for avoiding the guards.

Tahl spun back just as the man rounded the corner into the alcove. The guard's face was red, though from anger or exertion, Tahl didn't know, nor did he care. He braced the crown against his ribs and charged the guard.

Startled, the man reached for his sword too late. Tahl bounded past him and bolted down the hall.

"Sound the alarm!" the guard roared to his partner, still beside the emperor's door. The second guard echoed the command and elsewhere in the palace, more voices raised the call.

That was one way to gain notoriety. The second guard positioned himself in the middle of the hall, sword drawn, stance wide. Tahl checked his breathing and picked up speed.

A handful of strides before he met the second guard, he veered hard left and leaped against the wall. His momentum kept him going and he scaled the wall in three steps to flip over the guard. The carpet cushioned his roll when he landed on the other side and he dared a glance over his shoulder as he popped to his feet. The guard watched, his jaw slack.

No time to gloat, Tahl reminded himself on the way to the stairs. The sound of voices grew louder in the halls below. The clatter of weapons and armor rose to meet him. His mind raced ahead. There were more stairways from the third floor down to the second. He'd seen them, if not followed them. All he had to do was make it out of the main halls. Habit would work against the guards from there.

He was halfway down the stairs when a group of men with red tabards over their polished armor appeared below. The Emperor's Elite. Tahl lurched to a stop and swung his free arm to regain his balance. His toes teetered on the edge of a step, one short tip away from disaster. Pinning the crown harder to his side, he spun on his toes and went back the way he came.

"He's got the crown!" one of the Elite roared.

Tahl coughed a laugh. They'd only just noticed? Had they only been chasing him because he'd come from the queen's quarters? He leaped over the last stair and came face to face with the two guards he'd evaded before. Both were red and flustered. Behind them, the queen stood outside her quarters, looking like a spirit in her flowing white nightgown.

There was no worse place to be cornered than the top floor of a castle with only one exit. Tahl's eyes flicked past the guards, to the glass doors. Only one *intended* exit. He feinted to the side and then darted between the two men. One guard's hand brushed his collar, but his fingers closed a moment too late, and Tahl was past them again.

The emperor's door opened and Atoras himself appeared, his eyes ablaze with fury. Tempted as Tahl was to throw him a grin, he ran for the doors instead. He still didn't know where the latch was, nor did he have time to find it.

Time for a trick. Tahl shut the guards and the oncoming Elite out of his thoughts and trained his attention on the doors. A wisp of smoke stirred before the glass, like the first spurt as a fuse caught. Then thick, churning clouds spewed forth from nothing to flood the hall.

A sharp, crackling sense of power filled the air and Tahl's hair stood on end.

A mage. They had a mage.

He dove into his cloud of smoke and almost slammed into the glass doors. The balcony beyond was clear of sentries and a long center path led to the railing at the far end.

The flows of energy twisted around him without disturbing his smoke. Tahl braced himself to be snared, knowing he couldn't fight it off.

Instead, the prickling sensation of magic rolled through him and past him, and the latch on the balcony doors snapped open. The doors swung outward and Tahl stumbled a half step before he caught himself. He threw a look over his shoulder as his smoke poured out through the doorway and left the hallway clear. The guards were not far behind. He slammed the doors shut and hoped the latch would slow them down.

Sweet, soothing scents filled the balcony's garden. Tahl breathed deep as he ran. He relied on aromatic oils to relax his muscles now and then. After hours stuffed inside a bear, he doubted a single whiff would help, but he could hope.

The balcony itself slanted ever so slightly downward, but leveled out at the far end. The castle's entrance was just below the rail, the platform higher than the courtyard surrounding it. A two story drop instead of four. He could make that.

Somewhere in the courtyard, a shrill whistle blew. *Word spreads fast.* Tahl ran through the leap and landing in his head, even as his feet carried him toward the rail. The crown jangled against his elbow, hard and uncomfortable. He slid it farther up his arm. Why had he come without a bag? Even something to tie the blasted crown in place would have helped.

The courtyard opened before the end of the balcony, wide and filled by guards with torches.

Tahl vaulted over the railing and the drop launched his heart into his throat. He'd misjudged. It was more than two stories.

The elevated platform before the castle's doors rushed up to meet him. He twisted to land in a roll, but the stone was still unforgiving and chased the air from his lungs. The edge of the platform threatened to spill him down the stairs. He caught the edge in his roll and thrust forward to vault over the stairs and roll again when he hit the ground. Stone scraped the skin off his knees, shoulders, and shins, even through the sturdy wool of his stolen uniform. Around him, guards gaped.

He only had a moment to take advantage of their shock. Tahl sprang to his feet and let the momentum of his rolls launch him into a sprint. Guards in gray and red swarmed the front gate, reminding him he was on the wrong side of the palace. Even if he could get past them, Tahl wasn't positive he could lose them in the city, where their hounds already bayed and pulled against their chains.

Tahl veered toward the side where the stables waited, away from the barracks where dozens more guards dragged themselves from their beds and hastened to join the pursuit.

Whistles and bellowing alarm horns filled the air. Tahl skidded around the corner and almost collided with one of the Elite. Yelping in surprise, Tahl jerked backwards and narrowly missed a sword that would have had his head. He ducked wide and bolted before the Elite could take another swing.

The yard ahead filled with guards determined to stop him. Tahl dared not draw his knives. He could fight, but not so many, and trying to fight would only slow him down. This wasn't like escaping the Queen's Museum. If he did anything other than run, he was dead.

Might be dead anyway. He grimaced as he dodged another blade. Beside him, something pinged against the cobblestone and bounced away with a clatter.

Crossbow bolts.

Lovely.

Already, a familiar heat laced his muscles in a warning that he couldn't push much farther. Adrenaline coursed his veins and overruled his body's concerns. There was no stopping. Stopping was death. Tahl tore past a cluster of men, hoping their bodies would shield him from the crossbow archers on the walls. He was fast, and the guards were many. Using their own numbers against them was his best chance for survival.

The crossbows fire ceased, but resumed the moment Tahl slipped beyond unsheathed swords and grasping hands. A bolt tore through the loose fabric at the back of his calf and a hot sting followed in its wake. Nothing more than a graze, but too close for comfort. Then a bolt pinged off the crown on his arm and his guts clenched.

These were nothing like the guards at the Queen's Museum. How had he ever thought their skill level might be similar? Tahl trained his eyes on the stables ahead—and the white horses that wheeled and milled in their small paddock—and struggled to focus his thoughts.

Hints of warmth answered his call and Tahl drew them to the surface. Skittering streams of smoke crawled from the cracks between stones. He willed them to grow, to shield his movements and protect him from the bolts that streaked from overhead. The plumes thickened and around him, the guards began to cough.

The paddock fence emerged from the smoke before him, sooner than he'd expected it. Tahl leaped and cleared the top rail, but crashed to the turf on the other side. He skidded in the dirt and gritted his teeth. A shade too late, he tucked into a somersault and found his feet, though he stumbled twice when he tried to run.

Hands seized him from behind and Tahl sucked in a gasp.

"Got him!" a guard roared.

Tahl craned his neck until he saw a hand. Then he tucked in his chin and twisted inward to grab a finger between his teeth and bite down hard.

A startled curse escaped the guard and his grip loosened just enough. Tahl dropped to his knees and swung a leg behind him in a low, sweeping kick.

Caught off guard, the man went down with a cry. Unwilling to stay and fight, Tahl redoubled his efforts and ran.

Smoke thickened the air and Tahl urged it to keep swelling. He couldn't split his focus between running and generating smoke for long, and whatever screen formed would have to be enough.

Something white flashed in the haze before him. The horses. They had to be close.

A powerful gust of air tore past him, scattering his smoke. Alarmed, Tahl spun. There was no way he could face a mage.

Instead, a handful of men walked with giant, fringed fans spread as wide as their arms, the sort one expected to see waved over a pompous noble on a stifling summer day. It took two men to move each fan, but each heave dissipated more of Tahl's smoke than he would have thought possible.

"There!" someone shouted. Spotted again.

A crossbow bolt thunked into the soft earth beside Tahl's boot. A soft cry of alarm went up from guards somewhere behind him.

Nearby, a horse wheeled against the fence, its eyes rolling white with fear. The horses. Of course no one would dare shoot at the emperor's horses.

Tahl spread his hands and made soft, soothing sounds as he approached the horse, too slow for his liking and yet too fast for the animal to be comfortable. Still, it paused to swivel one ear in his direction and let him approach. He seized a handful of its mane and vaulted onto its back. He'd ridden a thousand times in his youth, but hadn't been astride a horse in years. Tahl gripped with his knees and curled both hands tight in the horse's mane, kicked hard and let out a whoop of encouragement.

The horse burst forth like a spring and surged over the fence. Its horseshoes hit the cobbles with a clack and Tahl rocked forward against the horse's neck so forcefully, he feared he'd bust his nose on the animal's crest. He regained his seat a scant few seconds later, leaning close and holding tight as the white horse streaked across the yard.

"Grip with your knees, steer with your legs, heels down, heels down!" Tahl chanted through clenched teeth. The horse darted between clusters of guards without breaking stride. Tahl pressed with his legs, urging the horse toward the curtain wall. It didn't need much encouragement.

The last of the magical smoke he'd created cleared and Tahl saw the horse gate for the first time. The portcullis was closed.

"Oh, for the love of leaves," Tahl groaned, loosing his legs against the horse's sides and tugging back on its mane as he pulled up his knees. "Whoa!"

The horse slowed and Tahl pulled himself into a crouch on the animal's back. "Sorry, this is going to be uncomfortable," he muttered to the beast as they neared the gate. From the ground, he never would have made it. But from a horse...

"Now! Shoot!" someone roared.

Tahl leaped from the horse's back. His hands caught the edge of the walkway overhead and the rest of his body crashed against the wall and the gate.

A cacophony of protests rose from the gatehouse as Tahl caught the very top bar of the grille with his toes and thrust himself upward. He hauled himself onto the walkway just as a pair of men appeared with spears.

Tahl bent and twisted like a dancer to evade the jabs of the wicked, jagged-edged spearheads, each step carrying him closer to the far side of the wall.

Both men plunged with their spears at the same time. Tahl leaped backwards to escape and his heel hit the edge of the the walkway. Grinning, he flicked a salute to the guards and let himself fall.

Cries of surprise and alarm went up from the guards as Tahl fell to the soft earth below. He rocked backwards, morphing his landing into a backwards roll that brought him back to his feet. A hint of dizziness took his head and he fought it with a deeper breath. Fatigue couldn't get the better of him now. He wasn't free yet.

His hand went to his arm. The crown was still there, somehow. For a moment, he'd forgotten to keep track of it. Had he dropped it, he surely would have noticed, but the fact that it had slipped outside of his awareness for even an instant was nerve-wracking.

Crossbowmen appeared atop the wall, but they hesitated to fire. The far side of the wall was dark, and Tahl had already moved beyond the light that spilled through the gate and into the field. He ran—or tried to run. His injured leg protested after a handful of strides, but he couldn't favor it now. He wanted to curse. It hadn't seemed a bad wound. It felt like a scrape. But now he felt the cold, sticky slap of blood-wet fabric against the back of his calf, and the pain grew more intense as he ran.

Beyond the castle yard, the moonlight seemed dim, and it took a moment for Tahl's vision to clear. White blotches moved through the field, most of them together. More horses. He cut toward them, unable to keep a limp from growing in his stride.

The portcullises of the horse gate groaned and screeched as the gate opened. Already, the sound of horseshoes on cobbles echoed in the night. On horseback, they'd run him down in an instant.

Tahl gulped for air and faltered in the grass. Even at his peak, he'd never run like that. His muscles throbbed, his head throbbed, and strange shadows that weren't of the night tinged the edges of his vision. Too little air for a man who was bleeding. He reduced his pace and struggled to fill his lungs. Better that he not run, he decided. It would be easier to entice a horse if he approached at a normal pace.

The white animals were not far off. He swallowed hard against a thick, dry sensation in his throat and wet his lips just enough to whistle.

A few heads went up, and several horses turned his direction.

"Come on," Tahl coaxed. He didn't dare look to see if the guards followed yet. "Come here, horse. I need you."

Several animals returned to grazing, disinterested in his approach. A handful more watched, wary. Only one seemed curious. Its hooves thumped softly in the lush grass as it inched toward him.

"There, that's a good horse." Tahl reached out one hand and a soft muzzle pushed into his palm, searching for treats. Chuckling, Tahl stepped to the side and slid his hand down the horse's neck, making his intent to mount and ride clear. "I need a favor, horse. Are you a boy or a girl? Too dark to see." The words meant nothing to the animal, he was sure, but he kept his voice soft and friendly despite how hard his chest heaved.

The horse stamped and whickered as Tahl gripped its mane and clambered onto its back. Pain shot up his injured leg, as if he could have forgotten it, and he sighed in relief when he settled on the animal's back and the pain lessened.

"Go," he whispered, nudging the horse's sides with his heels. It started slow and he clicked his tongue at it. The sound seemed to encourage it, and the horse picked up its pace. The rough trot was agony on his tired body and Tahl nudged the horse again in an effort to inspire a canter.

Shouts behind him came with hoofbeats. The small herd of horses in the pasture scattered and Tahl's mount tried to follow. He pulled the white mane with both hands and pushed with his leg, urging the horse northeast.

"Pikes ready!" a hoarse voice ordered from halfway across the field.

Tahl fought a groan, but the threat was apparently enough to inspire his stolen horse. It snorted and wheeled the direction he'd been pushing, then lit off at a startling canter.

Despite the protests of his bleeding leg, Tahl squeezed harder against the horse's sides and raised his seat from its back, knowing the pressure would urge the animal to keep moving and the way he hovered over its withers would keep him from falling. If his legs weren't exhausted first, that was. Hovering over a horse's neck seemed easy with a saddle. Bareback, it was all he could do to hold on, and he slipped precariously from one side to the other as he caught himself and over-corrected his posture again and again.

With such an unpracticed rider, the speed of the horse wasn't enough. Pikemen appeared to the left and surged closer. Tahl ducked to the side, but without a saddle, he couldn't hold on. His legs slipped and the horse cut right. Rather than be dragged, Tahl let go of its mane and tumbled hard when he hit the ground. The crown slipped past his elbow before he clamped his arm to his chest, trapping his treasure in place.

The pikemen shot past on their horses and turned back in wide loops. To Tahl's surprise, his own horse circled back, too.

"Bless you," he whispered to the horse as he mounted up again. Blood already smeared the horse's white coat where his injured leg had pressed and Tahl dreaded the sense of hope that would inspire in the pikemen when they saw it. His whole body shook with exertion and fatigue as he spurred the horse onward, just as the pikemen circled back.

Shadows crept in on Tahl's vision again and he shook his head as if to dispel them. As if sensing its rider's distress, the horse lengthened its stride and lunged into a full gallop. The four-note rhythm of its hooves drummed through Tahl's being, hummed in his head as if to lull him to sleep. Deep weariness clawed its way over him and he felt his hold on the horse's mane give way.

Without warning, the horse put all four feet down and squalled. Tahl flew over its crest with a startled shout, clearing the fence that came from seemingly nowhere. The edge of a cliff raced closer. He hit the rocky ground shoulder first, tumbled twice and rolled off the ledge.

The crown slipped from his arm. Tahl spat an oath as it brushed his fingertips and plummeted toward the river below. Then he twisted to catch the stone. His fingers found purchase and he swung in hard. The crunch that came from Tahl's ribs when he hit the cliff face yielded a wince, but he didn't dare scream. His hands burrowed deeper into the crevices he'd located, even as tears of pain squeezed from his eyes.

Scraggly brush sprouted from the cliff here and there. It wasn't much, but it was the best he was going to find. Tahl shimmied closer to a gaunt shrub and gasped in relief when he saw the small alcove beneath it. His foot scouted the ledge. It was no more than a foot deep, but it was enough.

Above, armor rattled and a pair of voices conversed in inquiring tones as they approached the ledge.

Using the bush for leverage, Tahl angled his body into the alcove and pressed close to the cool stone wall. Sweat slicked his temples and trickled uncomfortably down his spine. Tremors racked his slim frame, but he kept his breath steady. The slinking shadows hovered behind his eyelids, weighting them down. He closed his eyes and rested his head against the wall.

"Nothing," a man said above him, his voice disappointed.

"It's a long drop. Think he could have survived?" a second voice asked.

"Doubt it. You saw the blood, besides. Even if he landed in the water, he'd bleed out and be dead in no time."

Was the blood that bad? Tahl touched the back of his calf through his torn pants. The fabric was sticky, but it seemed the gash had dried. The injury was wider and deeper than he'd expected, his skin hot to the touch. He'd have to find a priestess before long.

"What do we do now?" one of the men asked, dismayed.

"Head back, I suppose. There's a fisherman's shack down there on the shoreline, across the river. If we come straight across from there, we can look for the crown."

A small sound of assent came as reply, and the crunch of booted feet against loose stone retreated from the ledge.

At last, Tahl allowed himself to gasp for breath. The risk of hyperventilation was past, and the darkness slowly began to recede from his vision. The alcove was still too dark to see clearly, but it was cloaked in the soft, natural blue of night instead of the creeping black of unconsciousness.

More than anything, he wanted to stay in the hollow of the cliff face and recover, but time was short. Even if the riders took their time carrying their pikes back to the castle, they'd move on horses, and Tahl needed to be far out of the area before they came to search for the crown. He leaned his head out of the alcove to look at the drop. Tahl wasn't afraid of heights, but the distance to the ground was intimidating.

Slowly, he slid his good leg down the cliff face in search of another foothold. Inch by inch, he eased himself out of the alcove and down the sheer stone wall.

Had he been less experienced a climber, he wasn't sure he would have made it. More than once, the stone crumbled beneath a hand or foot and sent him scrambling for a new hold. The cliff angled inward at its foot, which meant slipping would send him straight down instead of sliding along the stone.

"Just have to not slip, then," he grumbled to himself. The chalky stone dust kept his hands dry, despite the profuse sweating of the rest of him. Now and again, he paused and lingered in a secure place, resting his head against the stone and willing his body not to give out.

His feet hit the ground and the loose stones shifted beneath him. The river did not run all the way to the cliff—at least, not this time of year—and the narrow shore seemed like paradise as he sank to sit and catch his breath once more.

The shadows began to lighten. Hints of color tinged the sky and, uncertain, Tahl forced himself to get up. His legs quaked beneath him and he staggered a few steps, but by now, half the emperor's army had to be on the way to the river's north bend.

Injured and defeated, Tahl slipped in the debris and put a hand out to steady himself against the cliff.

The first rays of light spilled over the horizon and across Tahl's face. He raised a hand to shield his eyes and a glint caught his eye.

At the edge of the water, the river lapped at the crown.

CHAPTER 9

Delicate paper maps formed a pile of rolls on the bed. Someday soon, Tahl would replace them with fine quality parchment. Most of his maps were ones he'd drawn himself. The guild would need something finer than that.

All of his belongings—previously stashed under floorboards and inside walls—had been gathered onto the bed. Piece by piece, he sorted them into bags.

A familiar thumping of someone on the ladder to his loft reached his ears. The hatch in the floor creaked open. He'd never oiled the hinges, simply because their groaning complaints meant no one could sneak up on him while he was home.

Niada's head popped through the hatch. "You're here."

"Where else would I be?" Tahl offered a tired smile. No matter how his body ached for sleep, he couldn't spare the time.

She crawled into the loft and closed the trap door. "I don't know. On a gallows in the plaza?"

"I didn't know you had so little faith in me." He folded his heist shirt into his favorite bag.

Her eyes followed it. "Where are you going?"

"That's a secret. For both our safety." A hint of apology colored his tone, but Tahl didn't look her way. He'd gone to the temple to beg for healing the moment he'd made it back into the city, but healing only took care of wounds. It did nothing for the exhaustion that came from a harrowing night. The dark smudges under his heavy eyes would make her worry. "I'm not leaving. I have a guild to lead, remember? But it's safest if you don't know where I sleep anymore."

Niada made a soft sound of understanding. "The posters are already up. How did you get back into the city?"

"The cave connected to the sewers. The bear was out. I saw it in the field." If he hadn't, he never would have dared take the tunnels again.

"Where's your uniform?"

"Ditched it. Paid a beggar to bring me some clothes." Tahl paused. After today, the beggars would be as big a threat to him as anyone. Most would happily share his whereabouts for a few half-mites. "How big is my bounty?"

Nia shrugged. "One hundred thousand pims."

"Ah." That was disappointing. He would have thought swiping the crown from the pillow beside the sleeping emperor's head would be worth more.

"It makes you the most wanted man in Orrad's history," she added.

Tahl brightened. "Does it?" He'd never paid much attention to wanted posters. He was a thief, not a bounty hunter. He grunted. "Ah, posters. That reminds me. Do you still have that letter I gave you? The instructions for today?"

She nodded and wiggled the crumpled envelope from her pocket. "Do I need to read it now?"

He held out a hand and she crept closer to deposit it in his palm. The wax seal was still intact. Satisfied, Tahl ripped it into pieces.

Niada's mouth fell open.

"No need to leave incriminating evidence. We're together, so I can just tell you now. I wasn't sure we'd have a chance to meet up again, I didn't think I'd be able to get back into the city immediately." He squeezed the torn bits in his hand and willed them to burn. Magic tingled in his senses, but as always, he wasn't strong enough in his Gift to summon a flame. Instead, he stuffed the paper into his pocket.

"Makes sense," Nia agreed, though she eyed him with suspicion. "What do we do next?"

Only a few things remained loose on the bed. Tahl gathered all of them and jammed them into his pack. "That's the easy part. Start a rumor among thieves that the Ghost's guild is open to new recruits. That's the first part of your next job. You working in the taverns should let you seed rumors without anyone suspecting you. We'll need to establish a secret meeting point, somewhere we can easily escape from if the guards catch on."

"What about the caves?" she suggested.

Tahl lifted a brow.

"Prospective members have to find the caves from the sewer system," Nia said. "We hang out in that big cavern on certain days of the week. If the guards make it in, we can escape through the tunnels. They won't follow us if they see the bear."

"That's a ridiculously unsafe idea," he said. "It'll work."

Nia flashed him a grin. "I'll start sowing rumors tonight. I just have one question."

He motioned for her to ask.

"Can I see it?"

Tahl grinned to hide his hesitance. There was definitely something magic about the crown, and he was reluctant to let anyone else touch it until he'd had a chance to figure out what it was. He knew Nia well enough to be certain a look wouldn't satisfy her. "Trust me, you will. I need to move while the market's busy. Easier to hide in the crowds. I have one more job for you, though."

She perked up, eager to contribute.

"I need you to try to find information on something." He spoke slowly, unsure how to explain what had taken place. He'd paid so little mind to the situation when it happened; all he'd cared about was escaping alive. It wasn't until his long trek home that he had time to reflect on the situation. "There was a mage in the castle."

Her brow furrowed, but she waited for him to go on.

"Whoever it was, they helped me." In the grand scheme of things, it had only bought him a few seconds, but those seconds could have been what saved his life. Tahl hated to admit he hadn't done it all on his own. "I think... I think it was the queen."

Nia gaped. "Why would the queen help you steal the crown?"

"I don't know. There's a lot I don't know." Admitting that, too, stung. "I don't even know why she's called the *queen* when she's married to the *emperor*. But she had the chance to call the guards on me and she didn't. She let me escape without a word, and then I think she was the one who opened the balcony doors. I don't know why. I want to find out."

"So gather information on the queen." Niada nodded. "Got it."

"Thanks." Tahl shouldered the bag of his most valuable belongings, the crown stashed safely in the bottom. He'd have time to investigate what magic it held in coming days, while he waited for the rumors to take root. "If you can, meet me in the basement of the Queen's Museum tomorrow night."

"I will," Nia said as she watched him tie his maps into a bundle and slide them into a sack. "Just promise you'll be careful between now and then."

"Nia," he replied with a grin. "When am I not?"

Her gaze settled on the scar under his right eye and it was all he could do not to laugh.

"Fair enough." He swung the last bag against his back and patted her shoulder as he crossed to the trap door to the stable below. "You just worry about your part for now. I'll see you tomorrow."

"He's coming," Niada whispered. The soft plink of water dripping into a puddle somewhere punctuated her statement.

Tahl tried not to roll his eyes. "Took him long enough." The longer he sat in the dank of the underground, the more his nose itched. He hadn't realized he had any sort of allergies, but using the cavern as a rendezvous point made him glad they'd opted to use the museum's basement as a headquarters instead.

"Be nice," Nia chided. "Not everyone is as skilled as you." She wasn't one to praise him often. That she did now made Tahl grin.

The sound of someone in the corridor reached him now, too. Niada sat on the terraced stone outside the end of the sewers, close enough to hear anyone coming long before their steps echoed through the cavern.

"Good thing we didn't include a test of stealth," she grumbled.

"To be fair, I don't think they'd be able to sneak up on you." She'd praised him, now it was Tahl's turn to repay the favor. "You've come a long way in your training the last few weeks."

A hint of color rose into her cheeks, but she did not reply. A light glowed in the depths of the tunnel and they both grew quiet as it drew near.

A figure came into sight. A young man with a calm face but a nervous, halting step. Given that he'd come looking for Orrad's most wanted criminal, Tahl couldn't blame him for his trepidation.

"State your business," Nia ordered when the youth reached the end of the tunnel, her tone as flat and disinterested as could be.

The thief stared at her, confused. "I'm here to see the Ghost."

Niada turned her head to peer into the darkness. Uncertain, the thief lifted his lantern and followed her gaze.

Light spilled across the high table of stone where Tahl lounged and glinted off the jeweled crown he wore.

The thief's mouth fell open.

"You found me," Tahl said, mimicking the flat quality of Niada's tone. "What do you want?"

The young man swallowed hard and lifted his chin. "I want in."

A spark of amusement lit Tahl's eyes and a smirk twisted the corners of his mouth. "I thought you'd say that."

DON'T STEAL FROM DEMONS

A WESTKINGS HEIST SHORT STORY

CHAPTER 1

"Tahl!"

The sharp whisper made him tilt his head, but Tahl still crunched into his apple before he answered. "Yeah?"

A number of thumps and a low grunt came as reply. Niada's head popped up above the edge of the rooftop and she grimaced as she dragged herself onto the shingles. "I need help," she panted.

"After an ascent like that, I'd say I agree." Tahl swiped a bead of juice from the corner of his mouth with a fingertip he then licked clean.

Her nose crinkled as she crawled closer. She was a little more graceful on top of the bakery, but everyone inside had to know she was there. "I'm serious." Her hand went to her pocket, for something stashed inside. He raised a brow when she withdrew a bundle of cloth.

"I took this earlier," Nia said, "but not on purpose. I missed the mark's purse and got this out of his pocket instead."

"And you decided it was worth keeping." He bit into his apple again.

"Well, no, it's just... every time I get ready to drop it..." A hint of worry furrowed her brow and she shook her head. "I'm not superstitious, okay? I promise I'm not, but there's something weird about this thing, and every time I try to drop it somewhere, something happens."

Tahl squinted at the bundle as she extended it toward him on a flat palm. He wiped his hand on his trousers and folded back the fabric around whatever it was, revealing the most unremarkable knife he'd ever seen. He considered it for a time, trying to decide if she was messing with him. From the way concern pinched her face, it seemed unlikely. "What made you decide to bring it to me?"

"Because if anyone in the city can escape it, it'd be you." She inched closer, thrusting the wrapped knife toward him as she crawled, desperate for him to take it.

He rolled his eyes and reached to pluck it from her hand.

The moment his fingers brushed the hilt, a jolt of power shot through his arm. Tahl yelped and jerked his arm back. The knife tumbled from Nia's palm and bounced off the roof.

She squeaked and started down after it. As her foot swung over the edge to search for holds, a glint of metal caught Tahl's eye. He lunged after her, snagged her by the back of the shirt, and dragged her up the roof.

"Hey!" Nia kicked, but her legs were too short for her to connect with him from that angle. He hauled her over the roof's peak and shoved her down until they both disappeared behind it. Below, a half-dozen booted footsteps marched into the narrow street in front of the bakery.

"She came this way," a man's voice said. "I'm sure of it."

"Guards?" Tahl whispered, so close beside her ear he was sure no one else would be able to hear him.

Nia nodded once and hunkered lower against the shingles. She gripped the ridged wood so tightly, her knuckles grew pale.

"Were they following you before?"

She hesitated, then rocked a hand from side to side. Not a helpful answer.

"Either they were or they weren't," he whispered before he

slipped away. Unlike Nia, Tahl's movements on the rooftop were soundless. She scuffled after him, the toes of her shoes knocking on the edges of all the shingles she passed. "I think they saw me take it. Every time I think I've gotten away, I try to drop the knife and they show up again."

Tahl motioned for her to join him behind the chimney. "That just means they followed you, numbskull. You have to be sure you've shaken them before you try to drop it."

"But I have!" Nia protested. He hushed her with a sharp gesture and she tucked her chin into her chest, sulking. When she spoke again, it was little more than a whisper. "I took this from a mark on the east docks."

That was enough to make Tahl's brows climb. Perched near the west gate as they were, there were few places farther away she could run. As far as he knew, he was the only thief in Orrad the guard might find worth following from one end of the city to the other. Why would they pursue her so relentlessly?

He rose just enough to peer over the peak of the roof and watch the guards disappear. Then he flicked his fingers in a signal for Nia to stay put.

Her lower lip jutted out, but she didn't follow as he slid down the roof and dropped from its edge to alight soundlessly in the yard. The knife hadn't gone far; Tahl spotted it almost immediately, its wrappings lost and its blade stuck in the earth. He flexed his fingers, unsure he wanted to touch it again.

Had Nia felt that power? She wasn't a mage, so she shouldn't have. Still, she'd brought the knife wrapped. Curiosity tingled in his fingertips as he swept the cloth from the dusty ground and draped it over the blade's hilt.

When his hand brushed the pommel through the fabric, he felt nothing.

"You're an unusual thing, aren't you?" he murmured as he wiggled the knife free from the dirt. Whether he intended to talk to the blade or just mumble his thoughts aloud, he didn't know.

It wasn't as if he'd never talked to inanimate objects before, but this one gave him an eerie feeling.

Nia descended from the roof a shade more gracefully than she'd climbed it in the first place. "What do you think?" she asked as she dusted off her boyish breeches. "Is it cursed?"

"Why'd you wrap it?" Tahl glanced down at his hands, then looked around his feet. He'd been eating an apple. What had he done with it? He didn't remember putting it down, and he didn't see it, either. That the prick of magic in the blade had been enough to distract him meant nothing good.

"It gave me the creeps when I touched it. I don't know why. It felt better after I wrapped it." She scrubbed her hands against her hips as if to remove a sensation the knife had left behind. A look of concern pulled her brows together. "It's not cursed, is it?"

Tahl snorted. "Unlikely."

She didn't appear convinced. "But there's something funny about it."

"Yes." He turned the knife in his hand, studying the way the light glinted off its edge. Even without touching it directly, magic buzzed in his senses.

"Is it dangerous?"

For a moment, Tahl wasn't sure how to answer. The shock that had traveled up his arm hadn't been pleasant, but he hadn't held the blade long enough to know if it was dangerous. He wasn't willing to touch it again to find out.

Yet without touching it or exploring its energy, he had no way of knowing what the magic *did*. He frowned, unsure what to do next. There didn't seem much point to touching it. It wasn't like he'd had any more luck sussing out whatever the crown he'd stolen did.

"Don't know," he said at last. He almost stuck the knife into his belt, then thought better of it. Instead, he wrapped the square of fabric around it more securely and fished a piece of string from his pocket to tie it closed.

The action made Nia wrinkle her nose. "So that's a yes."

Tahl touched a hand to his chest. "What, you have that little faith in my powers of deduction?"

"You dropped it," she replied dryly. "Considering your incredible lack of slippery fingers, I can do my own deduction from that."

Fair, he thought with a smirk, though he was unwilling to concede that out loud. He kept the knife in his hand and turned toward the street.

"Where are you going?" Nia asked, trotting along behind him as he started walking.

Tahl waved the little bundle. "To give it back."

Niada almost tripped over her feet.

"You're going to do *what*?" Nia squeaked.

"To give it back," Tahl repeated. "It's pretty obvious you don't know what you have, here."

She hurried to match his longer strides. "Some kind of cursed blade that's out for my blood?"

The suggestion was so odd he had to stop and squint at her. He certainly hadn't felt *that* in that single shot of magic that lanced up his arm, but he also hadn't taken the time to analyze what it had done. Whatever it was, it hurt, and that was enough for him to conclude the knife wasn't worth the trouble.

A sheepish look flitted over her face. She opened her mouth to say something, but he silenced her with a wave of his hand.

"You can't just fence magic items," he explained as he ducked into an alley so narrow, he could hardly walk without his shoulders brushing the walls. Slim as he was, he could fit into almost every nook and cranny he'd run across in Orrad. But he wasn't done growing. He couldn't count on every passage being easy to traverse forever. The stablemaster back in his home city of Ashor had sworn he would fill out in his early twenties, when his shoulders widened and he started growing a man's muscle. Or, that was what the stablemaster had called it.

Tahl took a longer step over a pile of rat droppings and forced his thoughts back to the task at hand. "Imbued items aren't common. Especially not weapons. No merchant will touch them, and if I'm being honest, this isn't pretty enough to keep in my collection. Think you can identify the mark again if you see him in the city?"

Nia tucked in her chin and rubbed her arms, as if the thought alone was unpleasant. "He's hard to miss. I wish I'd chickened out when it crossed my mind."

It wasn't like her to confess such feelings. Nia was a cautious thief, but once she picked a mark, she could be brash. Tahl raised a brow, though he didn't say anything, lest she clam up.

She went on unprompted. "He was creepy. I didn't realize it until I was right up on him, but something about that guy was weird."

"So in other words, you'll gladly point him out so I can put this back in his pockets," Tahl said.

Reluctant, she nodded. After a moment, curiosity claimed her expression. "You think it'll be that easy?"

"Pickpocketing works backwards, too. I'm just as adept at planting things on people as getting things off them." He stopped at the end of the alley to peek into the roadway. People flowed past without noticing him, distracted by their own business. Satisfied, Tahl waited for a gap to slip into the throng.

"There she is!" someone cried behind him.

Tahl spun on his heel. Nia yelped and bolted past him as a pair of guards he swore hadn't been there a moment ago burst from the crowds.

Biting back a curse, he put himself in their path at the last moment.

One of the guards plowed straight into him, bowling him to the ground. The other tripped over the two of them and landed hard on the cobblestones.

"Hey!" Tahl protested, struggling to remove himself from the tangle of limbs.

The larger of the two guards—the one who had tripped—planted a hand on his face and shoved him down.

"Brant's bloody branches," the other guard spat as he freed himself and staggered to his feet.

Tahl curled up on the cobbles with a groan, covering his face with one arm. He didn't think the wax covering the scar on his face had come loose, but if it had, it would make putting himself in a guard's path the most dangerous thing he could have done.

Yet the guards never looked his way again after they were back on their feet. The one he'd entangled stepped over Tahl's legs and marched onward in search of Nia, without looking back.

Tahl unfurled himself slowly and peeked out from between his fingers. Under the guise of shielding his face out of fear, he probed the wax over his scar to ensure it was intact before he lowered his hand. He watched as the guards disappeared around a corner, momentarily unsure what to do.

Nia had nothing on her now. The knife was still on him. Even if they caught her, they had no evidence to support the claim she'd stolen something.

Unless, of course, they took her before her mark and had him identify her.

That was another problem. He could roam the streets all day, but without Nia at his side, he had no hope of finding the target. It was just as easy for him to abandon the knife somewhere; the blade meant nothing to him. But if the guards caught Nia and she was identified as a thief...

Tahl halted that thought before it could go any farther. "For the love of leaves," he muttered as he pushed himself up. There was no avoiding it. He retreated back into the alleyway and peeled the wax from his scar.

If anyone could draw attention off Nia long enough for her to escape, it would be the Ghost.

TAHL WOULD HAVE LOVED to have his heist clothing.

He could still climb walls and leap rooftops without it, but the close-fitting navy blue outfit had come to be as much a part of the Ghost's image as his scar. Some tiny, vain part of him had considered having his emblem added to his ensemble somehow. Perhaps not to his clothing, as it would have been foolish to add anything that stood out from the dark fabric, but maybe a scarf. Or a symbol on his bag. Right now, it would have been useful. Something, *anything* more that made his identity obvious would have been.

Instead, he had to hope his scar would be enough.

Tahl rubbed the cuff of his sleeve against his cheek as he bounded across the gap to another roof. The last traces of wax came free, and he threw himself into a sprint.

The guards had disappeared around a corner somewhere ahead. He had to find a way to cut them off, separate them from Niada long enough for her to make an escape.

Angry voices rose from the city below and he veered toward them, ignoring the instinct to keep quiet. Tahl breathed deep as he dashed across the rough wooden roof tiles of the poorer district they were in. They were easier to keep his footing on and he pushed ahead.

He knew every inch of Orrad by now. Just ahead lay a handful of shops—a perfect place for a distraction. From the sound of it, that was where Nia had gone.

Hope this means you have a plan. Tahl ran through his memories of which shops were where, then adjusted his course. When he reached the last roof before the wide shopping avenue, he slowed and gripped the roof's edge to swing down with as much force as he could muster. His heels struck the shop's glass display window and crashed through.

A chorus of shrieks rose as he swung back and released the roof. He landed lightly on the cobblestone street as broken glass hit the ground and splintered. The jeweler had already appeared on the other side of the window, his face distraught.

"I need to borrow this, sorry," Tahl called as he seized a fistful of jewels from the display and spun to scan the streets.

More cries went up through the shoppers nearby when he turned. "It's him!" a woman screamed.

"The Ghost!" a man added.

Tahl fought not to cringe. Thieving in broad daylight wasn't his style, and the number of eyes that turned toward him was uncomfortable. But at the far end of the street, he caught the gleam of armor as a pair of guards turned back his direction.

A pang of regret struck him like a punch to the stomach.

It's part of the plan, he told himself as he took two hopping steps backwards and raised his stolen jewelry overhead. "I'll bring these back, promise!"

From the obscenities the jeweler shouted at him through the broken window, the man didn't believe it.

Before the jeweler could make it through the door, Tahl ducked between a handful of startled shoppers and raced toward the oncoming guards. He'd barely taken a few steps before they were close enough for him to recognize them and be certain they were the guards after Nia. The fine hairs on the back of his neck prickled and an unpleasant shudder tore down his spine. Racing toward guards in broad daylight was another thing he didn't do, but here he was, cutting straight toward them and praying they didn't call for reinforcements.

Tahl had expected to see Nia somewhere past them, but she was nowhere to be seen. *That better mean you got away.* He skidded on the cobbles to keep from crashing into someone, then cut toward a side street.

He crashed into Nia, instead.

"Hey!" she cried as she tumbled to the ground. Tahl sprang over the top of her to keep from tripping, then spun back to offer her a hand.

She blinked at the gold laced between his fingers.

"Come on!" he snapped.

Setting her jaw, Nia grabbed his wrist and let him help her up. Then they both darted into the narrow street. "I don't need you to save me," she said, the edge in her voice sharper than the window's broken glass.

"Really? It looked to me like you were headed for the gallows!" He slapped her arm to get her attention and veered into a narrow alley. A few steps in, he kicked off the wall and started his vertical ascent, bounding back and forth between the close buildings.

She followed, but grunted and struggled to keep up. "You climb like a squirrel."

"Yeah, I've heard that." He swung onto a roof and leaned down to offer his hand. When she took it, he hauled her up and then glanced at the jewelry that still decorated his hand.

Nia nodded toward it. "What's that for?"

"Getting the attention of the guards. Come on, we have to keep moving." He backed up a few paces and took a running start to leap to the next building over. Nia landed next to him with a quiet thump. Before he could offer any directions, she lit off on her own.

"Where are you going?" Tahl called after her, uncomfortably aware of the noise of the city growing louder in the street below. They wouldn't have long to gain a head start.

"The docks!" Nia shouted back. "You still have it?"

Tahl was beginning to regret taking the knife. He nodded once and took a step forward, only for a crossbow bolt to thud into the rooftop at his toes.

"Archers," he breathed. "Perfect."

A second bolt cracked against the rooftop. Tahl launched into a sprint to follow Nia onto the next roof over.

A volley from the crossbows followed.

Niada yelped as one skimmed past her head, taking a few raven strands with it. "How did you manage to make things *worse?*" she cried.

Tahl vaulted over the peak of the roof to hunch on the other side, hoping that removing himself from sight would slow down the bowmen below. "You're the one who wanted me involved!"

"Yeah, to help me fix things! Not to bring half Orrad's guard after us!"

Offended, he put himself directly in front of her as she crested the roof and slid down beside him. She squeaked in surprise, clearly not having expected him to be so close. He pressed his fingers to his chest in a gesture of hurt. "Who helped you get out from under them, exactly? They almost had you."

"We aren't out from under them, stupid. They're right there!" Nia ducked reflexively as a bolt arced overhead.

Below, someone shouted, and an argument broke out. Whoever had fired didn't have permission. It seemed their reckless shot would earn them an earful—and hopefully buy Tahl a little time.

"Come on," he whispered, motioning her to the next roof. It was a longer jump, harder to make without a running start, but he bounded across the gap without difficulty and then spun to catch Nia. She didn't need his help, though she landed hard. They put two more rooftops between them and the crossbowmen before he motioned toward a narrow alley at the back of a building.

Together, they descended into the shadowy space.

"We need somewhere to hide," Nia whispered.

Tahl arched a brow. What did she think he was doing? He bit back a retort and waved for her to follow him, instead.

The alley snaked farther toward the edge of the city before it finally opened into a familiar yard. A round stone cap covered a sewer access tunnel in the middle of the weedy cobbles. He braced a foot against it and pushed. It didn't budge.

"Help me with this," he ordered as he dropped to the ground, braced his toes against the uneven paving stones, and pushed with both hands. Nia knelt to do the same, grunting with exertion. Perspiration just rose on his brow before the stone shifted. With the crust of dirt broken, it moved more easily, but he didn't fool himself for a second into thinking they'd be able to move it back. Tahl stopped with the stone halfway across the opening, swiped the back of his hand across his brow, and plucked a loose pebble from the ground. "Down."

"Don't have to tell me twice," Nia muttered. She slid over the edge and disappeared into the gap.

Tahl followed, too aware of the sound of people approaching. They stood a chance of escaping in the sewer, at least, but how easily the guards seemed to track them through the city made him uncomfortable. He'd never had that difficulty before.

They hurried down the tunnel until the light from the opening was no longer visible, then walked a bit farther, trailing their hands on the walls to find their way. Once he was certain they wouldn't be spotted easily, Tahl pushed a tendril of power into the pebble in his hand. It took a soft, warm glow, but he kept it faint. If anyone looked into the tunnel, a light could be visible. If he kept it faint enough, the mage-light wouldn't illuminate much beyond the ground beneath their feet.

"Think we made it?" Nia asked softly as they padded onward.

"Hopefully." Tahl's sense of direction rarely failed him, and he'd set a path toward the eastern side of the city. He'd explored a good portion of the unused sewers that had fallen short of expectations and ended up paved over, and he was confident when he assumed they could get close to the docks, but he had a stop planned along the way. He rubbed his mage-light with his thumb and fought back a frown. "Let's go a little farther. Once we get around a corner somewhere up ahead, I think we should sit down and have a proper look at this knife."

She made a soft sound of assent and said nothing more.

The tunnel carried on for some time before they found a branch. Tahl shifted their path north and continued for a while before he took another eastern branch. Not long after, he lowered himself to the ground and allowed himself a sigh.

Nia frowned. "You okay? It seems like that run took more out of you than usual."

"Fine. I wasn't planning on escaping any guards today, but at least they weren't Elite." He withdrew the knife and poured a little more magic into the mage-light, letting it brighten before he pushed it into Nia's hands. "Here, hold that."

She leaned forward, curious, as he unwrapped the blade. After the unpleasant shock of touching it before, he chose to keep it on the cloth. That shock was what made it all the more confusing that he didn't see anything out of the ordinary.

Now that he inspected it close up, he saw it was a nice blade. Plain, but good quality. Ordinary of appearance, anyway, yet clearly unusual. Ordinary blades didn't bite with magic when you touched them.

"See anything strange?" Tahl asked. He didn't expect she would. Noticing things was what kept him alive and made him a good thief, but he wasn't arrogant enough to think nothing could escape his attention. Especially when magic was involved.

Nia shook her head. "It's just a regular knife." She reached for it, then hesitated.

Tahl raised a brow. "What?"

"What happened when you touched it before?"

He snorted. "It hurt. It was like shuffling across a carpet and then poking someone to make a spark, times ten."

Now her face twisted with bemusement. "When I touched it, it just made me feel creepy-crawly. Should I touch it again? Is it safe?"

"I don't know," he admitted. "I get the feeling it's a lot more special than it looks. None of the mages at the academy are able to imbue objects with magic, you know. They call it a Lost Art."

"Can't be that lost, if someone's still making magic knives."

"That or this is a lot older—and more important—than we thought." He studied the knife for a moment longer, then folded the wrappings closed once more. "I know this is going to sound weird, but I think the guards are able to follow it somehow."

Nia tilted her head. "Like sensing it?"

"No, I don't think so. I didn't feel any mages in their group, and even I don't really pick up anything odd about it. But they might have an artifact that lets them know where it is. I don't think they'd pursue us so with this much determination otherwise."

She sat back on her heels, rolling the mage-light between her forefinger and thumb. "Why do you suppose they'd have something like that? Or be after a plain old knife?"

"I don't think they are," Tahl said. "If they've got something like that, I suspect they're looking for something else. We may have just tripped their alarm by mistake." He had a good idea of what sort of magic-imbued item they might be looking for, but he'd keep that to himself. If there was any way to sense the crown from outside the vault-turned-office he'd stashed it in, their headquarters would have been discovered by now.

"Then we definitely want to give it back." She stood up and dusted off her knees.

He blinked twice and rose after her. "Really? You seemed like you hated that idea."

"I do, but I hate the idea of getting caught worse."

Tahl couldn't help but laugh. "Fair enough. We're halfway to the docks now, but we've got one thing we need to stop and get before we move on."

"Really?" Nia asked. "What's that?"

"Disguises."

"Ready," Nia announced.

Tahl glanced over his shoulder and bit his tongue. He'd elected to wear the simple gray uniform of a soldier out of armor, something he'd liberated from a guard's house after his romp in Orrad's fortress-like palace. She, on the other hand, looked little different from her everyday appearance as a barmaid.

"You're going to need to do better than that." He fastened the last button of his coat and turned to help her. The dress she'd chosen was ordinary and suited a peasant girl, but she'd done nothing with her black hair. He slid his fingers along her hairline and gathered it all behind her ears to smooth it into a braid.

Nia scrunched her nose. "I can do my own hair."

"Really? How come I've never seen you do anything but tie it back, then?" His fingers were deft and with her hair little more than shoulder-length, it wasn't long before he'd tied off the braid and coiled it into a simple bun against the back of her head. But he didn't have any hairpins on him, so he caught her hand and clamped it over the bun to make her hold it in place until he could find some.

"Because I don't like it being fancy," she replied with a sniff.

Tahl snorted and pulled the box of treasures out from underneath his bed. "All the more reason to do something fancy, then. The goal is to avoid being recognized, remember?" He fished around in a smaller wooden container inside the box until he produced a few hairpins. He couldn't recall where he'd gotten them or why he'd decided to keep them, but the container was filled with bits of wire and string and miscellaneous pieces of who-knew-what he'd always assumed would come in handy. More often than not, he was right.

Nia rolled her eyes, but stood still while he worked the pins into her hair.

Satisfied, he stepped back to give her one last inspection. "Ready?"

"No, but if we get shot at again, I'm blaming you. I don't think I can run or climb in this skirt." She gathered the fabric in both hands and gave it a swish. It wasn't an impressive dress, but it was all he'd been able to procure for her on short notice.

Brant forbid she appreciate that it fits, he mused. "Fine. Let's get to the docks."

Though she groaned, Nia followed him out of his latest hideout.

He moved, every now and then; he still missed the cozy space above Ebitha's stables he'd called home after he'd been ejected from the academy, but it was safer not to be in any one place for too long. More often than not, it was Nia getting herself in trouble that prompted his moves. Tahl shut and locked the door behind her, lamenting the packing he'd have to do as soon as this was over.

With his stolen guard's uniform, no one bothered them on the trek to the docks east of the city. While they traversed the city streets, he found it a boon. Once they passed the gate and he saw how many men in armor swarmed the riverfront, his choice of disguise sent a trickle of sweat down his spine.

"I've never seen so many guards in one place before," Nia murmured. "Not even when you—"

"Now would not be the wisest time to discuss previous exploits," he said through clenched teeth. He expected her to come back with a retort, but she blushed, instead.

Keenly aware of the cosmetic wax that hid the scar on his face once more, he squared his shoulders and tried to look as if he belonged.

Together, they walked the crowded street, and it wasn't long before something brushed the edge of Tahl's senses.

"I think I see him," Nia whispered.

He nodded and slowed just enough for her to take the lead.

The farther they went, the more the sense of *something* prickled. A presence, a power unlike anything he'd ever felt before. The prickle turned to an itch and he rolled his shoulders, fighting the urge to scratch.

Nia tugged at his sleeve. "There. That's him. I'm sure of it."

"All right," he murmured. The itch turned to a burn, a heat that rolled over his skin like the air from a baker's oven. He fought back a shudder and made himself walk on. Magic had never put him so on edge before, but it felt raw, wrong, and the closer they got to their target, the worse it seemed to be.

It *was* the target, Tahl realized. The brown-cloaked figure that stood on the pier and watched cargo be loaded was a mage. That presence grew stronger, stranger, flooding him with a sickening urge to run. Nia must have felt it too, for all that she wasn't a mage. She stopped at the end of the pier and watched with wide eyes as Tahl forced himself to continue on.

Heat. Power. His heartbeat quickened and his stomach lurched.

Stealing was easy.

Returning something should have been easy.

Instead, he struggled onward, fearful he'd be ill.

The figure shifted, its hooded head canting to one side. It seemed the target had sensed him, too. It grew still as Tahl approached.

Power rolled off the stranger, more wild, more sickening than Tahl ever imagined magic could be. The sheer weight of its presence poured over him and threatened to drive him under.

The stranger turned.

Unable to resist, Tahl sank to his knees and presented the stolen blade on his upturned palms.

"You are not the one who stole from me," the mark said, his words thick with an accent Tahl had never heard before.

"But I'm the one who's giving it back," Tahl said.

A soft chuckle answered. "You've learned a lesson?"

All Tahl managed was a nod.

"This was not for you." Rather than anger, amusement colored the man's voice. He reached for the blade, and instead of fingers, it was claws that curled around the hilt.

Startled, Tahl lifted his head as that subhuman hand—and the dagger—vanished into the stranger's cloak. From the depths of the hood that shadowed the stranger's features, a pair of deep violet lights stared back.

The pit of Tahl's stomach dropped.

A shout from the ship beside them drew the stranger's attention and he turned away. With a grace as inhuman as the rest of him, the man swept up the gangplank and disappeared without a word.

All of a sudden, the crushing weight of power lifted, and Tahl's shoulders slumped with relief. Beads of sweat marred his brow and he swiped them away with the back of his hand. He'd never felt anything like that. Silently, he prayed he never would again.

Hurried footfalls thumped behind him, earning a few curious looks from passers-by, but not even the armored guards on duty watched them for more than a moment. Their luck, it seemed, had changed.

"What was that all about?" Nia asked as she knelt beside him. Her hands curled around his arm, and for a moment, he wasn't sure if she was seeking comfort or trying to offer it to him.

"A lesson," Tahl said. He freed himself of her grasp and pushed himself up.

Nia glanced toward the ship as the sailors pulled in the plank and prepared to set sail. "What lesson?"

His eyes glazed and he swallowed hard. "Don't steal from demons."

TO STEAL THE QUEEN

THE THIRD HEIST

CHAPTER 1

THE NUMBERS IN THE LEDGER DIDN'T ADD UP. TAHL CHEWED THE inside of his lip and tapped a finger against the desktop as he skimmed the columns again. The pad of scratch paper beside him was already full.

"No wonder Ebitha can't afford her horses," he muttered as he closed the ledger and put it back. If not for the odd jobs he'd done for the woman, he wouldn't have known where to find it. The widow's estate was a mess, to say the least, and had only grown worse after Tahl left.

He ripped the top sheet of scratch paper off the pad and stuffed it into his pocket. The next few pages bore impressions from his borrowed pen, but he doubted Ebitha—or whoever managed her money these days—would notice. They probably wouldn't have noticed if the office was out of order, either, given the state of things around the manor, but he still returned the pen to its cup and ensured the chair was in the same position it had been when he entered. Satisfied by the overall appearance of the office, Tahl stalked to the window and slipped outside.

Moonlight bathed the house. It wasn't the best night to be climbing, but Tahl was not concerned. Out of everyone in Orrad, Tahl could only think of one person he trusted more than Ebitha, and she waited below the window. The moment his feet touched the ground, Niada emerged from the shadows. Tahl didn't need a lookout, but after leaving Nia out of the jobs that put him on the map, he felt he owed her a few nights on the prowl.

"Get what you needed?" Nia asked in a whisper.

Tahl grunted in response. Had he? The numbers in the ledger were suspicious, but they weren't exactly important to anyone but him. Knowing someone had it out for the old widow who had fed and sheltered him after he'd been expelled from the mage academy bothered him more than it should.

"I'll take that as a yes." Nia glanced up the back of the house, but Tahl hadn't left anything out of place. The curtains were drawn and the window was closed. No one would ever know he'd stopped in for a visit.

"Not yet." Tahl made his way to the stables to steal a peek inside. A handful of equine heads lifted when the doors opened and he took a quick count. One was missing. He frowned.

Nia watched his back, puzzled. Without another word, he motioned for her to follow and together, they slipped into a narrow, winding alley.

"See anything interesting?" he asked once they were safely away from the widow's manor.

"I didn't see anything at all," Nia complained. "This part of the city at night is more dead than the emperor's grandmother."

Tahl quirked a brow at her choice of words, but let them go as he caught hold of a drainpipe on the side of a building. "Maybe it's time to liven it up, then. Think you can keep up?"

Her eyes brightened and he didn't wait for a response. He darted up the wall and kicked off the top to land on the roof of the lower building across the alley. Below, he caught the scuffle of Niada following. They'd have to work on that; Tahl's ascent hadn't made a sound.

Soon, she landed on the roof next to him. He spun in place and lit off in a sprint, building momentum to vault the alley and land on the next roof over.

Even three months ago, it wouldn't have been safe to travel the city by roof. Tahl wasn't sure *safe* was the right word to use for it now, but bounding from rooftop to rooftop no longer carried the same perils. He would have felt safer in his heist clothes, but those were reserved for important jobs, not for breaking into an old woman's house to nose through her financial statements.

Orrad had changed in the wake of the Ghost's return. His return, Tahl thought with a hint of smug satisfaction. Not every thief in the city was part of his guild, but their numbers grew daily and his reputation was enough to scare the rest into submission. Even some of the guards had now fallen under his sway. The city was easy to corrupt when you had coins to press into the right palms.

Behind him, Nia landed hard. She grunted as her knees cracked against the tiled roof, but he moved on. He needed to make her train more often. As the Ghost's second-in-command, she should have been the second most capable thief in the city. In reality, she wasn't far up the ladder in terms of skill. It was easy to hide her lack of ability when all she did was shuffle paperwork and pass orders to the lower-ranked thieves, but sooner or later, they'd be stuck in a situation where he'd need her to be at the top of her game.

The Queen's Museum loomed ahead and Tahl slowed his pace. His pulse drummed in his ears, but it was strong and steady and though his breath came quick, he was far from winded. He'd missed the freedom that came with his rooftop acrobatics, even if he hadn't missed the scrapes and bruises. On a particularly low roof, he worked his way to the edge and contemplated the best descent. He preferred a challenge, but he'd also left Nia behind several buildings ago.

She reappeared on a roof across the alley as he tried to work out an easy way down. "I give," she gasped, bracing her hands against her knees. "That last... last one was... a lot taller... than I thought."

"Maybe you should have said you couldn't keep up." Tahl smirked, but pointed at handholds in the uneven stone face of the building. "Swing over the edge and you should be able to climb down."

Nia groaned and hung her head.

"I'll go first," he offered as he slipped off the roof and caught a stone with his toes. The alley was narrow enough that he could have shimmied down with his feet braced on either building, but Niada's legs weren't long enough for that. Instead, he demonstrated the path down the side of the building. There were no windows facing the alleys through most of the city, so their chances of being seen were slim. All the better, considering how long it would take her to descend.

Though Nia grumbled, she followed. "So are you gonna tell me what we were doing at your old place?"

"I wasn't planning on it." Tahl paced backwards down the alley to give her more space.

"What do horses have to do with it?"

"One's missing." Which horse was missing hadn't escaped his notice, either. Tahl frowned at the thought.

Nia dusted her hands against her pants when she reached the ground. "Stolen? Is this a rival thief vendetta thing?"

Tahl led the way down the alley. Though the museum was their destination, he and his guildmates took care to never be seen near the building. "No."

Unconvinced, Nia narrowed her eyes at him until they were little more than slits. "Something more personal?"

"I don't expect you to understand." It also seemed unlikely she was going to drop the subject. Tahl rubbed the back of his neck, unsure how he could explain.

"Is it because it's the sweet old lady whose horses you took care of?" she goaded. "I didn't think altruism was your thing, Tahl."

He rolled his eyes. "It's not." Ahead, a ring of stone with a wooden cover lay hidden in shadow. He waited to be sure the alley was clear before he pushed off the cover and slid into the hole underneath.

Niada followed with considerably more confidence than she'd shown the first time he'd taken her down a manhole. She stopped partway down the ladder and wrestled the cover back into place. "Why are you always so secretive when you're planning a heist?"

Startled, Tahl turned back to face her as the cover thunked into place and the last sliver of moonlight disappeared. "What makes you think I'm planning anything?"

"Because you got secretive." Her soft shoes rasped against the rough ladder on her way down.

Tahl grunted in displeasure. Instead of answering, he dug a coin from his pocket and poured energy into it to make a mage-light. The cold illumination stung his eyes after the pitch black of the sewer and he grimaced. Someday, he'd learn a little finesse with his lights. He didn't practice it as often as he practiced with his smoke.

"Speaking of heists," he said as casually as he could, "have you found anything else on the queen?"

Nia shook her head. "Nothing much. She married Atoras just before his father died and he took the crown, but the ceremony and celebration were private. It was just the old emperor, Atoras and the queen, and the chief clerics from Brant's temple. Nothing else about the ceremony is public record."

"Huh." Tahl suspected he'd find more information than that in the museum. He made a mental note to cover the scar on his face and explore the exhibits one afternoon.

"It's weird, Tahl. It's like they tried to stick her in front of the city like she'd always been there. They even destroyed all the old currency, the coins that had the old empress's face on them."

The new coins offered precious little information, themselves. Tahl frowned as a thought flitted through his head. "What's her name?"

Nia paused and gave him a blank stare. After a moment, her mouth dropped open.

"Exactly." He shook his head. Nameless queens and missing horses. Two things that pricked at his mind, and the two couldn't be more different. Unsettled, he focused on the ground under his feet. To his relief, the distraction worked, and Niada asked no more questions.

They padded through the underground tunnels in silence. Eventually, they reached another ladder, this one newer. Tahl went up first and fit his fingers into a hollow on one side of the slab that blocked the way. The hidden pins were cold to the touch and he manipulated them with a practiced ease. Seconds later, the slab slid aside.

"I'd still like to know how Jeran did that," Nia muttered.

"I'm sure you'll have a chance to pry the schematics out of him someday," Tahl said as he extinguished his mage-light and climbed through. The trap door really was a feat. Jeran had been one of their first recruits, chosen primarily because of his background in engineering. Most of the doors in the new thieves' guild headquarters had been outfitted with contraptions of Jeran's design. Every lock functioned differently, and no two doors used the same hinge system. It would have been easier to blast a hole in the wall of the Queen's Museum than figure out the complex mechanics the young man had built.

A hint of a smile pulled at the corner of Tahl's mouth as Nia emerged from the hole behind him and the trap door closed. He had no room to think of Jeran as young; the other thief had four years on him. Whether or not Tahl was the leader, he'd only just turned eighteen two weeks prior and was among the youngest members of the growing guild. Nia was the youngest of all, though no one harbored her any ill will. If anything, her age had granted her favored status among the rest of the guild members. Tahl had already heard a half-dozen different outlandish stories hypothesizing what she had done to impress the Ghost enough to be made second-in-command.

The moment the door to their hidden headquarters opened, a half-dozen thieves inside leaped to their feet. Tahl motioned for them to settle as he strode in. The group eyed him with mingled reverence and wariness. Although they seemed to fear him—or at least, feared his reputation—Tahl didn't trust any of them. Complacency was what had landed Bahar Eseri in a grave. The old guild had shattered after the former guildmaster's death, and Tahl had no doubt any thieves connected to Lord Eseri's guild might find reason to plant a dagger in his back. Regardless, he'd allowed them in thus far. Safety—and control of the city's underbelly—came with numbers.

"Nia," Tahl said as the door latched behind them, "get the green books and bring them to my office. Is Ashyl in here?" He scanned the faces in the front room for his answer.

"She was after the wharfmaster tonight," someone called from among crates at the back of the room.

Tahl nodded. "Good. Send her to me if she returns in the next two hours. Nia?"

"On it." She wound her way between numerous crates and baskets to disappear into her own makeshift office.

Though most of the museum's basement had been outfitted to meet their needs, there were only a handful of finished, private rooms. The need for secrecy in construction outweighed the need for doors, so the shared quarters the rest of the thieves used remained unfinished. Even the latrine—the true crowning glory of Jeran's engineering feats—had only a curtain to keep eyes at bay. Tahl's office, on the other hand, bore a reinforced door with a lock only three people could open. Tahl himself, Nia, and Jeran had the code, and Jeran only had it because he'd built the thing. Unsurprisingly, the office on the other side of the door was dark, its contents untouched.

If only that was what Tahl had wanted.

"Send Jeran in, too, if you see him," he called over his shoulder. Skilled as the engineer was, he was also given to distraction. Blueprints for the rest of the unfinished headquarters should have been on Tahl's desk.

The back end of the museum's basement had been easy to appropriate for his needs. The first thing they'd done was shuffle the stored art and artifacts to the front, where the stairs descended into the cool storage space. After that, they'd built a wall. Tahl and Niada had done most of that themselves, smuggling in stone through the underground tunnels the rest of the city had forgotten. Jeran had joined before they finished; his expertise meant there was a door hidden in the wall, its edges blending perfectly with the mortared stone. Without knowledge of the hidden switches, there was no way for anyone to access the headquarters from the museum side. No one used that entrance, but it would have been foolish to leave themselves with only one way in and out.

Designing a layout for the rest of the basement the guild had claimed was Jeran's special assignment, but the thief was scatterbrained and often distracted with his more legitimate work. Tahl had offered him a more generous salary in hopes he would leave his job elsewhere in the city, but Jeran had refused. The man was passionate about his work; Tahl couldn't fault him for that. He felt the same way about the guild.

"Here are the books," Nia said as she trotted into his office. Most of the time, he left the door wide open when he was present. The last thing he wanted to do was shut himself off from the rest of his guild. Tahl found other ways to remind his followers who was in charge. He removed the crown from its stand at the back of his office and settled it on his head as Nia dropped the books onto his desk.

A few older members had been startled by his age, but with the crown he'd stolen from Emperor Atoras on his brow, no one questioned his leadership.

Nia swiped a strand of black hair off her forehead and planted her hands on her hips as she stared down at the books. "What exactly are we looking for?"

Tahl pulled one of the green log books off the top of the stack and flipped it open. Dozens of names filled each book, listing professions and residences beside them in tidy rows. It was impossible to keep track of everyone in the city, but anyone involved in noteworthy business got their information written down. "Transport companies, livestock management... Anyone who might be interested in buying horses."

"That could be half the people in the city." She pulled her own book off the pile.

"No, it couldn't. Most people in Orrad have no reason to keep horses. Ebitha's horses are a guilty pleasure she can get away with because she's got a large parcel of land. Few people have that kind of space in the city." He pulled out his chair and sat. One name on the page stood out. He groped blindly in the top drawer of his desk until his fingers found a pen. "Her horses cost her a fortune in feed, since there's not room for them to graze properly. But her husband cut deals with the farmers before he died. The feed hasn't gone up in price, but her money's evaporating, just the same."

Niada paused to peer at him over the edge of her address book. "And what does that have to do with horses and heists, exactly?"

A frustrated sigh escaped Tahl's throat and he glared back at her. "Would you just write down the names? I have a hunch, okay? Something's not right."

Her brows flicked upward before her expression settled to something cool and neutral. She wasn't good at hiding her thoughts and never had been, but Tahl didn't know how to explain what drove him to want to find the missing horse. He'd learned to trust his intuition a long time ago. If something struck him as odd or important, he knew it was.

A shadow appeared in the office doorway. "You wanted to see me, sir?" Ashyl's small voice asked.

Tahl didn't even look up. "Get the lamps." He'd forgotten to light them and hadn't noticed until she'd blocked the doorway and blotted out the light.

The thief made a quick circuit of the office to light the three oil lamps on the shelves. She finished with the one on his desk and eyed the pile of books. A hint of curiosity showed in the way she tilted her head.

"Report?" Tahl prompted before she could ask any questions.

Ashyl straightened. "The wharfmaster isn't going to be easy to convince. He's already reported the guild activity on the docks and even asked Atoras to posts more guards. I scouted his office. Turns out he had it out for Lord Eseri, too."

Nia lowered her book and frowned. "How do you suppose Eseri got things out of port, then?"

"Through a different port," Tahl said. "That man has been wharfmaster for thirty-seven years. If Eseri didn't sway him, my chances aren't great. I know this may come as a surprise to you, but there are still honest men out there in the world. Not everyone can be bought."

The girls exchanged looks. Eventually, Nia shrugged. "So we need another port."

"We'll try heading south," Tahl said. "We don't need anything big, and there are smaller ports all up and down the Ranton."

"What about northwest?" Nia suggested.

Tahl raised a brow.

"There are those new manufactories being built up there. They've expanded the docks there to move freight without it having to pass through the city from the east side." She pursed her lips. "Judging by what I've heard in the city, I think they'll be easy to sway."

"I'd agree with that," Ashyl said. "And since the manufactories are outside the city walls, the guard has fewer eyes in place."

"Then we'll look northwest." Tahl reached out and tapped the stack of the book. "Ashyl, read. We're looking for people who might want horses."

Ashyl's brow furrowed. "Horses?"

"Don't ask," Nia muttered. "You know how he is when he gets a wild hair."

Tahl elected to ignore that. He scribbled down a handful of names and addresses.

A slim finger slid into view, a nicely rounded fingernail pointing out a name on his pad of paper. Tahl blinked twice and let his eyes flick to Ashyl's face. She was close to his age, dark-haired and brown-eyed like most people in the Westkings. Niada had often called her pretty. He wasn't sure he agreed.

"This is one I'm familiar with," Ashyl said. "Do you want me to check some of these out?"

He pushed her hand away and went back to writing. "I want you to look through the address books and write down names, like I asked you to."

She raised a brow. "What's this for?"

Frustrated at the relentless questions, Tahl leaned back in his chair and stared at his notes. "I think..." he began, half-aware of the tingle of magic in the crown against his brow.

Both girls leaned forward and he looked up, determination in his green eyes.

"I need to steal a horse."

CHAPTER 2

SOME TIME AFTER ASHYL AND NIA HAD HELPED TAHL WORK HIS WAY
to the bottom of their list of possible contacts, he closed the door
to his office and buried his face in his hands.

It wasn't unusual for his work to take from dusk til dawn,
especially in the summer, when the nights were short and had to
be used wisely. Summer was now behind them, but this hardly
seemed like a wise use of time, and he slouched in the chair
behind his desk as weariness fell over him. Sometimes he slept
in his office. There was a blanket stuffed under the desk for just
that reason. Suspecting this would be one of those days, he
found the edge of the blanket with his toe and dragged it across
the floor. The crown shifted on his brow and he pulled it off his
head.

The emperor's stolen crown was a pretentious thing to wear,
but the other thieves both respected it and thought it a grand
joke. In truth, he kept it close because he hadn't yet figured out
what it *did*. To someone like him, with just enough of a Gift to
make himself a nuisance, the sense of power about the crown
was barely detectable. He'd taken to wearing it at home for a
while, where he could watch the streets below his windows and

see if anyone came to retrieve it. But no one ever appeared, and Tahl had concluded quickly enough that whatever power rested in the crown, it wouldn't let anyone track him.

What it *did* allow was still a mystery. Mage-enhanced items were more than just rare. The skill it took to weave magic into a physical object was all but a mystery. When Tahl had been part of the academy, he'd spoken to his teachers about such artifacts, more out of curiosity than truly caring how to do it. Such a feat would have been well outside the realm of what he could do. As it happened, it was beyond what anyone could do; his teacher had called the act of enchanting items a Lost Art.

Which means the crown is either older than the empire itself, or the art's not quite as lost as they make it out to be. He ran his thumbs over the gems as he thought. More than once, he'd prodded the crown with his own feeble magic, hoping he'd be able to sense something more than the faint tingle of power. Nothing had ever answered. So he'd worn it for a dozen things, trying to determine if the power in the crown let him detect lies, or think more clearly, or influence people more easily, or any number of other things it had not, in fact, done.

"Maybe it doesn't actually do anything," Tahl muttered to himself as he put it down.

In truth, he didn't know why he kept poking at it. For all he knew, the magic the crown was imbued with only served to ensure it never needed to be polished. He dragged his blanket off the floor, wrapped it around his shoulders, and slumped.

The crown wasn't the only investigation that seemed to be going nowhere. He couldn't learn anything about the crown, couldn't learn anything about the queen, and now it seemed even the horse problem was going to leave him scratching his head.

If Tahl was being honest, his primary concern over the missing horse *was* the old woman's wellbeing. Ebitha was one of few people in Orrad—in his entire life, blight it—who had been kind to him. He'd had guilt over leaving the widow without a stableboy, and he'd never felt guilt over much. Tahl owed it to her to ferret out whoever was destroying her fortune. He didn't know how to begin without staking out the manor, and after taking up the mantle he'd earned and embracing his role as the Ghost of Orrad, that was time he couldn't spare. *But I can get the horse,* he reassured himself as he squinted at the notes spread across his desk.

Most of those notes were unnecessary, but to leave anyone off his list would have given Nia and Ashyl clues as to what he intended to do. Finding Ebitha's horse wouldn't be hard. The missing horse was white, and there was only one person in Orrad interested in obtaining white horses. Finding a way to make sure the horse's absence wasn't *noticed* was the challenge.

"That and getting the stupid thing out of the pasture," he said, scrubbing his eyes with the heels of his palms. Brant's roots, but he was tired. Frustration and exhaustion mingled in his head and as he closed his eyes, he used his Gift to snuff the flames of the oil lamps scattered around the room. The last thing he saw was the crown on his desk, its multicolored gems glittering in the light of that final flame. The memory of clutching it tight to his side as his blood ran down the flank of a snow-white horse made the scar in his leg ache, but Tahl paid it no mind. A cat nap, he promised himself. Then his new heist could begin.

TAHL'S 'CAT NAP' lasted until early afternoon. He fought the urge to grumble as he scrubbed grit from his eyes and stuffed his blanket back under his desk. It wasn't like him to oversleep, but the previous night had not been the only night he'd pushed. There was always something to do in the guild, something to oversee, someone to train. His guildmates seemed to appreciate that he did not believe himself above training exercises. There were few secrets to share beyond suggestions on how to land or where to practice, but it was easy to outpace most of them, and Tahl admitted he got a hint of competitive satisfaction from knowing he was still at the top.

He covered the checkmark-shaped scar under his right eye with wax before he left his office.

Headquarters was empty. Since his sleep had gone uninterrupted, Tahl assumed Jeran hadn't yet returned and likely wouldn't until that night. With luck, those blueprints would be on his desk by morning.

A small, makeshift kitchen area stood in one corner and Tahl stopped there to retrieve something to eat. One of the puzzles the engineer had been working on was figuring out ventilation for fires so they could have proper meals instead of things that could be prepared cold. The museum had a boiler system it used for heat, and Tahl had suggested they figure out a way to vent their fires into the boiler room, but all that had done was send Jeran off muttering about masonry.

Someone had left a box of dried meats and roasted nuts. Tahl considered it, then swiped a piece of unblemished fruit instead. He didn't trust anything he didn't witness the others eating. Desperate as Tahl was for a proper meal, he'd have to make plans to go home that night or he wouldn't get it. *After work is done,* he reminded himself. He retrieved his bag of supplies on the way out.

When he emerged from the sewer tunnels and into the cheery afternoon sunlight, Tahl was tempted to go home then and put the job off for another night. He knew better than to procrastinate, but the draw of a full stomach and a soft bed was almost as irresistible as a siren's call. Resigned to his apple, he started the winding trek across the city. Halfway through the market, he paused to swipe a stick of fried and honeyed treats. Protein was a better fuel, but sugar was a quick boost that satisfied his sweet tooth, too. He'd snatch a bag of almonds or something later to make up for the splurge.

Against the northern sky, the palace stood like a looming cliff. Tahl had not been back since the daring escape that sent him over an actual cliff, and a hint of unease crept up his spine. Even the wax over his scar would do him little good there; he'd entered the castle in disguise. While Nia had pulled off the wax before he began the actual thieving, it was always possible the serving staff would recognize him and put the pieces together. Tahl kept his head down and worked his way toward the north gate.

The gate guards watched people come and go with little interest, but Tahl still waited for a chance to hide from clear view before he slipped past. The chance came when a farmer with an ox-drawn cart came in, his cart heaped with goods to trade. Tahl angled his shoulders and face toward the cart as he walked, pretending to watch his toes, so the guard to his right would only clearly see his back.

Nia sometimes chided him for paranoia, but she didn't understand. The Ghost's face decorated dozens of posters across the city, and all that separated Tahl from the now-infamous thief was a thin ribbon of flesh-colored concealing wax. Bahar Eseri had been sent to the gallows for crimes much smaller than stealing the crown. Tahl couldn't fathom what horrors might wait for the Ghost.

He shook off the thought and breathed deep as he passed beyond the city and wandered into the mess of businesses that lay just outside the walls. The largest part of Orrad's shanty town was on the east side, facing the Ranton river, where work was plentiful in the fisheries and warehouses that lined the docks. North and northwest of the city, there were fewer houses outside the walls and more businesses that no one wanted nearby. Farriers, tanneries, and any number of manufactories lined the roads.

The manufactories were largely new. The first had sprung up a handful of months prior. A half dozen more followed, the buildings in various states of construction. Their existence had caused quite a stir among artisans who had plied their trade in Orrad for generations. Some believed the massive buildings that churned out product would destroy their business. Others merely criticized the smell. Even well away from the first manufactory—more accurately described as a blast furnace for smelting iron—an acrid stench hung in the air.

Given how badly people hated the place, Tahl had long since decided it was a perfect place to hide. If Niada was right about the guild winning over the dock workers that supplied the manufactories, then they could prove a valuable asset to his own brand of business.

He ducked into an alley behind the iron refinery and held his stick of honey treats between his teeth. With his hands free, it only took a moment to climb to the lowest part of the roof. He'd wait for the sun to set, then head for his goal. Tahl took the stick from his mouth and bit into one of the fried treats with a satisfying crunch.

Below, a scrape signaled the opening of a door and Tahl leaned forward to peer down from the shadowed side of the roof, more out of boredom than curiosity. He admitted he knew little about the manufactories and their business. Several processed wool and produced textiles, but none could yet replicate the fine knit that made his heist outfit, so he wasn't particularly interested. They could churn out blankets and broadcloth all day, but until they could make something close-fitting that flexed like a second skin, he had little reason to care.

But the men that shuffled out of the refinery cast furtive glances down the alley before they hustled toward the far end. Tahl frowned. Thieves? They weren't his, nor were they faces he recognized from run-ins around the city. Nor could he fathom what could be inside an iron refinery that might be worth stealing. They hadn't carried anything that he could see.

Worth investigating, he mused as he slipped one of the fried goodies off its stick and stuffed the whole thing in his mouth.

There was always a chance it was nothing; it was possible they weren't doing anything out of the ordinary. Sneaking an extra break, perhaps, or trying to skip out on work. Tahl simply found everything suspicious.

The men did not return. Tahl considered delving inside to see what he could find, but dismissed the idea as reckless when there were people inside. Good as he was at sneaking about, he didn't enjoy taking unnecessary chances, and exploring the refinery—or any of the manufactories—was not why he'd ventured north of the city. He could return another time, perhaps roll the exploration into the job of determining whether or not people in the refinery could be brought over to their side. *A job for Ashyl,* he decided. *She can do it tomorrow.*

The early autumn days had already begun to shrink. By the time Tahl had finished mentally assigning new tasks to his recruits, the sun had dropped low in the sky and the streets began to fill with people leaving their jobs for the day. Seizing the opportunity, he abandoned the roof and moved through the bustle. People were the best disguise, especially when the crowd was full of people who were scarred and shabbily dressed. Tahl took comfort in how he blended in.

Ahead, the docks and their moored ships loomed, dull shadows against a bright streak of reflected light. The river always gleamed at sundown. White at first, then gold. Without any clouds to catch the light, the sunset would be unremarkable. It would also give way to a brighter night, meaning he'd have stars and the wandering soldier moon to contend with. *Nothing I haven't done before.* In some respects, it might help. For one, it would make finding his target easier.

Tahl studied the docks as he approached. Niada was right; they had expanded considerably since the last time he'd ventured northwest. A number of tall-masted ships awaited cargo at the ends of the long piers. Sailors strode between them, some hefting bags and crates, while others merely looked bored.

There were no taverns nearby to catch their interest—something Tahl found unusual, but the new construction along the roads might capitalize on the opportunity—but a handful of makeshift gathering places lined the shore. Men sat at barrels to drink and roll dice, most too distracted to notice Tahl as he crept to the river's edge and cut back toward the east.

Thinking of his last venture toward the promontory gave him a thrill, though without an opportunity to scout beforehand, he had no way of knowing if his plan would work. He knew he had no chance of getting past gate guards, but after his escape with the crown, there was a possibility guards would patrol the entirety of the promontory. But there were ways past guards, and Tahl wasn't about to let the fear of what *might* be scare him off.

The Ranton river was low after the dry summer. Wide swaths of rocky riverbank lined the shore like a low beach. To his right, a dun-colored cliff rose. The rocky face reached higher as he ventured onward, towering overhead like the sheer walls of the palace itself. Fewer people wandered this far from the docks, though the few fisherman pulling traps from the water did little more than glance Tahl's way. It never failed to amuse him how simply acting as if you belonged somewhere made people look the other way.

Near the peak of the bend where the river turned south, Tahl found what he was looking for. The growing dusk hid his movement as he worked his fingers into handholds in the stone and began his ascent. Halfway up the cliff face, he found the hollow where he'd hidden during his escape from the palace. Tahl crawled into the narrow cranny and made himself comfortable to wait for the deepening night. Sheltered on the north side of the promontory, he'd be hidden by thick shadows once the moon rose, and no ships moved on the river to see him when he climbed. He pulled his legs close and flexed his ankles, stretching and limbering what he could in preparation for the challenge ahead.

When night deepened, Tahl drew a deep breath and peeled the wax from his scar. "Okay," he whispered to himself as he swung out from his hiding place and resumed his slow ascent. *Let's go.*

CHAPTER 3

HE'D FORGOTTEN HIS CLIMBING CLAWS. TAHL MENTALLY CURSED himself for the lack of preparation, but didn't let the frustration last long. He couldn't afford any distractions, and it wasn't as if he couldn't climb without them. They'd merely been an investment toward ease in future jobs, purchased shortly after he'd stepped up to claim the title of Ghost. His fingers still found solid handholds with relative ease, his hands strong enough to support him with next to nothing to grip. More than once, Nia had remarked that he climbed like a spider, skittering up walls where she couldn't find anywhere to put her hands or feet. More reasons to train her better, he concluded as he climbed.

The edge of the cliff was not far ahead and Tahl steadied his breathing as he made his approach. Instead of swinging up over the ledge and putting himself back on solid ground, he clung to the cliff face and waited. If there were guards on patrol, he'd hear one eventually.

Long minutes crawled past. A small quiver began in his arms and Tahl shifted to easier handholds. He could hang in one place for some time, but that didn't make it pleasant. A fine mist of sweat beaded on his brow and his heart beat a little harder. He deepened his breath but kept it steady, his ears trained on the sounds of the night on the ridge above.

Nothing.

Satisfied, he slid up over the rocky edge and rolled onto the scraggly grass. It was nowhere near as soft as it had been when he'd escaped with the crown. It prickled through the thin fabric of his shirt and Tahl rolled his shoulders as if to shrug off the itch. He pushed himself to his hands and knees and peered past the fence. Evidently, Emperor Atoras still considered the headland safe. The sprawling field was devoid of people—at least, as far as he could see. At the far end of the pasture, a small grouping of animals stirred, their white coats gleaming like stars in the moonlight.

Either they did not fear the animals would be stolen, or Atoras simply didn't learn.

Guess we'll see which one it is. Tahl brushed prickling bits of dried grass from his dark hair and slid over the fence with ease. Some small part of him was disappointed by the lack of a need for acrobatics, but sense drowned it out. Not every heist was dangerous. Some weren't even challenging. As much as he enjoyed the thrill of a challenge, this job wasn't about prestige. It was a personal mission, and something he felt he owed the old woman who had shown him kindness.

Tahl trotted across the field, mindful of his footing in the dark. He doubted he was clumsy enough to hurt himself walking across grass when he spent most nights vaulting from rooftop to rooftop, but injury often came with complacency. The horses did not seem to notice his approach, or if they did, they didn't care. If Ebitha's horse was among them, the gelding would recognize him and mounting up wouldn't be hard. If he was wrong, then all he had to do was leave. *But nobody else in Orrad collects white horses, so I'm not wrong.*

His confidence proved justified when one of the horses lifted its head. They all looked the same in the dark, but the ghostly outline of the horse's head seemed right. Tahl clicked his tongue softly, hoping to entice the animal. Its ears swiveled toward him as if interested. A hint of hope and anticipation sparked in Tahl's chest. If he could get the horse out of the pasture, getting it back to Ebitha's stable before dawn would be easy. He'd have to find tack to get the animal past the gate guards—a halter and lead, at the very least—but those could be found anywhere in the west fields.

Tahl lifted a hand to invite the horse closer. Instead of pacing toward him, its head swiveled the other direction. Something buzzed against the edge of Tahl's senses.

Almost imperceptible against the dark of night, a shadow moved.

The horse whickered and paced backwards. Tahl darted in to catch its mane at the same time the shadow moved to the horse's other side.

A guard?

No, a *thief*.

Tahl spat a curse.

The sound caught the stranger off-guard and the cloaked figure recoiled. Around them, the other horses startled and milled. Tahl's target horse—Ebitha's gelding, he was sure of it now—tossed his head and huffed.

Before Tahl could murmur reassurances to the animal, the cloaked thief vaulted onto the horse's back and dug booted heels into its sides.

The gelding spooked and bolted, the stranger's cloak billowing as the horse streaked toward the west.

"Of all the horses to steal tonight," Tahl snarled beneath his breath as he caught another animal and swung onto its back, "why *mine?*" He gripped the beast's mane in both hands and squeezed with his legs. The animal turned and tossed its head as it trotted westward. Deeply regretting how rough the bareback ride would be, Tahl kicked hard.

The other rider was small and light. A woman, Tahl decided;

she'd been smaller than him, and though he had grown, his stature was not impressive.

Ahead, Ebitha's horse had already slowed. The thief clung to the horse's neck for dear life as it trotted onward. An inexperienced rider, it seemed. Tahl urged his borrowed horse into a faster canter. The wind whipped at him, the gusting air and charging beast beneath him stirring unpleasant memories of his almost-blundered escape. The long-healed injury in his calf ached at the thought and he chased it away, drawing up his legs, preparing to move.

The thief's horse caught the hoofbeats closing in behind it and picked up its pace. Tahl nudged his mount's flanks and its stride lengthened. Three beats later, he drew up beside the thief and his hand snapped out to grab her arm. The woman cried out when Tahl yanked and the two of them tumbled to the ground.

Silver flashed out from underneath her cloak and Tahl rolled backwards, separating them before the knife made contact.

The horses ran a short distance before they slowed and looped back in opposite directions, like the petals of a flower peeling backwards in bloom. Tahl shook himself. Now was *not* the time to be distracted by details.

The knife flashed at him again and this time, he snapped a dagger from his belt and deflected the blade.

"Take any other horse," Tahl said, his eyes tracking the animal he wanted. "This one's mine."

"*Yours?*" The thief almost choked on the single word, offense thick in her voice.

Tahl tried to dart past but she moved like lightning, lunging at him with her blade ready. Again, Tahl met it, the *ping* of metal on metal sharp in his ears. This time, he pushed into his defense and flung her back. The thief teetered in a moment of lost balance and he whipped a foot forward to sweep her legs out from under her. She yelped and went down hard.

The horse circled wide. Tahl clicked at it again and darted forward to catch it. Nervous, the horse snorted and stamped.

"Shh," Tahl breathed, knowing he didn't sound as soothing as he hoped. "Hey, boy. You remember me." He twisted his fingers in the gelding's snowy mane and softened his knees to spring onto its back.

Something struck his back, hard enough it hurt, but too high for its target. His kidney? She'd tried to punch him in the *kidney?* Instead of leaping onto the horse, Tahl lashed backwards with his foot and took the woman off guard. Her breath left her in a rush and the horse shied. Refusing to let go, Tahl let himself be dragged along. He found his footing a few steps later and swung onto the gelding's back. His arm swung back to swat the beast's rump with the flat side of his dagger. "Get up!"

The horse leaped into action, a moment too slow. Hands snagged Tahl's leg as he sailed by and the thief almost dragged him from his seat.

"Would you give up?" he shouted, hooking his arm around the gelding's neck as the animal surged toward the western gate. The thief latched onto his leg moved a hand farther up to clutch his thigh. She wasn't going without a fight.

Tahl's eyes darted between the cloaked woman and the rapidly looming western gate. There would be no escaping that way, the main entrance guarded by two tall stone watchtowers guaranteed to be swarming with guards. Instead, Tahl shifted to let the woman's weight drag him farther to one side. The pull turned the horse a shade to the north. If they could vault the fence while running parallel to the cliff's edge... It was the only place Tahl knew they could get away.

"Get off!" the woman snarled. She clawed her way up Tahl's side inch by inch. Her hand closed around his arm and he tried to fling her off without losing hold of the horse. Confused and alarmed, the gelding slowed to a tooth-rattling trot, then halted altogether. Abruptly, Tahl's grip gave way and they both fell to the ground.

The woman was on him in an instant. "You bloody thief!" Another knife—not the same one as before—appeared in her hand. She slashed toward his throat, but he struck her arm and the blow went wide. He hitched his hips and writhed, sinuous as a snake, and slid out from under her.

Across the field, lantern light appeared at the foot of one of the guard towers.

"Would you be quiet? Tahl whispered.

She struck at him again and he caught her arm. Though her strength surprised him, she couldn't stop him from wrenching the knife out of her grasp. Her breath caught as it left her fingertips and he wrestled her to the ground.

Voices rose from the towers. Ebitha's horse lifted his head and trotted toward them.

"Brant's bloody branches," Tahl spat.

More lanterns lit. The horse would have to wait until another day.

"Get off me," the woman whispered through clenched teeth.

He wanted to wring her neck. "You started this!" Still, he released her and staggered to his feet. He hadn't realized he'd gotten out of breath.

Shadows milled at the foot of the towers. Men moved toward the gate. Tahl fought a groan and sprinted toward the northwestern corner of the pasture. He could escape down the cliff face if he had to.

Dry grass crunched behind him and he threw a glance over his shoulder. The cloaked thief was close behind him, casting worried looks toward the gate as guards poured in.

All he had to do was outpace her and escape would be easy. They'd catch her, drag her off for questioning, sentence her the way all other thieves were sentenced. The thought put an uncomfortable lump of cold dread in his belly.

The last thing he wanted was for another thief to die. He'd sentenced more than his share to an untimely end, creating a name for himself and waiting while others fought to steal it. The Ghost was supposed to unify the thieves in Orrad, not kill them. Rival as she was, she had to be good to make it into the pasture.

Climbing the cliff face was no small feat, and the only other way in was to make it past the emperor's guards. *She could be useful,* he mused.

As if she hadn't just cost him this heist? He snorted. He owed her nothing. Yet the way her breath came in short, panicked bursts behind him tugged at his heart. If he outpaced her, then her blood may as well have been on his hands.

What a time for chivalry to rear its head, he silently groaned.

"This way." He cut more toward the north. The fence was just ahead, nothing but open air beyond the cliff's edge.

Her step faltered for a single beat. Then her pace quickened behind him.

Tahl vaulted the fence and bounded the short distance to the cliff's edge.

"What—" the thief behind him squeaked. She didn't have time to finish before he dropped to the ground and swung over the edge.

The cliff was not quite so high as where he'd plunged off it before, or where he'd chosen to climb up tonight. The rock was smoother, though, and he struggled to seek handholds she'd be able to follow. He didn't know her climbing capabilities from their short scuffle before. It was safer to think her closer to Nia's level than his. When one foot peeked over the edge of the cliff above and scouted for somewhere to go, he judged his assessment correct.

"Left," he whispered.

Her foot slid left and caught. Slowly, she eased herself down the rock wall.

If he waited, they'd both get caught. Only willing to stick out his neck so far, Tahl hurried to the bottom and breathed a soft sigh of relief when his feet reached the rocky riverbed. He clung close to the wall, watching the woman's descent. Above, the voices of men came closer. There was no way to know if they'd been seen, but now that he was down, there was little chance they'd catch him. He'd been raised on the coast; he was a strong swimmer and could disappear into the river if he needed to. The woman, on the other hand...

She panted as she neared the ground. Her descent had slowed even further. When she came within arm's reach, Tahl grasped her by the back of her heel and yanked. A quiet yelp of fright was all that escaped when she fell.

He caught her and promptly deposited her on the ground. "This way," he whispered. They'd been headed northwest when the guards would have spotted them. Tahl cut due east, hopping across the stones on his toes. He would have loved to have his split-toed shoes, with their soft, flexible doeskin sole, but there was nothing for it now. The woman followed a shade more noisily in his wake.

When they rounded the northeastern point of the promontory, Tahl turned to speak. A knife flashed for his throat and he ducked. How many of the bloody things did she have? He darted in low and brought his shoulder up into her stomach. The thief wheezed and he snared her wrist, immobilizing her knife hand and hitching her over his shoulder. *Brant's roots, she's heavier than she looked.* Tahl fought a wince as he spun to pin her against the rock, his green eyes flashing fire. "I just helped you!" he snarled, voice barely above a breath.

Defiant eyes met his, an angry spark in their depths. He hadn't realized until that moment that her face was covered, a fine, flexible knit fabric pulled up over her nose. The collar of her shirt, he thought. Blight it, he needed a shirt like that. Silently, he promised himself a visit to the old woman who'd knitted his heist outfit.

"You cost me my horse," she snapped.

"His name is Cotton," Tahl retorted, "and he's not yours. Move." He shoved her in the direction he wanted to go. It was a much longer trek back to the city that way, but it would be easier to get into the shabby neighborhoods that framed the city's main port. Those gates were always open; passenger ships arrived all hours of the day and night, and it wouldn't do for visiting dignitaries to arrive by ship only to be shut out of the best parts of the city.

The thief glowered and put down her heels.

"Move," Tahl repeated, his jaw clenched. This time, when she resisted, he grabbed her arm and hauled her over his shoulder again.

She squeaked and kicked hard, but he'd twisted her specifically so she wouldn't be able to reach him with her flailing legs. Her free hand went toward her belt—for a knife, he assumed—and he caught her wrist before she could reach it. Heavy as she was, Tahl had already decided he'd drag her along if he had to. She'd caused him enough trouble for one night. He wasn't about to turn her loose and let her muck things up a second time.

Half a mile downriver, he reached his destination. The shack belonged to a fisherman and was nestled on what had to be the only outcropping of solid ground against the cliff face. More often than not, the man spent his nights drinking and gambling beside Orrad's main docks. It was only chance that had put the man in the new guild's pocket, but his tiny house had proven an asset for Tahl's thieves more than once.

Tahl retrieved the spare key from the underside of a barrel and unlocked the door so he could haul the woman inside. She hadn't stopped flailing or fighting, but at least she had the sense not to scream. Had the guards found them, there was no doubt it wouldn't have ended well.

The shack was empty. Tahl shoved the door shut and thrust the woman into a chair. She lunged forward but he planted a palm on her forehead and shoved her back again, no longer caring if he hurt her. Any number of ropes hung from walls. He caught hold of one and looped it around her, dragging the coils tight before she could wiggle free.

"I've had enough of this," he muttered as he bound her tight.

She tried to kick him as he tied her feet to the legs of the chair and he scowled up at her as he jammed her heel against the wood. He knotted those cords twice.

"What are you doing?" A note of panic rose in her voice.

"What are *you* doing?" Tahl stood and shot her a glare. "I tried to help you and the moment we were safe, you pulled a knife on me."

The woman writhed against her bonds. "You should have run away."

"With you free at my back to try and stab me again? I don't think so." He gave the rope one final tug.

She wriggled a little harder. "Why are you doing this?"

"So you can't follow me home."

"I have no interest in you," the thief growled.

Tahl snorted. "Yeah, well I trust you about as much as a northern green-adder now. If you're a halfway decent thief, you can get yourself out of there by morning."

Her eyes darkened with anger. "I am not a thief!"

"Then what are you?" he challenged.

The woman stared back, defiant. Something in her eyes pricked at him.

Tahl stepped forward and pulled the mask from her face.

CHAPTER 4

THE KITCHEN'S BACK DOOR SLAMMED SHUT. "I STOLE THE QUEEN," Tahl gasped.

Nia spun to face him, alarmed. Her eyes darted toward the door into the inn's main room. It stood open, but they were alone. She hurried across the kitchen to close it. "You did what?"

His heart hammered so hard he could hear his pulse in his ears. "She was in the pasture, trying to get a horse." He'd run the whole way and his breath still came ragged. A scratchy dryness in his throat threatened to choke him. "I threw her over my shoulder and carried her down the river. She's tied up in a fisherman's shack."

"You did *what?*" Nia squeaked.

Tahl couldn't help but cringe. The panic that had to be sprawled across his face was uncharacteristic, but he didn't know how to keep it at bay.

She closed the distance between them in a few steps. "Okay, first off, that's called *kidnapping,* Tahl."

"I'm not a kidnapper," he protested, "I'm a thief. I steal things, I don't kidnap them!"

Nia grabbed hold of his arm and lowered her voice. "What were you thinking? You'll get us all killed!"

He swallowed hard. "I couldn't let her go, but I don't think she can get out on her own. I don't know what to do." That part was hard to admit. His words faltered, but he gave Nia a pleading look. That much came easily, at least.

"Does anyone else know?" she asked.

Tahl shook his head.

"Better keep it that way." She wet her lips with her tongue. "Are you sure it's her?"

"I broke into her room at the palace, Nia. I know what she looks like."

She spread her hands and made a gentle, soothing motion. "All right, all right. We're going to have to untie her. Maybe there's some way we can convince her to ignore us."

His mind turned somersaults at the suggestion. "Untying her isn't enough to convince her we don't mean any harm?"

Nia scowled. "If you just walk in there, untie her and try to leave, you'll hang by dawn. You're going to have to give her something she wants to get her to look the other way." She paused and her eyes narrowed. "Why was she in the pasture after dark? Without guards?"

"I didn't think to ask any questions after I realized she was the bloody *queen*," Tahl said. He hoped he wouldn't have to mention how long it had taken him to realize it. As a thief, himself, he hadn't thought anything unusual about her need to hide her face.

Rolling her eyes, Nia turned him toward the back door. "Wait outside. I'll tell my boss it's an emergency and I'll be out in a minute."

"I'm your boss," Tahl muttered.

"Only half the time." She pressed a finger to her lips and motioned for him to leave.

He retreated to the small yard behind the inn. His breathing had returned to normal, but his heart still thumped an unpleasant cadence in his chest. Part of him felt foolish for fleeing the shack and seeking Nia's help, but he tried to silence its protests. She was his second-in-command for good reason, not simply because she'd known and supported him before he was anyone worth knowing. Nia had a good head on her shoulders.

Better than that, she always put up with his wild schemes. If there was something good to come out of his accidental stealing —kidnapping, he thought with a grimace—of the queen, Nia would know how to find it.

"At least this will be an interesting addition to my reputation," he murmured to himself, rubbing his face with both hands. All he'd wanted was the horse. Why couldn't the job have been simple?

Warm light spilled across the yard as Nia slipped out the back door. She had left her apron behind, but still looked the part of a barmaid, her dark hair up and her long skirt stained with spilled ale. "All right," she said. "Let's go."

Tahl eyed her sleeves, pushed to her elbow. She'd been halfway through preparing vegetables when he'd burst in. "Your boss let you out willingly?"

"I told him my brother got himself in trouble. He knows enough about you to know it's not unusual." Nia stuck out her tongue, but gestured for him to lead.

Unsettled, Tahl turned toward the river.

Though Nia worked in a number of inns throughout Orrad— he liked to consider it gathering intelligence—she seemed to favor those near the east docks. It made sense when Tahl considered how many people came and went by ship. Large as the Westkings were, the ridges of mountains across the center of the conjoined continents were a hindrance for travel. Most goods were transported by ship.

He led the long trek back to the shack, silently praying the fisherman hadn't chosen the short window of Tahl's absence as an opportune time to return home. Whether or not the man worked with the guild, Tahl doubted he'd know what to do if he opened his door and found the queen tied up inside.

As they walked, Nia remained silent. Unusual for her, and Tahl took it to mean nothing good. Even so, her company was reassuring, and he walked with his usual confidence and composure again by the time they reached the shack. A dim light glowed inside. Tahl hoped it was only the lantern he'd left on the table.

Nia went in first.

The queen was still there and the fisherman was still absent. The bound woman raised her head and gave them a dark glare. She couldn't do more with the gag in her mouth.

Something crawled across Tahl's skin, a sensation it took him a moment to place.

Magic.

That was right; he'd already suspected the queen was a mage. Now he was certain, the presence of her Gift tingling in his senses. No doubt she'd feel him, too. The knowledge made him frown. If she was Gifted, why hadn't she tried to free herself with her magic? Or perhaps she had tried, and had failed. Or perhaps the discomfort of being tied and gagged was just enough to keep her from concentrating enough to grasp the flows of power around them.

"Your Majesty," Nia offered in greeting, her tone prim. The queen's expression only darkened further.

Tahl locked the door.

"We have some questions for you. First off, do you know who we are?" With nimble fingers, Nia undid the gag.

"Soul-blighted thieves," the woman spat the moment she was able.

"I am not soul-blighted," Tahl replied dryly. "The priestesses said so themselves."

Nia put out a hand as if to tell him to settle. "So you don't know."

The queen's brows twitched.

"I hope you know this wasn't any plot or plan against you,"

Nia said. "You were just unfortunate enough to be in the Ghost's way."

"The Ghost?" the queen repeated, blinking in confusion.

Nia glanced toward Tahl. He raised an eyebrow in response.

The queen's eyes raked over him. "But you're a child."

"I'm eighteen," Tahl replied, irritated.

Again, Nia motioned for him to settle. "He is the Ghost of Orrad. I thought you would recognize him after he took the crown."

This time, the queen's lips parted with her look of surprise. She studied Tahl again, focused on his face. The feeble lantern light did little to illuminate his features.

Tahl pulled a coin from his pocket and curled his fingers around it. A moment later, it flared to life, glowing softly with the hint of magic he'd used.

The queen's eyebrows flew up. "You're a mage?"

He hesitated. Hadn't she known? Her Gift prickled unmistakably at the edge of his awareness, her power calling out to his. He could have sworn she would feel it, too. "If I was," he said slowly, "I'd be bound to the service of the emperor. The law is that all trainable mages are to be sent to the academy and put beneath Atoras's thumb, is it not?"

"Yes," she replied, cocking her head. "But you're..."

"Not," Tahl concluded for her. He put the mage-light on the table and slid it across the wood with a fingertip. The light remained when he let go. "What were you doing sneaking around the horses?"

"Not trying to steal one," the queen retorted.

Nia choked back a laugh. "Knowing who he is, do you expect anything different?"

"Why that horse?" Tahl asked.

"He's mine."

A halfway useful answer, he mused. "Out of every horse in Orrad, why is that one yours?"

"I bought him." A flicker of uncertainty crossed the queen's features. "I'm not the most skilled rider. I was told he belonged to an older woman."

Which meant Ebitha hadn't been directly involved in the sale. Tahl fought back a frown. "What if I told you the horse was stolen?"

The queen glanced between Tahl and Nia. "From you?"

"From who doesn't matter," Tahl replied coolly. "My job is stealing it back."

"Strangely noble for the thief who stole my husband's crown." The woman lifted her chin, a hint of defiance returning to her eyes.

"He's not evil," Nia said. "He's just..." She stared at him, her hand groping at the air as if to find the answer.

"Unusually motivated," Tahl suggested.

From the odd look both women gave him, perhaps that wasn't the best answer.

"What do you want from me?" the queen asked at last.

Tahl and Nia exchanged glances. He wanted the horse. And for his hide to be intact after they let the queen go. From the desperation in Nia's eyes, he suspected she wanted something else. He spread a hand and motioned for her to go ahead.

She cleared her throat. "Firstly, Your Majesty, we'd like to know your name."

The queen's jaw went slack. "I beg your pardon?"

"Your name," Nia repeated.

"You know who I am."

Tahl crossed his arms and leaned against the table. "That's the funny thing. We don't. Your face is on our currency and the museum's named after you, but by that, I mean it's called the Queen's Museum. We know you're the emperor's wife. Beyond that..." He flicked a hand in helpless dismissal.

"After the Ghost took the crown"—Nia gave him a sidewise glance as she avoided his name—"he realized nobody seemed to know anything about you."

"But I'm your queen," she insisted.

"Shouldn't you be our empress?" Tahl asked.

Evidently, she didn't appreciate the question. Her eyes grew stormy and her face crumpled with a scowl. "Oria."

Nia tilted her head. "What?"

"My name is Oria," the queen said.

Tahl's arms tightened across his chest and he drummed his fingers against his bicep. "Wasn't that the name of the last queen before the first emperor? The woman who founded Orrad?"

"My great-grandmother," Oria said. "Yes. I'm surprised you would know that."

He shrugged. The academy had found it important. "She was the last of the mage queens."

"Not the last," Oria murmured.

A suspicious look drifted over Nia's face. "Mage queens?"

"Before the First Empire, Orrad was the capital of a smaller country that was ruled by matriarchy," Tahl said. "The mage queens were the last bastion against the empire's expansion. That's why Orrad is the capital of the empire now. The emperor saw it as an opportunity to gloat, taking what was once considered an impenetrable city as the heart of his holdings."

"Well look at you, with all your fancy schooling," Nia intoned.

"Indeed," the queen said. Her eyes weighed too heavily on Tahl for his comfort.

He stared back. "Well, now we know why you're called the queen. So is it your choice to keep the people from knowing your name, or is Atoras responsible for that?"

Oria did not reply.

Nia shifted on her feet. "I don't think we're going to get any more answers out of her right now."

"Probably not," Tahl agreed. "But considering how many times she tried to knife me, I don't think untying her is the best idea."

"I thought you were after me," Oria said.

Tahl raised a brow. "I was after the horse. Which still needs to be addressed, by the way. I'm getting it back, one way or another."

Again, her eyes weighed on him, but this time it was with thoughtful consideration. "You said it was your job. You're a thief for hire?"

Curiosity ran through him like a tingle. "I can be."

A slow, devious sort of smile wreathed itself across the queen's face. "Then I have a job for you."

CHAPTER 5

THE ENTRANCE ALONE WAS STILL ENOUGH TO MAKE TAHL uncomfortable.

"Rupert's not going to like this," Nia murmured.

"We don't even know if Rupert is home."

"He was home last time."

"Well then we go left," Tahl said. "Rupert never goes left."

Between them, the queen wriggled in her bonds. They both paused.

"She doesn't know who Rupert is," Nia said.

Tahl couldn't help his grin. "If she's lucky, it'll stay that way." He waved Nia into the narrow mouth of the cavern and tightened his grip on Oria's arm. The queen had given up fighting a while ago, but he felt no more inclined to trust her than when she'd kicked and flailed before he'd stuck her in the fisherman's shack.

Nia trudged on ahead, Tahl's mage-light in her hand. He'd replenished it once they made it to the countryside, safely away from prying eyes. Getting upriver with a bound and gagged woman without drawing attention had been a considerable feat.

"One last thing, Your Majesty," Tahl said as he turned to face her. She still glowered at him, but it was a look of frustration now instead of contempt. He offered his best apologetic smile before he swept her cloak up over her head and wound it so it wouldn't easily come undone. Oria grunted her protest behind her gag.

"I apologize. I know it's inconvenient, but so is bringing you along in the first place." Tahl guided her into the tunnel. "Which, I'd like to remind you, could have been avoided entirely if you'd not pulled a knife on me. Three times."

"He doesn't like unnecessary confrontations," Nia called back.

Tahl cringed. "Rupert," he prompted.

A hint of color rose in Nia's cheeks and she lifted a finger to her lips to indicate she would be quiet. Good.

They wound through the leftmost tunnels of the cavern without incident. If their makeshift guard was present, they saw no sign of him. The cavern connected to the sewer tunnels beneath the city, and by now Nia knew the path well enough to lead without needing Tahl to give directions.

After what seemed an eternity, they reached the foot of the ladder. Nia opened the stone trapdoor while Tahl unwound the queen's cloak from her head.

Oria sucked in a deep breath through her nose the moment she was uncovered.

Tahl pointed up the ladder as Nia scurried through the hole. "You'll have to climb. I'm going to check you for weapons."

The queen started to backpedal, then scowled behind her gag. Undeterred, Tahl stepped closer and skimmed her form with his hands. A dagger in her boot was first to go. Nothing on her arms or thighs. A ridge at her back drew his attention and her eyes widened with fury as he untucked the back of her shirt and his fingertips explored. Tahl unsheathed the knife at the small of her back and twirled it between his fingers.

"A lot of weaponry for a mage," he remarked as he added both her blades to his own small collection. Counting the three she'd pulled on him and lost before, that was five. Enough to rival his own equipment, most days. Satisfied she was disarmed, he loosened the ropes that bound her wrists. "Why not just use your Gift?"

Oria tore the gag from her mouth and threw it on the ground. "Why not use yours?"

Without knowing why, Tahl smirked at her. The expression seemed to be off-putting, for the queen huffed and turned to climb the ladder.

"I'll get the door," Nia said from above.

Tahl politely averted his eyes while the queen scaled to the museum's basement. Unlike Niada and her dress, Oria wore close-fitted pants and a curve-hugging knit shirt that resembled his own heist shirt too much for comfort, but there was something both unseemly and uncomfortable about watching a queen's backside as she climbed a ladder into one's lair. Once she disappeared, he made his way up.

The three of them strode into the guild headquarters together, and everything happening in the front room slowed to a halt. One after another, each of the half-dozen thieves present turned their eyes toward the queen.

"Sir?" Jeran asked, his voice shaky.

Tahl cleared his throat. "Guild, Queen Oria. Queen Oria, this is my guild."

The queen offered a tight smile.

As if nothing were out of the ordinary, Tahl strode toward his office door. "Did you get me those blueprints?"

Jeran almost bounced to the door to meet him. "Yes, sir. They're on your desk, along with a full list of materials necessary for the... project." His eyes darted toward the queen.

"You really are the Ghost, aren't you?" Oria asked softly.

"I'm surprised you still had any doubts." Tahl unlatched the door and let it stand open, as was customary when he was present.

The queen leaned forward to peer inside. "Where are we?"

"Guild headquarters. You don't need to know anything else."

Tahl paced around his desk and pulled back his chair. He sat without taking his eyes off her and pointed toward a set of chairs beside the door. "Come in. Make yourself comfortable. Let's discuss this business proposition of yours."

Oria sat on the edge of a chair, resting her hands on her knees. "I would like to know who Rupert is."

"He's our bear," Jeran put in helpfully from the doorway.

Her eyes widened.

"He's *a* bear," Tahl corrected. "He doesn't technically belong to anybody. Which is why we like to know when he is home."

"It's also entirely possible that he is a she," Nia added as she posted herself at Tahl's back. "We're waiting to see if there are cubs in the spring. Then we'll have three Ruperts."

"This doesn't sound entirely sane," Oria said.

Tahl flashed her a grin. "Welcome to the guild."

"What makes you think there would be three?" Jeran asked in a low voice.

Tahl flicked a hand. "Out. I'm doing business."

Jeran ducked his head and disappeared from the doorway. They'd have to discuss the blueprints, but that was best left for another time.

"So," Tahl said, lacing his fingers together as he let his attention settle on the queen. "You want me to steal something."

Oria offered a grim smile. "Assuming you can find it."

"Thieves are treasure hunters with a higher risk tolerance. Trust me, I can find it."

"Perhaps." One of the queen's slim fingers tapped a nervous rhythm against her knee. "It's a shipment. Somewhat large, multiple crates. I want them all. But I don't know where they're coming from. I don't think the contents originate in the empire. I think they may be coming from the north, but I can't rule out the possibility of Raeldan."

Tahl watched her hand. Her finger grew still when she finished. Was it the information that made her nervous, or the contents of the crates she wanted? "Intercepting cargo at point of import should be easy. Even if it's brought by land, it can only enter Orrad through so many avenues."

The corner of her mouth twitched.

"It is entering Orrad, yes?" Tahl asked, careful to sound neutrally disinterested.

She gave a single nod. "I believe so." No finger taps that time.

Nia's hand brushed his shoulder. One finger pressed against his collarbone. She'd noticed it too. He glanced up, pretending she only wanted his attention.

"Water?" Nia offered.

Tahl shot the queen a questioning look.

"No, thank you." Oria gave him that solemn smile again.

"Just us. Thank you." He motioned between his chest and Nia with a thumb and watched her leave. Then he returned to his questions. "Who's importing it?"

Oria's hands tightened against her knees. "That's none of your concern."

"Your husband?" he guessed.

Her eyes hardened. "Who is importing it isn't relevant to the job."

"No, but knowing who I'm getting myself in trouble with is." Tahl reclined in his chair and stroked his chin. The hint of stubble there startled him. He needed a chance to go home, rest, and recuperate.

"You're already in trouble with my husband," Oria said.

Tahl allowed himself a chuckle as his eyes swept toward the crown nestled among the belongings on his shelf. "So I am."

The queen followed his gaze and studied the crown with a hint too much interest.

He stroked his chin again. "You know what it does."

Oria shifted forward and hovered at the edge of her seat for a moment before she rose. "You know a lot about magic for someone who claims not to be a mage." She paced around his desk to stand before the shelf and study the crown, her hands clasped behind her back.

"It's important knowledge." Tahl watched her, but did not move.

"You've worn it?" Her hand lifted, as if she wanted to touch the glittering gems, but she forced it back down.

"Have you?" he countered.

The queen blinked at him. Then a faint smile pulled at her delicate lips. "I have a crown of my own."

"It would seem so." Tahl straightened as Nia returned with a pair of cups in hand. They were simple earthenware, nothing like the collection of fine crystal and molded silver that decorated his shelves. From the look on Oria's face, she found the difference interesting, too. He took a cup and took a sip. "We haven't discussed payment."

"Two hundred thousand pims."

Tahl choked on his water.

"For cargo retrieval?" Nia asked as she rested a hip against the corner of the Tahl's desk. "What's in the boxes, bricks of gold?"

Oria lifted her chin. "That's what I'm willing to pay. Take it or leave it."

Water dripped from Tahl's chin and he swiped it away with the back of his hand. "You're asking me to go into this practically blind. You've given me no real information about the job. You can buy ignorance from peasants, but not from me." He thunked his cup onto the desk.

"I don't think you have a choice." Annoyance glittered in the woman's dark eyes. "You can aid me or you can die for kidnapping the empire's queen."

"Only a fool would make a decision based on the money alone." He stood and circled the desk with Nia at his heels, putting himself between the queen and the door. "Besides, you can't do anything to me. You're trapped here."

Her eyes widened and she lunged forward, but Tahl caught

her and flung her back. She crashed into the shelves, trinkets and treasures raining to the floor around her. He grabbed Nia by the arm, hauled her out of the office, and slammed the door.

"All of you, come here!" Tahl roared.

All across the headquarters, thieves popped to their feet. There were never more than a half-dozen people in the headquarters at once, aside from Nia and himself, a rule Tahl had established based on safety more than space. The six present now were quick to answer his call.

"Jeran," Tahl began, "you're on guard duty, since you know the code to my office door. The door is not to be opened unless your life depends on it. Hadren, I want maps of every known trade route across the Westkings, prioritized by the amount of use they receive. Danella, pull names for every importer you can find in the books."

The thieves nodded and dispersed, while the others tensed, awaiting command.

"Chata and Minn, you two set up a rotation schedule to have two fighters in here at all times to play backup to Jeran. Perton, pull contacts. I need someone in the palace and someone at every dock."

"Aye, sir," Perton said, flicking a salute from his brow. The others scurried away.

"Nia," Tahl said, "you're with me."

She bounced on her toes beside him. "What are we doing?"

"The most fun thing of all." He forced a smile. "Research."

THE WINDING ALLEYS WERE LESS FUN THAN THE ROOFTOPS, BUT THEY were safer during the day. Tahl paused at a corner to rub his eyes. They'd started to burn, reminding him of how little rest he'd gotten curled up in his office chair. When he finally had a chance to collapse into bed, he suspected he'd sleep like the dead.

"Your mark is still there," Nia said as she crept to his side. She'd inched ahead some time ago, less of her own volition and more because Tahl suggested their mission presented a useful opportunity for her to practice. Her stealth skills had come a long way, but she wasn't the sneaking sort of thief like he was. She had sticky fingers and impressive sleight of hand, which worked well in conjunction with her day job. Nia was always able to coax a few extra coins from a drunk's pocket, or spirit away some of the winnings when she helped a gambler scrape his pile of silver pims into a cup.

Tahl rubbed his eyes again and squinted against the morning light. "Is it?" He'd been back by the academy a dozen times since his petty act of vandalism, but he admitted he had never really *looked*. Sure enough, the emblem he'd adopted—the hooked lines and oval that resembled a hood and leering eye, a symbol Nia had designed—still adorned the front of the building.

It wasn't exactly a surprise. He'd blasted the sooty marks into the stone with his Gift and exhausted himself in the process. The mages had eliminated the black marks, but a pale outline of the symbol remained where the stone had been etched away.

Odd, Tahl thought, to see his mark emblazoned in black and then scrubbed away to leave it light. Something about the difference made the back of his neck prickle.

"I guess not even the academy has the power to undo it." He rubbed his neck and willed the discomfort to subside. He turned to share instructions for their impending infiltration and found Nia staring at him with a subtle frown. Tahl blinked. "What?"

"You never say much about the academy." Nia's eyes darted toward the building. "You told me they put you out and said you couldn't learn. But you can make your smoke, and those little lights. I can't imagine that's all they've taught you."

He snorted. "The fact they kicked me out should tell you everything you need to know. As far as they're concerned, I may as well not be Gifted at all. Come on." He slipped out of the alley and strolled across the plaza with his hands in his pockets, gazing up at the building's front. Staring didn't seem to be unusual. A handful of the people crossing the plaza as they went about their work watched the place, either studying Tahl's handiwork or puzzling over the existence of the mages themselves.

Nia's curiosity wasn't unusual, either. The mages didn't welcome outsiders. Those who were not Gifted were shunned— as were those who weren't Gifted *enough*. Tahl had sometimes wondered what their benchmark for proficiency was and how far short he'd fallen. Then he reminded himself it didn't matter. Study only offered control over the power one had been given. No amount of study could expand the reach of one's Gift.

He was weak. He'd been born weak, and short of divine intervention, the depth of his magic would not change.

They circled to the back of the academy by a narrow access road Tahl suspected was only ever used for delivery of supplies and for sneaking in through the back door. The latter, somewhat amusingly, was precisely what he intended to do. It wasn't unusual for students to sneak in and out, and while they always acted as if it was some close-guarded secret, every student he'd crossed paths with had known the kitchen door was often unlocked.

"What are we hoping to find here?" Nia asked. She did not whisper, but she kept her voice so low he almost didn't hear.

"Information." Tahl peered into the stately yard behind the academy. There were people present, but that was not unusual. The medicinal garden out back required a lot of attention, and those Gifted with healing often rose early to tend the plants. "I learned a few things, but not enough, apparently. I was under the impression Oria—the founder Oria—was the end of the mage queen line."

A small wrinkle appeared between Nia's brows. "What does that have to do with this job?"

"When it has to do with your potential employer, it has everything to do with the job." Tahl drew back as a student emerged from the back of the academy's main building and meandered into the garden. After she was gone, he motioned Nia forward. "I'll explain more when we get into the library. This way."

Together, they tip-toed across cobblestones with thick veins of velvety moss between them. The garden behind the academy was quiet, peaceful, and despite the hint of tension that crept between Tahl's shoulder blades, a sense of calm settled over his mind. He'd never been fond of the gardens when he'd been in the academy, had never spent much time outdoors. He'd always preferred the basements, where students challenged each other to games of petty thievery and pranks. Perhaps he'd missed another calling. *A houseplant,* he decided. *Once we're finished with this, I'll get a houseplant.*

Nia hung close at his back and for the first time since their expedition had begun, Tahl couldn't hear her footsteps. Good. That was progress. He slid the kitchen door open and crept inside.

Despite the stealth, there was no chance they wouldn't be noticed. Nia froze just inside the door. The kitchen beyond was filled with workers, Giftless men and women who scrubbed pots and baked bread. The aroma reminded Tahl he hadn't had a proper meal yet, either. *Later,* he promised himself.

Though a handful of people paused to squint at him, Tahl waved Nia in and continued to sneak, ignoring the workers around them. The attitude was normal among mages and it only took a moment for the watchers to roll their eyes and return to their jobs.

Nia hurried to follow him, though she cast worried glances toward the kitchen staff. Her reaction wasn't unusual for an outsider either, something he'd counted on to get them through the door. To anyone in the kitchen, Tahl would simply appear to be a student sneaking a girl to his room. That wasn't unusual either, he thought with a hint of chagrin. The last thing he wanted was for anyone to assume he had an interest in *Niada,* of all people, but he wasn't above using such an assumption to his advantage, disgusting as he found the idea of romance with a girl who could have been his sister.

He beckoned her into the hall and she raced after him, her eyes wide.

"Everyone saw us," she whispered.

"They saw what they wanted to see," Tahl whispered back. "Not us."

She blinked at him, clearly not understanding what he meant. He waved a hand to dismiss the subject. He could explain later. Right now, they had a goal.

Tahl straightened his spine and strode onward. Though most mages hailed from noble families, many had become nobles because they were mages in the first place. Every student who walked the halls had a hint of swagger in their step. Tahl wasn't one to swagger, exactly, but he did channel confidence, walking with his head up and his jaw set with determination.

By the time they reached the end of the hall, Nia had picked up on the changes in his behavior and mimicked them. Tahl grinned. From the lofty way she held herself, he might have sworn she was one of them, too.

"The library is upstairs," Tahl said, less mindful of his volume as he rounded the stone banister of a grand staircase and began to climb. Mages did not need to whisper, as long as they weren't doing anything suspicious. Visiting a library in a school was the farthest thing from suspicious Tahl could imagine. "Hopefully they'll have what we need."

Nia's eyes roamed the fine carpets and expensive paintings as they ventured through the halls. "I can tell Orrad's mages have an appreciation for the finer things in life." She kept her voice low, but she'd added a hint of an accent. Western, he thought, envisioning her as a young woman from beyond the mountains that ridged the center of the continent. A good disguise, and something he could work with. She didn't have to be a lover, which was good, given how repulsive the notion was. She could be a relative come to visit, who wanted to see the school where her brother—or maybe cousin, he'd have to decide —studied.

"Shouldn't we? Aside from the royal family, we're the highest-ranking nobility the city has."

Nia sniffed. "Well, some of you are higher-ranking than others."

A hint of a smirk curled the corners of his mouth. Other members of the royal family—cousins, nieces, and nephews of Emperor Atoras—had attended the academy during Tahl's stay, and many nobles had their own ties to the throne. Yet she was right, and she didn't even know it. Even amongst themselves, the mages had a pecking order, and it didn't often correlate to how strong in their Gift they were.

"Perhaps," he agreed, allowing just a hint of mystery into his tone.

Mages roamed the upper floors, filtering between their classes and quarters. Tahl's skin itched around that much magic and he fought the compulsion to scratch. Everyone described the presence of magic a little differently, though most agreed it was something of a tingle. For Tahl, it felt more like the pins-and-needles sensation of a limb gone to sleep, uncomfortable and distracting.

His own Gift offered a hint of protection now. The mages—none he recognized, fortunately—cast him sideways glances, but disregarded him just as quickly. They could assume he was a new student for all he cared. It wasn't as if he was going to stay.

He led Nia to the far end of the hall and through a door, into a large library crammed with so many shelves there was scarcely room to walk. Nia studied the books and a hint of hesitance broke through her comfortable facade. Tahl had spent more time tutoring her since the new guild's formation, but she'd started from a disadvantage and was slow to catch up. She had become a competent reader in most departments, but the stiff academic language in history books still posed a challenge.

"I'll help," he offered quietly as he delved between the stacks, motioning for her to follow. "We're looking for a specific book, but I don't remember who wrote it."

"Do you know what it's called?" Nia asked in a whisper.

"If I remember right, it's *Pre-Empirical Colonies and Cultures,* but I might be wrong on that. It's been a few years." Tahl allowed himself a rueful smile.

She snorted. "They make it sound like it was a long time ago. Atoras is only the fourth emperor."

Tahl made a soft sound of agreement. "He took the throne the year I was born. The empire was hardly a hundred years old when that happened."

"I guess a hundred years is a long time."

He shook his head. "Not to mages." He trailed his fingers

across the books. "Mages live a lot longer than other people. Magic extends their lives. To a mage, especially an angry mage who feels her bloodline has been wronged, a hundred years isn't that long."

Nia pulled a book partway off the shelf and paused. "Tahl?"

He glanced over his shoulder.

"Will that happen with you? Living... longer?"

Somehow, he'd never stopped to consider the possibility. "I don't think so," Tahl said. "It's different for skilled mages. I mean... all I can do is this." He snapped his fingers and a plume of smoke wafted from his hand. A scent like that of a recently extinguished candle filled the air.

Nia waved it away. "Better not do that in the library," she said. "You'll upset the librarians."

"Fair," he chuckled, returning his attention to the books. "See anything?"

"No. It would help if you could remember the name of the author. Colonies and culture whatever isn't going to get us too far." She put back the book and wandered around the corner. "Why are we looking for a book, anyway?"

Tahl crept into the next row over. "I think she's lying."

"That would be no surprise. You have a reason?"

He had several, but it was best to keep things simple. "She said the founder Oria was her great-grandmother, but Oria was a powerful mage and the empire is only one-hundred-and-twenty-two years old. The founding queen was old when the empire rose, but not that old. Depending on how rich her mage blood was, she could have lived three hundred years or more."

Something clunked against the shelf. Nia had dropped a book. "Three *hundred?*"

"Maybe longer," he reminded her.

"So if this Oria isn't that Oria's great-granddaughter, who is she?"

Tahl rubbed his chin and pulled a book from the tidy rows. It wasn't the one he was looking for—he knew that one chronicled the bloodlines of the mage queens—but it might share the same information. "I think... well, she's a strong mage. I think she's that Oria's daughter."

A thump sounded near the door. "Who's in here? Library hours are over!"

"Time to go," Tahl announced. He cut through the row where Nia searched and caught her arm on the way. She barely had time to put back her book. Tahl held on to his.

"I'll be taking this to my room," he announced as he emerged from the stacks. "I need to—" His eyes fell on the mage in the doorway and he froze.

"Tahl?" The young man's brow furrowed and his gaze locked onto Tahl's face.

One important element of his disguise had been forgotten in his haste, Tahl realized. The mage's eyes raked over the distinctive scar and he grew pale as recognition struck.

"You're the Ghost?"

CHAPTER 7

TAHL DRAGGED NIA BEHIND HIM, WHERE HER SMALL FRAME WAS safely hidden by his form. He lifted his chin and met the mage's eyes. It was defiant, a challenge, and probably unwise, yet he had seethed with resentment toward the academy and everyone in it for so long that he didn't know how else to react. Even Colbin, the mage in front of him, couldn't escape that, and he'd been as close to a friend as Tahl got. Nia didn't count; she was family.

"I'd heard the Ghost was a mage," Colbin said, his eyes round with disbelief. "I hadn't thought it was true. I didn't see how one of us... Blight it all, you're the most wanted criminal in Orrad."

Tahl held up his book. "I'm taking this."

The mage looked troubled. "I should stop you. I'm stronger than you are."

"Your magic is more powerful than mine," Tahl replied, a shade more hotly than he intended. "Don't confuse magic for strength."

Colbin's frown deepened. His eyes returned to Tahl's scar. "What happened to your face?"

Nia shrank against Tahl's back as if to seek shelter. He reached back to touch her arm and steady her. If they had to run, she had to be ready.

"One of the Elite," Tahl said.

The mage sputtered a moment before he found words. "And you survived? Brant's roots, Tahl!"

"Like I said," Tahl murmured as he tucked in his chin, "don't confuse magic for strength. Step aside, Colbin. I won't hurt you if I don't have to."

Again, the mage's face twisted in a deeply troubled look. "I'm a librarian now," he said softly. "I can't let you take the book. I'd get in trouble."

Tahl released Nia's arm. "Well, that's inconvenient then, isn't it?"

"Tahl," Nia whispered, a hint of fear in her voice.

He spread his hand behind his back in a gesture for her to be quiet. "But if you're a librarian, maybe we can work something out. Shut the door for a few minutes and let me read. Once I get the information I need, I'll be more than happy to leave the book here. As well as the ones in my bag."

Nia touched his arm as if to ask a question. Tahl ticked a finger at her. He knew the question before she asked. That he hadn't brought his bag wasn't important.

Colbin's tongue darted over his lips, betraying his nervousness. He stepped forward and shut the door. "I'm going to have to report that you were here. There's no way nobody will know. Someone will have seen you."

"They'll have seen the Ghost," Tahl corrected. "My name is not to be mentioned. If you play along well enough, we'll earn you a commendation for your skill in deterring me from the library. Let's not forget that nobody's foiled me yet." He raised a brow as if in invitation for Colbin to dispute the fact.

Instead, the mage grew more pale, though a hint of something familiar lit his eyes. Ambition. Greed, perhaps. "Ten minutes," Colbin whispered. "That's all I can give you before someone will notice I'm missing. I'm supposed to be aiding a lecture down the hall."

Satisfied, Tahl nodded and opened the book. Ten minutes wasn't likely enough to find what he needed. The book in his hands wasn't even the one he'd come for. He licked his finger and turned a page. "I don't suppose you have a copy of *Pre-Empirical Colonies and Cultures* handy, mister librarian?"

"What?" Colbin's brow furrowed. "No, it was pulled from our collection about a year ago."

Tahl's eyes darted up. "Who pulled it?"

"Well, maybe pulled wasn't the right word," the mage said. "It just disappeared. It wasn't culled, I don't think. It was still part of the curriculum. I actually tried to replace it, but there wasn't a copy to be found anywhere in Orrad."

"Brant's bloody branches," Tahl muttered.

Nia peeked out from behind him. "Let me guess. Oria?"

"Or Atoras," Tahl said. "Someone who doesn't want us to find what I'm after."

"Which is?" Colbin asked.

Nia and Tahl both regarded him with skeptical stares.

The mage crossed his arms and shrank back against the door. "I'm a librarian. If you're here for information, maybe I can help."

Tahl conceded there was little doubt of that. If Colbin had gone hunting for *Colonies and Cultures* out in the city, Tahl was certain the mage knew what the book contained. He was less certain he wanted one of the mages to know what he was looking for.

A hint of worry crept into Colbin's expression when Tahl did not respond. "It's an unusual subject for a thief to be studying. If you could tell me more about what you're after..."

Did he genuinely want to help? Or was he prying so he could tattle? Tahl's eyes narrowed as he turned another page. "Orrad is a rich city with an equally rich history."

"A treasure from the old kingdom?" the mage guessed.

"That's one way to put it." Tahl could work with that assumption. He didn't have to verify it, and it wasn't as if the words had come from his mouth. Sometimes the best way to mislead someone was to let them mislead themselves. "They were powerful mages. Would *Colonies and Cultures* mention if the mage queens were Gifted in the Lost Arts?"

Colbin perked up. "You're looking for an artifact? I don't think *Colonies and Cultures* touches on that, but you might be interested in *Annals of Archaic Arts*. It's a first-century title, published immediately after the empire's founding." He hurried into the stacks.

"Tahl," Nia murmured uncertainly. Her fear was understandable, but Tahl pressed a finger to his lips. He'd already decided to shift his focus to a safer subject.

He followed the mage. "Do you know anything about the crown?"

"Like the old kingdom's monarchy? Not a lot. The queen was slain when the city was conquered, but most of the royal family was already gone." Colbin pulled a book from the shelf and skimmed its index.

Tahl raised a brow and cast Nia a smirk. She scowled back at him. He didn't care. If the royal family fled prior to the siege of Orrad, it made his suspicion about the queen that much more possible. "That's interesting, but I meant the actual, physical crown."

The mage froze with his finger on the page as if he'd suddenly remembered who he spoke to. "You mean the one you stole?"

Tahl flashed him a grin.

Suspicion and a hint of fear mingled on Colbin's face for a time before curiosity peeked through. "You think the crown is an artifact? If I could see it—"

"No," Tahl and Nia replied at the same time. He planted a hand on her forehead and pushed her behind him again.

"Right," the mage muttered. He cleared his throat as he skipped a few pages and held out the book. "Here. Chapter four is about pre-empirical artifacts. They all belong to the crown, you know. I mean Atoras, not... your... thing." His face crumpled into a scowl.

Tahl shrugged as he skimmed the page. It was longer than what he'd be able to read in a few minutes, but he hoped some piece of information would jump out at him. "If he didn't want anyone to take it, he shouldn't have left it on his pillow."

"His *pillow?* Blight it, do you have a death wish?"

"There's a gallows with his name on it at this point," Nia remarked dryly.

Colbin looked at her for the first time. "Who's this?"

"Sparrow," Tahl said without missing a beat. "My second-in-command. This says the crowns of the last three mage queens were destroyed when the first emperor took power. The gold was melted into a new crown for the emperor. Would that allow the magic in an artifact to be preserved, or would it be destroyed when the object lost its original form?"

Forgetting Nia was there, Colbin stepped forward to look at the book. "I don't know. I don't think artifacts can be destroyed at all. Something about the magic in them protecting their form. But it's hard to say, because artifacts are so rare, and the mages who could make them have been gone since—"

"Since Orrad fell?" Tahl suggested. "How strong were the queens?"

"I don't know," the mage admitted. "They say the old blood was still thick enough in them that their ears were pointed." His hand drifted to his own ear to rub the smooth, rounded helix.

Tahl almost wanted to do the same. "They must've been incredibly strong, then. Even the most powerful Masters in the Westkings barely have any point at all."

"Strong enough to make artifacts, I'm sure. But they wouldn't have been involved in the forging of the emperor's crown."

"No," Tahl agreed. "But maybe she wouldn't have needed to be there. All she had to do was get to it afterward."

Nia cleared her throat. "I think it's time for us to go."

Tahl clapped the book shut and pushed it into Colbin's hands. "Agreed. Although..."

The thoughtful note in his voice was apparently alarming, because Colbin took a step backwards.

"I have a job for you," Tahl said.

Behind him, Nia groaned.

"I'm not helping you," the mage replied. "You were excommunicated. You're not even a mage, as far as the academy is concerned. I'm going to get in enough trouble just talking to you."

"Aw, Colbin," Tahl started in his best persuasive tone, pressing a hand to his chest as if to signal hurt. He took a step forward, and for all that his gesture was earnest, he knew the movement would be threatening.

Colbin shrank back.

Tahl advanced on him and grinned. "How would you ever get in trouble for being kidnapped by the Ghost?"

"Sparrow?" Nia's tone was flat and unamused, though Tahl thought he saw a glimmer in her eyes.

"You're small and flighty," he said. "It's a good name."

Between them, Colbin groaned. Tahl had pulled the sack off his head after they'd made it halfway through the sewers, but he still dragged his feet and stumbled about as if he'd been blinded. The dramatics had begun to wear on Tahl's nerves.

Nia didn't seem bothered. "What if I wanted to pick my own name? What if I wanted to be something else? Like... Lark, or something."

"So you're okay with the bird theme, just not Sparrow?"

"I never said that."

Colbin groaned again. "The headmaster is going to kill me."

"We're all going to make sure that doesn't happen." Tahl tried to sound reassuring, but he suspected his flat tone fell short. "Having a mage I can rely on would be useful. I promise we'll make it worth your time."

"But I don't want you to rely on me!" Colbin protested. "I just want to sit in the academy with my books!"

Nia prodded his side when he slowed down. "Keep going. Tahl's got something figured out already that'll keep you out of trouble."

"How do you know?" the mage moaned. "He hasn't said anything that—"

"Because I know him," Nia snapped. "You don't question the Ghost."

The anger in her voice caught Tahl by surprise. Where had that come from? He motioned for her to settle. "She's right. About me knowing what I'm doing, not... questioning. People are allowed to ask questions." He shot a reproachful look at Nia behind Colbin's back. She tucked in her chin as if she meant to sulk.

Colbin didn't seem reassured.

"The point is," Tahl continued, "I know what I'm doing. All you have to do is play along. You do one small thing in my headquarters for me, and I do one big thing to benefit you."

"What big thing?" The mage's voice quavered.

Tahl nudged him toward the ladder that led to the museum's basement. "You'll see."

Though Colbin groaned, he did climb.

Still sulky, Nia leaned close enough to share a whisper the mage couldn't hear. "You're still sure he won't attack us?"

"I don't think he can at this point," Tahl whispered back. "We just have to watch him."

The mage had tried to fight them off in the beginning,

thinking his Gift had the two thieves outmatched. But he'd forgotten one tiny element Tahl hadn't. Magecraft took concentration. Fear disrupted power. With two thieves to wrestle, both of them armed and ready to jab him with a half-dozen daggers, he wasn't granted much time to focus.

Normally, Tahl would have ushered Nia up next, but he didn't trust his former classmate with the slight girl. Alone, Colbin might try to overpower her, and probably could. Tahl scurried up the ladder instead, then turned to offer Nia a hand. She waved it away with a scowl that said she didn't appreciate the gentlemanliness.

Shrugging, Tahl slipped a knife into his hand, caught Colbin by the arm, and steered him toward the door.

"Where are we?" the mage asked.

"Home." Tahl thrust open the door and urged him inside. Heads popped up across the room as he escorted his new prisoner into the guild's headquarters.

Jeran rose from his chair in front of Tahl's office door. "Another one, sir?"

Colbin sucked in a breath, but Tahl spoke before he could ask. "To help with the first."

The thief nodded and scooted his chair aside. Tahl had expected a racket inside the office, but it was deathly silent. A mage's presence prickled at his senses. From the way Colbin tensed beside him, he felt it, too.

Tahl let him go. "Here's your task. There's a mage in here. When the door opens, I guarantee she's going to attack me. I want you to hold the flows of magic outside of her reach so that she can't use them against me. My goal is to speak with her without either one of us coming to harm."

"How'd you get a mage in there if you can't do that by yourself?"

"Well..." Tahl scratched his chin with a thumb. "She went in willingly. It was the getting shut in that she wasn't happy with."

Colbin muttered something about a death wish.

Another thief joined them without being beckoned. She and Jeran positioned themselves behind the mage, along with Nia. Tahl gave them a nod. It helped when his guildmates worked without direction, and it helped to know he wouldn't have to watch his back while he spoke with Oria.

At least, speaking was what he *hoped* would happen. He'd half expected her to break out. Since she hadn't, either he'd underestimated the complexity of Jeran's locks, or she'd decided to bide her time until Tahl came back.

Bracing himself, Tahl fitted his fingers to the latch and pushed in the code. The current of magic in the air shifted as Colbin seized the flows and rerouted them. The door eased open. The office beyond was dark.

Tahl stepped inside.

Almost instantly, the leg of a broken chair swung for his head.

He ducked, and his hand shot out reflexively to catch the queen's arm.

She gritted her teeth and his senses tingled as she reached for magic. The flows skirted her grasp and her eyes widened.

Tahl spun hard and slammed her into the wall. She sucked in a sharp breath and the broken chair leg fell from her hand.

"Your Majesty," Tahl began.

Oria twisted in his grasp and swung a knee for his groin. He shifted sideways and she struck his thigh instead, yielding a grunt.

"Let go!" she snarled as she kicked again.

This time, Tahl spun aside, still holding her arm, and caught the back of her leg with his ankle. He swept it out from under her and together, they toppled to the floor.

Nia jerked forward but Tahl's hand flashed up in a signal for her to stop.

In the single moment both her hands were free, the queen slapped him hard enough to rattle his teeth. Tahl twitched his head once, as if to shake off the blow, and wrestled both her arms to the ground. Her limbs writhed like snakes and it took every bit of strength he had to pin her hands over her head so he could shove back her fiery hair.

She gasped in indignation, but he'd seen enough.

The edges of her ears were scarred.

Tahl gripped her wrists with both hands and glared down at her. "You lied to me. You're old blood. You're as old as the empire itself."

Oria spat at him.

He didn't even flinch. "Why did you lie?"

The queen's jaw tightened.

"Intercepting shipment," he muttered. "You'd be the first person in line to undermine the emperor's rule. What's in the shipment, Oria? Artifacts?"

Her eyes widened.

Just outside the doorway, a low murmur passed between the thieves.

"This might come as a surprise, Your Majesty, but I *like* the empire," Tahl said.

"And you believe I don't?" Oria snapped. She twisted her wrists in his grasp.

He tightened his hold. "What's in the boxes?" He expected she'd reach for magic again, but she didn't. Instead, she merely met his gaze, a steely glint in her eyes.

Frustration bunched between Tahl's shoulder blades. "I know who you are. I know what the first emperor did to your mother. Give me one good reason I shouldn't truss you up and hand you back to Atoras as a traitor."

"Because we're on the same side." Her words were clipped but clear, her voice low enough that the thieves just outside leaned closer.

Tahl's eyes narrowed. When he said nothing, she went on.

"If I had been honest, would you believe me when I say that? When I say I love Orrad and want the city to prosper, with or without me as its leader?" Her chin lifted, just a shade. She no longer struggled beneath him. "Atoras is a hard man, but a strong ruler. My mother was not, which was why her kingdom fell. If I am to protect my people, then I must protect the empire."

"Noble," Tahl said.

Frustration crinkled her brow. "If I am to protect this city, these people, I need help. Please."

His grip on her wrists eased a shade. "Then answer a question."

Oria's brows rose in expectation.

He couldn't see it in the darkened office, but if the queen was still there, it had to be there, too. "What does the crown do?"

Her mouth tightened and for a moment, he thought she meant to refuse. Then she sighed and closed her eyes. "I am not skilled at imbuing. My mother was, but I didn't have time to learn. I..." Her lips twitched and she shook her head, as if to dismiss the tangent. "It's to soften his disposition toward me. To make him warmer and more receptive to my suggestions and advice."

Tahl bit back a curse. "Mind control?" He hadn't realized that was possible.

Oria shook her head. "Magic can't control anyone. But it creates a... a fondness. It grants him a sense of comfort and wellbeing when he listens to me. That's all. It serves to open his mind and heart so he will consider my words. Without it..." A rueful smile touched the corners of her mouth. "Well, if he still wore it, perhaps I wouldn't be here."

"He won't hear you now that you can't influence him?"

"As I said, he is a hard man. If he will not hear my concerns, what can I do? The fact he wouldn't listen to me is what allowed this situation to begin." Her smile faded. "If only you'd worn it when I met you. Perhaps you'd be more inclined toward helping."

Tahl studied her face for a time, but it told him little. The anger had left her eyes, her expression soft and genuine.

"What's in the shipment?" he asked.

This time, a shadow filled her eyes. More than just worry.

Fear.

"Weapons," Oria said. "The kind that could change the world."

CHAPTER 8

"Wʜᴀᴛ ᴅᴏ ʏᴏᴜ ᴛʜɪɴᴋ, ʙᴏss?" Asʜʏʟ ᴋᴇᴘᴛ ʜᴇʀ ᴠᴏɪᴄᴇ ʟᴏw. A handful of others crowded nearby. Colbin was among them, his face pinched with worry, but Tahl would deal with the mage later.

"I don't know." Tahl scrubbed his face with one hand. "It's a lot of money. A team of five could finish and be set for for the rest of their lives."

Nia snorted. "As if you'd be happy with a few thousand pims."

"I would be," Jeran murmured. "Could invest in new tools. Set up an office with a drafting table the size of..." He trailed off as he caught the way everyone stared.

"Regardless," Tahl said, "it's a big risk. And outside our wheelhouse. We'd be going from stealing the crown to working for it."

"But it is thieving," Ashyl said. She tapped a fingernail against Tahl's desk. "And the money's good."

"I know." Tahl wanted to rub his face again, but he made his hands remain still. A handful of the maps he'd requested decorated his desk. He tried to make himself study them.

Now and then, Nia cast a worried look toward the queen.

Oria had not stirred since Tahl had let her up off the floor and bade her sit. She was outside the office, prim and proper in her chair, her hands folded in her lap. The queen watched them, but if she heard what they were saying, it was hard to tell.

Eventually, Nia tore her eyes away. "All that's assuming this isn't a trap. It could be a setup from the very beginning."

Tahl allowed himself a frown. "I don't think so. She had no way of knowing I was going to be in the pasture." And he still hadn't gotten Ebitha's horse back, blight it. "But I'm not ruling out the possibility that wanting to involve us is a trap she came up with along the way."

"The job is your call," Jeran said, though a hint of worry pinched the corners of his eyes.

Tahl shook his head. "If we do this, it's going to be a small team. Me and four others. I'm not about to tell four other people to risk their lives."

"So you're saying you'll do it?" Nia cocked a brow at him.

"I said *if*. I'm good, but I don't think I have enough muscle on my own to move crates full of... whatever this is out of a transport caravan. Which is what we're looking for, most likely. You've seen the problems we've had at the docks." Tahl tapped the maps in front of him. "I find it hard to believe anyone else could smuggle things through the main docks if we can't. And if they're not coming in through the main docks, they're coming from the new ones north of the city. With the construction mess up there, those will be easy for us to watch."

Ashyl crossed her arms and shrugged. "I'm in."

"Me too," Nia said before anyone else could draw breath.

Colbin cleared his throat. "Does part of this plan involve getting me out of here safely and ensuring I'm not executed for aiding a legendary thief in interrogating the queen?"

Tahl had almost forgotten the mage was there. "We'll make sure to have Oria pardon you before we head out. You can hardly be blamed for what I made you do, and the queen saw that dagger to your ribs. Jeran?"

The thief flinched at the sound of his name. "I'm an engineer, I don't think..."

"You just said you'd be happy with the money," Ashyl said. "You shouldn't back out now."

Jeran ducked his head.

"There was a dagger to my ribs?" Colbin asked in a whisper.

Tahl held up a hand to silence him.

"Fine," Jeran sighed. "I don't think I'm the best one for this, but—"

"You are," Tahl said before he could finish. "The group that goes needs to be diverse. You're my mechanical genius. Ashyl's the sweet-talker, I'm the stealth, and Nia—"

"I'm the scout?" she put in hopefully.

"—is staying here," Tahl finished.

The girl almost squeaked. "What?" Hurt filled her eyes and her face crumpled with anger.

Before she could argue, Tahl raised a hand. "Because I trust you. Not because of anything you did or can't do. If this is a trap, the stupidest thing I could do would be bring my second-in-command along to spring it."

"But I can help!" she protested.

"I know. And you will, by staying here and keeping the guild under control." The look of betrayal on her face tugged at his heart, but Tahl refused to let it sway his decision. "I need someone here who knows how I work, inside and out. Who the guild already looks to for guidance, in case I need to call reinforcements. You're the only one who can handle this job."

The other thieves nodded in agreement.

Nia sank into the chair behind the desk with a pitiful sigh.

"If Nia's staying here to keep things under control, I'm guessing we need two more?" Ashyl asked, catching Tahl's eye.

"One more," Tahl said. "The queen's with us."

The frustration and dismay on Nia's face deepened.

"You're taking her?" Colbin asked. "Does that mean I'm coming?"

"To make sure she can't use her magic against us?" Jeran glanced toward Oria, who still sat calm as could be. "That's not a bad idea."

Tahl shook his head. "Except then he really would be aiding us, instead of doing what he'd been ordered at knifepoint."

A hint of a smirk pulled at Ashyl's lips. "I'd wager Oria would still pardon him, since he'd be doing *her* bidding."

The flat look Tahl gave her made that smile evaporate. "Oria's using us for this job. Nobody should expect to be pardoned. If we do this, it's for the money. She already knows that's how we operate. That's why she's offering twice my bounty."

Jeran shifted uneasily. "What do you mean?"

"All of you are here because you haven't tried to collect the hundred thousand Atoras put on my head." Tahl glanced between them. "She knows the amount needed has to be big enough to do two things. It has to entice us, and it has to be enough to make assembling a team worthwhile. Two hundred is enough to make it worth working for a split."

Ashyl tilted her head. "But what does that have to do with collecting your bounty?"

"Because if this is a trap, she's probably going to use a chance at all that money to sway you to her side."

Everyone at the table fell silent.

Comforting, Tahl thought with a grim smile. He could almost hear the gears in their heads turning as they tried to decide if it would be worth it.

He curled his hand to a fist and rapped his knuckles on the desk. "Oria's four, we need one more. We're all on the lean side. We need someone big."

"Rupert?" Jeran suggested.

Ashyl dug an elbow into his ribs. "Hadren used to work as a porter."

"Hadren will do," Tahl said. "If you find a way to get the bear to cooperate with the guild, Jeran, I'm all ears."

"I'd like to throw Oria to Rupert," Nia muttered.

Tahl scarcely managed to keep from rolling his eyes. "I'm sure he would appreciate that. Ashyl, track down Hadren. You, Hadren, and Jeran will find your instructions at the third drop-off point."

"What about me?" Colbin asked.

"Right," Tahl muttered. "We'll take care of getting you out of here right now."

The mage's shoulders slumped in relief as Tahl rolled up his sleeves and rounded the desk. "How are we leaving?"

Tahl plowed a fist into Colbin's jaw.

"THAT WAS UNNECESSARY, WASN'T IT?" Oria asked in a low tone.

Tahl brushed his hand against his trousers and shrugged. "If he wants people to believe he got kidnapped by the Ghost, then he needs to look like he got kidnapped. He's a mage. You should know better than anyone that if he didn't want to go, we couldn't have taken him."

The queen barked a laugh.

He'd insisted on having the queen be the one to help him carry Colbin out of the guild's headquarters. They'd dragged him along with a bag over his head, only to eject him onto the museum's main floor. The trip hadn't been far, but his sudden appearance in the museum would be more disorienting than the sewers. With Jeran's invisible door in the stone wall, there was no way to see where they had come from. The thieves had long since cleaned the basement of dust that might betray their secret entrance.

"You disagree?" Tahl raised a brow.

They were the only two people who remained in the headquarters, everyone else having gone. Nia had carried Tahl's written instructions to the drop-off, though not without shooting any number of baleful glares at the queen.

"I didn't want to come here," Oria said, gesturing to the room around them. Her eyes caught on the shelves of goods that weren't quite fine enough to be deposited in the treasury. Though her face twisted with displeasure, she forced herself to go on. "You didn't give me a choice. You know how to keep a mage just distracted enough that their Gift is out of reach."

"Unlikely." He crossed to the makeshift kitchen and plucked an apple from a basket. The crunch was satisfying, but the light, sweet flavor only served to remind him that he still hadn't had a decent meal. "You're old blood. You could have killed me any time you wanted. But you didn't." His eyes met hers and he stared at her for a long time, thoughtful.

She shook her head. "I didn't have a reason to kill you."

Tahl wiped a bead of juice from his chin with a thumb. "You didn't have a reason to help me, either. But you did. When I was escaping the palace."

"I don't know what you're talking about."

"The door to the balcony," he said. "You unlocked it, didn't you?"

The queen stared back, her face betraying nothing.

"I felt the magic. The flows shifted. Parted around me like water and unlocked the door. I don't know if I would have found the latch fast enough to escape, but it seemed like the best chance for survival I had." He studied her expression again. It was calm, smooth. Even her eyes gave nothing away. How long had she been practicing that? Judging by what he knew, it had to be a long time.

He leaned back against a table. "Do you love Atoras?"

Her brow furrowed, the facade broken. "What?"

"Your husband. Do you love him?"

Oria blinked twice. "No."

"I figured." Tahl crunched into his apple again. "You don't have any kids yet."

"Having children has nothing to do with loving one another."

"No, but it probably helps. Want an apple?" He motioned to the basket by his feet.

Her gaze flicked toward it, then lifted to his face. "What are you doing?"

He shrugged. "Eating. Thought you might be hungry."

"You're asking questions," Oria said. "Irrelevant ones."

"Every question is relevant. If you think it's not, it just means you haven't figured out its purpose yet." A seed crunched between his teeth. Tahl pushed it to his lips with his tongue and removed it with his forefinger and thumb. Sometimes he ignored them. Today, the bitterness was unpleasant. He turned to drop the seed into a large jar of scraps someone else would dispose of later. "You're going to be working this job with us. I want to know who I'm working with."

"That won't change my performance."

"But it'll change how comfortable we are with you. Everyone on the team looks to me for leadership. If I don't trust you, they won't, either." He finished his apple and tucked the core into the jar, too.

The queen's brows drew together as if she didn't quite understand. "And knowing how I feel about my husband makes you trust me?"

He sucked sticky apple juice off his fingers, one at a time. "Well, it paints a fuller picture. I understand politics. I understand arranged marriages. But if you loved him, it would be easier to understand your loyalty and believe that you really do have the empire's best interests at heart."

Oria snorted. "And you expect me to believe you care about the empire's best interests? You're a thief."

"A thief who lives here." Tahl ticked a finger at her. "Life is better when the empire prospers. And you might not want to admit it, but I'm good for the city. The thieves in Orrad answer to me now, and those who don't watch their backs because they're afraid of me."

"Afraid of a child?" Her eyes narrowed.

"My age has nothing to do with my accomplishments. I infiltrated the palace and escaped with the crown of Atoras, ruler of the largest empire in the world. I did that, and I'm still alive." Scarred, but alive. He turned to the table and filled a small basin with water. Jeran had schemes for a water system that would refill itself and make life in the museum basement easier. Tahl hoped he'd live to see it.

He washed his hands. "So here's a question you may find more relevant. Would you have come to me, to the Ghost, with this job if you'd known how old I am?"

The queen hesitated.

"That's what I thought," Tahl murmured.

Silence fell as he wiped his hands dry on a rag. When he faced her again, Oria studied him.

Eventually, she clasped her hands in front of her. "I had not intended to seek you." Her voice carried a tinge of something. Embarrassment, Tahl thought, but that made no sense. Her hands tightened until her fingers grew pale, betraying her feelings. She did not want to tell him anything, but some part of her felt compelled to. Why, Tahl couldn't say.

She swallowed before she went on. "I knew I couldn't hunt down the shipment on my own, but I thought I could recruit people to help. I knew it would be dangerous to venture into the city alone, but without the crown, Atoras doesn't listen to me. I did not see any other options."

Progress. Tahl crossed his arms. "You married him before he took power."

Her brows twitched. More subjects of conversation she didn't understand, it seemed. "Yes."

"Does he know who you are?"

A hint of color rose into her cheeks and for the first time, Oria seemed less an angry queen and more... well, human. "Yes."

"I'm surprised he would agree to marry you, then. One would think he'd spend every day fearing a knife in the back."

"I was surprised, myself," the queen admitted. "But it probably would not surprise you to hear he is a stubborn, power-hungry man. He enjoyed the idea of being wedded to the woman who should have been Orrad's ruler. It gives him a sense of delight to be a power over both my political and personal lives."

Tahl's lip curled with distaste. "Not surprising, but still unpleasant."

"He is a strong ruler. I never said he was pleasant." Though her face was stern, a hint of softness touched her dark eyes.

Satisfied, Tahl paced toward his office. "This isn't going to be an easy job. And I expect the full amount. You don't get to dock me anything just because you're coming along."

The queen followed. "I'm surprised you're taking me, after you disposed of the mage. What's to keep me from turning against you now?"

"Your honor." He pulled the dark-colored satchel containing his best gear out from under his desk. "Turn around, please. I'm changing."

Amusement flitted across her face. "You're surprisingly honest, given your occupation."

"Turn around."

She gestured in apology and turned away.

Tahl stripped out of his everyday clothing and slipped into his close-fitting navy heist clothes. One by one, he stashed his favorite knives on his person. Then he stuffed his satchel with a few supplies snatched from around the room. Aside from the one small wooden chair she'd shattered to use as a makeshift weapon, his office had been strangely untouched. Out of everything Tahl stored there, only the crown had been moved.

"I'm surprised you listened," he said as he fastened his split-toed shoes. "Most people would fear a knife in the back."

"As I said," the queen remarked as she cast a tentative glance over her shoulder. She smiled when she saw him dressed. "You're surprisingly honest."

"Hopefully when everything is over, I'll be able to say the same about you." He did not smile back. "Let's go."

Oria's cheer evaporated, though she gave a grim nod and followed him as he led the way to the sewers.

Without a plan or any leads, the new heist began.

CHAPTER 9

A COLD DRIZZLE HARBORED THE ONSET OF AN UNPLEASANT NIGHT TO come. Oria pulled the hood of her cloak up a little farther, but Tahl walked with his shoulders squared and pretended he didn't feel the rain.

He'd considered blindfolding the queen on the way out of headquarters, but after she'd helped him eject Colbin, there had seemed to be little point. She already knew where they were, but her chances of finding her way through the sewers to get to them again were slim.

"I begin to understand why our guards couldn't catch you," Oria panted as she followed him through the winding alleys.

Tahl raised a brow. He'd set a brisk pace, but he hadn't thought it that hard to follow. "Would you believe me if I said you were slowing me down?"

"Yes. I think I would."

He glanced toward the rooftops. He would have preferred to be there, leaping from roof to roof in the gloom. Wet roof tiles were always a unique challenge, a good way to hone his acrobatic skills. Occasionally, he was less enthusiastic to admit, they were a good way to earn bruises.

"Of course, you're part of why they didn't catch me. Aren't you?" Tahl cast a knowing glance over his shoulder. Oria still hadn't admitted her involvement, but her silence made him smirk. Of course she'd done it. There hadn't been any other mages there.

After they crossed a wide street and vanished into another alley, he slowed so she could close the distance between them. Her presence tingled in his senses, an uncomfortable sensation that crawled over his skin and his soul at the same time. He'd never known how to explain the feeling of another mage, but his short jaunt back into the academy with Nia had reminded him how glad he was to leave that world behind. Being a formally recognized mage would have been prestigious, made his family proud, and he would always be angry at the way they'd shunned him. But magic was unsettling by nature, and he'd come to realize he didn't miss the lessons or his peers.

"I have a question for you now, Ghost," the queen said after a time.

"No one's stopping you from asking."

"I want to know more about the horse. The one you sought to take from me."

Tahl raised a brow. "I thought we went over that already."

"Yes," Oria conceded, "but I want to know why you, the Ghost of Orrad himself, thought recovering one white horse was a job worth your attention."

Which meant she probably already knew the answer. Even thieves had loved ones. Tahl wasn't sure he'd call Ebitha that, but the old woman had earned his loyalty. He'd declared her estate to be among the properties in the city that were off-limits. Nobody had questioned the choice. The guild protected those who were useful, and no one seemed to care what made the wealthy old widow part of their number.

Not that wealthy anymore, Tahl reminded himself. He needed to figure out what had happened to Ebitha's fortune. *And* retrieve her horse. Unconsciously, he rubbed the crease that had formed between his brows.

"I see," Oria said. Her voice was soft, far from accusatory, but it held a note of knowingness that rubbed him the wrong way.

"I don't need to explain my reasons for accepting a job." He tried not to snap, but the words still came out hot. "My guild brings me leads, I choose which ones we take."

She straightened her cloak as she trailed behind him. "And which ones you take for yourself?"

"I do what I please," Tahl said. "That's the best part of being who I am."

The queen said nothing else.

The rest of their trek through the city was silent, save for Oria's ragged breath whenever Tahl moved faster than what she could easily keep up with. More than once, his eyes drifted toward the sky as if to check the moon's position. With the cloud cover, it was nowhere in sight. He had a strong internal clock and didn't need it, but some part of him felt like the wandering moon would give him something to point at and hurry the queen along. Tahl bit back his frustration and remained outwardly cool and calm.

That facade was so practiced that half the guild thought him unshakable. He wished he was. His powerful flight instincts had kept him alive through a number of scrapes. Only occasionally did that panic break through to the surface. With the queen close on his heels and the meeting point looming ahead, he felt a little more shaken than he wanted to admit.

"Where are we?" Oria asked in a murmur as they reached a narrow but well-lit road.

"Just outside the garden district. I'd think you'd know that, considering this was supposed to be your city."

An angry flush colored her cheeks, but she ducked her head and the fight in her seemed to subside. "I've spent a great deal of time in the palace. I no longer know the city as well as I once did."

Tahl paced backwards down the avenue. "Oh, so you wouldn't know that in approximately thirteen minutes, there will be a brief guard rotation at the district gates that leaves an opening where we'll be able to slip in unnoticed."

She blinked. "That's strangely specific."

"Strangely specific keeps us alive, Your Majesty."

"How could you know the time with that much accuracy?"

"I do a lot of jobs here." He flashed her a grin. "There's a certain satisfaction that comes from infiltrating the security of people who've sequestered themselves off from the rest of the city. But then, I've noticed all my favorite heists involve walls."

The queen gave him a disapproving look, but he ignored it as he gently directed her into a narrow gap between two tall buildings.

"Eleven minutes," he whispered.

She frowned, but settled in the shadows to wait.

Tahl leaned against the wall and watched the guards, though he remained aware of the queen in his peripheral vision. At this point, he had little reason to fear she might attack him, but that did not mean it wasn't a possibility. He kept his senses open. At the first hint of magic, he could strike.

The guard slipped inside for shift rotation.

"Let's go," Tahl said. He set a brisk pace, but this time, Oria was right on his heels.

Together, they slipped through the gate without notice and disappeared into the shadow of the garden wall.

"Has this district always been under guard?" the queen asked in a whisper.

He shook his head. "Not like this. One of many things I've ended up changing in this city." His footsteps were soundless on the wet grass as he led her behind and around a number of tall houses. "There's the meeting point."

With how slow she'd made them, they were the last to arrive. The other three thieves lounged around the garden district's fountain with varying degrees of boredom on their faces. Hadren saw him first. He elbowed Jeran and pointed their way.

Had Tahl not wanted to be seen, they never would have known he was there.

"We're meeting out in the open?" Oria asked.

Tahl walked slowly and kept her close. "Anyone who sees us will assume we're supposed to be here. The district is guarded, remember? No one in their right mind would sit out in the open after sneaking in."

"Comforting," she mumbled.

"And yes," Tahl said, "I'm aware of how that makes me sound." With the absurdity of what he was doing, he couldn't guarantee it was that far off the mark. Taking a job that could be either a trap or an attempt to undermine the empire he loved and called home certainly seemed like lunacy, but it was also the only way he could know the queen's intentions for sure. If she truly posed a threat to the empire, he'd be in a perfect position to stop her.

Though Hadren had been the first to see them, Ashyl was the one who stood and strode to greet them. "I think you'll want to see this, boss." She cast Oria a wary look as she extended a small, folded pieced of paper.

"Notes, or something you found while scouting?" Tahl studied the texture of the paper. It was ordinary, the common wood-pulp paper found anywhere in Orrad. He unfolded it and paused.

"Can you read it?" From the note of uncertainty in Ashyl's voice, he guessed she couldn't.

Tahl strode toward the fountain and did not reply. The plaza around the fountain was well-lit, and he had no difficulty seeing the sepia ink. "Where did you get this?"

"The iron refinery. Sort of."

He raised a brow.

Ashyl squirmed. "It was in the pocket of a worker who was

leaving by the back door. He looked like he was in a hurry. He kept looking over his shoulder."

Tahl fought back a frown. He'd seen men leaving the building the same way. Maybe he should have sent Ashyl to investigate sooner. "When?"

"About two hours ago. Long after work should have ended."

The queen glanced between them. "What is it?"

"Schematics," Jeran said.

Tahl shot him a glare and stuffed the paper into his pocket. "Not just schematics. A proposal. It's written in one of the northern alphabets. There aren't a lot of people who still use it outside of Daribur, which is one of the larger kingdoms that emerged from the Claiming Wars."

"So you can read it?" Ashyl asked.

He did not acknowledge the question. "They're trying to find someone who can replicate it."

"But what is it?" Jeran rubbed his chin. "Ashyl let me look. I know it's some kind of mechanism, but I don't know what it's for."

"It's impossible to say without more context. Could be a door latch, for all I know," Tahl said. "But we don't have a trade relationship with Daribur. In fact, they're considered one of the biggest antagonists against the empire."

Hadren grunted. "Think this is where our shipment's coming from?"

"It's a possibility," Oria said.

Tahl nodded. "Probably the best lead we've got, too. But Daribur is on the western side of the continent's northern half. Transporting anything by ship would be cumbersome, since they'd have to go all the way around the Westkings in one direction or the other."

"So you think they're coming by land?" Jeran rubbed his chin a little more aggressively.

"That would be my wager." Tahl crossed his arms and shifted

on his feet. Once he had his gear on, he always found he wanted to move, even if it was just an uneasy shifting of his weight. "They could go one of two directions once they hit the break in the mountains where the north and south Westkings meet, but that divide is where anything coming from Daribur is most likely to pass."

The thieves quieted. Hadren had traveled a great deal as a porter, but Ashyl and Jeran had never ventured beyond Orrad's surrounding countryside. Traveling as far as the neck of land that connected the north and the south had to be intimidating.

"Of course," Tahl added to waylay their concerns, "I'd want more evidence we should look that direction before we try to make that kind of trip. One piece of paper from an unfriendly country is hardly proof of where the queen's mystery shipment is coming from."

The other thieves visibly relaxed.

"Where to, then, boss?" Hadren asked.

"The refinery." He touched two fingers to his pocket. The paper stashed inside crinkled. "If someone's sneaking out with a proposal, there might be more paperwork in the building that could give us an idea what this is, or if it's worth pursuing."

Oria grimaced. "I recall Atoras granting permission for the structure to be built. It was quite a fuss in court, being so much larger than a typical bloomery."

"It's also outside the city limits," Tahl said, guessing at the reason for her grimace. "And you can't exactly slip in and out of the city gates unnoticed."

The rest of the group fidgeted.

Eventually, Hadren slapped his thighs and stood. "Well, we'd better get on, then. Hope Rupert's not hungry."

Beneath the shadow of her cloak's hood, the queen grew pale.

"REMEMBER," Tahl said as they stopped in front of the gate that led to the natural caverns, "keep right. The right path only forks once. When you find it, also keep right. I'm putting out the mage-light as soon as we start walking. We'll all be walking blind, and hopefully staying as silent as possible."

"Right?" Oria asked.

"Correct."

She frowned at him. "Last time, you said keep left."

"Because we were going the other direction. We were going in, not out."

A hint of color rose in her cheeks. "I was blindfolded. You can't expect me to have a sense of direction."

"True enough. Now, be quiet. The last thing we want to do is wake the bear. Rupert's never gone down that tunnel, which is why we use it most, even though it's longer. But we can't overlook that fact that Rupert is a bear, and animals are unpredictable." He glanced between his companions to make sure they understood.

When everyone had nodded their agreement, Tahl curled his hand around the glowing coin and unwound the delicate strands of energy that constituted the light. The mage-light extinguished and a hint of suffuse warmth spread through his hand. He resorted to magic less often now, most jobs easy to achieve without his smoke tricks. Tahl was careful to keep the skill honed, practicing when he was working in the guild headquarters or when he was home alone, but it was rare to need his Gift. With Oria present, he doubted his ability would be of any use beyond occasional lights.

They padded on down the tunnel with Tahl in the lead, the quiet shuffle of feet and puff of nervous breath close at his back. Now and then, someone came close enough to brush fingers against his arms or shoulders. Every touch made him grimace and twitch a hand toward his favorite dagger. He liked the crew he'd chosen—aside from Oria, as he wasn't sure what he thought of the queen—but only Nia escaped that sort of reaction from him.

Somewhere ahead was a point where the passages converged. The faint sound of movement reached his ears and Tahl reached back to catch hold of the next person behind him. One after another, he propelled the rest of the group ahead of him with a near-silent whisper of "Go."

It wasn't as if he'd be able to escape the bear if he was in the back, but as far as he was aware, he knew the cave's tunnels better than anyone else. His chances of evading the beast were the best, and putting himself at the back gave him the opportunity to distract the bear if need be.

The group hurried on in tense silence. Tahl's heartbeat hammered loud in his ears and he breathed a little more slowly to reduce the speed of his pulse. It wasn't as if the bear could hear his heart, but with it beating that loud, he couldn't hear the bear.

Eventually, the scent of fresh air reached his nostrils and a sense of relief came down on his shoulders. It wasn't exactly safe at that point, but the cave's mouth gave way to a wide slope where it would be easier for the group to split up and escape. Jeran took the lead as they emerged into the night, cutting straight north from the exit. He was sure-footed and quick, almost as much so as Tahl, and the other thieves had difficulty matching his pace. The queen lagged so far behind that Tahl decided she was most likely to be mauled, should Rupert emerge on their heels, so he posted himself at her back and managed not to be frustrated by their lack of speed.

The field beyond the cave hosted little more than farms, but as they trekked north, the city's growing industrial region came into view. Large warehouses and manufactories sat still and empty in the night. A faint glow came from closer to the river, where workers caroused until the small hours of the morning. Tahl expected the sounds of life would fill the air there and he wished the iron refinery were closer to the river. Noise was a buffer of safety, something to hide the sounds of their activity. He, Jeran, and Ashyl could probably get into the refinery without making any noise. He was less certain about Hadren, and he assumed Oria would not be proficient at sneaking. Nobles were occasionally surprising, but as they approached the refinery from behind, a look of uncertainty painted her face.

Ashyl had taken the lead. She motioned them through a narrow alley and flashed a quick hand-sign to Hadren and Jeran as they passed. *Scout. Guards?* The question mark was implied by the tilt of her hand at the end, her little finger hooked. The men nodded. She had no instructions for Oria, or for Tahl. Wise of her, considering this was his operation.

The men disappeared from sight. Ashyl hung back, waiting for Tahl and the queen.

"I don't think there are guards, exactly," she whispered as they approached, "but there are definitely still people inside."

Tahl tilted an ear toward the refinery's wall. Even from outside, he could hear the steady whoosh of bellows and the occasional ping of metal against metal. "How many were here when you stopped by?"

"I didn't go in," Ashyl whispered back. "I didn't think I should, specifically because of how many people were here. They were working later than I expected."

"Manufacturing things they don't want people to know about?" Tahl raised a brow at the queen.

Oria shrugged. "Or increasing output to meet the demand that comes with all this construction." She waved a hand at the area around them. "Orrad's an old city. I don't think it was prepared for this sudden economic boom."

"I think I'll have questions about that, but not now." Tahl joined Ashyl as she inched toward the back door. Jeran had reappeared and waved for their attention.

"There are still people here. There's a sort of metal grid above the main floor, and a walkway along the top where they're throwing iron into the furnace." Jeran wriggled his fingers at the equipment inside the building, as if he wasn't sure what to call it. Tahl nodded in encouragement for him to continue. The rather esoteric names of the refinery's tools didn't matter to thieves. Jeran's eyes swept up a nearby stairway. "Most of the building is metal, so sneaking will be hard. My footwear's not as soft as yours."

"I'll scout, then. Ashyl's with me. You and Hadren keep an eye on the workers. And the queen." He kept his voice low, but with the rattle of equipment, the roaring fire, and the noisy gusting of the bellows, there was no need to whisper.

Above them, footsteps clattered on the walkway. Everyone looked up, but the worker carried on without notice. The back door was still open, but perhaps the workers found that a blessing. The cool air that rushed in had to feel good.

Tahl crept forward and motioned for them to close the door. His fingers flicked in a few silent instructions for Ashyl. *Go. Far right. Up. Scout.*

She nodded and stalked off in the other direction. The hand signals had been Niada's idea. Every time Tahl ventured out with other thieves, he was glad she'd invented them. The words they'd developed were limited, but they were useful, and he wouldn't have thought of them on his own.

When Ashyl reached the staircase far to the right, he slipped up the stairs nearby. Despite the metal treads, his footfalls were silent, each movement tightly controlled.

A handful of workers in thick leather gear moved around the walkways. It was hotter in the upper part of the building and the air was acrid and dry in Tahl's nostrils. Even so, it was less sooty and dirty than the floor below and Tahl had no doubt an office would be on the upper level, where a foreman could watch the day's activity and spare his papers from the grime.

The walkways were something of a maze and it wasn't long before Ashyl disappeared from sight. Tahl trusted her to find what they needed and focused on his own footing and movement. Smokestacks rose through the ceiling and most of the walkway was dangerously cluttered with boxes and carts, offering no shortage of places to hide. More than once, the proximity of a worker forced Tahl to duck behind something until the footsteps passed. Grateful as he was for the shelter, it made it hard to see the rest of the refinery.

At the far end, near a stairway that led to an open space near the front door on the first floor, a boxy, windowed room sat nestled in the corner of the building. The crude glass windows were gray with soot and practically useless, but no light came from inside and Tahl saw no hint of movement in the shadows behind the dirt. He reached the door at the same time as Ashyl and she ducked her head in deference.

Tahl hovered a hand above the door's handle, testing for wards or other strands of magic that might impede entry. Nothing tickled his senses, so he tried the door. Unsurprisingly, it was locked.

Watch, Tahl signed. Ashyl nodded and shifted so she could see every walkway path that led to their location.

Behind her, Tahl sank to his knees and opened his bag. Sometimes he missed the old one, the worn brown leather satchel he'd always used in the beginning. But his new bag was custom-made, super-soft leather dyed to match his midnight blue heist clothes and lined with pockets to fit all his tools. He removed his lock picks without needing to look and set to work.

Before any of the workers came back into view, he wrenched the lock open and slipped inside with Ashyl right behind him. The door made no sound when he closed it.

"You want to take the records, while I do the desk?" Tahl asked.

She grunted a halfhearted response, but crept to the rows of shelves and stacks of crates beneath the windows. The ledgers were mostly clean. The foreman probably didn't dirty his hands often. *At least, not physically,* Tahl thought with a wry smile. He sorted through the papers on the desk with a practiced eye, skimming for anything out of the ordinary. Shipments of coal and raw iron came from all over the empire. Pig iron didn't go far from Orrad, though a few loads had departed by ship. The youth of the refinery made Tahl raise a brow at the numbers involved, but the place was novel and rumored to be the most efficient refinery in the world. If those output numbers were standard, he was inclined to believe it.

"Do you want connections to Daribur specifically, or anything that looks suspicious?" Ashyl asked.

Tahl paused his sorting to look at her. "That depends on why you're asking. Find something?"

"No. Just asking, in case I do. I think this is just employee records. There are a lot of people on staff here."

"There would have to be, with all the work they're doing." Tahl abandoned the papers and pulled open a drawer. A trinket inside caught his eye and he lifted it to inspect. "This looks like the mechanism on that diagram."

"Sample, maybe? Was it made here, or sent here to see if someone here can replicate it?"

"Don't know. Haven't seen anything that answers that question." Tahl touched his pocket, where the diagram still waited for further study. He wasn't able to read the alphabet well, but he'd gotten the gist. He slipped the mechanism into his pocket alongside the paper and pulled open another drawer.

Ashyl paused. "Do you smell that?"

Tahl sniffed. The air was hot and acrid, but he didn't detect any new odors.

She inched toward one of the crates stacked beside the shelves, inhaling deeply. "It's in here."

A sense of uneasiness wriggled up Tahl's spine and crawled across his scalp. He abandoned the desk and stalked toward the crate. He and Ashyl reached for the wooden lid at the same time. It was tacked shut and they both pried to loosen it. As it came open, the scent of sulphur reached his nose.

Ashyl slid the lid aside and reached for a stack of papers in the top of the straw-filled crate. More schematics, plans for whatever lay inside. She paged through them and squinted down at the crate's contents. "What is that?"

Tahl leaned forward as the same sense of uneasiness wrapped itself around him and tightened to a knot in his belly. "What the queen's afraid of."

CHAPTER 10

Tahl's pack thudded against his back, its contents as heavy as the burden of knowing what they'd found. Ashyl had pocketed all the papers, but he took the crate's contents for himself before they closed it and escaped the office. It protruded strangely from the top of his bag, but he'd balanced it carefully before emerging onto the walkway. This time, he and Ashyl went the same direction.

They skirted around the workers and tip-toed down the stairs, one after the other. No one waited at the bottom.

Tahl scanned the first floor of the refinery before he darted past the door to investigate. Not far from where he'd left them, the queen crouched behind a number of heaping ore carts with Hadren and Jeran.

Jeran pointed at the object that stuck from Tahl's pack and hooked his little finger to signal a question.

Later, Tahl signed. He motioned for the group to come.

Ashyl waved for them to stay still. Booted footsteps clomped toward their hiding place and the group of thieves shrank back into the shadows.

The man didn't seem to notice them. He threw the back door open and sucked in a lungful of fresh air, then stepped outside.

Instead of leaving, he lingered on the back step. Taking a break, it seemed.

Jeran pointed toward the front door and shrugged.

Could they make it out the front? Tahl tried to recall what the street was like. He'd only been out there a handful of times. Tempted as he was to try it, he didn't trust Oria to make it out the door unnoticed. He shook his head and signaled toward the back.

Hadren, Jeran, and Ashyl all mirrored the signal and followed it with a flurry of surprised gestures.

Tahl jerked his head toward the back again, then rolled his eyes and planted a palm on the ground. Thieves, all of them, and yet somehow they'd forgotten how to sneak. He squeezed his eyes shut and focused on the sense of heat around him. Pursuing his power was always easier in places like this, where his fire affinity was fed by the flames in the furnaces and the heat in the air.

He coiled the flow of magic underneath the palm of his hand and felt warmth bloom against the stone. It swelled in his senses. Behind him, Oria twitched.

Smoke poured from between his fingers, denser than he'd anticipated, his power augmented by the nearby fire. Thick clouds billowed around them, flooding the air and cutting off all visibility. Beyond their hiding place, startled shouts and coughs rose above the noise of the furnaces and bellows.

Tahl darted through the thick of it. The smoke continued to churn, pouring out of the back door. The man on the steps doubled over coughing and spun to face the refinery. His eyes found Tahl instead.

The man scarcely yelped before Tahl tackled him and clamped an arm around his neck. Tahl squeezed. The man clawed at his arm and gasped uselessly, but Tahl's wiry arms were as strong as the smelted iron. After a few seconds of struggle, the man collapsed.

"Go," Tahl whispered. He dared not lift his voice any more than that.

The queen emerged from the smoke first, though Hadren was just behind, gripping her arm to steer her through the smoke clouds. Ashyl and Jeran followed together.

"Split up," Tahl ordered as they started down the alley behind the refinery. "Teams of two. The fisherman's shack. Meet me there."

The thieves all nodded. Oria squeaked as Hadren jerked her along.

Tahl spun back, his attention locked on his smoke. It grew thicker as he focused, masking their escape, but not masking *him*. A factory worker launched out of the smoke with a massive hammer raised over his head.

His attention snapped from his magic to his adversary and Tahl ducked aside. The hammer plowed into the earth.

Without the smokescreen between them, the man was no threat. But the others hadn't gone far, and with Tahl's orders to split up, there was no way to aid all his comrades. Instead, Tahl opted for a distraction.

He darted closer to the hammer-wielding factory worker. Before the man could react, he twisted to one side and dashed toward the door.

The smoke inside had not yet cleared. Tahl tried to concentrate enough to fortify it on his way through. It responded, though weakly, thickening and spreading farther throughout the refinery.

Coughing came from several places throughout the building. Tahl counted and noted their locations at the same time. Seven; eight, counting his friend with the hammer who stumbled his way back to the door in pursuit. Tahl ducked up the stairs, ignoring the way his hurried footsteps clanged against the metal. It was hard *not* to be stealthy. Making noise so the workers would follow him went against his nature, but every minute they followed him was another minute between them and his team.

"Upstairs!" someone shouted. Good. Let them try to follow him across the narrow metal walkways that spanned a grid of bars.

Tahl stuck to the path until someone rounded a corner to cut him off. Then he grinned and leaped the rail to land on the grid. The rounded bars were little thicker than his thumb, but they were solid and still. He followed one toward the front door while the man who'd tried to intercept him raced across the walkway in an attempt to beat him there.

Toward the front of the refinery, there was little smoke in the air and Tahl saw people below. A pair of men had grabbed poles. They jabbed up at him, but they were clumsy and the blunt poles were little threat to begin with. Tahl hopped from bar to bar across the grid to evade. As long as he kept moving, he didn't need to worry about balance.

A number of wide access doors lined the front of the building. Ore carts stacked with coal and raw iron sat before some. Those were his best bet. Tahl chose one farthest from the wide path where the workers pursued him on the ground floor and cut toward it.

It took a second for those below to change direction. They wove around equipment and materials, but Tahl's path was unimpeded. He dove between the widest-spaced grid bars and landed atop a cart of coal. He skidded down the side of the pile, jumped before he hit the edge of the cart, and landed on the stone floor with coal clattering around him.

The second he turned to the door, a worker rounded the corner of the ore cart with a hand axe.

Tahl unbarred the door and flung it wide. "Sorry, I've got enough scars." He grinned at the man and darted out the front.

Refinery workers converged at the doorway, shouting orders and epithets as Tahl raced down the street toward the new docks. He didn't know anything about the guard presence beyond the city walls, but he was willing to wager the patrols were few and far between compared to the city streets.

Out in the rain-fresh air, he sucked deep breaths and freed his lungs of the smoke he'd created. Running warmed his muscles, and he ran with a comfortable, lengthy stride. Behind him, the heavy, booted steps of the refinery workers faded as he outpaced them.

First leg down, he told himself. A handful of night-owls that roamed the developing dockside area shouted and tried to draw attention to him, but just as many ducked back into doorways or behind buildings to try and avoid his notice. To his relief, there wasn't a guard in sight.

Tahl ran until he reached the rocky shore. Then he allowed himself to slow, out of breath and regretting the unpleasant burn in his legs. He'd need to add more running to his routines; climbing and vaulting across the rooftops was more of a full-body exercise. It hadn't been that far, and he couldn't help but feel he shouldn't be breathless. He'd have to blame the smoke.

The river's edge was vacant and after he'd checked to make sure no one followed him, Tahl took his time. It was still a long trek to the fisherman's shack and he didn't know what would await him there. With that in mind, once he rounded the tip of the promontory, he stopped and sat beside the cliff. The object protruding from the top of his pack hadn't shifted much. He slid his pack's strap off his shoulder and opened it to loose the thing from what held it. Oh, he'd present the object for the others to inspect, but not until he had a chance to look at it, himself.

It was not iron. Nor was it completely metal. He slid his fingers down the fine steel's smooth length and frowned at the soot left on his fingers. It wasn't the sort of remnant one expected to see on anything new, and when he sniffed his hand, he caught the distinct scent of sulphur that had drawn Ashyl's attention in the first place. How had she smelled that? It was so faint, he could hardly pick it up above the petrichor.

Now that he had a chance to properly investigate, he saw the base of the thing wasn't metal, either. Instead, it was a wedge of wood that had been lacquered black. Preventing the soot from staining, perhaps. A gap between the wood and the long steel tube caught his attention and Tahl probed it with his fingers. Something was meant to go there. Something like...

His brow furrowed and he dug the strange mechanism from his pocket. It fit almost perfectly, a peculiar device with a chunk of flint wedged between pins.

Flint and black powder.

"Lifetree's mercy," Tahl breathed, wiping his face with one hand.

He was in over his head.

"It's called a musket," Jeran said as he examined the papers Ashyl had liberated from the crate. "The real thing is supposed to be much longer. This is just a sample indicating what they want. The schematics have the proper dimensions listed."

Tahl crossed his arms a little tighter across his chest. "Does it say anything about who wants it?

"Nothing. Just the number requested." Jeran licked his lips and lowered the paper. "They want five thousand."

The team around the table grew quiet.

Five thousand weapons like nothing they'd seen before. Tahl closed his eyes long enough to exhale. "So this is what we're looking for."

Oria bowed her head. "I had no idea it would be this severe."

"Now would be a good time to tell us everything you know, Majesty," Ashyl said, a sarcastic edge to her voice.

The queen gave a humorless laugh. "If I knew as much as you seem to think I do, perhaps none of this would have happened."

"I think telling us the rest of what you do know would be wise at this point." Tahl studied her as he spoke, but he felt none of the suspicion that flowed across the faces of his fellow thieves. Oria was secretive, obviously, but nothing in Tahl's instincts had indicated she was lying now. There was bitterness in her tone and regret on her face, but no hint of deceit—or nervousness, which would have betrayed any ill intentions.

Oria sighed and spread her hands to indicate helplessness. "I know little, but I'll tell you what I can. All this began shortly after the crown was stolen."

Her choice of words made Tahl raise a brow. Even knowing he'd done it, she didn't accuse him of anything.

"The Westkings Empire is constantly threatened, but I'm sure that's not surprise," she continued. "The Claiming Wars left everyone bitter. Atoras believes his empire should have encompassed the northern portion of the continent, as well, but the northern kingdoms banded together to drive the empire back."

"The Claiming Wars weren't in Atoras's time," Tahl said. "What does his opinion matter? This was something that happened to his great-grandfather."

"Half of what keeps the empire safe is that the northern kingdoms eventually turned on each other." Oria twisted a lock of her hair around her finger and stared at the unfinished musket on the table. "But rumors surfaced after the theft. People were questioning the empire's security. And the kingdoms in the north began to discuss new alliances."

A new war, in other words. Tahl bit the inside of his cheek.

The queen touched the musket's barrel, traced the steel bands that anchored it to the wooden stock. "I tried to caution Atoras, but he wouldn't listen. I began to realize that without the crown, nothing I did would sway his opinion. He believes the empire is infallible. I fear someone is ready to prove him wrong."

"From the inside," Hadren murmured. He'd been quiet through most of Jeran's explanation of the musket's schematics, his face twisted with thought.

"I doubt it." Ashyl straightened some of the papers. "Do you know how much weapons like these would have to cost? The only people who could afford that would be the nobles, and then only if they pooled their resources. But the empire was built to favor them. Why would they turn against their ruler?"

Tahl's eye twitched. "Maybe they don't know they're funding it."

Everyone looked at him.

"What do you mean?" Hadren asked.

"I noticed something odd about Ebitha's books the last time I was there," Tahl began, his eyes locked on the weapon between them. "The numbers are all wrong. Huge amounts of money disappearing from her estate, but it's a slow bleed. A few pims here and there, but almost every transaction was off, and there were some that didn't make sense or came too early. That's half of why she had to sell her favorite horse." He gave Oria a hard look.

She stiffened. "I thought you said that horse was stolen?"

"I thought it was. But now I think otherwise. She's a responsible old woman. Cotton was the youngest of her horses, and probably the most valuable. If she couldn't figure out why her fortune was evaporating, I imagine she would sell him willingly to try to keep the other two for a little while longer."

Ashyl raised a finger. "So, wait. You think someone's stealing money from a wealthy old noble and funneling it into funding that?" She lowered her finger to point at the musket.

Tahl nodded. "You said it yourself. The only way someone could afford to pay for weapons like these would be if the nobles were pooling their resources."

"So if people are siphoning money from the nobles to pay for this, all we have to do is follow that money." Jeran stroked his chin and then smoothed a hand over his brown hair. "We start at this Ebitha's?"

"We start at Ebitha's," Tahl agreed.

CHAPTER 11

Tahl peered up the back of the tall manor house, his fingers itching to climb. He'd planned to enter by the balcony, but a lamp still glowed in that room. Entering on his own wouldn't be a challenge, but there was no need to tempt fate, and even his luck only went so far.

No one had been happy about being left behind, but they hadn't argued too heartily when Tahl insisted on visiting the old woman's estate alone. It wasn't just that this was his personal mission. Tahl had a good rapport with Ebitha, and was the least likely to be in trouble if something went wrong. He'd covered his scar as soon as he'd reached the old woman's stables, just in case. Scraping the wax back off was faster than putting it on. If he ran afoul of guards, it would be easy to remove it before they got a good look at him.

He dusted his hands together before he scaled the wall. The office window was his best shot for getting in unnoticed, but it was also hard to unlock and the casing was old and stiff. Instead, he aimed for the guest room. The drawn curtains made it impossible to know if someone was inside, but the window opened with hardly a sound.

Tahl clung to the wall, listening for signs of life. When

nothing caught his ear, he slipped over the sill and crouched behind the curtains to close the window behind him. The office was just down the hall. He stalked to the door and lingered beside it.

Elsewhere in the house, soft notes of music rose into the silence. He'd seen the harp in one of the parlors, noted how clean it was, but hadn't considered the widow might play. Much less in the middle of the night. The desire to investigate pricked at Tahl until it made him uncomfortable, but he made himself focus and crept to the office instead.

The office door was locked.

Tahl blinked at it and checked again. The office was never locked. He'd been certain his tampering was invisible, too. Why would it be locked now?

Frowning, Tahl removed his picks from his bag and knelt beside the door. Bright color flashed beyond the old-fashioned open keyhole and he froze. Someone was in there. The soft, slow harp music still flowed from downstairs.

Blight it all. Tahl gritted his teeth and sat back on his heels. Did he wait? Or did he barge in and try to catch whoever was in there?

The possibility it was Ebitha crossed his mind, but he dismissed it. She wouldn't lock the door to tend business in a home she lived in alone, even if there was company downstairs to pluck the harp strings. He also doubted the musician could be anyone else, or that anyone awake in the small hours would lack the decency to ensure the house was quiet enough for guests to sleep. Nobles were peculiar that way. A great deal rode on their reputation, or so they believed, and few would willfully mistreat a houseguest.

From that, Tahl concluded the old widow must have believed she was alone. He slid his pick into the lock and worked it open.

Even for a thief as skilled as he was, the lock picks were not silent. The soft sound of movement on the other side of the door grew still.

Giving the enemy time to prepare, Tahl thought. *Giving them the advantage.* He'd have to compensate. He thought of his smoke, but he'd just used it in the factory. He didn't want to leave a conspicuous sign that might connect the two events if he was seen. The fewer people who knew he'd found the trail, the better.

Tahl gripped the doorknob and stilled his breath. He shifted back as he twisted the knob and flung the door open. A glimpse of bright clothing was all he got before he darted backwards into the hall to shimmy up the walls and join the shadows.

An unfamiliar man charged out of the office with a blade in his hand. He spun to face the way Tahl had retreated, his lip curled back like a growling dog's.

Ever so slowly, Tahl allowed himself to breathe. His reach was just wide enough for him to span the hallway and hold himself with his back pressed to the high ceiling. Fortune had favored him again. Soft illumination spilled from the office, but the man had no light.

The stranger lowered his knife and looked the other direction. His anger faded to wariness when he saw nothing. "Ebitha?" he called, his eyes darting one way, then the other.

Tahl cocked his head. Who was this?

The soothing music halted. The man stared down the far hall, listening. He sheathed his blade and paced forward, uneasy. "Ebitha, was that you?"

Unwilling to miss his opportunity, Tahl dropped to the floor and bolted into the office.

The man spun back, mouth agape, but he was too slow. He got one syllable of a shout out before Tahl slammed the door. He couldn't lock it without a few more moments, but he snatched a book off a shelf and jammed it under the door to keep it from opening. A split second later, the stranger jostled the doorknob and shouted again.

So much for getting in unnoticed. Tahl allowed himself a grim smile as he dragged the chair out from behind the desk and wedged it under the doorknob. *Time to make this fast.*

A handful of ledgers and a small oak box sat on the desk. Tahl's eyes raked over them and he stifled a curse. He'd known someone was stealing from the old woman, but he hadn't expected to walk in on it.

Tahl pushed the box aside. Inside, coins clinked together when he jostled it. A piece of paper lay atop everything else, a handful of notes and numbers scribbled across its surface. He studied them as he rearranged the books and figured out which was which.

The stranger hammered at the door. "Ebitha, call for the guard!"

"Don't call the guard, Ebitha," Tahl murmured. He squeezed his eyes closed and tried to gather his wits. All he had to do was focus, wait for something to leap out at him. Everything he did was led by intuition. He couldn't doubt it now.

When he looked at the papers and books again, he skimmed the names and numbers until a pattern began to emerge. He paused and looked again.

"Thirteen pims a fortnight," Tahl muttered. A lot of money to bleed from someone, but not so much that a wealthy noble would think it suspicious, in the midst of all their expenses. But where was it going? And who was the man who was taking it?

A soft, familiar voice rose in the hall, the words too muffled to make out, but the alarm in them clear.

One easy way to find out. Tahl rounded the desk and jerked the chair out from under the doorknob. The door flew open and Tahl retreated, positioning himself in front of the desk.

The unfamiliar man stumbled in a step, his dark hair disheveled and his eyes burning like embers. Behind him, Ebitha stood in the hall. When she saw Tahl, she clamped a hand to her mouth.

Tahl's gaze locked with hers. "He's stealing from you."

The old woman's jaw dropped. "Tahl? What—"

Before she could finish, the man surged toward Tahl with his knife drawn. Ebitha shrieked, but her fear was unfounded. Tahl ducked to the side and caught the man's arm with one hand, hooked his ankle with a foot, pulled him off balance and drove him to the floor. The stranger cried out in mingled pain and anger as Tahl wrenched the blade out of his grasp and dug a knee into his back.

"Don't hurt him!" Ebitha cried.

Tahl motioned for her to calm down. He stashed the knife among his own hidden blades and kept the man's arm twisted. "Who is he?"

"My nephew," the widow said. "He comes twice a month to help me."

The man groaned.

"Enough!" Ebitha cried. "Let him up. Oh, Veris, are you all right?"

Begrudgingly, Tahl released his hold on the man. He darted behind the desk before Veris could rise.

Ebitha hurried in to help her nephew to his feet.

"He's coming to steal from you," Tahl said firmly. "Twenty-six pims a month, enough to hire two or three farmhands for the same amount of time. He's not helping you at all."

They both gaped.

Finally, Ebitha seemed to give him a proper look. "Tahl, why are you dressed that way?"

"Because he's a thief," Veris spat.

"You're the thief," Tahl retorted. "Twenty-six pims a month, thirteen a fortnight. He had your money box out and everything." He pointed at the desk.

Ebitha's expression faltered and she cast a questioning glance toward her nephew.

Tahl pretended to relax, though every muscle remained tight-wound and ready to spring. "Check his pockets. If he won't let you, then I will."

Veris paled. He shoved Ebitha aside and bolted for the door.

Tahl darted after him like a viper, striking hard and fast. They toppled to the floor together and the man's panicked cry bounced off the close walls in the hallway. He tried to fight, but Tahl was too fast, his wiry strength more than the nobleman could overcome. Tahl produced a cord from his pack.

Ebitha emerged from the office with a hand pressed to her chest, her white hair falling loose around her face.

Tahl bound Veris tight and turned him over.

"Brant blight you," the man spat.

"He's had his chance and hasn't done it yet," Tahl replied dryly. He plunged a hand into the man's pocket with an uncomfortable grimace, but found what he was looking for. When he removed his hand, a fistful of silver coins gleamed in his grasp.

"Veris!" Ebitha gasped. "What is the meaning of this?"

Tahl crossed to her and pressed the coins into her hands. "I'm sorry for entering your house like this, Ebitha. I never wanted to alarm you. But when I happened by the other day and saw Cotton was gone, I knew something was wrong."

The old woman's eyes filled with tears and she looked him over again, taking in his unusual fitted clothes and the assortment of knives on his person.

Lifetree's mercy, what was he supposed to say now?

"Can we go down to your parlor?" Tahl asked. "There's a lot to explain, and I have questions for your nephew, too."

Concern and uncertainty warred on the old woman's face. Tahl admitted it wasn't a good look, but there was little he could do about that now.

"I want to get your horse back," he added. "I know where he is and how we can do it. I just need you to trust me."

Slowly, Ebitha nodded. "Come downstairs. I'll... make some tea."

"Thank you, Ebitha." Tahl touched his chest in a gesture of sincerity and dragged Veris to one side of the hall as the old woman passed.

Uncooperative as the man was, getting Veris to his feet proved harder.

"I know who you are," the man growled.

Tahl snorted softly. "Maybe, but you definitely don't know why I'm here. Move."

The man resisted, but when Tahl drew a knife to press to his back, he became suddenly more cooperative and inched toward the stairs.

Together, they descended to the widow's parlor, where the tall harp sat. Something rattled in the kitchen down the hall, and Tahl took advantage of the privacy to shove Veris into a chair and bind him in place with the last of his rope.

"The money's buying weapons," Tahl said as he tightened a knot. "I know that much. Now give me the name of the buyer."

"I'm not telling you anything."

"Really? I thought you knew who I was." Tahl stood and traced a finger over the wax that hid his scar, indicating the checkmark shape that crossed the bridge of his nose and hooked beneath his right eye.

The man's eyes widened in fear.

Tahl raised a brow. It seemed Veris hadn't known, after all.

"Will you kill me?" Veris's voice quavered.

"Not if you cooperate. Give me the name of the buyer."

"H-how do you know my aunt?"

"She was good to me when no one else was. Your aunt Ebitha is a good person. Better than you deserve." Tahl drew the blade he'd taken from Veris and brandished it before the man's face. "And if you care about her at all, you'll give me the name of the weapons buyer before they destroy Orrad and everyone in it."

A rattle from the porcelain cups on Ebitha's tray heralded her arrival in the doorway. "Here we are."

Tahl's weapon disappeared in a blink, hidden safely where it wouldn't give the old widow undue fright. He hurried to the door to take the tray from her hands and help her to a chair. She eyed him dubiously, but did not refuse the assistance.

The disdain of another had never unsettled him before. Pretending he was unbothered, Tahl put the tea set on the low table beside Ebitha's chair and filled a cup for her first. "I know all this is strange. I promise I can explain everything."

"But can *you* explain, Ebitha?" Veris sneered. "I'm sure the emperor would love to hear why you've sheltered Orrad's most wanted criminal."

The old woman's eyes widened. For the first time, when she looked at Tahl, she was afraid.

He'd never expected how badly that would sting.

"It's not what you think," Tahl said softly as he poured his own tea and sat cross-legged on the floor.

Veris snorted. "I would love to hear your explanation."

Tahl ignored him and blew on his tea. "I feel like I have to apologize for what your nephew's done. Or what I didn't catch him at sooner. This shouldn't have escaped my notice, and I'm sorry."

"I don't understand," Ebitha said shakily. "What has he done?"

"Someone is importing weapons into the empire. A kind unheard of in Orrad. Your nephew is stealing money from you to help fund their production." He sipped his tea and savored the warmth. He hadn't had time to sit and enjoy a cup of tea in... he didn't know how long.

"You can't prove it," Veris snapped.

Tahl offered him a tight smile. "I don't have to. You've already done it."

The man blinked, taken aback. "How?"

"Because you never denied it. You weren't surprised when I told you I knew. You expected to get caught and you aren't even ashamed. You just didn't expect me to be the one to catch you." Tahl gazed at him over the rim of his teacup, a gleam in his bright green eyes.

Veris faltered.

"Is this true?" Ebitha asked. A note of sorrow touched her voice.

Instead of replying, her nephew glared. "How can you

believe him? I thought you were honest! And here you are, with the Ghost of Orrad under your roof!"

Again, worry and fear pinched the widow's face.

"Easy," Tahl reassured her. He reached to touch her hand and she did not shy away. A small comfort, that. "I'm here because I want to help. Not just you, but I want to help Orrad, too."

"The emperor will see you both hang," Veris spat.

"The emperor will do nothing," Tahl replied calmly. "I'm working for the queen."

A small glimmer of hope sparked in Ebitha's eyes.

Veris heaved a sigh. "Come, you can't possibly believe him. He's a thief, a liar, and a killer."

"I've never killed anyone," Tahl protested. "I don't kill people."

"But you don't contest the lying and stealing?"

"This job is sanctioned by the queen. I do what I must to ensure it gets done."

"But not every job you've done is sanctioned," the man goaded.

A hint of annoyance burned between Tahl's shoulders. He fought to ignore it. "I'm not going to let you redirect this toward me. The fact stands that you're part of the group siphoning money from nobles and using it to fund a force the queen believes means to attack and destroy the empire. You're going to tell me where the money's going."

"I won't help you."

Tahl's eyes narrowed. "Then you'll hang."

Silence fell over the comfortable parlor.

Irritation churned to frustration and Tahl made himself exhale. How was he going to make progress if he couldn't make the man talk?

"Tahl," Ebitha said slowly. "If you're being truthful, perhaps... that is, if you could prove..."

The suggestion sparked an idea, and he nodded. "Yes." Tahl rose and returned his teacup to the tray. "But you have to swear, under honor to the crown, that he'll still be here and be tied up when I get back."

"Ridiculous," Veris muttered.

Tahl ignored him. "Do you swear?"

Ebitha glanced between the two of them, her wrinkled brow furrowed deeper than ever before. "Yes," she whispered, and the single word carried all the finality of the thud of a headsman's axe.

CHAPTER 12

When Tahl returned, he went to the front door.

"Are you certain this is wise?" Oria asked as he knocked.

"You should ask Nia how often anything I do is wise. I function on instinct, not wisdom." Still, despite the admission, Tahl bounced on his toes, eager to continue the night's proceedings before the sun rose. A faint rosy hue had already begun to color the eastern sky.

The queen did not seem impressed. "I had guessed as much, given how many times we've passed through that bear's den."

"If you know of any other good secret passages that lead in and out of the city, that would be welcome knowledge," he said.

Oria's mouth clamped shut, her lips puckered like she'd just tried one of the sour lemon tarts sold in the coastal markets.

The door opened a crack, Ebitha's weathered face peering out into the night.

Tahl straightened. "Here's your proof. Let us in, please."

He expected the old woman to question him, but instead, she opened the door wide and ushered them into the foyer. He and Oria were quick to comply.

"Is Veris still tied?" Tahl asked as Ebitha closed the door behind them.

"Guessing by how tight those knots are, I couldn't have let him out if I wanted to." The old woman tried to smile, but the expression was strained.

Tahl nodded and motioned for her to lead the way. More than once, Ebitha cast a thoughtful look toward the queen, but Oria's hood was up, her face shadowed.

They returned to the parlor together. Veris had slumped to one side of his chair and proven unable to straighten. He glowered when he saw Tahl.

"Here he is, Your Majesty," Tahl announced as he stopped before the man's chair.

On that cue, Oria pushed back her hood. Ebitha gasped and Veris grew pale. There was no way he wouldn't recognize her. Her face decorated every pim he'd stolen.

"What do you mean to do with him?" Oria asked. She sounded appropriately disinterested for a queen and looked down her nose at Veris with disdain to match.

Tahl squared his shoulders and clasped his hands behind his back. "He knows who commissioned what we're looking for, but refuses to surrender the information. By your leave, Majesty, I think an interrogation is in order."

"Interrogation?" Ebitha repeated, aghast.

Oria gave a single nod. "Very well."

The last thing Tahl wanted to do was frighten the old woman. With that in mind, the best thing he could do was let her to witness the entire thing. He allowed himself a grim smile and leaned close to the queen to share a conspiratorial whisper. "My affinity is fire, what there is of it. I need you to do me a favor."

The queen raised a brow as he finished his request in a breath so light, he was sure no one else had heard. He drew the knife he'd confiscated from Veris and looked at the man from the corner of his eye. A fine mist of sweat emerged on the man's brow.

Tahl positioned himself behind the chair. He caught Veris by the collar and pulled him upright. "Now," he began, "you have the opportunity to tell the queen where the money is going and who else is involved, or you can try to see how long you're able to hold out against questioning."

"The queen has no authority," Veris sneered.

"Suit yourself." Tahl slid the knife down the back of the man's shirt and sliced it open with one good flick of his wrist.

Ebitha gasped, but covered her mouth with her hands. Veris seemed confident Oria could do nothing to him, but Ebitha lacked that certainty.

Tahl raised the blade and held it where Veris could see. All his training had never helped his magic develop, but he could do enough. He funneled power into the blade and it began to glow. Most mage-lights were cool in tone, but he'd learned to alter his. The metal reddened, then brightened to yellow, and finally white, imitating extreme heat. In truth, a subtle warmth was all he could conjure, something to radiate from the blade and imply the metal was scorching hot. The rest of his magic, he coiled close and held ready.

The beads of sweat on Veris's brow began to swell and roll down the sides of his face.

Oria paced around the chair to join Tahl. With one hand, she pulled the fabric of the man's split shirt wide open.

"This is your final warning," Tahl said. "Tell us where we can find the buyer."

"I can't," Veris gasped.

"Veris!" Ebitha cried. "Tell the queen! What you're doing is treason!"

"Too late." Tahl flipped the blade in hand and jammed it down the man's shirt. At the same time, he swiped the chunk of ice he'd asked for from Oria's hand. He flashed Ebitha a wicked grin and let her see the glittering icicle in his hand before he rammed it against Veris's spine.

The magic he'd gathered surged at that moment. The ice hissed as his fire magic hit it. Thick, acrid smoke billowed from the point where the icicle met the noble's skin.

Veris howled in agony.

Ebitha stared in disbelief.

"Tell us," Tahl demanded as he slipped the glowing blade to the queen. Oria took it, her nose wrinkled. By now, she had to think him mad.

"It goes to the pool!" Veris wailed.

Tahl removed the icicle.

The man slumped, panting. "Everyone adds funds to the pool. I don't know who's in charge of spending it."

"Who is everyone?" Tahl demanded.

"An organization. They call themselves Crownwatch."

"Arrogant," Oria muttered. She tilted the knife in her hand. The magic had already faded, the blade dull and lightless once more.

"The Crownwatch council is all nobles, but I don't know anyone on the council. I'm at the bottom. The money was supposed to help me move up." The sweat that tracked down Veris's face mingled with tears. For a moment, Tahl almost pitied him. But pity wouldn't answer questions.

"Does all the money come from the bottom?"

"I don't know."

Tahl jabbed the icicle against his back again.

The man's back arched, a howl of pain and fear tearing free of his throat.

"Blade's not quite hot enough," Tahl muttered as he removed the ice. "I apologize, Your Majesty. He's bleeding." He winked at Ebitha, who appeared too horrified—and confused—to speak.

Oria leaned forward and frowned. Fat droplets of water rolled down Veris's back where the ice had been pressed. "It's hot enough," she said. "I imagine even his blood feels cold after that." A ghost of a smile played across her lips and Tahl blinked at her in surprise. He hadn't expected her to comment, much less join in his deception.

Before them, Veris slouched and gasped for breath between

panicked sobs. "M-most of the organization is n-n-nobles like m-me. No w-wealth of their own, but access to it."

"Even the council?"

Veris bucked forward before Tahl could move. "I don't know!" he cried. "I haven't met them. All I have is names!"

Perfect.

"Give them to us," Tahl ordered.

His hand had begun to go numb from gripping the ice, but they were close. He could hold out a few minutes more.

"Ryald Aldiss," Veris said.

Tahl shifted enough to remove a notepad and a stub of a pencil from his bag. He passed them to the queen.

The man continued. "Norel Rohede. Arl Endelor. Bahar Eseri —" He cut off with a scream as Tahl jabbed him with the ice again, the smoke pouring out thicker than before.

"Don't lie to us," Tahl snapped. "Bahar Eseri is dead!"

"He's not!" Veris gasped between breaths. He slumped forward and his shoulders trembled with his sobs. "He's still alive."

Tahl shook his head vigorously. "Half of Orrad watched him hang."

"He's the leader of it all, I swear he is!"

Before Tahl could say anything else, Oria held out a hand in order for him to be still. Irritated, Tahl stepped back. He was supposed to be in charge, but he recognized when his head wasn't clear.

"Where do we find him?" the queen asked.

Veris panted a moment before he could speak again. "He's not here. He's gone north to meet with a caravan."

"The shipment," Oria murmured.

Tahl nodded. "We go north." He reached forward and dropped the half-melted icicle into Veris's lap. A moment later, Oria dropped the man's knife onto the cushion beside him. Then the queen drew up her hood and swept toward the door without another word. Subdued, Tahl followed at her heels, though he paused in the doorway.

Ebitha already knelt beside her nephew, cradling his tear-streaked face in her hands.

"You'll find he's unharmed, if being proven a coward hasn't bruised his ego," Tahl said flatly.

The old widow stared at him in disbelief. "Who are you?"

A strange question. Somehow, Tahl didn't know the answer, himself. "I'll be back with your horse." He turned to follow the queen, though a new sense of uneasiness churned in his belly like a knot of snakes.

Bahar Eseri had been hung. Tahl hadn't witnessed it himself, but it had been the talk of Orrad for weeks. The hanging had happened; he was sure. But if Lord Eseri wasn't dead, who was?

TAHL SCRUBBED his face with both hands and struggled to hold in a yawn.

"You okay, boss?" Hadren asked. The uneasiness in the large man's voice made Tahl uncomfortable.

Normally, he wouldn't have let anyone know he wasn't at the top of his game. Things were far from normal, though, and Tahl wiped his burning eyes with the heel of his palm. "I'm tired. I don't know about you, but I haven't had a decent night's sleep in days."

"Maybe we should stop for a break," Jeran suggested. "Make a camp. That's what people do on quests like this, right?"

Tahl snorted at the idea of being on a quest, but he supposed it wasn't far off the mark. The five of them had departed almost immediately after he and Oria had returned from questioning Veris. Though Tahl would have preferred a decent chance to eat and rest, a sense of urgency had clawed at him and drove him to lead the way out of the city without more than a few minutes to pack. The lightweight change of clothes he kept in the guild's headquarters wasn't well-suited to the chilly nights, but he suspected they'd sleep more often during the day. Under the cover of night, they could move along the main roads without notice.

"I hope we're going to take a break soon. I'm starving." Ashyl rubbed her stomach. If it had growled, no one seemed to notice.

"Food's going to be sparse unless some of you can hunt. Didn't have much time to pack provisions." Hadren scanned the horizon.

Tahl did, too, though for different reasons. Most of the empire's settlements were on the eastern half of the continent. The west coast was all but untamed, save a select few port cities positioned to intercept trade from the Chains of Raeldan, a twisted series of landmasses that resembled large islands. But the Chains were often split by political strife, and shipments from Raeldan were irregular. Most trade passed through the eastern side of empire—and followed the main roads.

Thus far, they'd seen no sign of traders.

"We'll rest in a few hours," Tahl said, forestalling any further discussion. "I don't think any of us brought a tent, so I'd prefer to wait until we're a ways into the foothills and can hide among the trees."

Jeran glanced toward the treeline in the distance. "Is that really necessary? We have a good explanation for why we're out here. Even you're safe as long as we've got the queen with us."

Tahl doubted that. From the way Oria's mouth twitched, she doubted it, too. He did not reply, but none of the other thieves pressed any more questions. The night had left them all wearied, it seemed.

When they reached the pines, Jeran, Hadren, and Ashyl all ate and chose trees to use for shelter. Tahl was halfway up his chosen tree when he caught the queen watching the others with a pained expression. After a moment of consideration, he let go of the branch he still dangled from and dropped back to the ground.

A still moment passed between them before Oria nodded her thanks.

"Not used to this, are you?" Tahl asked as he settled with his back against his chosen tree. It wasn't much protection, but it was better than nothing.

She sniffed. "Why, because I'm a queen?"

"Because you look miserable." He couldn't help the little smirk that tugged at the corner of his mouth. "The climbing part's not that hard. I could teach you."

"Not that hard for *you*. You climb like a squirrel, scampering all about. Up and down trees like it's nothing."

Tahl grinned as he stretched, legs extended, and leaned forward to grasp his toes. "I've heard that before."

Despite her disdainful tone, Oria offered a slight smile. "You're so young, but no one could deny your skill. You've been practicing long?"

"Since I was a kid." The backs of his legs ached. He slowed his breath and willed the tired muscles to relax. "Not for this purpose, but I guess that doesn't matter."

The queen tilted her head. "Why did you learn?"

"Because it was fun." It still struck him as odd that some people expected a deeper explanation than that. He'd been lonely. Bored. As the son of mages who had little interest in anything outside their political machinations, he had little in common with his family. As a child, he'd been left to his own devices.

The acrobatics had simply been fun. Looking back, he marveled at how easily they had fed into less innocent habits.

"And is this fun?" Oria gestured to the trees around them with an open palm.

"Verdict's still out on that one. Come on." He popped to his feet and pressed his knuckles to his back as he stretched one last time. "Let's climb."

"Queens do not climb," she protested.

Tahl squinted up at the trees. "Really? I'd think queens get to do whatever they want."

She rolled her eyes, but crept closer. "If it were so easy to do what I want, I wouldn't be hiring gangs of thieves to do things for me."

"Fair enough." Tahl slipped behind her and scooped up her cloak. She started to turn, but he motioned for her to stay put. "Cloaks are like skirts. If you're going to climb, you'd better gird up." He showed her how to twist and tie the bulky material to keep it out of her way, mindful not to touch her in the process. He wasn't particularly interested in touching her at all, but she was royalty, and he preferred the notion of keeping his head attached to his shoulders.

Oria shifted about experimentally when he finished. "Do you climb in cloaks often?"

"I climb all the time. In everything. But wearing something like this does help." He pointed at his own attire briefly. His heist clothing provided the best range of movement one could hope for, outside of being naked. Tahl did, he decided, prefer to climb while clothed.

Keeping that thought to himself, he showed her where to put her hands and feet and launched into the same sort of explanation he'd used in teaching Nia to climb.

Before long, she was halfway up the trunk.

"It's not as hard as I thought," Oria said as she scouted out another handhold. "I'd assumed it only looked easy because you were good at it."

"I'm not the only one who was climbing." Tahl jerked a thumb toward the next tree over. He'd opted to climb behind the queen, just in case she slipped.

"And if you're smart, you won't stay down there," Ashyl called softly from the tree beside theirs. "Someone's coming."

Tahl slipped to the other side of the pine's trunk and scurried up to Ashyl's level, nearly at the crown of the tree. He couldn't see her, but she switched to a soft series of whistles that could easily be mistaken for birdsong.

South. Guards.

Tahl could have cursed. He parted the branches just enough to get a look. Armor glinted on the road between their group and Orrad, the city little more than a gray smudge on the horizon. He retreated down the tree to offer the queen a hand. "Best get up top, Your Majesty. I have a feeling if they see us, they won't let us continue this little adventure."

Oria accepted the assistance without comment. He hurried her into the branches and helped her settle against the trunk, then pressed a finger to his lips in signal to be silent. Once she nodded, he took a leap to the next tree.

Had it not been so close, he wouldn't have been able to light on a branch and bound over to Ashyl, but he still allowed himself a small chuckle of amusement. A squirrel, Oria said. He'd been called worse things, too.

"I saw red," Ashyl whispered. "Why would Atoras send his Elite outside the city?"

"Hard to say." Tahl rubbed his chin and looked south again. He couldn't see anything without moving branches, but he'd seen enough. "It doesn't have anything to do with us, though. We'll wait for them to pass, then we'll move, but we'll stay off the roads."

Her eyes narrowed. "How do you know they're not after us? This could be the team sent to set up a trap."

He snorted a laugh. "You don't send someone to set up a trap after the quarry's already on the move. If there is a trap, it's already set up at the destination, and they'll be waiting for us."

"Reassuring."

They both fell silent as the group of guards came close enough they could see the gleam of armor through the trees. The road was not particularly close by, but given who they were and who they traveled with, Tahl had no doubt they'd become targets if they were seen.

He crouched close to Ashyl, gripping a branch overhead to aid his stability. She was closer to the trunk, and he was subtly aware of the way she shifted closer to him. A thread of uneasiness trailed through his mind and he glanced down, but she didn't seem threatening. Instead, her brow furrowed with concern as she pressed near to his side. Seeking protection? Or comfort? Either one struck Tahl as odd, but she wasn't hurting anything, so he didn't try to dissuade her.

Distant voices carried near enough to give away the guards' location, but it was impossible to make out the words. The bored tones in those voices told Tahl everything he needed to know. They wouldn't discuss anything important or useful while they were on the road. At night, when they met to review orders and plan accordingly, he might have heard something they could use, but he'd dealt with the Elite enough for one lifetime. Without thinking, he touched the scar that marred his face.

Unexpectedly, Ashyl touched his arm and gave him a look of sympathy. He blinked at her for a moment before he lowered his hand and waited for the noise to pass. His legs grew stiff beneath him before he decided it was safe.

When he dropped from the tree, his thieves followed.

"They're a good mile and a half north by now," Jeran said as his gaze swept up the road carved into the countryside. "What do we do?"

"Not rest," Tahl said. "We'll cut into the hills and try to get past them. Keep rest breaks short. We're going to need to get as far ahead of that group as possible."

"Why?" Hadren asked. "What are you instincts telling you?"

Behind them, Oria made her noisy descent from her tree.

Tahl turned to fix her with a stare, considering that question. The queen had seemed disdainful of the way he operated, relying on gut feelings and intuition to lead the way. His crew seemed to take it in stride. Until he'd noted her uncertainty, he'd never found that odd.

Something to think on later, he told himself as he checked to make sure he had his things and finally answered Hadren's question. "That they're after the same thing we are."

CHAPTER 13

Tahl fought to keep his teeth from chattering as he trekked over the fresh snow and down the long slope between one rise and the next. Moving kept him warm enough that he wouldn't suffer, but the wind still bit.

They moved single-file to hide their number, but there was no hiding the trail in the fresh powder. The snow wasn't deep, nor was the snowfall heavy, but it would take several hours of sun the next morning to eliminate the sinuous line they'd left behind.

Ashyl had suggested they cut as far west as possible. Tahl considered it wise advice, but that took them higher into the hills than he'd anticipated. The terrain was not difficult to climb, but the incline slowed them down. They set a hard pace to compensate. Under the cover of night, when they didn't have to worry about being seen, they moved faster.

Levity had evaporated with the knowledge the Elite trekked north. Behind him, Tahl heard the quiet conversation that passed between the others. He made no effort to join. His mind was elsewhere.

Bahar Eseri's name hadn't been common knowledge until he'd been tried and found guilty. The evidence that tied him to the old guild had been powerful, undeniable, and the man's death was part of what had instilled fear of the Ghost—of Tahl—in the city. If Lord Eseri had lived, there was no way the man would have allowed Tahl, of all people, to seize power over Orrad's thieves.

Someone could have adopted the name, Tahl supposed. It carried weight and a reputation. Had Lord Eseri been alive, pretending to be him might have offered valuable connections to smugglers. But why take the name of a man widely known to be dead?

"Hadren," Tahl called absently, his voice almost carried away by the wind.

The man hiked up to join him.

Tahl wouldn't confess to being short of breath or out of energy, but their newfound need for speed had pushed him to his limits. "Take lead for a bit, will you? All the fresh snow's making my toes numb."

"Sure, boss." Hadren inched ahead and Tahl fell back to join the others. For the first time, he found himself envious of Oria's wool cloak.

Everyone looked tired. They'd opted for cat naps instead of setting up for hours at a time, uncertain how fast they had to move to beat the Elite to the valley between mountain ridges where the shipment was sure to come through.

Now and then, Tahl sent one of his crew back toward the road to monitor progress. From a hill or two over, it was easy to see the winding road, but none of them were familiar with the route and no one was certain how far it was safe to stray. The notion someone should go look again had just crossed Tahl's mind when Hadren's voice rose from ahead.

"Hey, boss?" Hadren crouched at the top of the hill and spoke again, lower. "You're gonna want to see this."

Concerned, Tahl jogged ahead to crouch beside him.

Below, the hills fell away in gentle slopes to leave a wide, sprawling valley. Shadowy shapes marked with tiny, glittering lights inched along the roadway that snaked toward the northwest.

"Lanterns?" Ashyl whispered as she knelt on Tahl's other side.

"Looks like a caravan," Tahl murmured.

"Wagons," Hadren confirmed. "Blight it, I thought the snow would make it easier to see. All those bare patches on the slopes make it confusing."

Tahl squinted up at the moon. "Snow's going to make it hard for us to get down the slope without notice."

Jeran and Oria joined them a moment later. The queen peered down without comment.

"So do we think this is who we're looking for?" Ashyl asked.

It was impossible to tell from atop a hill at least half a mile away. Tahl rubbed his chin. "Traveling through the night certainly isn't normal."

"So we send someone to check," Hadren said. "Who's most qualified to sneak up on a caravan, get into a wagon, and check out the cargo?"

All eyes turned to Tahl. He bit the inside of his lip and drummed his fingers against the cold, damp earth. "We're going to need to work out a signal if it is what we think it is. If I make it in, it'll be easier for me to stay put and have the rest of you come help."

"Which means you need a plan before you go down there," Oria said. "I suspect instinct doesn't lead your colleagues nearly as much as it does you."

"No," Tahl agreed. He studied the caravan train through narrowed eyes. "From here, I can't tell if those lanterns are lamps or mage-lights. I guess it doesn't matter. I can work with both."

"A light signal?" Ashyl asked.

He nodded. "I know we haven't used those as much as the hand signals. I'll keep it simple. I'll signal 'help' if I find what we're looking for. If I don't, I'll signal 'no' and meet you back on this hill."

"The caravan's moving pretty steadily south," Hadren said. "We'll keep pace with it up here."

"Just make sure you stay out of sight." Tahl shot Oria a meaningful look before he waved them all back.

Jeran took the queen by the arm and gently tugged her down the slope they'd just climbed. Ashyl and Hadren flattened themselves against the top of the hill as Tahl began his downward trek alone.

Avoiding the snow patches meant taking a more circuitous route that put Tahl farther ahead of the caravan. It was safer to hide in the hollows beside the road and wait for the wagons to pass than to try to catch up from behind. He huddled against the hillside, regretting his lightweight clothing a little more with each minute that passed. Snow was not uncommon in Orrad, but it rarely accumulated within the city, where the heat of life was insulated by stone. Tahl crossed his arms over his chest and tried to stay focused.

The caravan crawled toward him, providing ample time to study the distribution of wagons and people. There were a surprising number of gaps in their security. Those who rode alongside the caravan seemed more like travelers than guards, milling about to converse with one another instead of remaining posted near the gaps between wagons or taking up the rear. Tahl counted seconds between movements, searching for a pattern, but there seemed to be none.

Not what I'd expect from a caravan carrying weapons, he mused.

The first few wagons rolled past his sheltered nook without drivers or riders noticing him. Tahl waited until the last wagon passed, then darted toward the unguarded back. It was the easiest point of entry, which meant he was unlikely to find anything, but one never knew. The less they guarded whatever they hauled, the less likely it was anyone would find them memorable.

The back of the covered wagon was closed with nothing more than cloth flaps and Tahl leaped in without resistance or notice. He landed with little sound, his hands braced against the wagon's floorboards. Part of him was surprised there was space at the back of the wagon, but it wasn't as full of cargo as he expected.

Boxes and sacks lined the wagon's walls with a narrow walkway between them. Tahl crept between them, their shapes near-impossible to make out in the dark. What little light there was came from the moon, a dim sliver of illumination that flashed every time the wagon swayed.

He tugged open a sack and promptly shut it, unimpressed. Dried beans were hardly the makings of warfare. A gentle probing of the other sacks indicated they held similar goods. A barrel at the back held salted fish. Frowning, he turned his attention to the boxes. Those that were sealed were not sealed well, nor did they hold any muskets. Determined to be thorough, Tahl checked them all. Then he sat back on his heels, tapping his fingers against his thighs.

Was it worth checking the other wagons? He supposed he had to, though he hadn't spent much time thinking about how he'd get there.

Something to figure out in the process, he told himself with a wry smile. Slowly and silently, he slipped out the back of the apparent supply wagon and kept pace close behind it, his footsteps soundless beneath the groaning axles and the squelch of wheels on roads made soggy by melting snow.

For a moment, Tahl considered trying to go up and over the top of the wagon, but the cloth covering made that seem like an unappealing and unlikely possibility. Instead, he peered around the wagon's sides and waited for an opportunity to move. Part of him wished he could hide behind a smokescreen. Most of him knew that would be foolish. Still, the thought played in the back of his mind as he waited for the people on horses to move out of the way.

People, he thought again. Not soldiers, not men. Both men and women rode alongside the caravan, conversing in low voices. One of the riders wove between the wagon Tahl shadowed and the one in front of it.

A small opportunity.

He took it.

In the split second the wagon's driver was distracted, Tahl darted into the shadows just off the side of the road and arced up to the next wagon in line. He approached it from the side, shoved the rough canvas covering up a few inches, and wriggled his way inside.

He bumped into something soft and warm and froze.

Whatever it was, it didn't move. Tahl pivoted on his toes and stayed crouched as he craned his neck to see where he'd landed. *Oh, for the love of leaves.*

Instead of cargo, the wagon was filled with sleeping children.

This is definitely *not the caravan we're looking for.* Tahl gripped the frame of the wagon's covering as the rough terrain under the wheels made the wagon sway. He chewed his lip and closed his eyes. If there had been any mages in the caravan, he would have sensed them when they came near. Still, he focused his attention on his Gift and searched for power in anyone else nearby.

When nothing tickled his senses, he shifted his thoughts to the lanterns he knew were by the driver's feet. The flame called to him, as fire always did. Weak as his own power was, getting it to bend to his will would be the hard part. Tahl set his jaw. He didn't need much, just enough of a flicker to send the signal.

To his surprise, the flame leaped to answer. It flared brighter in his senses and his heart skipped a beat. *Not brighter, dim.* In an instant, its presence dwindled. He drew it back to life and made it dim again, blinking the pattern his crew would be waiting for.

"Oi," a voice rose from right outside. "Check that lantern, will you? It's flickering something fierce."

Hoofbeats drew closer. Tahl released his magic and opened his eyes. Moonlight illuminated a child's face peering up at him, round and pale with dark eyes glittering in curiosity.

Startled, Tahl stared back for longer than he ought. Then he offered a nervous grin and lifted a finger to his lips to ask for silence.

A guarded look crossed the boy's face.

Tahl couldn't blame him. What must he look like, crouching in the back of a wagon with knives bristling from his belt and wrists?

But the boy didn't scream. Instead, when Tahl lowered his hand, the child shifted in the blankets and squinted as if to see him more clearly. "Who're you?"

"The Ghost," Tahl whispered.

The boy's eyes grew wide. How far had his reputation carried?

Before the child could act, Tahl motioned for him to wait. His sleight of hand was useful for more than just lightening purses, and he showed the boy his empty hands before flexing his fingers and making a silver coin appear.

The boy's eyes grew wider still.

"I was looking for someone," Tahl whispered. "He's not here. Try to forget you saw me." He offered the single pim between his first two fingers.

The boy's chubby hand reached for it, but the wagon lurched.

"Whoa, now. What's that?" someone outside called.

Tahl glanced toward the wagon's rear flaps and then turned an ear toward the wagon's front.

Horses huffed as the caravan came to a stop. The riders moved ahead.

"State your business," another voice called, farther away.

Tahl winced and pushed the coin into the boy's waiting

fingers. He motioned for silence again and slid out the wagon's side, the same way he'd gotten in.

"We're farmers," someone else answered. "Packed up our families to move back to the capital. Our field's to sit fallow this coming year. We thought it best to travel before winter."

The statement yielded an unimpressed grunt. "Check the wagons," a man ordered.

Tahl ducked underneath the wagon. It wasn't exceptionally large, but he could barely suspend himself between the axles to press his back against the underside of the bed. The wheels turned slowly as the wagon's driver positioned for inspection.

A pair of familiar boots passed by and Tahl made himself grow still.

The Elite.

Of course.

"This roadway is now closed," the soldier at the head of the caravan said. "Imperial business only."

"Closed?" a man exclaimed. "This is the only road to Orrad."

Tahl watched the boots circle the wagon he hid under, mindful to keep his breath quiet. Above him, children stirred and small, worried voices rose into the night. Concern edged its way into his mind. They wouldn't do anything to children, would they?

"Nothing unusual at a glance, sir," one of the Elite called. Two pairs of boots trudged back toward the front. "Should we take a closer look?"

With the soldiers gone, Tahl eased himself back to the ground. The wagons had shifted while he hid. Instead of single-file, they now waited in a wide row. He could have escaped easily, but instead he inched backwards and stood by the back of the wagon, listening.

"No," the commander said. "There's no need. They're not what we're looking for."

Which indicated the Elite *were* after the same thing as the queen. Did she know? Or was it an ill stroke of luck that the emperor had decided to humor her concerns only after she'd disappeared?

The commander's voice hardened as he addressed the drivers or riders. Tahl didn't know which and supposed it didn't matter. "Have you encountered anyone else on this road who might impede our travel?"

"Another group," a woman said. "Camped a ways north. They're why we decided to keep moving through the night. Unfriendly lot."

Now that sounded like what Tahl was after.

"Well, we'll see them move, too," the Elite said. "You need to get your wagons off this road. There's a smaller access road farther east. If you cut due east across this field, you'll find it."

Tahl retreated into the shadows. The caravan had rolled on some distance, but he doubted his companions had experienced any difficulty in following. Instead of backtracking, he trekked straight into the hills, weaving around the snowy patches that decorated the slopes.

He couldn't hear or see his thieves, but he knew they were there. Once he crested the hill, Tahl stopped trying to hide.

"Always pushing your boundaries, aren't you, boss?" Ashyl asked from somewhere in the dark.

A small tingle of surprise and concern ran through him when she stood, not an arm's reach away. He'd wanted to be detected, but that he hadn't detected her *first* left him unsettled. He skimmed the hillside for the others and found Jeran before the man rose. Oria and Hadren did not appear to be present.

"We figured we'd be more effective without the queen in tow," Jeran said, as if predicting what Tahl would ask. "We left them on the next hill over. Close enough if we needed them, but far enough back to be out of the way."

Tahl nodded once. "We're headed back north. We'll pick them up along the way."

"You sound like you have a plan," Ashyl said.

"Right now, my plan is to get as far away from the Elite as

possible." Tahl jerked his head toward the north and turned to lead the way. "That caravan down there was inspired to keep moving by another group they say is camped up north. If we can hit them while they're settled, it'll make our job a thousand times easier."

Jeran made a soft *hmm*ing sound. "I'm not sure I'd agree with that math."

"I'm a thief, not a mathematician," Tahl replied. "The only counting I do is coins, *after* I've gotten away with them."

"That's not true," Ashyl said unhelpfully. "You've got entire books full of numbers you're always scribbling together. You're no professor, but you're definitely some kind of scholar."

Tahl decided it was best not to honor that with a response. He paused on the next hilltop until he saw Hadren and Oria settled next to a large stone. Her dark cloak almost let them disappear beside it. He joined them and related his intentions as they jogged onward together.

A new sort of urgency pricked at him, something Tahl couldn't quite identify. A sense of restlessness and a need to move fast, both tempered with a sense of dread that only grew heavier as they moved on.

More than once, the party rearranged themselves, changing order to let someone new take the lead. Tahl led as often as he could, but the wind had shifted, the bitter gusts cutting through whoever stood at the forefront of the line. Lean as he was, he could only tolerate it for so long before it felt as if his bones had turned to ice and he would never be warm again.

Eventually, the stars began to fade overhead, the depths of night receding. It was still long before sunrise when Jeran topped a hill and dropped to his stomach, his hands flashing urgently in a signal for extreme caution.

The dread that had been growing for hours congealed in the pit of Tahl's stomach, morphing into a frigid ball of something far more sinister. For all that his instincts made him flighty, the feeling was uncomfortably unfamiliar. Icy tendrils lashed out from it, tangling his limbs and making his feet grow heavy as he knelt, then crawled to the top of the hill.

Fear, he concluded, more to himself as an effort to acknowledge it and brush it away than anything else.

He crested the hill and pressed his chest to the frozen grass.

Below them spread an army.

CHAPTER 14

"WHAT'S THE PLAN?" JERAN ASKED IN A WHISPER SO THIN, TAHL almost didn't hear it above the wind.

The army camp below was still quiet, but it wouldn't likely remain that way for long. Paler shades of blue already touched the sky, and the soldier moon had disappeared as its endless patrol across the sky carried it beyond the horizon. Any time, the camp would begin to rouse.

"Someone needs to go back," Tahl said absently, his eyes investigating every inch of the camp. Theirs was a good vantage point. "Someone needs to warn the Elite."

Ashyl inched up beside him. "Warn them? They want to kill us!"

Tahl gave her a hard look. "Even the Emperor's Elite won't stand a chance against all this. There have to be at least five men for each Elite in that squad."

"You think the Elite can't handle that?" Jeran nodded toward the camp below. Dozens of wagons sat in a ring the center of the camp, tents arranged outside them in a lazy spiral.

"They couldn't handle *me*," Tahl said. "They're good, but they're not infallible."

"I think the real question is why he doesn't want the Elite

smashed flat." Ashyl's voice took a sour note. "Having them out of the way could only make our job easier."

"Maybe you should consider how your client feels," Oria chimed in. She crouched low on the hillside behind them, as if she didn't dare look over the hill at the disaster that surely awaited.

Tahl nodded once. "If we're going to do this, we're going to do it clean. Which means someone needs to backtrack and let the Elite know what they're up against."

"And risk us getting sandwiched between the Elite and that army?" Hadren thrust a finger toward the camp. "We don't even know if they have the shipment."

That, Tahl couldn't argue. They didn't know. Not for sure. He had an inkling of confidence that they'd stumbled on the right place—Brant knew he couldn't fathom what else would justify that sort of escort—but he could only ask the others to trust his intuition so many times. "Then we find out," he concluded. "And then we act."

At last, Oria inched up the hill to look down at the camp. Her mouth tightened and a faint furrow creased the space between her brows.

Tahl leaned toward her. "What are you thinking?"

"The tents are mismatched," the queen murmured. "There are horses, but not enough for all the men that must be down there. No campfires. No signs of cooking. They must have dry rations."

"What does that have to do with anything?" Hadren asked.

"The queen has her own credentials as a ruler," Tahl reminded him. "Let her speak."

Oria nodded in appreciation. "It's a mercenary force. I'd put money on it. Atoras's father forbade the existence of mercenary forces."

"And the only reason for someone to hire mercenaries to escort something coming into the empire would be..." Tahl trailed off with a vague hand motion, hoping someone else would pick up on the importance of her words.

"If they were escorting something of dire importance," Jeran finished. He rubbed his chin and fixed his stare on the wagons in the middle of the camp. "Such as delivering weapons to an uprising in the city."

Precisely what Tahl thought. He glanced to Ashyl on his other side. Her face was twisted with displeasure, but he thought he saw a hint of grudging acceptance in her eyes.

"Oria," Tahl prompted softly.

The queen turned to him, her silent question painted on her face.

"Your Majesty," he corrected himself with a wince. Better late than never, though she hadn't seemed to mind the familiarity. "You should be the one to go. Not only are all of us likely to get ourselves arrested or killed, but the Elite have no reason not to listen to you."

Ashyl gave him a look so sharp, it could have cut. "You want her to go alone?"

"And give her a chance to betray us?" Hadren added.

Tahl ignored them both. "The rest of us will take on the camp. Oria, hurry. The sooner you catch the Elite and turn them back toward the city, the better. I have an idea, and having a bunch of Atoras's men showing up at the edge of the camp would ruin it."

The queen's eyes took a stormy, stony look, but she nodded in confirmation and put out a hand to touch Tahl's arm. "Good luck."

He blinked, staring at her hand until she pulled it away. The warmth in that touch had been strange, foreign, unlike anything he was used to. A message of confidence. A statement of trust. Oria slipped away and pulled up her hood as she departed. Everyone watched her leave, none of them comfortable.

"You're a madman," Hadren grumbled.

"I think we already knew that about him," Jeran said. "So, boss, what's the plan?"

Tahl stared after her until she disappeared in the shadows and even his eyes couldn't pick her out. How often had anyone trusted him? His mouth worked a moment before he found his voice again. "Powder."

"Powder?" Jeran repeated.

Blinking to clear the vision of the queen's trusting hand against his arm from his thoughts, Tahl mustered a grin and trained his thoughts on the half-hatched scheme that had the gears in his head turning. "Tell me," he began as he slid his bag off his shoulder and flipped it open. "Who all brought flint?"

***

THE SULPHUR-SOAKED INCH-STICKS Tahl kept in his bag always left an unpleasant residue on his hands. He rubbed his fingers together as if that would make it disappear, but he'd just have to handle the little slivers of pine again anyway. No matter. If everything went according to plan, the foul sulphur sensation on his fingertips would be the least of his worries.

"Are you sure that's enough?" Hadren counted out his inch-sticks for the third time before he put them away.

"It'll have to be. Mage or not, I can't do much without them." Tahl still hated to admit the lacking extent of his power, but he had no reason to hide it from his fellow thieves. They found his smoke creations useful and his mage-lights convenient, but in the end, he suspected the rest of the guild liked the fact their leader couldn't do anything *too* out of the ordinary. Acrobatics like his could be learned without needing anything more than mundane skill.

Jeran studied his sticks with the sort of thoughtful, bemused frown that indicated he was developing some sort of engineering idea. Any other time, Tahl would have been eager to know what the man was thinking. Right now, that sort of distraction could prove dangerous.

"This is going to get us killed," Ashyl muttered.

From the way Hadren snorted, he didn't agree. She raised a brow at him, and he gave her a more pointed look. "Speak for yourself. An attractive woman in the middle of a camp of lonely mercenaries? They'd be more likely to build you a throne."

"I doubt the queen would appreciate having Ashyl as a rival," Tahl said. "Let's go."

A few grumbles answered, but at least Jeran pocketed his inch-sticks and seemed ready to move. He wasn't the best fighter, but he'd been the most cooperative. Tahl would remember that when it was time to dole out the mission's rewards.

"The line of tents is most narrow on the northeast side," Tahl began. "That's the direction we'll leave by, once we get the wagons. The fact the horses were left in their harnesses means the army's planning a quick start, so expect men to come out of their tents armed and ready to fight."

"Should have brought more thieves," Hadren remarked under his breath.

Tahl ignored the complaint. "Remember, we only need one wagon to make this work. Adapt as necessary to keep the plan on track, but don't take any unnecessary chances."

Everyone nodded in confirmation. Tahl nodded back, and the group split up.

They didn't need everyone to make it to the wagons. For everything to work as planned, they only needed one point of contact. Splitting up was their best chance to make it. It also gave Tahl the opportunity to pursue his own side mission. He closed the distance between their hill and the camp in little time. The soft, subtle sounds of life—whuffing horses and snoring men— hid the near-silent sound of his footsteps in the grass.

The fact the nobles watched Emperor Atoras with contempt was unsurprising. Almost everyone coveted the throne. Tahl was a rare exception; he didn't want more than what he made for himself and a fun challenge or two along the way. Who ruled made little difference to him, so long as the person who governed the empire provided healthy opportunities for Tahl's ambition. An organization like his would thrive best in a stable country, where there were fewer rivals and a burgeoning economy to fatten coin purses throughout the city.

The existence of this Crownwatch Ebitha's nephew had mentioned was not necessarily a problem, but Tahl would have to be a fool to ignore the group's existence and merely hope for the best.

Had he been headed for the wagons, he did not doubt he would be the first one there. Instead, Tahl wove his way toward the tent he'd chosen from the hillside, the large, well-made one that promised to either be a brilliant target or a terrible idea. It could house nobles, members of Crownwatch that Tahl could observe and evaluate, possibly even sway toward a tentative alliance with the guild. Or it could be the leader's quarters, a possibility that could send the rest of Tahl's plans up in flames.

It wouldn't be fun if it was easy, he reminded himself.

Then again, not much about this ordeal had been fun. After so many days on the move, all he really wanted was a good meal, a hot bath, and a long night's sleep.

He paused against the back of a tent. Someone had roused inside. Grunts of displeasure and the soft clank of armor issued from inside. Maybe they'd waited a few minutes too long to start. Tahl forced the possibility of failure out of his mind and pushed on.

The big tent glowed, its thick canvas walls illuminated by lamps inside. Tahl fought back a wince. *Too late to nose in, then.* Unless he wanted to get himself skewered right off the bat. Getting skewered at all didn't sound pleasant and wasn't part of the plan, but if it had to happen, he hoped that came later in the mission.

Not being able to nose through the private belongings of

whoever was heading up the small army was a disappointment, but Tahl refused to let his side trip be wasted. He scanned the tents nearby, determined which was least likely to lead to him being noticed, and positioned himself on that side of the large tent. He'd already caught voices inside, but they were low and cautious, and he couldn't make out anything that was being said until he grew still and listened hard.

"...unlikely we'll be able to move much farther unnoticed, but we already knew that."

"It's not much farther until we're supposed to split up, anyway. Once we head to our individual meeting points, each of you will be on your own. I hope you're ready for that."

Each of them? Tahl's brow furrowed. How many people were inside? He eyed the bottom edge of the tent, wondering if he could lift it enough to get a look without being noticed. It was staked down at regular intervals, but if he wiggled a peg free, perhaps...

"Waiting will be the hard part." That was a third voice, so that offered a hint. "If there were any more docks open—"

"We've been over this already. The shipments will be broken up and separated by several days." That one was familiar. If that man was doing the most talking, perhaps he was the leader.

All Tahl needed was a peek, a look just long enough to commit faces to memory. If they were planning to enter Orrad, he'd see them again soon enough. He flattened himself on his belly as he locked his fingers around a tent peg and began to wiggle it free from the ground.

"Hey!" a voice bellowed behind him.

Tahl spat a curse and thrust himself from the ground, abandoning the peg. He wasn't supposed to be caught. He definitely wasn't supposed to be the *first* to get caught. Not waiting to see who had been talking inside, he sprinted off between the tents with angry shouts rising behind him.

All through the camp, mercenaries emerged from tents in mismatched clothes and armor, and the alarm spread.

Ashyl's path intercepted Tahl beside the wagons that had been their original target. "What did you do?"

"Detour went bad. Go!" He motioned her toward one of the wagons at the same time he almost slammed into the back of another.

Ahead, Jeran poked an eye around the corner. "What happened?"

Tahl silenced him with a sharp cutting gesture, then flung open the back of the wagon. A familiar scent greeted his nostrils and he couldn't help a grin. He slipped into the wagon and drew a knife to help pry open the nearest crate.

Dozens of polished steel barrels gleamed inside, stacked in neat rows.

Hello, reward. He slid his fingers down one of the muskets. Then he slammed the lid closed and spun to search the rest of the cargo. He could admire the workmanship later. Right now, there was still work to do.

"Where do we want these?" Hadren asked from beside the back of Tahl's wagon. He had a small barrel on either shoulder and didn't seem bothered by the weight at all.

"Away from the cargo," Tahl said as he uncovered a barrel of his own and rolled it toward the back. "Oria's paying us to steal it, not destroy it."

The larger man grunted. "Should've asked for money up front."

"Next time we pull a heist for the crown, I'll keep that in mind." Tahl hauled a second barrel out from between the crates. He'd hoped for more, but when he delved back into the depths of the wagon, he found no more of the barrels stashed anywhere. A few smaller boxes—heavier than he expected—proved to contain hundreds of small metal spheres. Balls to fire from the muskets, Jeran had explained. Tahl had spent more of that explanation nodding and pretending he understood than he wanted to admit. He shoved the boxes back into place and hurried back to the barrels.

Outside, the first boom rocked the camp—and the wagon Tahl was in. Outside, the horses hitched to the wagons shrieked and the wagon lurched again. Tahl swayed on his feet and regained his balance before he leaped out and hefted a barrel onto his shoulder the way Hadren had done. The former porter had made it look easy. The barrels were heavier than they looked. He clenched his teeth, silently praying the horses wouldn't bolt before he could get the second barrel.

The wagons were no longer in a line, the horses straining to escape from that first explosion. Ashyl teetered on the edge of her wagon's bed. Instead of trying to carry her barrels, she kicked them out the back of her wagon. Then she climbed over the top and let out a muffled cry. Tahl spun toward her just in time to see a soldier slice the harnesses and turn her wagon's horses free.

A moment later, his wagon stopped inching along and another pair of horses bolted into the field.

Shouldn't have tried to snoop. Tahl growled under his breath, frustrated he'd been the one to bring trouble down on the job. They would have been found eventually, but he'd been at fault. Maybe he should have gone the other direction, instead of leading the whole camp straight to their target.

"Change of plans!" he called over the sound of soldiers. "Jeran, horses. Ashyl, to me."

A few paces away, Hadren froze, his barrels still on his shoulders.

Tahl lowered his voice to address him. "Leave those. Get all the cargo into one wagon."

Hadren grunted, but lowered the barrels and sprinted away. Tahl swept in as Ashyl joined him. "Grab one of those," he ordered, tapping a barrel with his toes. Ashyl dropped to pick one up and grimaced at the weight.

The moment she had it in her arms, the first mercenaries were on them. Unwilling to let them strike, Tahl made his move. Gathering his power, he twisted the flows of energy in the air and focused them at his feet. Smoke spewed from the ground like a geyser, halting the mercenaries in their tracks.

Precious seconds gained. Tahl held the magic tight as he spun toward where Ashyl had been a moment before. With both his hands supporting barrels, he searched for her with an elbow, and she yelped when he found her.

"Cut south. Blow it up." he whispered as he sprinted past. The mercenaries would plunge into the smoke after a moment, he was sure. The last thing they wanted to do was linger where they would be found.

Ashyl vanished into the smoke without a sound. Tahl hoped she'd put together a good distraction without his aid. It was all he could do to keep the smoke blowing. Whether it helped Hadren and Jeran complete their jobs, he didn't know. Some distance into his smoke cloud, Tahl stopped and lowered a barrel to the ground. He slammed a knife into the end and twisted to make a crack.

A sword whistled through the smoke beside him and thudded into the ground. Tahl stumbled back to his feet and took his barrels with him. Black powder streamed from the crack he'd made, its unpleasant fragrance filling his nostrils as the coarse grains spilled down his back and left a trail across the grass.

The powder made him easy to follow. The thudding footsteps of pursuers multiplied behind him and Tahl released his smoke to let it dissipate.

The cloud had given him a head start. He hoped it had done the same for Ashyl. Tahl darted between tents as he wove his way back toward the large one he'd tried to infiltrate before. There was no better way to cause a distraction than to target the leaders.

Hopefully they're still there to *be targeted,* Tahl thought with a hint of chagrin. He hadn't seen anyone emerge. With luck, they were the cowardly sort of leaders that preferred to bark orders from the shadows while others were the ones to act.

Panicked cries and thick plumes of gray smoke rose from the other end of the camp. Tahl didn't dare risk more than a glance. For a split second, he feared someone had set Ashyl's powder afire. Then he remembered she hadn't punctured her keg.

Flashes of flame raced between the tents, churning up acrid clouds behind him.

Not her powder.

His.

Tahl spat a curse and flipped the leaking barrel on his shoulder to halt the stream of powder as he ran. He was supposed to blow them up, not the other way around. *Wouldn't that figure?* He didn't dare allow himself the harsh, bitter laugh that tickled the back of his throat. Or maybe that was the smoke tickling. It hung low over the camp, clogging the air and the lungs of everyone in it. The urge to cough tightened his chest. On a whim, Tahl grasped his power. His vision narrowed with his concentration. Without stopping to think, he forced the smoke from his lungs with magic. He hadn't realized he could.

What else can you do? He vaulted a rope that supported his targeted tent. Without stopping, he lobbed the powder keg at the canvas walls. It spiraled, spewing powder in loops across the ground.

Tahl skidded to a halt and slammed a hand against the end of the trail, power already in his grasp.

The powder trail ignited.

The keg exploded, the force pitching Tahl and a half-dozen mercenaries to the ground. A harsh whine rose in his ears as he scrambled to his feet amid his enemies.

"You!" someone roared.

Tahl spun toward the voice.

A familiar man emerged from the smoke left in the explosion's wake. Blood plastered his dark hair to his head, but Tahl would have recognized that scowl anywhere.

"I heard you were dead," Tahl called.

Bahar Eseri's lips peeled back in a snarl. "You're about to be."

CHAPTER 15

A SCAR ENCIRCLED LORD ESERI'S NECK. A DOZEN QUESTIONS flashed through Tahl's mind as he saw it, but he tamped them down and put them aside. It didn't matter. It didn't change anything. All it meant was that Ebitha's nephew had been telling the truth.

Mercenaries clawed their way to their feet with their weapons in hand. Before they could strike at Tahl, Lord Eseri drew a knife and advanced. "He's mine!"

Tahl couldn't have asked for a better distraction. He locked eyes with the former guild leader and drew a knife of his own. The mercenaries shifted uneasily, but none tried to strike. Fearful of Lord Eseri, it seemed. They should have been fearful of *him*. "You look good for a man who should be in a grave," Tahl said.

"Shut it, Ghost," Eseri snarled.

Tahl's brows climbed. "You know me? I'm flattered."

A deafening boom shook the ground underfoot. Plumes of smoke churned into the sky on the west side of the camp.

Pure fury crossed the former guildmaster's face. "Get the others!"

The mercenaries around them scurried to follow the man's orders.

Tahl cocked his head. "Just you and me then, huh?" Despite the curiosity that needled at him, the last thing he wanted was to waste time dueling Eseri when his team needed help. If no one was watching, the only one distracted was him.

Lord Eseri didn't give him time to think. He charged with his blade up, his face contorted with fury. He was fast, nimble, but he wasn't the Ghost. Tahl ducked and darted to the side as he reached for his magic. Smoke burst from every footfall, cloaking him with the haze. A few strikes. A few cuts. That was all Tahl could allow.

He rushed in as Lord Eseri hissed and flailed in the smoke. Tahl struck fast, aiming for the man's blade instead of his body. The metal chimed angrily as the blow threw the former guildmaster off balance.

Before Lord Eseri could recover, Tahl disappeared into his smoke again.

Come on, he urged himself. *More smoke.*

The scent of his smoke cloud was just as acrid as what spewed from the burning black powder.

Powder Tahl had all but forgotten. He retreated into his smokescreen and scouted out the second barrel he'd lost—and abandoned—when the first one blew up. He almost tripped over the keg.

"You can't hide from me!" Lord Eseri snarled, his form a dark silhouette in the pale blue smoke. He charged again, swinging his knife wildly.

Tahl danced away from his powder keg to continue the fight. "You've got no grace. How did you ever survive as a thief?"

"Survive?" The word stirred a new fury in the former guildmaster and his attacks grew more vigorous. "I barely survived at all, no thanks to you!"

"Yeah, that was kind of the idea." A spark of inspiration lit as Tahl ducked a swipe. He feinted upward, his blade coming just close enough to make Lord Eseri stumble back.

Tahl didn't give him time to recover. He flowed into the opening and with a single, hard swipe, dragged his dagger across Lord Eseri's face.

The man howled, clapping a hand to his bleeding cheek. His eyes blazed with rage.

"A scar to match the one I got because of you," Tahl said, flipping his blade in hand before he darted into the smoke. A roar of anger swelled behind him, but he didn't turn back. Though part of him wanted to fight, to sprinkle the battle with questions and glean answers for the things that swirled in his head, Tahl knew better than to try. A thief who fought was a thief who died, and his team still needed his help.

Tahl snatched his remaining powder keg from the ground and wove between the tents, ducking weapons and dodging arrows. He couldn't see Ashyl in the camp, but shouts and sounds of battle drew him farther west.

It didn't take long for the smaller thief to come into view, all but surrounded by mercenaries.

Tahl dove into the fray, parrying a sword with his dagger and praying no one would sweep in with a second blow. He lobbed his barrel toward a group of men and flung a hand after it, as if to cause the powder to ignite. Mercenaries shouted and scattered as the barrel hit the ground, but Tahl's magic didn't answer.

He stifled a curse.

"Took you long enough!" Ashyl cried over the clang of weapons.

Tahl ducked closer to help her defend. "What's that supposed to mean? We split up for a reason!"

Realizing the keg was no threat, the mercenaries he'd startled swept back in to pummel the two of them.

Ashyl grunted as she knocked a club aside. "Was that *reason* me getting teeth knocked out while you hobnob with the nobility?"

Nobility? Tahl's brow twitched. Had she seen Lord Eseri? He

swiped at a mercenary's arm and then caught Ashyl by the elbow to steer her south. They had to find the others. By now, he hoped Hadren and Jeran had escaped with the cargo, but he wasn't willing to bet on it. Not with the number of men around him—he and Ashyl weren't even important.

"Go!" Tahl hissed when she resisted his push.

Growling a complaint under her breath, she sprinted ahead, leaving Tahl in the thick of battle. A handful of men spun to catch her, but she evaded their grasp. The mercenaries shifted, closing the gap as Ashyl escaped.

"Thanks a lot," Tahl muttered as he drew a second knife. He strained to listen for sounds that might betray whether or not the others had been caught, but he couldn't split his focus.

Unwilling to let their prey escape this time, the men charged in a unified, organized pattern.

And here I expected simple-minded brutes, Tahl chided himself as he twisted to evade. Their numbers were threatening, but the men were so numerous they got in their own way. He bobbed under a sword and slipped under someone's arm, upsetting the man's balance in the process. The mercenary crashed into a colleague and Tahl bolted away, his eyes trained on the powder keg.

He almost stopped to grab it again. Instead, he rounded a cluster of tents and spiraled the mercenaries on his heels into a concentrated group, then locked his thoughts on the barrel. Tahl didn't want to kill anyone. He just wanted to inconvenience them as much as possible.

He closed his eyes and focused.

The powder ignited.

A shot of excitement streaked through him as the ground quivered underfoot, followed by a sense of awe. He'd never had the power to start fires, but he could light his inch-sticks. Was the powder that volatile? Or had he finally crossed some threshold into greater capability?

Unlikely, he reminded himself with a chagrined smirk. The

blast wouldn't distract them for long, but all he'd needed was a few seconds to make his escape. He pushed himself to run faster, streaking across the camp to rejoin the others.

If he could find them, that was. Ashyl had already disappeared, and though the mercenary force boiled in a frenzy, they charged south. Jeran and Hadren wouldn't have been foolish enough to take the wagon straight down the road, would they?

The answer came a moment later when a new rumble shook the earth. A thunderous noise reached Tahl's ears, muted beneath the quiet whine he'd almost forgotten, aftereffects of that first ill-timed explosion. He fought back a groan as the wagon swayed into view. It swerved between tents, only for the horses hitched to its front to trample right over another. Jeran sat on the wagon's tongue, lashing the reins against the backs of four beasts in crude harnesses fashioned from what looked like scraps of proper harnesses and... were those belts? Tahl could have groaned, but he didn't have time. The wagon veered toward him and he got a running start.

As the wagon barreled past, Tahl vaulted himself into the air and managed to catch a rail on the roof's edge. The wagon rocked dangerously and he dragged himself up. A second later and he would have been flattened by the wheels.

"Welcome aboard," Jeran called above the hammering of hooves and the mad clatter of cargo inside the wagon.

"Where are the others?" Tahl shouted back.

An arm raised from the back of the wagon so a slim hand could wave. Ashyl made it. Good. Tahl slid toward the back of the roof. He gripped the rail hard and leaned over to peer upside-down into the back.

Inside, Hadren rammed a steel rod down the barrel of a musket. "Not enough powder!"

"Powder? For *what?*" Tahl had a guess, but he almost didn't want to know.

"Jeran found instructions." Ashyl's voice was so small, Tahl could barely hear it above the clamor and the persistent ringing in his ears. "The balls get packed in there with powder. Then finer power goes in the... What was it called, Hadren?"

"Who cares what it's called?" the big man roared.

She shot him a glare, then returned her attention to Tahl. "They're basically handheld cannons. We found some powder in a few horns, but it's not enough."

"For all the good blowing up the barrels did out there," Hadren said with an angry jerk of his head. Smoke still lay thick over the encampment, but if the explosions had stopped anyone, Tahl didn't know. He hadn't stopped to see if anyone had been injured.

Or worse. Tahl tried not to cringe. He didn't relish the idea of killing anyone, but things had gone wrong so quickly, what else could they do? Somehow, he doubted the queen would care.

Unwilling to let himself stew over the possibility, Tahl gripped the roof rail harder with his left hand so he could wave for Hadren to stop with the right. "Put it down. All we have to do is get this to the queen. I don't know how far off she might be, but the mercenaries were headed—"

"Whoa!" Jeran cried above the shrill whinnies of the horses. The wagon skidded and lurched and Tahl almost fell from the wagon's roof. "Boss, we've got a problem!"

Of course they did. Tahl pulled himself upright just as Jeran tried to set the horses into motion again, the reins pulled taut in his effort to steer the beasts eastward.

Ahead, a sea of armor shone, men in red tabards leading the way.

"Brant's shaking branches," Tahl spat. "Go! Go!"

Ashyl's head popped out the back as the wagon lurched again. She opened her mouth to ask, but the horses veered and the sea of the Elite came into view. Her jaw went slack.

An arrow with red fletchings whizzed past her face.

Tahl planted a hand on the top of her head and shoved her inside. "Stay inside! Jeran, ride straight into the army and ask for the queen. Remember, you're not enemies. They don't know you. They—"

Something struck his shoulder and a shot of pain lanced across his ribcage and down his arm. Startled, Tahl looked down at the red-feathered shaft that protruded from his flesh. His grip on the railing faltered and his mouth worked a moment before he produced words. "Oh, blight it."

He fell.

The landing knocked every bit of air out of Tahl's lungs and left him paralyzed on the ground as precious seconds ticked past. He fought to regain control of his body, to overcome shock and move out of sheer determination.

As if something came loose in his chest, his lungs obeyed and he sucked in a deep, gasping breath. Pain came with the oxygen, filling every inch of his body, threatening to cripple him again. *Get up,* he growled at himself. To his left, the mercenary army surged to meet their new challenge. To the right, the wagon disappeared into the sea of Elite.

Gritting his teeth, Tahl dug his fingers into the earth and forced himself to draw another breath. Slowly, he peeled his head and shoulders up off the ground. The arrow embedded in his shoulder hurt worse than anything he could recall experiencing. That didn't seem right. It was just an arrow. He'd been cut, stabbed, had broken bones—there was no way a single arrow should... what? What couldn't it do? His vision hazed and for a moment, he thought the air was filled with smoke.

Poison, some small part of him answered the unasked question. *They're the Elite, and they know who you are.*

Tahl found his hands and knees and rolled to his feet. He rocked, unsteady, and grasped the arrow's shaft.

Precious seconds gone. Orrad's best soldiers upon him, no hope for escape.

"Wait," he croaked, lifting his free hand as if he could stop the emperor's oncoming army with just his outstretched palm.

As if the gesture meant nothing at all, one of the Elite slammed the hilt of his sword into Tahl's head.

CHAPTER 16

WHEN TAHL WOKE, GRIT STUNG HIS EYES. HE RUBBED THEM WITH the side of his hand. His body ached with more than just the cold, and as he pushed himself to sitting, he swore every inch of him had to be bruised. After the fall he'd taken, he suspected that was the case.

His hand went to his shoulder. The arrow was gone, though the hole in his heist shirt remained, the fine navy fabric crusted with dried blood. Tahl frowned and probed the skin underneath. It was whole, seemingly unblemished, betraying a mage's healing handiwork. Judging by how clear his thoughts were now, they'd cleared the poison from his system, too.

And why would they do that? His frown deepened as he lowered his hand and observed his surroundings. Maybe the poison wasn't completely cleared. Checking to see where he was should have been the first thing he'd done.

Yet part of him had known the answer, even before he opened his eyes. He'd woken on cold stone, the air thick with humidity and the musty scent of stale mildew. Tahl brushed his fingers over the ground beneath him and wrinkled his nose. It was slimy with something he only hoped was mold, instead of blood... or worse. Fighting back a shudder, he wiped his hand clean on his pants.

The cell was dim, but there was no mistaking that was what it was. He'd never seen the inside of Orrad's prison, but he'd imagined it. Three solid stone walls without a single seam framed the cell, the front barricaded by rusted iron bars. The lock appeared old-fashioned and simple, but a quick check of his person showed they'd been thorough in removing his weapons and tools. All he had was his close-fitting outfit and his split-toed shoes. Shoes that were not, he noted, closed. He wiggled his toes and found himself pleased to see his socks remained, but if his shoes were undone, they'd already checked there for lock picks.

Slowly, Tahl ran a hand—the one he *hadn't* slid across the floor—through his dark hair. So they'd decided not to let him die. That meant they knew who he was, and meant to make an example of him. No one would believe the Ghost was dead unless they saw it with their own eyes. A mistake he'd made with Bahar Eseri, he reminded himself with a grim smile.

But he hadn't been the only thief in that sea of red-accented armor. Tahl was alone in his cell, naught but a bucket and pile of straw to keep him company, but that didn't mean anything. He pushed himself up, wincing at the ache in his joints and muscles, and peered across the hall. The cell on the other side of the walkway was too dark to see, but he thought it looked empty. Given who he was, it wasn't a surprise if they'd chosen to isolate him.

Unsure how to proceed, he crept to the bars and leaned against the heavy door. It did not so much as shift when he put his weight on it. The lock was simple, but he couldn't open it without something stiff. He doubted the straw would cut it. Not that he was eager to escape before he'd determined who else had been captured. The word put a bitter taste in the back of his mouth, even though he'd only thought it.

He'd been the one to send Oria for the Elite. He'd thought that meant they'd have some layer of protection.

Naive of him, Tahl concluded.

His eyes focused better once he was on his feet. The cell across from his was definitely empty, the cell door a few inches ajar. It opened inward, he noticed. Harder for a prisoner to force his way out, perhaps? His fingers curled around one of the crossbars on the door and he leaned back. It still didn't shift.

Frowning, he leaned against the door again and turned his ear to the hall. Farther down the walkway, he caught the sound of someone coughing. Someone moving, too. The same person? He doubted the castle's dungeons would be so empty.

Deciding it best to begin planning, Tahl wet his lips and gave a soft, two-note whistle that ended like a question. *Here?* the signal asked. Something simple, something the guards wouldn't likely recognize that his crew undoubtedly would.

Silence filled the air.

He whistled again. This time, a soft clank and a scrape at the far end of the hall answered his call.

"Nobody's coming to help you, spook boy," a guard shouted.

Tahl craned his neck to see the guard station at the far end of the corridor. The other sounds in the prison had grown quiet. Did that mean the others had escaped? He worried his lip as he tried to put together the possibilities of what could have happened after that poisoned arrow sent him toppling off the wagon's roof.

Maybe the others had escaped with the cargo after all. Maybe they'd made it to the queen and Oria had protected them from the Elite. But that didn't explain why he was in prison and they weren't—unless their misgivings had been right all along.

Had it been a trap? One meant to snare him and nobody else? His stomach twisted with the thought of Oria turning his own recruits against him, bribing them to follow him into the job and then leave him to the Elite. Ugly as the possibility was, it could have happened. He'd left the queen with his team when he'd gone to investigate the first band of wagons. That would have offered enough time for them to plan.

Tahl rubbed his shoulder, the one the arrow had struck. It ached more than the rest of him, but from what he knew of magic-based healing, that was to be expected. Pain lingered after the wounds were gone. He stared down at the smooth stone floor of the hallway.

He'd only just begun to search his thoughts for options when voices rose at the guard station. They were just low enough that he couldn't make them out, but he lounged against the bars and turned that way, just the same. No matter what, Tahl wouldn't let them see him nervous. He'd only just started thinking, and there were some tools they could never take from him.

As if in response to the thought, his senses prickled. Tahl straightened as a pair of guards left the station and started down the hall with someone between them. Another prisoner? No—a mage, that was the tingle in his awareness. Tahl's eyebrows climbed as the pair of men stopped before his cell with Colbin between them. The guards looked to the mage, expectant.

A look of consternation and then resignation drifted across Colbin's face. "It's him." His shoulders slumped with the admission. He hadn't wanted to give Tahl up? Interesting.

"You're positive?" one of the guards asked.

The mage hesitated, then gave a single nod. "I—yes. I'd recognize him anywhere after he threatened me in the library."

Satisfied, the guards motioned Colbin back toward the front of the dungeon.

"Good to see you too," Tahl said sarcastically.

His one-time friend gave him a single, anguished look before he allowed the guards to escort him back out as quickly as they'd seen him in.

Tahl held back his sigh of frustration until he was sure they wouldn't hear. So they hadn't been positive of his identity when they arrested him. Or had they only needed confirmation before they could see him to the gallows? He thought of the scar that encircled Bahar Eseri's neck and raised a hand to touch his own throat. Clearly, there was a way to survive. It would have been nice to have learned how.

Disheartened, he trudged to the pile of straw and lowered himself to sit. Though his senses had itched when Colbin came close, Tahl was too drained to grasp power now. He'd wait, rest as long as he dared, and hope a solution came to him whenever he'd recovered enough to wield his minuscule power again. It had done something the night before, the fire in lanterns eager to answer his call, the powder under his fingers igniting easier than anything he'd ever touched.

Maybe, just maybe, that feeble power would be enough now.

SLEEP CAME FITFULLY, far from the deep, peaceful slumber Tahl hoped for. Every time someone stirred in the dungeon, the sound woke him. He'd grown used to every sound being a threat. In a place like this, that seemed the truth. The guards hadn't come to bother him again—as far as he could tell, he was at the very end of the row—but every time footfalls or the rattle of armor reached his ears, he expected them to appear.

After the unusual experiences of the past several days, Tahl's normally accurate internal clock had grown muddled. He thought it had been close to twelve hours since Colbin's visit when footsteps finally came down the hall between cells, but he wasn't certain. Tahl pushed himself to his feet and braced for a fight, but all that happened was a balding old man in coarse clothing dropped a wooden trencher on the floor, kicked it underneath the door, and leaned forward to reach between the bars and deposit bread and a wooden cup atop it.

Tahl stared at the offering with a sense of befuddlement until the man left. He'd never even looked Tahl's way.

A white spot decorated the bread's crust. Tahl considered it for longer than was necessary before he trudged over for a closer inspection. Against all odds, it seemed unlikely his captors might try to poison him. Orrad would demand a public execution. It would be a spectacle, maybe even rival a festival day. He was no good to them dead. With that in mind, he crouched beside the trencher and picked up the bread. He'd thought it was mold and was surprised to find flour instead. The yeasty bread was still soft and after days without a decent meal, its fresh scent made his stomach growl. The cup held water, which he sniffed and frowned at before deciding poison was still unlikely.

He sat back on his heels and ate.

Some hours later, he'd found his way back to the pile of straw and had just dozed off when voices snapped him out of his uneasy, half-dreaming state. Unsure whether or not he should meet them at the cell door again, he settled for sitting at the edge of the straw and staring past the bars. When the guards came into view, though, he flew to his feet and dashed to the front of the cell.

"Tahl," Nia cried when she saw him. She flung herself against the bars and reached in, her fingertips groping for his touch.

He put himself in her arms and reached through to hug her as close as he could manage. Then he stepped back, cradled her face in his hands, and lowered himself to one knee so they were closer to eye level. "What are you doing here?"

Tears brimmed on her eyelashes and she touched his hands. "You're alive."

A hint of guilt surged in his chest. "Not for long." The guards shifted uneasily at the comment, but neither tried to correct him.

"What happened? Why are you in here? I thought—" She leaned back, her eyes skimming his frame. Her attention lingered on the hole in the shoulder of his shirt like she knew what it was, then her expression grew more guarded. "Where were you?"

Something had changed in her voice, as if to cue something

should change in his, too. Recognizing it for the sibling act they often put on, he followed suit. Though part of him wanted to throttle her for coming to see him and doubtlessly putting herself in harm's way, he admitted it was the best way to relay information to the rest of the guild.

"I made a mistake," he said, shifting his hands on her face until she looked him dead in the eye. "I trusted somebody I shouldn't have."

"And now what? You're going to leave me?" Nia grasped his wrist and a tear escaped to roll down her cheek. She could act, but from how fat those tears were, he took the sense they were real. Fear for him shone in her eyes.

Tahl wasn't sure how to respond. He had a million instructions to give her, but the guards were right there. How much could he reveal without incriminating her? He needed her to escape, to get back to the guild. To keep the guild alive. "I have to take responsibility for what I've done. Now I need you to be responsible, too."

She shook her head. "What are you talking about? You can't just let them—they'll kill you!"

Frustrated, he made her hold still. "I can't change that now. You can. You're not part of this. Don't become part of this. Do you understand me? Stay out of it."

Nia lunged forward to wrap her arms around his neck in another hug. Sighing, Tahl surrendered to it. Behind her, the guards looked away, made uncomfortable by the sentimental display.

"I need you to go home," Tahl continued, his voice calm and level. "I need you to take care of the family. Do what I couldn't do, don't make the same mistakes I did. Keep your nose clean and remind the boys who's in charge now that I'm gone."

She squeezed him harder. "Don't say that."

He didn't know what else to say. "There's money in a box back home. It'll pay the rent this month, but not much else. I'm sorry. I can't do anything else."

"Time's up," one of the guards said, his voice gruff.

Nia didn't want to let go.

"Go on," Tahl whispered. "Fly home, Sparrow. Everyone needs you."

"They need *you*," she protested.

He pushed her back. "Go."

The guard laid a hand on Nia's shoulder and pulled her away. She clung to the bars until Tahl squeezed her hand. Then her fingers slipped off the metal and the guards steered her toward the entryway as a first strong, very real sob tore free of her throat.

Tahl gripped the bars and watched her go. It hadn't been enough time, not enough words, not enough instructions. He hadn't gotten to praise her, to reassure her she could take his place, that he trusted her to see the guild survived. His shoulders slumped. Something poked uncomfortably in the back of his shirt's high collar. Tahl's brow furrowed and he reached back to scratch it. Instead of the straw he expected, his fingertips found the shaped metal of a single lock pick.

A smirk twisted his features before he could catch it. *Clever little sparrow.* He hadn't even felt her slip it to him, distracted by her squeezes and the fat tears on the dark lashes that framed her childlike eyes.

She'd grown skilled at playing roles, at pretending to be innocent. No wonder the guards had agreed to let her see him. Who would have suspected a tearful child who just wanted to say goodbye to her brother?

The guards stopped at the far end of the hall. Only one continued onward to escort Nia from the dungeons. Tahl hid the pick in his hand as he brushed dust from his shoulder. If he'd had a dagger, he would have taken a chance and tried to get past the one armored man who remained. Unarmed as he was, it seemed wiser to wait until the man was distracted.

The chance didn't come. Moments after Nia and the other guard disappeared, the sound of many footfalls filled the prison.

An uneasy shuffling and a number of moans followed, hinting that other prisoners retreated farther into their cells.

Tahl's eyes narrowed and he leaned closer to the bars.

A half-dozen men with the red tabards of the Elite draped over their armor marched down the walkway between the cells, their weapons in hand. Tahl wasn't surprised when they stopped at his cell door.

"The Ghost of Orrad," the leader said, his face twisted with disgust.

"I seem to be quite popular today," Tahl replied, tone dry.

The Elite were not amused. The dungeon guard scurried into view with a ring of keys.

Tahl raised his chin in defiance, though his stomach churned.

The leader lifted a pair of shackles as the door's lock clacked open. "Let's go."

CHAPTER 17

ONLY TWO ELITE GRASPED TAHL BY THE ARMS. THE OTHER TWO pairs walked in front of and behind him, creating a barrier between him and the rest of the palace. None of the utilitarian structure appeared familiar, but he doubted it ever would. The palace was as cold as he believed the emperor to be.

The lock pick remained hidden in Tahl's sleeve, waiting for him to slide it free. He had no doubt the single pick would be enough to undo the shackles on his wrists and ankles, but he doubted he could undo the locks without the Elite noticing. Especially not the one on the shackles that bound his feet and kept him from taking more than shuffling steps no more than six inches apart. After his acrobatic escape with the crown, Tahl admitted they'd been wise to chain him.

Even if he had managed to undo the shackles, he wasn't sure he could escape the Elite. He'd made a point of avoiding them after one gave him the scar that marred his face. Luck had been on his side that night. If it was on his side now, he wouldn't have been captured.

All lucky streaks come to an end. He tried to show no emotion as they escorted him down featureless halls and came to a stop outside a pair of doors no more interesting than the bare stone walls. One of the Elite leading the group pushed the doors open —both of them—and Tahl found himself squinting into the room beyond.

The throne room was nothing like he'd expected. Unlike the rest of the blocky palace with its squared-off floor plan, the throne room was circular. Seats ringed the outer walls, as if it were a stadium or a gladiator's ring instead of the emperor's lair. *Then again, they do expect a show.* Tahl allowed himself a soft snort. People—nobles—packed the stone benches. Their heads turned to follow Tahl, reminding him of vultures as the Elite led him inside.

In the center of the room, the throne stood on a dais so tall, it almost seemed like a pedestal. Arrogant, Tahl thought, and yet fitting. Atop the throne, Atoras sat, and on his brow was the crown.

Anger turned in Tahl's stomach, writhing with a coil of disappointment it took him a moment to recognize. The crown had been in his office. Either Oria had stolen it back, or his guild had betrayed him.

The pair of Elite leading the group and the pair behind it knelt at the foot of the dais. The men holding Tahl's arms bowed their heads in reverence, but did not otherwise stir.

The emperor rose from his throne.

"Ah, the plague upon my city." Atoras's voice was booming, powerful, deep enough to shake Tahl's bones. "So we meet, Ghost."

Tahl met his eyes with a cool composure, though he very much wished to glare. "We met before, sire. The problem is, you were asleep."

The emperor did not respond at first, though he raised his head and peered down his nose to give Tahl a long, appraising stare. "I know who you are."

"A lot of people do."

"Tahl Athiat Ashor. Son of Duke Achaean Ashor, sent to my city to become a mage. You failed."

An intrigued murmur rolled through the spectators.

"That depends on what you think my goal was," Tahl replied. From the way Atoras stared at him, he suspected the emperor thought he'd be surprised. How could he be? He already knew Colbin had identified him.

The corner of the emperor's mouth twitched. "Your treason runs deeper than Orrad knows. Tell me, did your father recognize you as marquess?"

Tahl lifted his chin. "My father disowned me."

"Was that before or after you chose to make a mockery of me?" The emperor tilted his head, as if in thought. "I should hate to punish your father. He has been a good leader for the southern coast. And we are blood, after all. Distant relations, but blood, nonetheless."

"Well," Tahl said with a sneer, "I'm sure my father loathes me as much as you do."

Atoras sank back in his throne, drumming his fingers on its arm. "You know the punishment for what you have done." It was a statement, not a question.

"The usual punishment?" Tahl asked. "Or what you have in mind for me?"

A hint of amusement lit in the emperor's eyes, though it was fleeting. "You will hang."

Unsurprising. Tahl had assumed as much, the moment he'd awoken to find himself in prison. "Like you hung Bahar Eseri? I think one scar is enough."

Atoras did not react. Maybe he didn't know Lord Eseri had survived. Or else he hadn't cared. For a split second, Tahl considered that Lord Eseri's survival might have been intentional, then he discarded the idea. If they'd helped him survive and escape, why would Bahar Eseri join an organization that pitted itself against the crown?

"Where is your guild?" the emperor demanded.

Tahl blinked before he managed to wipe all surprise from his expression. He didn't know? But he wore the crown. "Waiting for me."

Atoras's lips peeled back in a sneer. "Then they can join you in the grave. Prepare the gallows."

One of the Elite in front of Tahl pressed a fist over his heart.

Behind them, the doors banged open and broad beams of light spilled across the floor.

"Atoras," a familiar voice cried.

The emperor stirred and sat straighter on his throne.

Oria hastened across the throne room. "You promised to wait for me!"

Atoras patted the air, as if the gesture would soothe her. "I am not a cat, who wishes to play with my prey."

"You promised!" she protested. "How dare you? You don't even know what you've done! Do you know who this man is?" She thrust a finger in Tahl's direction and glowered up at the throne.

The emperor stared at her, unthreatened by her glare. "A nuisance."

"He is mine!" The queen clenched her hand into a fist. "The chief of my spies, my window into the criminal world that plagues our city. And by bringing him before an audience, you unravel everything I've built."

"He is a child," Atoras replied dryly.

"A young man of noble blood who answers to the crown," Oria fired back. "Not some common criminal. Had you only stopped to listen to me before all this—"

Again, Atoras spread his hands and made calming gestures. "Peace, woman! Brant's mercy."

From the anger that twisted her face, she had no intention of settling. Tahl stared at her, his brow furrowed.

Oria drew a deep breath before she spoke again. "How is anyone to monitor the criminal activity in the city without being part of it? I've asked you to develop spy networks for years, and the moment I have one functioning, you tear it apart! How do you believe I found the weapons, Atoras? Without my network's information, we would have nothing!"

Anger flashed across the emperor's stony face and he thrust himself from the throne. "He stole my crown!"

"To lend him credence," she said, exasperation painting her face. "How else was anyone to believe he was worth following? How do you think he escaped? I orchestrated the entire thing. Thieves respect capability!"

For the first time, a hint of uncertainty showed in the emperor's eyes. He glanced toward Tahl, his gaze lingering there, questioning instead of hard.

Tahl stood straighter and stared back. He had no idea what Oria was doing, but if it kept him alive, he wasn't going to protest.

"He rooted out one of the leaders of Crownwatch once," the queen continued, plaintive now instead of angry. "To hang him for his service to the crown—for a service *I* sought—would be to shame us all."

Eventually, the emperor's eyes narrowed. "You said your father disowned you," he said, focused on Tahl.

"He doesn't know what I am," Tahl replied levelly. "Aside from Her Majesty, no one does."

"You forfeit your right to dukedom for this?"

"Frankly, sire, this is more fun."

Another murmur ran through the crowd in the stands and Tahl decided to curb his sarcasm. "I fell in love with Orrad as soon as I reached the mage academy. I miss Ashor, but Orrad is my home. You know I was sent to become a mage, that I wasn't strong enough to learn. How else was I to serve the crown? How else would I find a place in this city that would allow me to stay here?"

"Release him," the queen ordered.

The pair of Elite who still held Tahl exchanged worried glances before they turned to the throne.

Oria's brows knit together, pleading. "Please, Atoras."

The emperor remained on his feet, staring down at the group below him with an unreadable expression. "The stands are dismissed," he called.

More murmurs of speculation rose as the nobles ringing the room got to their feet and shuffled for the door. Long moments of weighted silence dragged past as they emptied into the hall.

At the flick of Atoras's finger, one of the Elite from the rear of Tahl's party retreated to close the doors behind them.

"You try me, woman," Atoras sighed, though there was a hint of fondness in his voice.

Tahl eyed the crown on his head and gave Oria a sideways glance. From what he had heard in the capital, *fond* was not a word anyone would ever use in conjunction with the emperor. He recalled what she'd told him about the crown's function. Perhaps that had been the truth. Was that why it was here now? Retrieved for this very meeting? He doubted it.

The queen rested her hands against her chest, either defensive or earnest. Tahl supposed it didn't matter. "I've begged you to let me aid the city," she said, "but you haven't given me the chance. I tried to tell you my plan to find those weapons, but you were angry with me and would not hear me out. Please, Atoras, you know I wouldn't try to undermine you, but I had to do something. I feared for Orrad. For the empire. I knew nothing else to do."

For a moment, Tahl wasn't sure Atoras would reply. He stared at her, his thoughts guarded, for what felt like an eternity.

At last, the emperor turned his attention to the Elite. "Escort him to the north holding room. Wait there for further instruction."

The Elite bowed in acknowledgement and dragged Tahl forward. He chose not to resist, letting the six Elite usher him into a small, private parlor off the far end of the throne room. He cast a glance over his shoulder as one of the men behind him closed the door. Two men positioned themselves beside it. Tahl's captives released him and took chairs at the end of the room.

Unsure what to do, Tahl sank to sit cross-legged on the floor. The lock pick was still up his sleeve. If he was careful, he could unfasten his shackles while he sat.

The parlor remained quiet for some time and he dared not try. Skilled as he was, he could not make lock picks silent. Or perhaps he could. Tahl tilted his head at that thought. He'd never progressed far enough in his studies to learn how to spin wards, but if he could make smoke, perhaps he could learn to make wards small enough to mute his picks.

"What do you think this means for the weapon recovery unit?" one of the Elite asked after a time.

Some of the other men spared glances for Tahl. "Possibly nothing," one added. "They were just following orders."

"Weren't we all," Tahl muttered. He fingered the iron that encircled his wrists, contemplating the pick hidden up his sleeve. How hard would it be to escape six Elite? It sounded impossible. He should have tried to escape the dungeon the moment Nia had been escorted away. One cell door and two guards seemed laughably easy now.

The men regarded him with what seemed to be deep consideration. Did they regret speaking in front of him? Eventually, one of the Elite sitting at the back of the parlor leaned forward and rested his elbows on his knees. "The queen really helped you steal that crown?"

Tahl offered a sarcastic smile, though he bit back the witty response that leaped to his tongue. The truth was both forthcoming and deceptive. "I wouldn't have made it out of the castle without her." He still believed that. Maybe that knowledge would help endear the Elite to him, too. Hints of doubt swam across their faces now and then, as if they weren't sure what to believe. "If I'd known how badly this particular assignment would go, I never would have accepted when the queen brought it to me."

The Elite who had spoken frowned as if he wasn't sure what Tahl meant.

Tahl arched a brow and rubbed his shoulder through the hole in his shirt, reminding them he'd been shot.

A soft click sounded behind him and he turned toward the door as it opened. Oria stepped inside, her chin up and her head high. "I will speak to the Ghost in private."

All six Elite exchanged looks, but the queen didn't give them a chance to protest.

"Go," she ordered, an edge in her voice.

The sitting men rose, all of them bowed, and they filed from the room. The door's latch snapped behind them, ominous in the still.

Tahl stood to face the queen and his shackles dropped away.

Oria raised one eyebrow. "Your resourcefulness has often surprised me over the past several days."

"A talent, Your Majesty." He was careful to ensure she didn't see his lock pick as he slid it back up his sleeve.

"One I hope you will retain," she said.

Though Tahl suspected she hoped he would, he did not reply.

Eventually, she cleared her throat. "I have done what I could. The crown was necessary to soften my husband's demeanor. I hope you can forgive me for the liberties I've taken with our story."

"Where is the rest of the group?"

A sad smile tugged at the corners of her mouth. "Safe. They were unknown. In some ways, you aided with that. When the Elite shot you off the wagon's roof, they assumed you had been attempting to stop them from hijacking the weapons. They believed me when I said the others were my infiltration team."

"But they didn't believe I was part of it." He didn't know if he should laugh or be angry.

Oria spread her hands and gave a helpless shrug. "I won't lie. I didn't try very hard to stop them. You were injured and in need of immediate healing. I cannot risk using my Gift in front of those who see me, lest they discover my identity and try to convince Atoras that marrying me was a foolish decision. Letting them take you into custody and heal you so you could stand trial seemed the best way to ensure your survival."

This time, he couldn't help a laugh. It escaped as a single harsh, humorless bark. "That was a trial? It looked more like Atoras single-handedly deciding to kill me."

"He has not decided that. He decided..." She hesitated, searching for words. "You have a choice."

He stared at her, waiting for an explanation.

Oria caught his eyes and held them. "You can become what I claimed, and he will let you live. Chief of my intelligence department, a spy operating within the empire and perhaps someday beyond it. Or you can hang."

"Not much of a choice," Tahl said.

She sighed. "He is willing to let you live, but I cannot convince him you truly answer to me without evidence."

He rubbed his forehead and exhaled. What other options did he have? Surrender his freedom and answer to someone else, or lose his life. "What about the guild?"

"I don't know," the queen admitted. "I don't think I can shield them. As it is, Atoras's patience with me is thin."

"So I lose them?"

"I believe so."

Tahl squeezed his eyes closed.

"There is also the small problem of the thieving," Oria continued. "Your reputation has grown. I believe you will remain feared and intimidating. But I cannot have you continuing to antagonize my husband or my city. If you work for me, you are a spy and only a spy."

"Then the guild is out of the question. They won't follow a leader without teeth."

"I am sorry, Tahl. Truly. I have seen how much your people mean to you."

"I don't know what I'm supposed to say." He fought to keep from throwing up his hands in defeat. "I don't have a choice, not really." The admission was devastating. Everything he'd built was gone, a flash of sparks that died as embers in the air. A chance for a legacy that never took root.

Oria studied him. "Then you accept?"

"I accept," Tahl said.

The queen nodded and slipped from the room. When the door closed behind her, Tahl felt more trapped than he had in his dungeon cell.

"But I never should have accepted that job," he muttered to himself.

Too late now.

CHAPTER 18

TAHL SLID HIS LOCK PICK FROM HIS SLEEVE AND RAN HIS THUMB down its length. He hadn't been sure what to do with it. His bag was gone, along with his set of favorite picks. Whether or not spies needed lock picks, he wasn't sure.

He stared at the trapdoor for longer than he probably ought, but it took time to put his thoughts in order. He'd been distracted during his trip across the city. Thoughts of home and rest called to him, but it wasn't the right time. He needed to do this. To finish what he'd started, even if the idea of ending it hurt.

Slowly, Tahl fitted his fingers to the mechanism in the stone slab and pressed the code that made it open. When the latch popped and the heavy trapdoor shifted, he exhaled in relief. He'd half expected the code to have changed.

Voices greeted him as he pushed the trapdoor open farther and crawled into the museum's basement. The second door stood open. Lantern light filled headquarters and cast shadowy outlines of figures against the walls. Whoever sat around the table set up in the center of the guild hall's main room, they were arguing. Loudly.

Tahl pushed the hatch shut until it locked and then stood.

Before he could announce his presence, someone screamed.

Everyone at the table spun to face him with a round of startled shouts.

At the far side of the table, Nia leaned forward with her hands on the tabletop. "Tahl?" she asked, her voice shaky.

His brow furrowed. "What? I can't look that bad."

A dozen gray faces stared at him in disbelief. Ashyl pressed a hand to her mouth, her dark eyes wide. Had she been the one who screamed? The sound had been so high-pitched, he'd thought it was Nia.

"Is this why they call him the Ghost?" Jeran asked in a murmur.

Tahl frowned at him.

Nia made a cutting motion and everyone grew quiet. She cleared her throat. "Why... are you here?"

"Uh, because it's my guild and my guild headquarters?" Tahl waved at the room around them. The space was packed with goods they hadn't yet shifted. "We need to talk."

"Yeah, we do," Nia said. "We were just trying to figure out a way forward, now that you're dead." She raised an eyebrow in invitation for him to explain.

Instead, he stared at her, confused. "What?"

"We sent Perton to watch the execution," Jeran said. "To confirm it was really you. He said you tried to escape as they took you across the courtyard. But you got hung, boss. Perton saw it happen in the square outside just a few hours ago." He jerked a thumb toward the ceiling, indicating the plaza outside the Queen's Museum.

Tahl's brow furrowed. "I wasn't... I was still in the palace with Queen Oria until about an hour ago." Perton's eyes were good. How did he make *that* mistake?

The thieves exchanged uncomfortable glances.

"Better explain what happened, Tahl," Nia suggested.

"Well, first off, executions here don't seem to mean a whole lot. I'm not sure if any of you saw him, but Bahar Eseri was in that camp. Everyone swore they saw him die, too." Tahl padded across the room to take a seat at the table. Lifetree's mercy, he hadn't realized how tired he was until he sat down.

A few faces frowned. Nia stared at him as if trying to see through a mask. "Are you sure?"

"Positive." He rubbed his forehead to smooth away lines of worry and weariness. "I thought they'd question me or something when I woke in the dungeon. Not sure how you learned I was there, Nia, but I appreciated your visit." He produced the lock pick from his sleeve and held it out in offering.

She blinked in surprise and took it from his hand. "No tricks, then. It is you."

Tahl snorted. Who else would he be? "Before I saw you, they dragged Colbin down and made him confirm who I was." He left out what exactly that meant. No one in the guild—not even Nia—knew his surname, and he planned to keep it that way. As long as word didn't escape with the nobles, that was. "Almost immediately after you left, a half-dozen Elite came and got me and took me to meet the emperor. I noticed he had the crown."

Jeran grimaced. "Some of the team was here. They tried to stop her, but..."

"But she used her power," Nia finished for him. "Her... magic, I guess. None of us could even get close enough to touch her when we figured out she was trying to leave with it."

"Doesn't matter." Tahl waved a hand. "We'll come back to that. The queen came in as Atoras declared I would be executed. She convinced him to let me live."

Everyone stared in silence.

"Yeah, there's a catch." He rubbed his forehead again. He was exhausted. "Starting tomorrow, I'm head of the queen's intelligence department."

The silence persisted.

Did they believe him? From the uneasy way some of the thieves eyed him, he wasn't positive they all believed he was really himself. Tahl fought not to sigh.

After a time, Ashyl cleared her throat. "What does that mean for us? The guild? If you're working for the crown, then..."

"Then a few things need to happen." Tahl tapped a finger against the table as he sorted through his thoughts. "First, you need a new headquarters. The queen knows where this is, which means none of you are safe. I recommend evacuating through the tunnels, past Rupert, so nobody can follow you. Where you go after that, it's probably better that I not know."

Nia's shoulders slumped. "You're not coming with us?"

"I can't," Tahl said. He'd spent the past several hours puzzling over how he could hold the guild together, but he couldn't find a way around Oria's conclusion that he could not continue as leader of the guild and serve the crown at the same time. "Not only would that be likely to end with Atoras putting a noose around my neck after all, I'd be a liability to the rest of you." He still wanted to know how they'd had a hanging without him there. It wasn't as if Tahl doubted the emperor would find someone to execute in his stead. It was more that he didn't know how they could have found a double so convincing that even Perton, one of Tahl's own men, had been fooled.

Oh well. He could look into that later. If Tahl was supposed to be head of the queen's intelligence department, looking into things would come with the job. He shook his head and went on. "After you're settled, you're to take this to the bank north of the garden district." He withdrew a small sheet of delicate, colored paper from his pocket and slid it across the table to Nia.

She leaned forward to take it. "What's this?"

"A treasurer's check. Two hundred thousand pims, as originally agreed upon." Tahl smiled bitterly. "The deal's been changed, somewhat, to match the story that's flooding the city. According to what everyone else has heard, the crown was ransomed back to the emperor."

Nia unfolded the check and the other dozen thieves huddled close to look over her shoulder. "Where's the money now?" she asked.

"My account."

Jeran blinked at him. "You have a bank account?"

"I have a lot of things." Tahl wasn't about to elaborate. "But we're out of time for conversation. By dusk, Atoras's Elite will be here to flush out the criminals hiding in the museum's basement. I suggest none of you are here when it happens."

Nodding, Nia tucked the check into her pocket. "You'd probably get in trouble for warning us, huh?"

Tahl flashed her a half-hearted grin. "I do seem to be good at getting myself in trouble."

She didn't smile back. Instead, she set to giving orders to the thieves who surrounded them. The group split as they rushed to carry out their orders and take news to the guild members who weren't present.

Tahl lingered at the table as his feigned mirth faded. He'd thought the guild hall would be his new home, somewhere he built his new family and the sort of life he wanted. Instead, he watched as his recruits—former recruits, he told himself with a hint of chagrin—stripped the place bare and escaped into the tunnels below the city. Just like his father's estate in Ashor, Orrad had become a prison. Maybe cages were all he was destined for.

"Tahl?" Nia's voice rose, soft and hesitant, beside him.

He turned his head.

She looked at him as if she wasn't sure what to say, her brows drawn with worry. After a moment of searching for words and not finding any, she lurched forward to wrap him in a hug instead.

"Good luck," she whispered.

Tahl smoothed her dark hair and fought back a wave of unfamiliar emotion. Leaving behind his blood sisters hadn't been so hard. "You, too. I suspect we'll be seeing each other again."

Nia nodded, wiped tears from her cheeks, and darted into the tunnels behind Ashyl.

Instead of following them, Tahl exited the guild headquarters through the door that led into the museum's basement. He tried to empty his head, to allow himself a moment of respite from the swirling thoughts and troubles that plagued him. Instead, they hung over his mood like a storm cloud, putting a damper on any relief that came from the fact he was still alive.

Without caring if anyone followed, Tahl made his way to the apartment he'd rented above a shop nearby, the home he'd kept secret even from Nia. He should have been hungry, but his appetite had evaporated. Unable to fight off his exhaustion any longer, Tahl collapsed onto his wide bed, pulled the covers over his head, and slept.

WITHOUT THE TREASURES that previously lined the shelves, Tahl found his office lacked any charm or appeal. Books and papers packed the space, none of them glittering or interesting. Part of him was still irritated the guild had taken *his* treasures when they'd moved. He'd collected them on his own across the months he'd served as guildmaster. Who would have expected they'd end up stealing from him?

Tahl laid a folder on his desk and ran his fingers through his hair. Just outside his door, furniture scraped across the bare stone floor and the steady knocking of a hammer promised more would be assembled shortly.

"Excuse me, sir?" A shadow moved in front of his doorway, blocking most of the light. They hadn't brought lanterns in yet.

Tahl gave the man an expectant look. He doubted he'd ever be used to being called *sir*, but a lot could change. A lot had, in the weeks after his arrest.

The liveried man in front of him cleared his throat. "We have a problem. A handful of men scouting the tunnels underneath the intelligence office reported the presence of, ah... well, bears."

A stray paper had caught Tahl's attention, but at the last word, his eyes snapped up again. "Bears?"

"Yes, sir. A mother and two cubs, they said. What should we do?"

"Huh." Tahl rubbed his chin, his eyes falling to the papers again. "So Rupert *was* a girl."

The man blinked. "I beg your pardon?"

"Nothing, nothing." Tahl waved a hand as if it didn't matter. "The tunnels aren't necessary, or a good idea. Call a mason and have them walled off." It was probably better that way. The fewer routes into the intelligence office, the better.

"Yes, sir. One more thing. There's an architect here who said he has an appointment to discuss alterations to the building."

That earned a raised eyebrow. Tahl hadn't made any such appointments, but there were half a dozen people involved in moving the intelligence office into the basement of the Queen's Museum, and any one of them could have saddled him with an architect. "Right now?"

The man in livery nodded. "Yes, sir. Now."

It took everything Tahl had to bite his tongue and keep from kicking the man out. The queen had given him his first real assignment a week before, and with all the people coming and going and demanding his attention, he hadn't even had a chance to open the folder. His fingers trailed over it, almost longingly, as he surrendered and followed the man into the front room.

The basement space the guild had occupied was worlds different now that it housed the budding intelligence office. Putting the office there had been the queen's idea. Tahl thought it was a cruel joke. Instead of crates of stolen goods and shelves full of treasures, the space now held comfortable sitting areas and less comfortable desks. Eventually, an entire team of intelligence officers would fill the space, and Tahl was expected to lead them.

A man in fine clothing stood in a corner formed by two couches in the sitting area nearest the door. He held a stack of papers and studied the door with a speculative eye, his back to the rest of the office.

The liveried man cleared his throat and the architect twitched.

Tahl blinked twice.

"Sir, this is Jeran Tachir," the man said. "Don't let his age fool you. I am assured he is one of the finest architects in Orrad."

Jeran met Tahl's eye in a manner that was all professional. "Ah, I prefer to think of myself as an engineer, first and foremost, but I've found architectural work provides a healthy income when business is slow. How do you do?"

"A pleasure to have you here," Tahl replied, barely able to keep his amusement from his voice as he clasped Jeran's hand and pretended not to know him.

Jeran offered a small smile. "I was referred by a colleague who said you have an unusual lock system in your doors. Being that engineering is my occupational preference, it was suggested I may be able to help you change the codes for the locking mechanisms and potentially improve the infrastructure of your location."

"That would be appreciated." In truth, Tahl couldn't have cared less about the doors, but he was already trying to think of a way to slip Jeran information about Rupert's cubs.

"Excellent, excellent. I brought some diagrams and a few revised designs I thought you might appreciate looking at." Jeran divided off half the stack of papers, grimacing when a few slipped out of his grasp and fluttered to the ground. "Ah, that always happens. My apologies."

Tahl accepted the ream of papers Jeran offered before the engineer bent to pick up what he'd dropped. A moment later, Jeran laid the other papers with what was already in Tahl's hands.

"It will be a pleasure to work with you, sir," Jeran said, offering a polite nod before he retreated through the door.

"Of course," Tahl murmured, his eyes drawn downward. On the very top of the stack, a folded piece of paper bore his first name in blue chalk. Questions for how Jeran really came across the job could wait for another time. For now, curiosity tickled, and Tahl trudged back to his office.

He closed his door and unfolded that note. Inside waited a few lines of familiar childish handwriting.

Con-grats on your first real job.
Here's who you need to question.

His eyes skimmed past the list of names, to a cute drawing of a fat bird at the bottom of the page.

Tahl couldn't help but grin. "Sparrow."

www.ingramcontent.com/pod-product-compliance
Lightning Source LLC
Chambersburg PA
CBHW061351190726
48288CB00005B/1679